THE KILL

Also by Richard House

BRUISER

UNINVITED

RICHARD HOUSE

THE KILL

PICADOR

For Nick

First published 2013 by Picador

First published in paperback 2013 by Picador
an imprint of Pan Macmillan, a division of Macmillan Publishers Limited
Pan Macmillan, 20 New Wharf Road, London N1 9RR
Basingstoke and Oxford
Associated companies throughout the world
www.panmacmillan.com

ISBN 978-1-4472-1486-1

This book was generously supported by fellowships from
The Corporation of Yaddo, Saratoga Springs, NY,
and The MacDowell Colony, Peterborogh, NH,
and with a grant from the Arts Council, England.

1 3 5 7 9 8 6 4 2

A CIP catalogue record for this book is available from the British Library.

Typeset by Ellipsis Digital Limited, Glasgow
Printed and bound by CPI Group (UK) Ltd, Croydon, CR0 4YY

Visit **www.picador.com** to read more about all our books
and to buy them. You will also find features, author interviews and
news of any author events, and you can sign up for e-newsletters
so that you're always first to hear about our new releases.

THE KILL

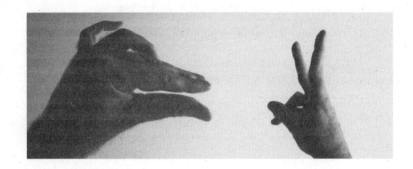

Mr Rabbit: He gives them a choice. It's the same in the film.
Mr Wolf: What kind of choice?
Mr Rabbit: They don't know. He flips a coin, and they have to choose. Heads or tails.
Mr Wolf: What if they don't want to?
Mr Rabbit: Not an option. Heads or tails. They have to choose.
Mr Wolf: And this is what you want to do?
Mr Rabbit: They get to decide what happens. Only they don't know. They have no idea.
Mr Wolf: It's a place to start.

YEAR 1: VIA CAPASSO 29

SUNDAY: DAY A

Early on the last Sunday of July, Amelia Peña, supervisor at via Capasso 29, rented a tiny basement room to Salvatore, who, with his sons, ran a modest grocery and eatery set into the corner of the palazzo.

They met at the small service door on via Tribunali, and Peña escorted the man across an inner courtyard to the basement stairs. The courtyard was cluttered and unswept, and as they walked Salvatore answered Peña's questions but did not chatter. He spoke quickly and in a soft voice, mellow enough so that much of what he said was lost to her. *No*, he said, *in all these years he hadn't seen these rooms before.* The windows overlooking the courtyard were closed and shuttered. *This wasn't for him. This wasn't for his business.*

The basement, Peña explained, was what remained of an earlier building: small square rooms carved into the tufa with barrel vaults that might have been used as storage for food, oil, wine, nobody really knew, as nobody knew how old they were. Every building abutting the Duomo had similar rooms dug at different levels, each sunk deeper than an ordinary basement. Their layout didn't conform to the layout of the buildings above and there were signs that they were once linked. Peña took the steps one by one, her hand fast on the side rail, and hoped that this effort wouldn't be wasted. The temperature dropped as soon as they stepped out of the sun. The walls, rough as pumice, shed a white grit, a kind of static.

The previous tenant had left the room in a poor state: flattened boxes scattered across the slab floor, a stained mattress tied into a roll and tipped against the wall, a stove stripped of fittings turned into the room out of square. A window slit let in a little dull natural light through a shaft carved up to street level. *And was that via Tribunali or via Capasso seven or eight metres above them?* Salvatore couldn't quite tell.

Salvatore stood under the window, cocked his head and appeared to listen. In all these years, he admitted, he'd assumed the door led to another apartment, or street-level rooms. Although he knew the city had subterranean vaults and passages, he'd never given it much serious thought. *In the war,* he said, and nodded. *Yes, in the war,* Peña supposed, *they would have been used for shelter.* Salvatore measured the room with strides. No one comes down here? he asked. It's secure? Peña showed him the key-ring and chain. If he was worried about security, there were only two keys, he would have one and she would have the other. The last time these were used – she had to think back – would be seven or eight years ago. Whatever he wanted to store down here would be safe. Nobody knows about the place to steal from it, she said. Pay the rent in full and on time, and everything will remain secure.

Salvatore took two or three photographs with his mobile phone, although, in truth, there was nothing to show, and he didn't seem to know what he was looking for. When he was done he snapped the phone shut and said he needed to return to the courtyard to get a signal.

Peña locked the door and laboured back up the steps. Not even halfway she paused for breath and asked if he was or wasn't interested and the man became flustered. It wasn't for him, he said. Hadn't he explained? He was working as an agent, a go-between for his associates. They were brothers, businessmen, French, they didn't speak Italian, and they were busy, so he'd agreed to check the room for them. Just as soon as he could send the images they would get right back to him.

He pressed ahead, and hurried through the door, and by the time she joined him Salvatore said he'd spoken with the brothers, they'd looked at the photos and they were happy. They'd take the room for one month, but they'd pay for two to cover any inconvenience or deposit. He could pay her now, in advance.

With money in her fist Peña repeated the terms of the lease. This was for one month, renewable before the end of the month. The first key would open the small door at the main entrance and the door to the basement from the courtyard. The larger brass key was for the room itself. Salvatore and his associates could come and go as they pleased, but they should not disturb the residents. As an afterthought she asked for the brothers' contact details, just in case, and he wrote a number on the back of a business card. The room would need painting, if she could arrange this, and the men would require a driver.

It was only later, once she was back in her apartment that she looked at the card and read: *Room 312, Hotel Grand, CMdS.*

MONDAY: DAY B

For six weeks Mizuki Katsura's clothes, hands, and hair reeked of a sweet vanilla. During the summer the bakery three floors below the language school on via Capasso produced small star-shaped biscuits, dipped in syrup and covered with paper then plastic and left to drip and dry on trays on racks in the courtyard. Throughout the day the sugar attracted a good number of wasps and the perfume rose as a fume and seeped, thick and unwelcome, into the schoolrooms and offices above.

The train arrived late at the Circumvesuviana station and Mizuki, phone in hand, stood at the door halfway reminded of the scent of burnt sugar. The morning sun cooked sweetness from the furnishings, the rubber seals, and the sticky floor. Idly stubbing her mobile against her cheek she squinted at the docks and recalled details of a detective story in which a man paused to smell jasmine before he was shot, but couldn't remember the title or the writer. She could chase this notion on her phone and hunt down the reference, but did not like the idea that she was leaving trackable data every time she switched it on. Even so, she quickly checked for messages, emails, SMS.

The train stopped with a gentle shove. On the platform, immediately in front of her door, stood a young and thin man with shorn hair and a drawn face: tall and puppet-like and handsome, as European men can be angular and handsome. A creaturely intelligence about him that held a kind of stillness. Sunlight, softened by the humid station air, cast a broad square over the man as he waited. Handsome, yes, and maybe even cunning.

Mizuki rode the escalator and the idea of this man stuck with her as she dug out two euro for a bottle of water. Once on the concourse she found, to her surprise, the same man already ahead of her, waiting. A little more alert now. The man stood with his arms folded, chin down, attentive to the steady line of commuters rising from the lower platforms.

The realization that there were two men, not one, came slowly, an idea she only properly understood after she'd paid for the bottle of water and turned to find both men waiting side by side under the station's awning. Dressed alike (one in a powder-blue shirt, the other in seamless white), and surely brothers; the man in the powder-blue shirt looked directly at her: a simple turn of his head as if he knew precisely where to look and what he would find.

Out of the station the traffic was stopped bonnet to boot. Horns sounded above the market and rounded hard off the buildings on either side. Mizuki walked by the market stalls and between the round walls of Porta Nolana, alongside tables of shoes and purses and undershirts, and a stack of birdcages. Agitated by the traffic the finch and quail squalled against the bars. Looking, even briefly, at their skinny necks made her skin itch. On Corso Umberto she found the focus of the delay: a long, low-slung tow-truck with a crushed taxi loaded on the truck-bed. Other cars looked only like cars, but the battered taxi had the bruised, gummy face of a boxer, its side compacted, slumped, the roof cut off and strapped back upside-down. At the head of the intersection by the newspaper stands and cash machines and racks of clothing the police fussed over an orange city bus stopped sideways and within metres of a smaller coach. The coach like the taxi had a mashed hood and a shattered windscreen. An ambulance turned in the corso, and Mizuki pressed her fingers to her ears and wished that she had walked some other way. When there were sirens it meant that someone was hurt, but worse, no sirens, according to Lara, meant that someone had died.

She deliberately turned her thoughts back to the brothers and sketched the differences between them, but couldn't measure the look the man had given her: clear and direct, an assessment. The man was taking weights and measures. Mizuki brought her phone from her pocket and regretted not taking a photograph. No messages. No email. In this way she avoided thinking about the accident.

Access to the school (on the third floor at the back of the building) was gained through a courtyard, and before that a set of massive carriage doors of solid black beams with a small inset port door, through which you had to be buzzed. Such buildings, a feature of the city, were referred to as *palazzi*. Palaces. The word lent a formal air and a sense of protection to the apartments and businesses inside, so that ducking through the smaller door was very much like escaping the ordinary world: except this ordinary world had narrow streets, black cobbles as big as shoe boxes, the constant buzz of Vespas. The hidden world housed wasps. Mizuki always paused at the door, tucked away her hair, drew her sleeves over her hands, and worried over the wasps and how she would cross the courtyard without being stung.

☆

At seven o'clock on the first Monday in August, Marek Krawiec picked up the coach from its lock-up on via Carbonara. Marek drove a small eighteen-seat transit bus and shuttled American servicemen between the military base at Bagnoli and the airport at Capodichino. He took civilian aircrew between their hotels and the airport as and when required. English Tony arranged the work, provided the vehicle, and paid him cash in hand. The job ran scattered: two being the fewest, and eighteen the most runs he'd managed in a single day. Marek didn't like flying and didn't much care for the people he transported about the city. While he tolerated the servicemen, he disliked the aircrew. The men were effeminate, the women aloof, and once they settled onto the bus they ignored him and talked among themselves, unless there were complaints to be made about the traffic, the congestion at the airport, or the delays before the tollbooths.

While the work was light the morning was hot and Marek began to sweat. He'd gained two kilos since the beginning of the year and felt himself to be slowing down, although he could see no reason for it, no change in habit or diet. As he sat in the driver's seat he avoided his reflection.

Tony waved him off with a floppy gesture, half-ironic and half not bothered.

At seven twenty, Marek returned to via Capasso to pick up his part-ner, Paola. *Partner*: her word. Marek waited outside the palazzo as Paola hurried about the bus, made no comment as she loaded the bags of shirts and struggled to close the door, then drove the short journey down via Duomo to take her to a machine-shop close by Porta Nolana that manufactured sports clothes. Paola worked at home, seldom less than a seven-hour stretch stitching sportswear logos onto pockets and collars for three cents an item. The house sang with the crank of the sewing machine and a kind of intense concentration she had with two hands down to the material, lips tight, willing the thread not to break, the material to hold. Most mornings Marek collected the shirts and vests and ran the loads back and forth, but on this day Paola wanted to negotiate the workload and the pay, and, he suspected, use this time to talk with him again about money, about why they never had enough. While Paola knew they were in debt, she didn't know the full extent: the loan from his brother Lemi, the payments for his mother's healthcare, a bank loan he could barely service, and back-standing rates and taxes on his mother's apartment. Running between his mother in Poland, his brother in Germany, his *partner* in Italy, was costing Marek more than he was making. His mother's unkempt slide into dementia hit his temperament and his pocket with equal force. To add to this Paola had decided that they would take a holiday this year. Somewhere nice. Not Poland. Not Germany. Maybe the Croatian coast? Like they were the kind of people who sat on beaches.

Paola remained testy from the previous night's argument and it became clear that she didn't want to talk. Where their disagreements had once refreshed them, they now brought drought. Delivered to her work in silence, she opened the door, tugged out the shirts, and muttered that she did not want him to wait.

Marek drove up Corso Garibaldi with a burn of irritation. At the corner of piazza Garibaldi he noticed a small red patent-leather purse in the passenger footwell, the kind of purse sold by African traders at the Stazione Centrale and along via Toledo. While he hadn't seen it before he guessed it was Paola's. Inside the purse he found a single twenty-euro note, a lipstick, and a small roll of receipts. She would be inconvenienced without the money and sorry to lose the purse. Without the money she'd have to walk home with the shirts.

With the purse in hand Marek missed the lights and failed to pull into the intersection. Horns sounded behind him, a taxi cut directly across his path – so close he automatically braced – the shock of this barely registered when the cab was struck by a city bus, punched sideways and shunted into Marek's coach.

Marek dropped to his side as the airbags pillowed over him, as the windscreen blew out, and found himself straddling the gearbox on his hands and knees. The impact itself seemed to come later, after its effect, as a mighty shove, something divine, out of scale.

The accident left a buzz in Marek's ears and dampened all other noise. He'd hit his head, not hard, but a knock nevertheless. Scattered birds came soundlessly down, and a kind of wonderment spread through him: if he hadn't been preoccupied with the red purse he would be dead, he would have driven directly into the path of the taxi, of this he was certain; being caught on the rebound was nothing, nothing at all. Glass in his hair, a shirt ripped in the seam, but no real damage, except to the coach.

Passengers stepped off the city bus and walked in a disconnected stumble to the kerb. To Marek's right a woman with bags tipped at her feet, groceries spilling into the road, pointed at the traffic lights and shouted, *red red*, in disbelief.

The instant it was over a bevy of car horns sounded along Corso Garibaldi and Corso Umberto. The first pneumatic punch brought people onto the balconies overlooking the intersection. Others hurried from the market stalls to catch sight of a crushed car and coach, a city bus stopped at an acute angle to the sidewalk. From under the cab rose a thin, violet quiff of smoke.

Marek studied the car in front of him, astonished that this – how many tonnes of steel? – had spun out of nowhere, as if the car had landed smack-bang out of the sky, as if the people stumbling from the bus were drunk. As if the men – the passenger slumped across the seat, his head resting on the driver's haunch, the driver lolling over a battered door, shirt rucked to his shoulders, arms flung out so he appeared to be reaching or pointing – were some soft part of the car.

A man in a doctor's coat, skinny and bald, hurried to the taxi. He leaned deep into the cab and as he drew out he sorrowfully shook his head, nothing could be done – an intimate gesture, Marek thought, which implied kinship: as if they knew each other.

Traffic locked the length of Corso Garibaldi and Corso Umberto, and in a slow outward spread the smaller side streets began to seize up. Marek could smell oil and rubber and the sun's heat rebounding on the smooth black cobbles. He looked hard at the taxi and the dead men and resisted the urge to lie across the seat and see how long it would take for someone to come to him. He didn't know what to do with himself. His job, he knew, was over. Without the coach Tony would not be able to hire him. The vehicle, too damaged to repair, would not be replaced. Without a vehicle there would be no work. Paola would need to be told.

Security guards from the Banco di Napoli escorted passengers from the bus; as the bus driver passed by he looked hard at Marek, his expression still and blank, one of shock, and Marek felt pity for him. The man in the doctor's coat helped passengers to the kerb and looked at Marek as if he knew him, and Marek realized the man was his neighbour, Lanzetti, Dr Arturo Lanzetti, the pharmacist who lived on the fifth floor with his wife and his son. He knew his son, knew of him, heard him almost every day.

The first police arrived on motorbikes and rode the pavement alongside the piazza. The corso sang with their alarm. Firemen trapped in the traffic abandoned their trucks and clambered between the cars to the intersection, and everyone stopped to look at the taxi, the two dead men, then Marek and the coach, and shook their heads at his undeserved good luck.

Lanzetti came to the coach and opened the passenger door. He brushed the glass from the seat with slow sweeps then sat down, uninvited.

'This will take a while.' He offered Marek a bottle of water and told him to drink. 'Will you let me?' He signalled Marek's head by tapping his own. 'You have a cut.'

'It's nothing.' Marek leaned toward his neighbour. Lanzetti looked and nodded, it was nothing to worry over. The pharmacist could give no information; a passenger on the bus needed to be taken to the hospital and although they had managed to get an ambulance to the intersection, it would be another matter getting it out. The medics were already in control.

The police slowly re-established order: the gathering crowd kept to the pavement, and drivers ordered back to their cars.

Marek leaned away from the sun and waited for the police to come to him. He showed the purse to Lanzetti and explained how it had delayed him, how otherwise, without the purse, matters would be very different. Lanzetti nodded as he listened, a slow gesture, one of comfort, as if he understood how the smallest coincidences of place and time could be of such startling importance. The difference between what did happen and what had nearly happened – which didn't particularly require discussion, but needed to be acknowledged.

The road was hosed down before the roof was cut from the car and both men watched, silent and respectful. A ring of firemen held up blankets to block the crowd's view and to prevent the curious from taking photographs. As the bodies were lifted from the squat wreckage Marek finally gave his details to the police and Lanzetti slipped quietly out of the cab.

The sight of the young men being laid carefully on stretchers and then covered with blankets struck Marek deeply; he looked hard, expecting some break in their stillness.

And what was their argument about? Money, sure, because every argument is about money. But this one started with a discussion about children, about how they could not afford, as a couple, to have a child, when really, the simple fact was that Paola did not want his child, and he wanted her to admit this truth. We have enough to look after, she said, with me and you. We have enough. Their arguments concertinaed, one to another, and while Marek remembered the insult he lost the particular words and phrases; Paola, however, recalled intricate points and details so that nothing was properly resolved. They each had their triggers: the uselessness of their work, their mismatched schedules, how lonely it was to go to bed alone or wake alone, how weekends when they finally spent them together were listless, empty, and how they both felt unattractive. Beneath this ran their own dissatisfactions (for Marek: his recent weight gain, his thinning hair, how easily these days he started to sweat. For Paola: the veins thickening on the backs of her calves, how tired she was and lately forgetful). Some of their disagreements grew out of their daily routine. Paola resented cooking, and Marek resented the half-efforts she would make, and how much food was spoiled through lack of care. How could someone prepare so carefully for sex (the gel, the foam, the condom slick with spermicide), and not have the wherewithal to make a simple meal? How could an Italian woman not cook? How could this be possible? And then there was the issue they usually avoided, the heart of every disagreement: Paola did not want his children. Who would want the children of a man who had no work?

When Marek returned he found Paola in the kitchen, deliberately positioned at a bare table with nothing about her, no cigarettes, no drink, so that her waiting would be obvious.

Tony had called. She'd heard everything from him, about the accident, about the coach, about his job. She stood up and walked to Marek and held him tightly.

'He'll find something. I know it.'

Feeling ugly and argumentative Marek closed his eyes. There wasn't any *something* out there for Tony to find. In his mind a sign in the building supervisor's slanted script, pinned under the mailboxes, 'Painter Wanted'.

Letting him go, the recriminations started. Why hadn't he spoken with her? Not one call. Why? 'I called. I sent messages. Why didn't you respond?' Wasn't she his partner? Didn't this mean anything to him? Didn't he have any idea what she was going through? My God, did he do this to her deliberately? He could have been killed.

She would be glad, he said. Happy if something had happened to him.

Paola's hand fluttered in front of her mouth, and then, inexplicably, she began to laugh. She waved a hand in defeat or exhaustion and surrendered, tonight she wouldn't argue. Instead, Paola walked queenly to the bedroom.

Once alone Marek looked for something to justify his meanness, and found Paola's keys and mobile phone beside the sink. He took the phone to the bathroom and checked through the log. The only number dialled that day was his. The incoming calls came from mutual friends. He recognized every number stored in the phone's memory.

In the wastebasket lay the packets of condoms and the spermicide he'd brought to her the night before in his demand that they be thrown away, and here they were, thrown away. Marek searched through the basket to see what else she had discarded, and found among the foil packets a slender box of contraceptive pills and didn't understand exactly what this meant, although he could see, right there, that this was exactly what he'd wanted.

That night he lay awake and fretted over his work. *Painter Wanted.* It wasn't a simple matter, even if the coach was replaced, he still didn't have the proper papers. The insurers, the police, would want details about the driver. When he finally managed to sleep he was woken by the sound of drilling, a sudden racket from the street.

He struggled to read the time on his watch. From the balcony he could see two workmen. Another man stood bare-bellied on an opposite balcony and shouted: *What are you doing?* The workmen ignored him, and the man shouted louder. A magistrate lived in the same building. If Marek leaned forward he could see the apartment on the top floor.

During the day via Capasso appeared respectable, students from the language school took coffee at the Bar Fazzini, but at night women worked the corner. They sat on mopeds, indifferent to business. Marek wasn't certain they were all women.

Behind him Paola drew the sheet over her shoulder.

The noise didn't matter. The sound of the men drilling gave him a reason to be awake, a reason not to be in bed, and another example of how this city drove him crazy. As he watched the workmen he again considered the accident and wondered if the police had yet identified the men and informed their families. He wanted to thank Lanzetti, he wanted to find the pharmacist and thank him, because the man's calm had made an impression on him. As he stood on the balcony a message came on his mobile from his brother Lemi, *call me*, which would give news of his mother wandering unsupervised from the care home a second time. A search by the police, and a requirement from the home to find her somewhere new, somewhere that could manage.

☆

At midday, as Peña returned to her apartment, she decided she would ask Marek Krawiec if he knew of a driver for the men who had rented the basement room. She took the stairs one at a time, her head swam with the effort. On top of the Duomo, perched on the dome, a hawk bobbed against the wind, sometimes sleek and sometimes ruffled. Peña watched from the second landing and felt her pulse calm and her head clear. When the bird launched the wind held it in place. Wings out, the hawk tested the updraught before it tipped backward and away. She watched it eat on occasion, some small bird held down and plucked, elastic innards and meat. A strange thing, if you gave it thought, a little repugnant, a bird eating a bird.

Ten years before, when Peña first arrived in Naples, Dr Panutti's apartment was halved by a flimsy dividing wall to make two apartments, one for Dr Panutti, Snr., the other for Dr Panutti, Jnr. The wall once had a door, so the younger Panutti could steer the older Panutti through his final illness. Peña, employed as a companion and respite nurse, made herself indispensable and invisible, and earned the right to stay in the apartment as specified in Panutti Snr.'s will, much against his family's desire. In taking out that door and sealing the wall, they turned the room into a sound-box, so that Peña heard the intimate comings and goings of the family who now rented the apartment: the pharmacist Dr Arturo Lanzetti, the voice coach Dr Anna Soccorsi, and their son, Sami. She knew when they ate, bathed, fought, and reconciled. More than this, the room duplicated the movement of sound: if Sami ran in some hectic game, his escape mapped a similar higgledy path across Peña's room.

They called the boy Sami although she knew his proper name to be Francesco. With his dark hair and olive skin the boy could be taken for a full-blooded Neapolitan. He mostly resembled his mother, a woman Peña believed to be ill-suited to city life: unable to shift and adapt she pressed too hard in one direction. Peña could read this stubbornness in the woman's thin-lipped mouth, in the sessions with her clients: the repetitive 'peh-peh-peh', 'zseh-zseh-zseh', 'tah-tah-tah' exercises, the insistent singsong rhymes she gave to stutterers, language students, and lisping adolescent boys. Their boy, Sami, often alone and unsupervised, played with his toys at his bedroom window, and Peña sometimes found these toys scattered in the courtyard. Small plastic figurines of crusaders, Roman and American soldiers, robots, caped action characters, and other figures she couldn't place. She would find them and she would pocket them, and she would take them to her room.

Most mornings before Arturo Lanzetti went to the pharmacy he sat with his son and read through the headlines from the previous day's paper. The child's voice, sweet and high, carried easily through the wall, and Peña, who spent her mornings cleaning the stairwell and courtyard, made sure she finished in time to enjoy the company of their voices. She began to associate the boy's voice with the morning light that flooded her room.

At night he dropped tokens into the courtyard, sometimes lowered on string: small figurines, notes, coins, folded scraps of paper, wads of bread, pieces of his mother's make-up. In the morning she would retrieve them.

Today, as on other days, Peña climbed into the armchair, restacked the cushions and scooted herself back so that her legs stuck out. Of the four places where she could listen to the family, three offered views into their apartment (the kitchen, the hallway, and the boy's bedroom), which ran around the courtyard and mirrored her own apartment. When the shutters were open their lives were offered up one to the other in merciless detail.

Sami read out the world's news with sticky precision. His ear was good and he repeated the phrases he couldn't grasp, softly correcting himself.

'Brasilia. A fire . . .' he read.

'Brasilia,' Lanzetti repeated, 'a fire . . . in the centre of the city.'

'Brasilia . . .' Peña softly whispered.

The older Panutti had taught her Italian in exactly the same way. Reading, repeating, reading, until her Portuguese bent to Italian. Later he helped in other ways, providing medication, then braces to help straighten her legs. The more you use them, he said, the easier this will become.

As she listened Peña took her medication. She laid the pills along the smooth walnut side-table and took a sip of water, a tablet, another sip. *The boy dropped toys into the courtyard and she retrieved them: the small soldiers, crayons, pens, a racing car, a diver with the yellow aqualung.* She listened to him read. The boy's pronouncements outlined a chaotic world. The tumble of an aircraft into open water; a fire erasing an entire city block; a mudslide sweeping houses, cars, caravans into a widening canyon, events which described nothing godly or divine, but simple laws of opportunity, matters Peña understood to her core. There was nothing, she considered, not one thing, which could truly surprise her. After reading the headlines Sami turned to the local section to read stories of disagreements, strikes and train stoppages, contracts for uncollected trash. After this he read the sports, although this was news they already knew.

A sip of water. A tablet. A sip of water.

Propped forward with pillows, Peña sat upright and motionless, her eyes fixed on a length of sunlight vibrating into the room. Her medication amplified her waywardness, a potential to slip away. Tiny things tumbled down the side of the building. A steady rain of falling toys: a cowboy, a diver, a mule, a racing car, a lipstick, a robot that was also a car, a troll or what she took to be a troll, a key-ring, a mobile phone, a face cut out of a magazine flickering down, a hawk – wings open, a number of pigeon eggs, one by one, a series of keys, an open can of paint, a boy who could swim through air.

*

At night Sami hitched himself onto the window ledge and pushed open the shutters. Too short to see into the courtyard, the boy shuffled on his forearms like some kind of creature, Peña thought. Dust stirred and sparked in the void between them. Peña stepped back from her window. It troubled her not to remember things. Names mostly. Places. But sometimes plain words.

It took some moments for her eyes to adjust; she watched as Sami edged himself forward, one hand set in a fist. With his chin on the stone lintel he stared into the courtyard. Small sounds skidded beneath them: televisions in separate rooms, honks and voices, the settling rattle of air-conditioners and the steady clap of water on stone, the less attributable snaps and tremors that came from deeper sources – the entire building contracting in the cooler night air.

There was something in the boy's hand, and he took time to stand this object right at the edge. Another toy soldier, Peña guessed by the size, another trophy.

About an hour after Sami had set the toy on the ledge Peña heard the clack of the lock on the small portal door, then a muffled conversation as two men came from via Capasso into the courtyard. Sami came to the window then quickly ducked away – and although she could not see him she guessed that he was standing in the dark away from view.

The voices were soft, too quiet to properly understand, and when a soft chuckle rode up the side of the building the boy cautiously returned to the window ledge. They were speaking to him in whispers, words she couldn't quite catch. *Come on*, they seemed to say. *Come on.*

The men continued talking while they smoked, the rising whiff of tobacco, their voices becoming a little less discreet. One of the men became boisterous and shouted through the courtyard, 'Hey,' for attention, and then softened into laughter. Peña slipped back into her room. The boy slid himself forward to watch.

In the kitchen, unaware, Anna Soccorsi stood over a kettle with her arms folded, wearing nothing more than a man's T-shirt.

Peña slept in her armchair. She woke once and heard the voices again, men whispering to the boy words she could not hear.

Arturo Lanzetti did not always live with his family. He stopped two months in Naples, sometimes less, but two months was his median stay, then he would be gone, leaving Anna with the child, or Anna alone. The period before his departure would be plagued with silences and bitter argument so that Peña could tell even before he was gone that he was going. While Lanzetti was away the phone rang late at night, and Peña became used to Anna's thin and unpersuasive voice sounding always like a complaint. Anna sometimes wore a ring and sometimes did not, and as was common she kept her own last name so there was no clear indication of their status. For Peña the mystery of their relationship was solved at different times to a different result.

TUESDAY: DAY C

As the train drew slowly toward the station in one long curve, Mizuki, by habit, stepped up to the door and watched the reflection, phone in hand. The towers of the business district, superimposed on the glass, slipped over the long grey container park that faced the bay. On this day she remembered a story about a woman who'd lost a bracelet, and again she couldn't remember the title: she found the lapse funny, because wasn't this also the subject of the story? In learning a new language she was forfeiting memories, or maybe she was simply tired? For two nights now her sleep had been broken. Nothing particularly troubled her, and neither was she hankering for something – the usual causes of unrest. She simply couldn't sleep. Both nights she'd lain awake with the notion of a river suspended above her, a current flowing through the room that would occasionally descend and engulf her (and she would sleep), then rise (and she would wake). The water looked nothing like water: black and slick and infinite as volcanic glass. The sensation was not unpleasant, but it left her unable to concentrate. A memory of the dream stuck as an insistent ache in her arms and a pressure in her chest as if she had wrestled a strong current.

Mizuki did not purposefully look for the brothers, but was pleased to recognize one of them as she stepped off the train. *Which brother is this*, she asked herself, *the older or the younger?* Once again the man appeared to be waiting, a little less present than the previous day, perhaps even bored. This time he leaned back, puppet-like, with one shoulder bent to the grey pillar and his hands dug into his pocket, so that his body turned – loose-looking, something set aside. When she passed by she hoped to catch his eye and paused to make sure that this would happen: when he finally looked at her he registered nothing. This, then, was the younger brother.

On the upper concourse she spied the older brother at the station threshold, beside him the newspaper vendor, magazines pegged in a line, others stacked in bundles, and drinks, water, cola, wrapped in packs. She stood beside the man as she bought a bottle of water, felt her pulse quicken. If she leaned to her right her shoulder would touch his upper arm. She paid, turned about, passed directly in front of the man – and noticed how he turned his head to watch her with the same intensity as the day before. Today the men were not wearing similar clothes and she could easily distinguish one from the other. French, she decided. Definitely French. She had an eye for this. The clothes (a summer suit jacket with new jeans, expensive shoes when sandals would do), but best of all a studied casual air, a kind of self-possession she had to admit she found attractive even while she found it arrogant. Generalities, sure, but she was usually right. And was he wearing perfume, some fresh aftershave or shaving balm? Or was it just the sight of him, so clean, a man in a pressed shirt, a man in a suit jacket, European, that made her expect this?

Today the corso was clear and Mizuki reached the school before the start of the lesson, and realized, again, that she had failed to take a photograph. At the large wooden doors to the courtyard she tucked her hands into her sleeves, pulled back her hair, and turned up her collar to protect her neck, readying herself to run from the wasps.

☆

Marek rose early. He walked about the house in his shorts, prepared breakfast for Paola and laid a place ready at the table, and considered what he needed and what he didn't. For example: he didn't need Paola on his case, organizing him, making plans. She would bother him with schemes and details. Finding him work would become her project. He didn't need this bother and he didn't need his brother calling or sending messages. He needed his mother to stop her midnight walks. He needed less advice and more money.

His first idea was to visit Nenella. A *fattuchiera*, a woman from Pagani reputed to have second sight. Pagani was Paola's village, and Paola had known Nenella as a girl. Nenella, she swore, could call out the bad fate of the most cursed. Often Paola would say that such a situation, or such a hope, such a notion could be divined by Nenella. The woman was able to advise, solicit, or intervene in any situation. Marek had no such faith, and ridiculed Paola whenever she expressed this belief, but today he thought he would see her.

A slow trickle came out of the pipes, not enough to shave and not enough to wash. He remembered the workmen and how the drilling continued intermittently for three hours, driving sleep out of the neighbourhood. He leaned over the balcony and looked for the pit the men had dug, but there was no sign of water, only a dry hole surrounded by bollards, nothing he could see, and no signs that explained the drilling. It was typical. They came in the middle of the night to disrupt his sleep and after all that noise they had achieved nothing. Further up the street he could see the magistrate's car and his driver leaning casually against the side. As he looked down he thought he saw the man look up. Glancing back at Paola it occurred to him that the magistrate's driver spent a great deal of time outside the apartment.

With what little water he could draw from the tap he made a coffee. As he waited for the coffee to boil he checked the wastebasket in the bathroom. Marek brought a small cup to Paola, and waking her set his hand on her stomach, and thought perhaps that he felt her flinch. Light bloomed between the shutters and Paola blinked, slowly wakening. Marek ran his hand softly over the curve of her hips as an overture, but remembering the discarded contraceptives decided against it: a child conceived today, out of duty, out of surrender, would be an unlucky child.

'Speak with Tony.' Paola hugged her pillow. 'See what he has. He promised he'd find something.'

Already. Not yet up and she's making plans. He told her about the water, happy to annoy her.

Marek hid in the café beside the *tabaccaio*. He watched Peña sweep the pavement, Lanzetti leave for work. The youth, Cecco, hung around the *tabaccaio* during the day and the Bar Fazzini at night, and seemed, oddly, to be friendly with Stefania, who otherwise sat at the counter and stitched all day without much of a word for anyone. For the boy she ordered coffee, Coke, *limonata* allowed him to sit with her and run errands on occasion.

At eight o'clock Paola sent Marek a message asking what he was doing. When he answered, *Speaking with Tony*, she responded immediately, *IMPOSSIBLE!!!! I just spoke w. him.* Moments later a third message: *He has a car for you.* Then a fourth. *Can you pick up more shirts? I need them this afternoon?*

I'll ask Tony.

As long as it happens.

He watched the palazzo. The supervisor, Peña, sat on an upturned crate in the long shadow beside the entrance. She looked like a doll, not only because she was small, but because of her high forehead, thin hair, tiny mouth and hands, and the way she sat with her legs stuck out. When she moved the action appeared mechanized. Unlike everyone else on the street she seldom spoke and he felt something in common with her because of this.

As Marek came out of the café Peña shuffled forward to slip off the crate. She waved to him, straightened her clothes, and signalled that she wanted a quick word.

Peña spoke formally but not coldly. 'You are a driver? Yes? I'm looking for a driver.'

'For how long?'

Peña didn't know. She'd ask Salvatore. Two men had rented a room from her. Two brothers. She believed they were French. They weren't from the city, and had an idea that they wanted to hire someone to drive them. She offered Marek a card with a handwritten number and asked him to copy it down. She also needed a room painted if he knew anyone who could manage this.

Marek said he'd see what he could do.

He found English Tony at the garage with Little Tony and Antonio. The three men discussed two cars raised on the loading bay; another car, a cream and grey old-style Citroën, sat on the sidewalk. English Tony broke away to speak with Marek.

'Use this one.' He signalled the Citroën. 'There's a pick-up in Bagnoli. Bring it straight back.' Tony looked him over with sympathy, and said he wouldn't know the extent of the damage to the coach until he'd taken a proper look. At an uninformed guess, worse scenario, the frame could be shunted back. If this was the case it would take a while to fix. Marek wondered what story Paola had told him, why he sounded calm about the matter, and why he would loan him the Citroën – a man who lost his temper at any provocation, and had once thrown a hammer at his son, Little Tony. Tony also did some dealing, nothing more serious than dope and maybe some light recreational blow for his American friends, and Marek clumsily implied that he could help, you know, deliver, you know, but English Tony didn't take up the invitation.

'Can I use the car this afternoon?'

Tony gave an expression Marek couldn't read.

'Paola needs some packages for her work. Some shirts.'

'Sure. Take it. But when you're done you bring it back.' English Tony gave a half-hearted wave, then added as an after-thought. 'But no accidents. OK? No damage. There's just one thing. Fuel. Don't go by the gauge. Sometimes she just dies.'

Marek drove to the *lungomare* at Mergelina and called Peña's number, and at first, because what was being said didn't exactly make sense, he thought that he was speaking to an answering machine – then realized that the phone had been answered by accident.

'If it's not in,' the voice said, 'we don't do it.'

After a rustle the call cut out.

Marek called a second time, and the answer came as a curt *pronto*. He spoke carefully, in Italian, and explained that he was a driver, and that he understood that they were looking for a driver. So . . . The call cut out a second time. Marek waited a moment before calling back. This time he spoke quickly and apologized for not having a name and said that he was a driver. The supervisor at the palazzo on via Capasso had given him the number. He understood that they needed a driver.

He felt that he had the man's attention.

'You need a driver?'

In the background he could hear another voice, in French, a man demanding to be given the phone.

'Hello. You are a driver? You know the city? Can you come at four this afternoon? We can discuss rates when you come. Room 312. Hotel Grand.'

The man gave an address in Castellammare di Stabia. Did he get that? 'It's on the hill,' he said. 'On the mountain. Looking at Napoli. The big white hotel. You will find us, yes? Room 312.'

Marek said yes, and once the call was cancelled he realized that he had not taken a name, just a room number.

They called an hour later and cancelled the meeting.

By the afternoon Marek found himself in the basement stripped to his waist with two tubs of white emulsion and a roller that didn't apply paint so much as drag grit off the walls. He couldn't quite believe how quickly the walls absorbed the water, and then flaked. Four hundred euro made the job worthwhile. Good money from the same men who'd wanted a driver then changed their minds.

Marek worked through the afternoon and grew resentful while he painted, what choices had he made to come to this: making do by driving cars and painting rooms? Falling deeper into debt while his mother slowly lost her mind. He set himself to the task, bought new brushes and a third tub of emulsion from the hardware store at the back of the palazzo. He stripped down to his shorts and felt the air wrap round him blanket-warm, and as he worked sweat stung his eyes. Once he was done the room seemed little improved. Brighter, yes, but otherwise no different. Four hundred euro would barely service his debt. Four thousand euro would pay the debt and leave enough, perhaps, for his mother or for Paola, but no money for himself.

He took a call while he waited in the courtyard for the final layer to dry. The men who'd rented the room wanted to know if the room was ventilated. Marek picked up a toy dropped by the door. A scuba diver, a black figure with moveable arms and legs, the mask missing and two small round holes in his back where an aqualung would fit. He described the room, said there was a window, high on one of the side walls, but the basement was a good six or seven metres below street level so there was little chance that air could circulate. He wasn't sure quite what they needed, because the air was dry and stale and the walls flaked as soon as you touched them.

The man became hesitant. That wasn't good news. 'It's going to be used for storage,' he explained. 'It's important that everything remains clean, you understand?' He seemed to think something through. 'You need to line the walls and the ceiling with plastic. Do it properly, nice and neat.'

Marek listened as the man outlined the job. Behind a row of railings stacked against the wall he found another toy, a small figurine of a green plastic soldier. He wasn't sure how to ask for more money, and broached the subject cautiously. The man appeared to sense his unease. 'We can pay, of course.' Marek could buy the materials, see to the work and they would reimburse him. If this could be done by Thursday they would double the money.

Marek returned to the hardware store and bought a roll of plastic. He explained what he needed to the clerk, a man with grey rheumy eyes.

The man swept his hair from his face and shuffled to the back of the store between racks of shelving.

'It's not the best way to do it. It's dry now, but when it rains the damp will come through the stone. You need to build walls.' The clerk returned with a long box on his shoulder, his expression – as if setting Marek's face to memory – remained stern. 'You need to know what you're doing. These days people don't know what they're doing.'

Back in the basement Marek cut lines of plastic to the length of the room. He carefully trimmed the sheets and set them side by side ready to tape together. He left enough plastic to make a lip to double over as a seam. By late afternoon he'd managed to cut the all pieces for the ceiling and walls.

Determined to complete the project in one day he worked late and found satisfaction in this labour, a level of pride, a return to the normal world of work and reward. The walls and ceiling were smartly lined, the floor scraped clean and painted, and the room reeked of a fresh chemical smell.

He called the brothers a second time. 'It's ready,' he said. 'It should stay up for as long as you need.' He crossed the courtyard for a better signal and blinked up at the square of pure blue sky five floors above him. Two windows open – Lanzetti's, and opposite, the supervisor, Peña – all others shuttered or blocked with the purring back-ends of air-conditioning units.

The men said they were pleased, one on the phone the other prompting in the background.

A helicopter crossed overhead, POLIZIA, too small for the noise it was making, smaller even than the swallows diving for ants. Marek waited for it to return but the clapper-like sound soon faded.

In the evening he sat with Paola, he drank two glasses of water without speaking, then started on the wine, and mentioned, because he couldn't help himself, that he was being paid eight hundred euro to clean up a room.

'It's hot down there,' he said, to excuse his appearance. He realized his mistake, regretted bringing up the money because now she would make plans. 'It's good to work with your hands.'

Paola explained that the water wasn't running but she'd set aside some buckets so he could wash. They could think about that holiday, then? Croatia, maybe? There was a place on the coast. 'The hotel is

close to the port and the beach and there are places to eat. It's convenient for the ferry. Easy.' How many nights did he think they should stay?

'Let's see about my mother.'

'One week,' she said. 'Six nights. No more.' She looked at him
closely. 'Good, we can decide this tonight otherwise the money will
just go. If you found work today, there will be more tomorrow.'

☆

Lila scooped up the bear and hid it under her jacket as she came out
of the room. On the dresser sat a number of other toys from a suitcase of examples, some unfamiliar – hand-stitched felt with glass
eyes – and others more recognizable, rubber-formed figures with hard
faces and outstretched arms: Topolino, Goofy, Pinocchio. Picking up
the toy to put it right and taking it was one continuous action.

Out on the landing Lila checked that the door remained closed
then wrapped the jacket about the bear. She shimmied her skirt the
right way round and fastened the zip. The tang of stale talcum still with
her, and right before her, looking down, a city bright with bare sunlight
and the rising scents of braised meats: infinitely busy, infinitely small.
Lila didn't like heights, or holes, or any kind of drop which presented a
proposition: to jump, throw, or hurtle into, difficult to resist.

The man had deliberately sat the toys upright in the suitcase, row
upon row, stadium-style, to face the bed: three stacked lines that
would have taken patience to arrange. He was happy to finish himself
off, he said, just as long as she watched, so Lila watched, ass tipped up
and head twisted on the pillow. Out of his shirt the salesman looked
underfed and pale, a dry man with a pinched, soapy face, and the same
soft eyes and calf-like lashes as Cecco – a coincidence she didn't like.
Once he was done he asked her to pass him the hand-towel and complained that she hadn't paid attention, but slipped off somewhere,
present but not attentive. He spoke Italian in a northern accent and
every comment came as a complaint. On the floor beside the bed lay
an open map, a pencil stub, and a single new shoe. When she thought-
lessly used the towel to wipe her thighs the man lost his temper.

Light on her feet Lila scooped up her clothes, took the abuse, nothing more than shouting, and snatched the panda as she opened the
door. If there was ever trouble Lila knew how to smartly break a nose
and run. Four times now she'd sped out of a building, clattering onto

some corso or piazza, her heart in her mouth and clothes in her arms. She wore plimsolls, large and loose, as per Arianna's advice to keep her shoes on – because *men can't run after sex. They just can't do it, as their energy, momentarily, lies elsewhere.* The shoes' loose slap drew memories of a wheel-less camper in a dry pine wood, in which she'd tolerated the same kind of attention she tolerated now. Memories of running across sand as a skinny girl, a spider – all legs and arms, all knees and elbows – weren't especially real, but this is how she saw herself, as something in flight.

Cecco was gone. Disappeared as soon as he'd received the money. The deal, arranged by Rafí, was simple: *Cecco goes along to make sure the men pay first, after which he does as he pleases, just as long as the money reaches Rafí by the end of play.* Lila became used to Cecco watching from a doorway, stairwell, or window (stealthy enough to keep out of plain sight and always a little sulky when she returned). Cecco, Arianna said, was a picture. She couldn't work out if he was dumb or not, and supposing he was an idiot, just how deep it ran through him: if you offered the boy too many choices he simply sat down, confused, head shaking, and he only washed when Rafí reminded him. Who could guess what Cecco wanted, coming back each night with pizza, *aranchini,* some days a bottle of wine, and other days pills? And who could guess what his business with Rafí actually involved, he just hung around without purpose, almost as if he loved him?

Lila headed down the wrong flight of stairs to a sudden view of the Albergo dei Poveri, a building so monumentally solid that she paused when she knew she had no time to pause. How in four months had she not noticed this? Finding herself at a secured gate she threw the bear and jacket first, then climbed over, eyes fixed on the long red roof of a building that could be a prison, or a barrack, or maybe a workhouse. Three flights down the air reeked of petrol. Everything about the day scorched and hard except the view of distant hills; Capodimonte, Vomero, and there, Vesuvius, the tip of it seen through fumes, blunt, jellied green.

She squeezed the bear as she picked it up and found a pocket stitched into the back, a pouch large enough to fit four fingers up to the second knuckle. She could feel the seam inside, the stitches beginning to loosen.

*

Lila avoided the traders grouped in the lobby at the Hotel Stromboli. Nigerians, Kenyans, sweaty men twice her height with blankets folded into sacks filled with belts, handbags, sandals, goods they sold on the streets. Quietly up the last of the stairs she paused to take off her shoes and slowly unzip her skirt. She stepped barefoot into the room, into the heat, breath held, toes testing for the edge of the mattress that took up most of the floor. In the late afternoons she preferred to lie beside Arianna, who was softer, less agitated, easier company than Rafí.

The salesman had worn two condoms, insisted on the detail, then was brief and rough, and she could feel him stuck to her guts and hated the idea that the man stayed with her and how it was getting harder to leave everything in place. Rafí told a good story about how she was stolen from her family, how she was naive, maybe even a bit simple, and while no one seriously believed this there wasn't a man who didn't find pleasure in the notion.

Arianna slept with her back to the window, a blade of sunlight across her shoulder. Lila shuffled out of her clothes then sat carefully on the edge of the mattress and waited for her eyes to become used to the dark. She set the panda against the wall then curled beside her friend and settled down as if slipping into water. She held her breath, slowly exhaled, attempted to empty her mind. As soon as she relaxed Rafí's dog began to bark, he sounded close, as if from a neighbouring room. Two floors below, tethered by a chain to an upright pole, Rafí kept a skinny white bull mastiff on an open rooftop. The creature slept outdoors without proper shelter or shade, it loped from one flat of cardboard to another to stay cool, ate whatever was thrown at it, and barked in pitiful, chuffing coughs. Scabbed and hairless, the animal stank.

Arianna slowly woke and reached blindly behind her, tap-tapping Lila's hip. 'You're back already. Oh? Cecco didn't wait?'

Lila's chin nuzzled Arianna's shoulder. Her arm crossed under her breasts, and she thought for a moment that she could smell Rafí's aftershave, a smell not locked to the skin but hovering above, separate.

'He wants us to go to the Fazzini.' Arianna yawned into the pillow and gave a sour chuckle. 'Tonight. I don't know though?'

There were whole days when Lila wouldn't speak. Not one word.

They began to prepare for the evening at nine o'clock. Arianna gathered clothes and make-up onto their shared mattress, along with what remained of Rafí's favours – crushed pills, halved tabs in foil and brittle plastic packs, treats from his associates at the hospital: for this, at least, he was useful. Arianna made no bones about it, these gifts were the only reasons she would tolerate him. For Lila the matter was entirely transparent. She knew three people in Naples: Arianna, Rafí, and Cecco. Between the four of them they knew only the district pinched between the Stazione Centrale, the Hotel Stromboli, and via Carbonara. While they could name the hotels alongside the marina they had little idea what lay inland.

Lila sat still as Arianna brushed her hair. She squeezed the panda between her thighs, teased its fur, and plucked stuffing from its pocket. Arianna worked herself into a sulk and asked why they should go tonight, what was so important about the Fazzini? Why did they always have to do what Rafí told them?

Lila looked up because the question made no sense.

'He has this man he wants us to meet,' Arianna scoffed. 'We can find men by ourselves. We can look after ourselves. We should never have come here.' By *here* Arianna meant Naples.

Lila sorted through the make-up. Rafí had his uses, even Arianna had to admit, and it wasn't like they had any choice. Rafí, in his scattershot way, provided clothes and food, arranged this room at the Stromboli and made sure they were secure and they had something to sleep on. Rafí found business for them, ensured the men paid, he picked out new names and refigured their histories so the whole mess of Spain was forgotten. It was Rafí's idea that Lila and Arianna should work together as sisters, and he bought them small gold pendants, an A for Arianna, an L for Lila.

In private they thought him ridiculous. To his face they were sulkily obedient. Arianna had forgotten how difficult life was before Rafí, how the traders harassed them for sex and money, and she was forgetting the trouble they'd had from other women, from the police, how easy it was now they didn't have to hustle for business: you couldn't work the city on your own.

Still, while he made business easier, he couldn't make it any more pleasant. Preoccupied by the salesman Lila imagined him checking out of the hotel, the toys secure in their suitcase, a phone nudged between his shoulder and ear; the man talking and walking to his car and speaking with his wife, his girlfriend, his mother, or perhaps a daughter who might be close to Lila's age. She couldn't understand why this especially bothered her.

Arianna brushed Lila's hair in measured sweeps. All in all Rafí demanded too much of their attention. She dropped the brush and drew Lila's hair back through her hands. 'I'm serious,' she said. 'We don't need him. And what about the dog? I hate that dog. Every day, bark, bark, bark, bark, bark.'

Lila found the lipstick she wanted. She held up the mirror, stretched her mouth to a smile, then drew a finger across her lips.

Arianna, now standing, said that Lila looked like the panda. Adorable.

As Lila drew the lipstick across her lower lip she had the idea that the salesman was polluting the toys, showing them something of the world before he handed them over to families and children who would take them into their homes, their beds.

They found Rafí at the bar, shirt unbuttoned to a grey T-shirt, sleeves rolled up, Cecco beside him with his elbows on the counter looking more boyish than usual. Rafí signalled out the man he wanted Lila and Arianna to meet.

'You know him?' Rafí asked. 'He's here all the time. His name is Salvatore, goes by *Graffa*. He lives in the palazzo opposite.'

Reed-thin, static, heron-grey and bald, the man wore workmen's trousers and a workman's shirt. Lila found his bird-like sharpness a little sickening and thought the man didn't belong in the bar. If such a man wanted company he'd pick up women along the marina. Such a man, being fifty-five, maybe sixty, would be married or separated, and almost certainly would prefer young girls.

By the time Lila and Arianna reached the counter, Rafí was already at the man's side. He rested his hand on the man's arm and whispered to him. Cecco, watching, appeared bereft.

Lila watched Cecco as Cecco watched Rafí.

Rafí bought the man a drink. Salvatore, he said, persuasive, over-using the name, Sal. *Graffa* then followed him outside when he wanted to smoke and stood so close that when the man exhaled he blew smoke over Rafí's shoulder. Arianna leaned close to Lila and said they should be going, her voice now hoarse. Although the bar was busy there would be no business, and she didn't like the way things were going with Rafí. The man, this Salvatore, wasn't interested – anyone could see. Lila shouldn't encourage Rafí. Tomorrow she'd have a word and find out exactly what was going on with their money. They shouldn't depend on him.

'Have you heard him talk?' She nodded toward the street. 'These stories?'

When they tried to leave Rafí stepped up to the entrance, sly and pleased with himself.

'It's good,' he said, his head turned so the man couldn't see him. 'He's interested.'

'In what? What have you told him?' Arianna steered Lila toward the street, and there, on a low stone wall, with the dark furred shafts of palm trees behind him, Salvatore sat waiting, expectant. Music from other bars slipped through the night air. Lila could smell jasmine, and looking up she saw a rusted sign of a star and realized that what she could taste in the air wasn't jasmine but scorched sugar and vanilla from a bakery. From the windows came the hum of fans and extractors.

Rafí whispered into Arianna's ear then stepped back. 'It's agreed. Right? You agree?'

Arianna looked to Lila then nodded. 'We do this, then we go.'

For a reasonable fee Rafí took the women to a car parked in the alley behind the bar.

Rafí shone a flashlight along the cobbles and spun the light over the sunken bags and newspaper packets bunkered into the doorways. Lila held her breath against the sweet boozy stink. Arianna became argumentative. A flashlight? A car? What was this exactly?

Salvatore turned his back to the group and spoke on his phone. When he was done he clicked his fingers to draw Rafí's attention. He nodded at Lila. 'Seriously. How old?'

'I told you. Fifteen.'

The man sucked on his teeth and shook his head, certain. 'She's not fifteen.'

Rafí gave a small confirming nod and called to Lila. 'Tell him. Fifteen?'

Lila nodded. Fifteen it was.

They kept their voices low, aware that above and about them were open windows to kitchens and bedrooms, the warren-like pockets of apartments dug side by side into sheer unornamented walls.

Salvatore repeated the information into the phone, one hand to his ear. 'Is she clean?'

Rafí held out his hands, palms up, as if insulted.

'Where's she from?'

'Originally?' Rafí blew out his cheeks, and slowly, indifferently, spun a story about how Lila was Sicilian, how her dark complexion came from Arab blood, but being too live a firecracker her family had packed her off to Mostra to the sweaty attentions of a retarded uncle and cretinous second-cousins. He'd found her in the Veneto, he said, picked her up on an autostrada, or some such flat un-sunny hinterland. Lila was a naive unfortunate who surrendered her ass night after night to every male member of her family, who might be imbecilic but knew enough about business to save that other temple for a paying stranger. So, in a sense, she was untouched, and yes, definitely clean. Unschooled but not uneducated. Dumped at the side of the road by her uncle after a final refusal she was making her way back home. This story played better than the earlier version where Rafí claimed that the women were sisters, who slept cat-like, entwined on a single bed in a small stone hut in some dumb coastal village. Driven by misfortune to the mainland to sell themselves, Lila and Arianna delivered nightly shows on hollow mattresses in dry, dirty basements right across the peninsula. In their primitive understanding there wasn't even a word for what they were, Arianna being a weird boy/girl hybrid so you couldn't actually call what they did lesbian. Any story played better than the truth, which, in Lila's case was nothing but bland. Lila came from Modena, and before that Skopje, the entire family uprooted when she was less than two years old, although she had no memory of this. End of story. Her father was a mechanic, as were her brothers. Her mother, gone too long for her to remember, had worked as a domestic. Now, Arianna, half-Spanish, was a more interesting bundle and told stories about her brothers who threatened her with knives, locked her in a room for an entire week the first time they saw her dressed as *Arianna*. The second she fled they told the neighbours she was dead. Rafí discovered her at a gas station ten kilometres outside of Pavia, where, he explained, she'd learned to suck the small change from a vending machine.

Salvatore listened without interest and repeated the information into the phone, and this time Lila could hear him repeating himself, as if the person he was speaking to could not follow the discussion. While the man listened he looked hard at Lila. 'Is what he says true?'

Lila shrugged.

Rafí pinched his tongue between his teeth and nodded.

Salvatore cleared his throat. 'What about the other one?'

Lila for her part was starting to tire; she couldn't see why they were waiting, or why they were doing business outside and on the phone. She hoped these men weren't Italian. Italian men talked everything to death, explained themselves and their sorry situations in endless preparation, each one of them secure in the notion that buggering a prostitute wasn't hard-line adultery. As soon as they were done Lila didn't exist, and this disregard seeded a real and terrible shame.

Rafí stepped away and shone the flashlight on Arianna, who stood with her arms folded, clearly unimpressed.

'And she has a—' The man whistled through his teeth and waggled his little finger. 'This one, she has a cock? Yes? A pistol?' He translated into the phone and then, speaking to Rafí, said that he needed to see for himself before they could decide.

Rafí turned the flashlight through the window to the back seat of the car. 'Just to look,' he cut his arm in a flat cross-swipe, 'anything different and you pay more.'

Arianna shot Lila a glance as she ducked into the car. She signalled Rafí to come close and whispered to him, the streetlight stroking his jet-black hair and greasing Arianna's forehead.

Inside the car Arianna sprawled across the back seat in an attempt to find a comfortable position. She raised her knees, struck up her feet and shimmied her hips lower and lower until her shoulders jammed against the door. Salvatore let her settle then took the flashlight and hunched through the front passenger door, folding himself inside as a man undertaking an unpleasant task.

Lila backed off and waited ten, fifteen paces away, poised on her toes. It wasn't fruit she could smell, ripe and spoiled, but a heap of flowers brought out of the chapel beside the music conservatory. The air fizzed with their perfume. On the brighter cross-street a woman sat side-saddle on the back of a scooter and whooped at friends out of sight on another bike. Hearing the scooter Rafí shrugged, indicating to Salvatore, ducked inside the car, that this was nothing. The scooter's buzz zipped across the shuttered shop fronts and the woman's shouts echoed up, teasingly unstable, mapping her route down via Tribunali, up via Atri, and back about the hospital. Lila listened knowing they would return, because that's what they did, these kids, they ran feckless circles round the Centro Storico until the police, or someone, stopped them.

Throughout the inspection Arianna lay across the seat, legs high and wide. It was hard for Lila to look without getting a little anxious. She wondered what it would be like if this car, the bags and newspapers, the armfuls of faded flowers, the mordant sticky stink itself, dislodged and tumbled down the hill with Arianna riding a tide of muck into the delicately detailed courtyard of the music conservatory.

Salvatore clambered out and straightened himself, tut-tutting, unimpressed. He wiped his hands on his shirt with the same distaste he'd demonstrated earlier. It wasn't Arianna that disgusted him, so much, but the task itself. The man spoke into the phone and then turned to Rafí. 'OK. They're interested,' he held the phone to his shoulder, 'but they want to see. I'll pay for one photo.'

'How much?'

The man ducked his head to listen. 'Twenty,' he said.

'Fifty.'

'Twenty-five. No more.'

Salvatore took less time on his second visit, and while he didn't touch Arianna, he shone the flashlight directly into her face.

Out of the car he straightened his shirt, and spent some time composing a message. Once he was done he shut the phone. Rafí stood with his hands in his pockets and bided time while they waited for a response. Lila wanted to go.

The phone gave one sustained trill. As he answered Salvatore coughed to clear his throat. He nodded as he listened. 'How much do they earn?'

Rafí shrugged and stepped back, his hands in the air.

'No. Don't walk away. These girls. How much do they earn?' Salvatore gestured at Arianna. 'Do you know how much she earns?'

Rafí gave no reaction.

'How much? Tell me what she makes in one night. Fifty? One hundred? Two hundred?' The man made a small seesaw gesture. 'How much?'

Rafí pursed his lips and refused to answer.

Salvatore redirected his question to Lila. 'You tell me. How much? You understand? How much do you earn?'

Lila kept still and refused to look up.

'They want to make an offer for both of them, for one night,' he said. 'What do you say? One hundred? Maybe two? Two hundred? Two hundred, let's say?'

Lila looked to Rafí then Arianna. If they made two hundred a night their debt to Rafí would have been paid a long time ago.

Salvatore held up his hand, and listening to the phone he appeared confused. 'How much do they weigh?' He kept the phone to his ear. 'Fifty kilos? Do you think she weighs fifty kilos? And the other? Sixtynine?' Salvatore cleared his throat. 'I will pay you two euro per kilo.' He squinted as he made the calculation. 'So that's – what – that's the final offer. There's a party tonight. A party with important people, businessmen, judges, people from Rome. Name a price and I'll pay you now, and the women are ours.'

Rafí looked to Arianna, who now leaned out of the car. She shook her head at that final phrase, it suggested intention, sleight of hand, a game with uncertain parameters.

'I have to be honest,' Rafí explained. 'Usually, the way this works, I bring men to them, or I take them to the men. Hotels, private parties, saunas . . .'

Salvatore nodded.

'. . . if people know they are working, then other people are going to start expecting things. Money. Favours.' Rafí softly rolled his head from side to side. 'You understand? And everything becomes difficult. If everything is quiet then everything is good.'

Rafí looked back to Lila, then Arianna. Arianna curtly shook her head.

'OK. You can all come with me.' Salvatore made a final gesture of agreement, and took out a wallet fat with cash. Fingers flicking through the notes he peeled off five, six, seven, and held them out. 'Here. OK? For you.'

Rafí accepted the money, but his eyes remained fixed on the man's wallet, on the new, unspoiled notes.

'It's for you, OK?' he said, 'and something for the photograph.'

Rafí counted the money as he folded the notes into a small roll.

Salvatore walked ahead and crossed the street diagonally. Rafí followed behind, arm in arm with Lila and Arianna. The street cut directly through the old quarter, a broad barricade of shop-fronts. The buildings rose six or seven storeys in one face, a long line undercut by an arcade, with regular balconies along the upper floors, shuttered windows, and huge tarred carriage doors. Salvatore hesitated at the entrance to the palazzo and appeared to have trouble opening the small portal door. In the shop beside the entrance, spelled out across the glass were the words S A L V A T O R E - G R A F F A / A R A N C H I N I / P I Z Z A, the end of the sign obscured by a banner.

Rafí stepped back to Lila and Arianna. 'They have a room,' he said, 'here, in the basement.'

Lila leaned backward to take in the full height of the building.

'They?'

'These brothers.'

'How do you know this?' Arianna blew smoke directly into Rafí's face. 'He said there was a party.'

'They want to look. The brothers. First they take a look, then they take you to the party.'

'You'll stay with us?'

Rafí handed the flashlight to Lila and told them to wait.

With the door now open Salvatore signalled that they should be quiet.

Lila followed Arianna into a square courtyard to find Salvatore struggling with a second door – this difficulty set Arianna into a giggle, and the man stopped, held out his hand and indicated that she needed to be silent. The door, metal, smaller even than the first, refused to pull open.

Lila stood in the centre of the courtyard and shone the torch up the wall. A square of low cloud yellowed by the street lamps stoppered the opening. All but one of the shutters were closed, and Lila thought she could see a figure leaning out. When she shone the flashlight directly at the window the socket appeared empty. Lila switched off the torch but kept her eye on the spot, and there, too indistinct to be certain, appeared a face – what she took to be a child. Lila tapped Arianna's shoulder, looked back up, but couldn't quite tell in the darkness if there was someone at the open window or if this was her imagination.

Salvatore finally turned the key, unlocked the door, and beckoned them forward. Lila looked up a last time, and there, bumping down the wall, came a small object tied to a piece of string. Arianna fussed with her skirt, Salvatore and Rafí ducked through the doorway. Lila, captivated by the thread and the lowering object – a toy, a small plastic figure – walked to the wall and waited for the toy to reach her, watched it twirl as it came down. Salvatore, irritated at her dawdling, hissed at her to hurry.

She raised her hands, let the toy settle into them, looked up as she drew the thread away from the wall. In the open window four flights up, she could clearly see a boy leaning over the edge, holding the other end of the thread and a torch. The boy flashed the light, twice, and Lila signalled back with two blinks. She directed her beam at the window and was surprised to see how young the boy was, his face all moonish, round, a little startled. Torchlight from the window strafed the paving, settled on her face. Lila smiled up and raised her hands so he could see the toy.

Salvatore shoved her out of the light so hard that she fell backward, and without thinking she punched, open hand, heel first, and blunted the man in the face, struck his nose – then scuttled to the doorway, and further, to the street, so fast that she didn't stop until Rafí and Arianna grabbed hold of her. What was she playing at? What was she doing? Arianna pulled her upright, drew her quickly into the streetlight toward the noise of the Fazzini while Rafí reasoned with Salvatore, salvaged what he could, saying: 'Calm. Calm. Let's all keep calm.'

Lila didn't understand the problem. Arianna stroked her face and said she shouldn't worry, 'but these men, they don't want to be seen. It's not so good to draw attention to yourself. You shouldn't have hit him.'

Arianna hectored Lila on the walk back.

'He was laughing at us,' she complained. 'What was he saying? How much we weigh?' She waited for Lila to catch up. 'The price of what, of meat? Who were these brothers? Who talks like this?'

Lila wanted to find something to eat. Michele's would be open, they could pick up pizza, Pepsi, *frittura*, but Arianna walked ahead without a word. She walked wide of the doorways and the shuttered booths, suspicious of every man they passed.

Back at the Hotel Stromboli, Lila settled against Arianna. Arianna complained about the dog, her long body stretched out, head turned to the window, straw-coloured hair loose about her face. Bark, bark, bark, she complained, every time they come back. No end of trouble. She spoke slowly, lazily, as if the words were too weighty to heft out, her arm hung over the side of the mattress. On the floor between them, mismatched shoes, a scrap of foil, three lighters – all spent – an envelope with two remaining pills, egg blue on one side and white on the other. Lila pressed her head back into Arianna's thigh.

'Did it hurt?' Lila asked. She could feel her voice vibrate through her collarbone. There had to be some science behind this, the way that people intuit sound, how some people sense danger, or how animals, dogs for example, or birds, know that trouble is coming, or feel threat in their bones, a coming earthquake, a lightning strike, a wall of water. The dog's barks also passed through her.

'Did it what?'

'Hurt. When you were in hospital?'

Another pulse ran through Lila's shoulders. She could smell Rafi's aftershave, a metal tang to it, old and sour.

Arianna crawled out from under her and sat upright. 'We need to think. We need to plan what we're going to do when he comes back. If he had to give back all that money . . .' She rested her hand on Lila's head and apologized. 'I should have been watching you.'

☆

In the late afternoon Peña swept the courtyard and kept an eye open for Sami's toys but found nothing. When Dr Lanzetti returned to the palazzo he passed by Peña and continued to the stairs without a word. A man who walks with his head down, his hands in his pockets, a man who used to show politeness, who passes now without the time of day, is a man in trouble.

That night Peña waited until Arturo Lanzetti and Anna Soccorsi were in bed. Neither of them had spoken much through the evening; Anna's mood infected the air. Again the palazzo settled into its own subterranean sounds, the tiny clicks of cooling tiles, the snap of contracting wood, of pipes tightening.

Sami appeared at the window some time after midnight, awake and ready. With his shoes over his hands he slowly pushed open his shutters. The boy must be standing on a chair, or a box, something to raise him level to the window so that he didn't need to scramble up.

This confidence made Peña anxious. The boy was becoming bolder and she worried that with any misstep he would fall, but he stood, framed by the window, the room a black hollow behind him. After half an hour she could not help herself and drifted into sleep.

The first disturbance of the night came as a scuffle, a woman's shouts and a confusion of voices, how many men how many women she couldn't tell, although one of the voices, she was certain, was Salvatore's. By the time she made it to the window the fuss was over, the entrance door shut, the courtyard silent. The boy's window and blinds now closed.

The second disturbance came several hours later when Peña was woken once again by a soft call, men's voices rising though the hollow. She looked out and saw the boy standing on the window ledge, one hand timidly touching the shutter, his toes tipped to the lintel. Four floors up and the boy stood at the lip of his window, knees slightly bent, while from the courtyard voices seemed to coax him forward with a baritone coo. Unsure of what she should do Peña picked up her water glass. Terrified that she might startle him and cause him to fall. She thought to drop the glass, but instead simply struck it lightly, a spoon against a glass – a slight sound, clear and distinct. The boy looked up. He stepped back, and Peña moved forward so that he could see her. The boy slipped further back from the edge, clambered down, then closed the shutters. With the shutters closed, the voices stopped, and she thought that she had imagined this. A startling image, a boy in a window, so high above the courtyard.

The third disturbance came at four in the morning. A shout from the boy's room, cries, the clatter of shutters thrown open: light cast directly across the courtyard to brighten her room.

A scene of unity, the three together in the boy's room, Lanzetti holding the child, the mother bent beside him, insisting that she look at his hand, prising it open, and the boy twisted away, stuck to his father crying slow ow-ow-ow's.

Anna came to the window, looked down into the courtyard and then shouted across to Peña. 'Who did this? You saw. You must have seen.'

Peña shook her head.

'It's impossible. You must have seen who did this. You see everything.' Anna leaned further over the ledge, fierce and unwavering.

Peña again shook her head.

Anna left the boy's bedroom. Lanzetti followed after – the boy fast to his side – asking where she was going.

'I'm going to talk to her,' Peña heard her say. 'I'll make her tell me who did this,' she said, 'that shrunken little bitch.'

Peña stood at her door and opened it knowing that the woman would shout at her, that there would be no containment, no reserve. Anna Soccorsi came across the landing with a toy held in her hand, a small metal car, the front end blackened.

'They heated this. Do you see? He burned his hand. It was deliberate. Do you understand? This is assault, and you saw who did it.' Now warmed up, she looked over Peña's shoulder and caught sight of Sami's toys laid out across Peña's kitchen table. Her voice immediately slipped gear, became incredulous, alarmed. 'What is this?' She turned to Peña. 'Those are my son's toys. Look,' she shouted to Lanzetti and pointed, 'look, she has his toys. It was you? It was you! I'm calling the police.' One hand covering her mouth, Anna turned and ran back to her apartment.

Back in her apartment Anna vented her rage at her husband. In one long monologue she lay out her dissatisfactions, her outrage, her unhappiness, and this, this assault, was the natural result of how they lived. A burn on his hand today, and what tomorrow? Lanzetti could not soothe her and found no consolation for her outrage.

Lanzetti came to apologize. Peña stepped aside and allowed him into her apartment. His eyes settled first on the table. She had cleared the boy's toys away, hidden them in a drawer. Uncomfortable, the doctor nodded at the windows – the closed shutters.

'All these people,' he said, 'so close. The way we live now.' Lanzetti meshed his hands together.

She asked if he would like a seat, but the man remained standing, the size of him, filling the room. 'How is your son?'

'It's not so serious. He has a blister.' Lanzetti forced his hands into his pocket. 'He was fishing,' he said, 'playing a game with people he couldn't see. He sent down a toy on a piece of string and they heated it up.' He began to apologize. 'She spends all of her time with him. She won't let him go to school. It's difficult for her. And Sami,' he said, 'believes all of these things, these ideas. He mixes them up.' Lanzetti smiled and shook his head. He spoke slowly and chose his words with care.

'He says that he can hold his breath for fifteen minutes. Fifteen minutes. This is what he says. He believes that he has special powers, that he can control things. He believes that if he concentrates hard enough he can shatter glass, or start fires, or flood a room. He believes that he can make the building shake.'

Lanzetti cleared his throat. 'He does not like to sleep, because he thinks that when he sleeps he cannot control these powers. He believes that when he is idle he makes bad things happen, that when he is asleep he is responsible for earthquakes and landslides. For accidents. I read the paper with him every day to teach him that these things are coincidental. That they have nothing to do with him, that the world works without him and he is not responsible. But unlike other children he isn't able to let this go. He thinks that there are people hunting for him. I'm not sure what we will do.'

WEDNESDAY: DAY D

Mizuki told the story in class about the brothers at the station. An ordinary moment, easily told, about how, on three successive days, she had noticed one man on the platform, the other up on the concourse, and how on that first day she was confused to see a man she assumed to be behind her, suddenly, so quickly, ahead. Today she'd found the men waiting side by side at the top of the escalator: both men had watched her walk by, hands in pocket, one without much interest, the other with a certain intensity. This time she had her phone ready, but didn't dare take a photograph, and didn't pause to buy water. In crude and cumbersome Italian she explained her confusion and delight in seeing one man doubled. Today, the couple (could you even call brothers a couple?) followed her to the station exit – although she couldn't be certain that this was deliberate. She used the words *attractive*, *handsome*, when what she wanted to say was brutish. *Bruto* in Italian meant ugly, and the word caused confusion.

The tutor nodded as Mizuki spoke: not in agreement, but collecting mistakes. The group discussed what the men could be waiting for – some crime no doubt, Mizuki should watch her bag. Those stations are dangerous.

The tutor shrugged. 'It's part of our culture to observe. It rarely means what you think.'

The women disagreed, and began speaking in English. It wasn't the looks, so much, but the comments, or the tutting, what was that about? Men tutting at women? And wasn't it worse in southern Italy than anywhere else?

Mizuki found nothing problematic in the men's interest. Nothing troublesome. It wasn't quite interest in any case. She knew the word in English, she knew it in Japanese: one of the men was *assessing* her. Collecting information. He'd looked at her, three times, with a kind of assessment that had little to do with catching her eye. When men look at you they usually expect a response. But this man didn't appear to want anything.

Although her story had nothing to do with coincidence, the class became busy with stories of happenstance: a woman who missed a flight that crashed into the ocean off Brazil, only to be killed one year later in a car accident in Austria; a man who survived one bombing in London to die four years later in another. Mizuki could not follow the logic. Europeans, she thought, Americans, are like birds in the way they collect information: greedy and undisciplined. How foreign this all seemed in comparison to the look she'd received three times at the Circumvesuviana, a look of solid concentration, a look signifying intelligence, a focused assessment.

With some effort the tutor drew the conversation back to the previous night, to conversations the students might have attempted in Italian. But the discussion slipped into rumour and could not be retrieved.

'I don't like it here. It isn't safe.'

The group nodded in agreement.

'It's no worse than anywhere else.' Mizuki shrugged and added that the city was beautiful, knowing this would please the tutor.

'It's not the city. It's the people.'

The other students keenly agreed. Something about the city just didn't feel safe. Mizuki flushed with embarrassment.

One of the military wives spoke up. 'They warn us not to go into the centre on our own. We aren't allowed into the Spanish Quarter. Don't even think about it.'

While Mizuki had spent time in Berkeley there were still some American accents she couldn't follow.

The tutor clapped her hands, 'Italian! We speak in Italian!' This was not what she wanted to discuss.

A French student shifted her chair forward. 'I couldn't live here. It's all the same. The restaurants serve Italian food and nothing else. There's a Japanese restaurant in Vomero, and guess what? They sell pizza.' She held up her hands, exasperated. 'Seriously. This is old Europe. It's important what village you come from, or street, or neighbourhood. It matters. People actually care about that kind of thing.'

Mizuki couldn't accept the point. How different was this, say, from New York, Paris, Tokyo, where people took you more seriously depending on your street, district, zone.

The American student held up her hand. And what about the Spanish student in Elementario Due who was chased through the Centro Storico *by a man with a machete*?

The tutor dipped forward in defeat. She knew this student, she said, and Erica, point of fact, wouldn't run even if her head were on fire.

'I heard this from an Italian,' the American continued regardless. 'There's an earthquake in the middle of the day, OK, and a house shared by two families – one family from Milan, the other from Venice – and it's totally destroyed. Which family die?'

The women fell silent.

'A family from Naples who broke in while the others were at work.'

Mizuki could not look up and didn't want to face the tutor. The class fell silent: when the tutor finally spoke she suggested they take an early break.

Mizuki waited in the stairwell for Lara to finish her class: she checked the messages on her phone then switched it off. She thought to leave, to return to the station although she guessed the brothers would be gone by now. A young man flapped a dishcloth out of a window; the sound dislocated and came softly across the courtyard to her, undiminished. People knew their neighbours because the courtyards amplified every detail: the TVs, radios, the clatter of plates and cutlery, the arguments and supple conversations, the flushing toilets, the water running through pipes, and with surprising frequency, people singing or coughing. To live here was to sense your neighbours at all hours, to taste the food they ate, to bear their good tempers and bad. It made no sense that she would like this city, being so opposite to home, so permeable and messy.

When Lara finally arrived the friends kissed in greeting. Lara said she looked tired and asked if she still wasn't sleeping.

Mizuki shrugged, who knew why these things happened?

'You should rest this weekend.'

They sat on the cool marble steps of the open stairwell, quietly sharing confidences, while other students (the military wives, the vacationing teachers) on their way to the café mixed with priests and clerks from the seminary offices. Mizuki, closest to the courtyard, kept an eye on the wasps, small specks chaotically charging the air two floors below. No one else appeared bothered.

She repeated the joke, knowing it would annoy Lara.

'They talk about this place like it's a zoo,' Lara slapped her hand to the step. 'Come on. I need a cigarette.'

Mizuki followed Lara through the courtyard and kept close to her side; her hands tucked away, her collar drawn up. Wasps zagged over the biscuits in untold numbers, their tiny shadows flitting across the wax paper, antennae dipping for syrup. A horror show. Mizuki covered her mouth, held back her hair, half-ran to the door with her eyes closed, suppressing a squeal – bad enough to be stung, far worse to swallow one.

Once outside Lara lit up, indignant now, unaware of her friend's small panic. Mizuki held her hand to her heart.

'And where does she get these ideas? She lives in Bagnoli.' Lara huffed out smoke. 'These houses are behind gates, no one can visit. Americans keep themselves locked away. They aren't houses, they're safes.'

The buildings overshadowed the street and drew out a cavernous darkness. A clean blue sky pinched above tight black alleyways of old stucco facades, of dim intestinal yellows and pinks. Above them hung a sign for the bakery, a simple tin star in a circle. How familiar this was now, this depth: straight lines buckled to time and gravity. Streets designed for walking, for carts, made perfect runs for scooters and dogs and channelled their noise.

'If they don't offer me something soon I'll have to go back.' Due to finish her course, Lara taught sessions at the language school as part of her placement. 'It's good to have work, but it's always temporary, and it's not enough. Everywhere is the şame.'

They watched students return from the cafe one by one, each buzzing first, then ducking through the small portal door. Mizuki looked over two dusty violas displayed in the window of an antiques store. She held her hand to the glass to see into the shop.

'They never sell anything. I've never seen it open,' Lara paused. 'You're wearing a wedding ring?'

Equally surprised, Mizuki looked at her own hand then held it up for Lara to see.

'I've never seen you wear a ring.'

'It was my mother's.' Mizuki automatically began to screw the ring about her finger. 'I wear it at home. Sometimes. I forgot to take it off.'

The first bell rang and they returned to the courtyard. Lara hesitated at the door, half-in, half-out, unconvinced by Mizuki's answer.

Mizuki let Lara walk ahead, worried now that Lara would ask bolder, more direct questions. She hurried by the bakery, did not look at the trays of biscuits, but noticed, up on the third landing, the American, Helen, arms up, flailing, and couldn't make sense of her gestures, how her hands slapped uselessly at the air. Up the stairs Mizuki kept behind Lara to avoid her questions, and the reason for the waving came to her. A wasp.

Mizuki fell immediately on the first sting, sudden and heavy, and upturned her bag even as the wasp, caught in her hair, stung her throat a second and third time. She frantically ruffled her hair, felt the insect between her fingers as something rough, like a seed head, caught then swiped free, she saw the pen, a red tube, tumble out of her bag with her lipstick, face cream, sun cream, tissues, hand mirror, mascara; her course books scudded down the steps, her phone. She snatched up the pen, snapped off the top, stuck it to her shoulder and injected herself.

By the time Lara reached her, Mizuki was done. The wasp, flicked out of her hair, spun circles on the marble.

And now the part she hated, a light woozy bafflement, how she might even seem a little drunk. How inevitable this was because of the biscuits, the syrup, the wasp's natural aggression, and how day after day for six weeks the odds were getting thin. Inevitable now that Lara would ask questions about the ring and Mizuki would have to explain herself.

Lara brought her to the office then returned to the stairwell to collect her bag and books. Mizuki sat by the computers expecting to feel sick, an awful anticipation. She took the water offered to her, insisted that she was all right, and explained to Lara once she returned that she took antihistamine each night as a precaution. Who could say if this helped, if this time there would or would not be a reaction?

'When I was a girl,' she explained, 'I was stung.' Once, on her foot – and her legs, her arms, her face swelled like she was some kind of windbag, or some instrument. And while her throat had not sealed, a mighty itch had troubled her afterward as if her neck was fur-lined, and the threat that one day she might choke stuck with her. Ant bites, spider bites, a scratch once from coral, and she swelled up, ballooned.

As if to prove her contrariness the insulin depressed her. She could feel the immediate effect. Not sick now but tired. A nurse from Elementario Due came out to check her pulse, her throat, and declared if something was going to happen, it would have happened. Mizuki wasn't sure that this was true. She hid in the toilet and hoped that Lara would leave her, but Lara stuck outside and waited in the corridor.

An undiscouraged Lara accompanied her to the station. Because of her tiredness, Mizuki felt a general disconnection from what she was doing; more than this, she felt empty, and this emptiness seemed evident in every spoken word and gesture, to the flow of passengers rising on escalators or paused on the stairs, the deepening sunlight, the presence of the scaffolding, of paint pots and rollers laid across the platform. She insisted that she would be all right; two hours now and there were no serious fears, no reaction. She just wanted to be home. Home? In the hot and still air it seemed possible that she could haul herself above the hubbub and swim free. In her dreams flying and swimming were the same action, but even when dreaming she never really lost what was troubling her, she never really became free.

Mizuki took off her sunglasses and shook her head. She pointed at the stubby towers of Porta Nolana, close by there was a café, she said, she had something she wanted to say.

Lara paid for the coffees, brought them to the window where they stood and faced the Circumvesuviana station. The sun sparked off windscreens and chrome of passing traffic. She couldn't help but scan through the waiting groups outside the station for the brothers.

Lara dusted sugar off her hands.

Unsure about how she should start, Mizuki took out her passport and passed it across the counter, the text inside was printed in Japanese and English. 'My name is not Mizuki Katsura,' she began. 'I didn't intend to lie to you. I haven't told you everything. I'm married. It's true that this ring belonged to my mother.' Mizuki rubbed her finger as Lara paged through the passport, conscious that her friend would not look at her. Mizuki looked to the station forecourt. 'When I first met my husband he told me he had two ambitions. He wanted to marry before he was fifty, and he wanted to see every building designed by Kenzo Tange. He likes this architect. Back home, in Tokyo, he has an office in a building designed by Tange. He sometimes arranges his business so that he can go to a new city and see Tange's buildings, and he has seen almost all of them, but he hasn't come to Naples. He hasn't seen the

Centro Direzionale. After we married he became busy with his work. He's away most of the time, and I was looking after his mother, who is very sick and very difficult. When I decided to leave, I couldn't decide where I should go, or what I should do. And one day he was talking about Tange and Naples. I don't know why, but I made up my mind to come here.'

Lara closed the passport and left it face down on the counter.

'Why did you leave him? Why change your name?'

'I don't know. I could say that he is nineteen years older than me. That he knows his mind. He never makes mistakes. He is always certain. I could say that I always make mistakes. I make too many mistakes.' Mizuki bowed her head. 'But I don't know that these are the right reasons.'

'He doesn't know where you are?'

Mizuki shook her head. 'Nobody knows. Not even my family. If they knew they would tell him.'

'What about your friends?'

'I had friends before I was married, but he didn't like them. He told me they were bad people, or they were stupid, or strange, and that they were not a good influence. Then, slowly, they stopped calling or inviting me out. It's complicated. When I'm with him I don't know my own mind.'

'But if he can't find you here. If he doesn't know where you are, he can't bother you.'

'My husband is very wealthy. I thought that if I told somebody they would find out how wealthy he is and they would tell him where he could find me. I don't think they would want to – not at first. But I'm certain that this would happen.'

Lara propped her elbows against the counter. Both women looked hard at the coaches and taxis under the station awning. 'This is my second attempt to finish my studies? I never finished – the first time – because I met someone. It was a terrible mistake. I gave up everything. When it was over, when I came back, I had to start from the beginning again. I had nothing. Nowhere to live, no money, no work. I had to start everything from the beginning.'

Mizuki fell quiet for a moment. It was sad, she said, when one person gives too much and the other takes for no proper reason.

'It's never that simple. But why don't you tell him where you are?'

Mizuki paused then closed her eyes. The story was not true, not quite. She hadn't left her husband exactly, but run away for an adventure, something happenstance, the kind of encounter suggested by the brothers at the station: one thing couldn't end without another starting.

Lara saw her onto the train and then left.

Immediately out of the station the line ran between empty warehouses and loading bays stacked with rusted shipping containers, the shore visible between the gaps. Mizuki sat beside the window, her shirt stuck to the small of her back, and she regretted explaining herself to Lara. Why had she done this? After spending six weeks as Mizuki Katsura, she had spoiled this illusion in five, less, three minutes of careless chatter. She couldn't understand why she would do this, and couldn't see what she could do to correct it. In an attempt to dismiss the day's events she began to take notice of the passengers, and sensed among the men an air of opportunity. They looked at the women dressed in thin skirts and tight summer tops with long glances and lowered heads. A dog-like expression, she thought, common, hopeful, indolent, and nestling threat.

Mizuki looked at the sea through breaks between the apartment buildings. Her mobile rang as the train came into San Georgio, and she was bothered to see that the call came from Lara. More questions. More explanations.

One man dressed in a business shirt, his tie loose about his neck, stood too close. Mizuki shut off the phone and closed her eyes. How disappointing these men were, and how unlike the brothers. If she saw them now what would she do? Would she speak with them, follow after them? The idea of two brothers took on a new shape and possibility. It wasn't the older brother who interested her, no, it was both of them, together, and how would it be to spend time with two men? One intense, the other removed.

The train slowed as it approached Torre del Greco; men drew out cigarettes, lighters ready in their hands. The businessman paused on the platform as he lit his cigarette. He caught Mizuki's eye as the door shut between them, then gestured, hands raised, unresolved.

Anxious that her sleep would again be interrupted, Mizuki prepared carefully for bed. She ate early and moderately, and then focused on completing her assignments. Once she was done she sat at the dressing table and declined verbs, then answered simple questions with direct answers and watched Italian bubble out of her mouth. Mizuki practised the tricky rolling consonants, the unchanging vowels, and wondered at how her expression, fierce with concentration, appeared to show anger, when she was seldom, if ever, harsh or bad-tempered.

In the hour before bed Mizuki set her books aside and took a long shower. She bathed the stings with antiseptic. She double-checked her tongue and throat. She turned the sheets, opened the shutters to refresh the room, laid out her clothes for the next day, so that even the smallest decision would not trouble her, and she knew, even as she did this, that she should call Lara and attempt to undo what she had said.

The call came after Mizuki had gone to bed. The line fizzed and a voice, immediately familiar, crackled out, saying nothing except an inquisitive, 'Hello, hello?' in Japanese.

'Hiroki.' She said her husband's name without inflection then cancelled the call. She checked the screen to make sure that the connection was cut.

The phone rang again, two bursts, and stopped.

Mizuki sat up, turned on the lights, assured herself that she was far away, that it was only her husband's voice which could carry to the room. How had he found her? Less than five hours after she'd spoken with Lara. How could this happen so quickly? Mizuki set the phone on the pillow and lay beside it so that her ear was close. She watched it ring and stop. Ring and stop. A counter clocked the number of incoming calls.

Lara answered on the first ring and asked Mizuki if she was all right. 'I was worried,' she said. 'You didn't answer.'

Mizuki wasn't sure where to start. 'What if everything I told you wasn't true?' she asked.

Lara said she didn't understand.

'What if everything I've told you came from another person? All of the details. What if I'd taken everything from somewhere else?'

Silent for a moment, Lara said she didn't understand. 'Why would anyone do that?'

A silence grew between them. Mizuki wanted to know details, she wanted to understand how Lara had found him so quickly, how she could have come to such a decision with so little thought. Not five hours even. Not even one night. But all she could ask was why.

'Are you in trouble?' she asked. 'Because if you needed money, I could have given you money. You could have asked me.'

Lara said she didn't understand.

Mizuki turned onto her side and changed her mind about talking. 'It's not important.'

Mizuki cancelled the call, rolled onto her back and looked up. The ceiling fan stirred hot air to no result. The phone rang and she looked at the small screen and decided that she wouldn't speak to Lara again.

Despite her best efforts Mizuki lay awake, aware of the passing minutes, the tread of traffic, the supple chuff of voices outside the all-night *farmacia*, and later, much later, the sharp and mournful caw of gulls – sounds so ordinary that ordinarily they would cause her no trouble. She wouldn't return to the language school. Naples had not provided what she wanted after all, or rather, if she was honest, she didn't have the courage to follow opportunity when it occurred. The brothers provided a perfect example: supposing these men were interested in her, she doubted she could follow through. She began to consider other cities. Milan, perhaps. Rome. Palermo. Genoa.

When she finally did sleep, in the moment she succumbed, Mizuki felt a weight descend upon her, a rolling tide that brought anxious but unspecific dreams.

☆

The sun crossed obliquely over the building and spilled through the window, drawing with it the noise of traffic, buses idling outside the station, car horns, the hiss and snort of hydraulic brakes, shouts from the market stalls. Lila woke to the dog's barks, which sounded less alarmed than usual, a colour to them, frisky, expectant. Today she felt soft, gummy, not one hard bone in her body, not one joint. She liked how Arianna inclined toward her, leaned on her, almost nestling, how their skin brushed lightly when she breathed in.

Rafí returned in the early evening and said nothing at first about the previous night but kept himself busy fetching water for the dog.

'So I'll make the arrangements, then?' His foot nudged Lila's thigh. 'What do you think? I'll get everything organized.'

Arianna turned over. 'Organize what?'

'With the brothers.'

Arianna cleared her throat and began to cough.

'Tonight. I'll set something up. They'll come and pick you up.'

Arianna rose herself onto her elbows and frowned at Lila, her face red. 'What's he talking about?'

Lila shrugged.

'I'm talking about the two men from last night,' he said, 'they'll pick you up in front of the station.'

Arianna shook her head. She blinked into the sunlight. 'You told them where we live?'

'I told them to meet you at the station.'

Rafí stood over Lila, raised his foot and pressed it onto her stomach. 'You're going to be nice tonight,' he warned.

They waited under the station hood, anxious about the police, the carabinieri, the station security, the taxi drivers. This surely wasn't a smart idea. In front of the entire square, fenced off and dug up, cranes reaching over, the belly of the piazza dug out to a vast black pit. A white car drew up to the kerb and the headlights flickered. Two men sat inside and watched the women approach. As they came alongside the passenger opened his door and stepped out. Lila looked across the piazza to the Hotel Stromboli and picked out the windows on the upper floor, imagining herself already in bed, and thought, How is it that this building always appears to be wet? Arianna began to heckle: who did these people think they were? I mean seriously, to pick them up at the station like common whores?

The passenger leaned on the car roof, smug, hands clasped, smiling. They only wanted to be nice, he said. Nice. Nothing more than that. Behind him, from a ring-fenced lot, steam rose from the building work, a new line for the metro, a pipe impossibly crusted with ice.

Arianna gave a huff. 'Nice. What is this nice?' She settled her hands on her hips and leaned forward, neck stuck out. With slender shoulders and waist, large hands, the passenger looked out of proportion, a long body of mismatched parts. Not a boxer, Lila decided, but a swimmer.

Now the driver stepped out of the car and Lila could see that the men, unaccountably tall and trim with similarly shorn hair, were undoubtedly brothers. The same features – noses, brow line, small inset eyes like field mice – the same swagger. Men who considered themselves handsome. The driver pointed to Lila and indicated that she should get in.

The driver approached, slid his arm about her waist and brought Lila to the car and opened the door, something gracious about the gesture, his hand in the small of her back. When Lila sat down she thought to open the opposite door and slide out but did nothing. On the pavement Arianna stood with her arms out wide, palms up, face set with disapproval. Ignoring her, the younger brother and the driver returned to the car, leaving Arianna alone on the pavement, behind her the long swoop of the station front, black windows of empty restaurants, chairs on tables, the certain presence of security guards. When the car started Arianna reached for the door handle.

With Arianna in the car the younger brother locked the passenger doors. Lila sat with her arms crossed and looked up at the Stromboli, a thought came to her, *wasn't this what they had talked about,* but she kept the thought to herself.

The passenger set his hand on Arianna's knee and shoved clumsily under Arianna's skirt. 'Now you are the one with the cock? Yes? Show me,' he grinned.

Arianna stopped the man's advances in a small gesture, a hesitation rather than a refusal. In response the man twisted completely about – and with a swift and sudden jab punched Arianna in the face. The sound of it, a snap, then Arianna's howl accompanied their acceleration about the piazza.

When they arrived at the farmhouse Arianna bolted from the car, hurtling into darkness, leaving one sandal in the footwell, another tipped on its side in the gravel, pointing to an orchard, a long wall, dimly lit by the car's red tail-light. Lila sat with the door open, the night air a soft drift across her shoulders, the realization slowly occurring to her that they would not escape this trouble. The passenger shot swift as a rat after Arianna and leapt on her with poisonous certainty. The driver pulled Lila out of the car, hefting her forward by her hair and dropping her at the threshold so that her elbows struck the flagstone. While Arianna fought and struggled, Lila shut down and made no attempt to protect herself. She focused hard on the details before her, the uneven floor, the tiles, broken but still in place; the peaty stink of rotten furnishings. She knew these smells. She knew this air, how the wind picks salt from the sea so that it can be tasted many miles inland.

THURSDAY: DAY E

Lila and Arianna were abandoned twelve miles outside the city on a slip road off the Domiziana. Hired pickers and farmhands working in the lower fields watched the women struggle out of the car naked and shoeless – and for one bad moment the vehicle jolted backward threatening to reverse and run them down but drew instead hastily off the side road. They had seen women squabbling in awkward brawls, hairpulling, kicking, ugly slap fights at the roadside, or more usually cars pulling slowly into the tree-line and dropping some girl off, often as abrupt, but never with such threat. Later, confirming the story among themselves, the workmen easily described the women but disagreed on the model of the car, mistaking its dusty coat for grey or tan or silver. The men had barely started work, and the last thin breath of mist clung stubbornly to the irrigation ditches, and there, right before them, two naked women scurried chaotically, chicken-like, across the fields.

First out of the car, Arianna zigzagged across the mud then clambered back up the embankment and stumbled alongside the road, falling more than walking, cars veered wide, her focus set on the distant lilac mountains, her hands covering her crotch. When the labourers caught up they beat their sticks and tools on the road and whooped to drive her down to an irrigation ditch. Trapped in the shallow black water Arianna began to bellow in a language they couldn't understand, and they could see for the first time cuts and bruises, soiled red skin and fatty white grazes, evidence that she had been brutalized – and they could also see, despite her skinny figure, her long hair and hard breasts, that she was a man.

Deaf to the labourers' hoots and jeers Lila tottered through the mud and slippy rotten sops of cut greens, her underarms, buttocks, stomach, legs, caked with dirt. She fled diagonally across the field, and ran with quick picky steps, but when she heard Arianna's shouts she simply stopped, sat in the mud, hung her head and covered her ears, waiting for whatever would catch up with her. Startled, the men also stopped. Keeping their distance they waited for the police.

In the ambulance the women faced each other, eyes wide at the strangeness of being brought from an open ploughed field into a box where they could hear themselves breathe. Wrapped in a rough red blanket Arianna shivered violently and would not look up, her ankles and forearms crossed with deep bramble scratches, her neck scored purple, swollen to show the clear imprint of a belt. Lila refused to be touched and sat forward, head down, hands tucked under her thighs. This was her fault. Clearly all her fault. As she slowly warmed, the punctures on her back began to suppurate. She fought against sleep, fearing the sensation that she was evaporating, becoming lighter than air; but sleep, or something like it, brought on by a mess of drugs came in soft buckling waves, impossible to resist. The accompanying officer, dressed in a smart and faultless uniform, looked out of the back of the vehicle and watched the road and fields recede. In full daylight the mountains took on the soft contours of a strong man's arm.

They were separated at the hospital and taken to small bright booths set side by side. Alone, Lila slipped off the high examination table and hid under it with the thin tunic drawn over her head. She squeezed hard against the wall. The pressure and the cool tiles soothed the sores on her back and the penetrating ache in her shoulders. Crouched under the bed she could smell cigar smoke in her sweat, and the sweet, cold stink made her retch. She did not want to sleep and she did not want to be awake, neither did she want to be alone. She called for Arianna. Her voice sounded separate, not of her making, so that the sound itself became something to fasten on to.

Almost two hours after they had arrived at the hospital a second woman officer returned with a photographer, a doctor, and two uniformed police. The woman spoke to Lila in a whispered singsong, supposing that Lila was as degraded as she appeared.

'Can you come out? Can you stand? Can you sit?'

Lila allowed the woman to coax her out. She sat where she was told and did not flinch as the doctor opened the back of her tunic and unpicked the temporary dressing.

The man spoke in a flat and practised tone, almost a private whisper as he described his actions. 'I'm going to lift and extend your arm. Let me know if this is too painful.'

Lila allowed the man to hold out her arm and softly turn her head, and made no complaint when he compressed the skin either side of the wounds. The dry sound of dressings being unsnapped from their packets identical to the sound of that first punch – a sharp crack.

'These are cigar burns.' The doctor began to count the blisters across her neck, shoulders, back, behind her knees, and on the soft underside of her arms. 'And these,' he said, 'are bites. Here, and here. Here. These marks are older.'

She said nothing.

The brothers, trading places, warned that if either of them spoke they would return to finish what they'd started. Lila didn't doubt their threats, she wasn't lucky, a simple fact, and she knew when to take advice.

The photographer took pictures of her back and shoulders. He took photographs of the nape of her neck, showing where her hair had been tugged out. Coming round to face her he photographed the bruises and lacerations to her thighs, wrists, and breasts, then took a single photograph of her face. The men who touched her now wore gloves. Lila waited for them to be done.

After searching for traces of fluids, the doctor began to inspect for matter, dirt captured on the rough skin on her feet and in the grazes on her knees, traces of ash and tobacco swabbed from the wounds. He measured the bruise about her neck, then one by one the bites, burns, the lacerations were swabbed, cleaned and finally dressed. The sounds of utensils set in their trays, of metal against metal, and metal against glass, sang unnaturally sharp in the small booth, sharp sounds tightened by the hard walls, unabsorbed and brittle, unexpectedly invasive.

With the examination complete Lila was left alone with the promise that someone would return with clothes. She waited, stared at the door until her eyes watered and wished herself, uselessly, elsewhere. The woman returned, apologizing, with two T-shirts held to her chest. A charitable order provided the clothes and this was all they had at the moment. The clothes were new, both with designs, smiling cartoon characters Lila did not recognize. She sounded apologetic. It was OK; no one else had worn them.

When the police returned she'd changed her mind, come around to the idea that it didn't much matter if she did or did not speak, and that the effort not to speak would require resources that she knew she didn't have. The choice was a simple economy.

They met the men at the station, she said. If they wanted to know exact details they could speak with Rafí at the Hotel Stromboli. They'd raided the hotel a number of times and they would know him.

The brothers were tall, slender, active, with sporting bodies, trimmer and fitter than the men she was used to. Their hair was cropped military-style. They had clipped their body hair, and one of them, the younger brother, had waxed his arms. Except for a thumbprint mole under the older brother's right nipple there were no tattoos, no distinguishing marks. She couldn't guess their ages, but they appeared younger than the officers now questioning her. They almost certainly weren't Italian, and weren't familiar with the city nor the autostrada: when they were driving they took a number of wrong turns. She couldn't swear to it but there were times when they spoke to each other in pidgin French, or slang, or in a private invented language.

After the first punch, when the passenger, the younger man, hit Arianna, the brothers had joked with each other. The older man was persuasive, and he kept talking about a party in Livorno, and that other women were being brought there. Rafí had promised this earlier, maybe the day before, and Lila in particular liked the promise that they would be introduced to influential men; judges, lawyers, businessmen, but knew that this was unlikely. In their long slow afternoons Lila and Arianna had concocted a loose plan where they would move to America, to Los Angeles, or stay in Europe and work together in Milan, Paris, or maybe even return to Barcelona. They wanted to be kept by one man, why not, or better still, to be able to afford an apartment of their own where they would establish themselves with a select and limited number of clients, men that they would choose, and their working lives would run to a timetable of regulated and well-paid fucks. This hope had underscored every discussion, and the brothers' hint that they understood this was one of the night's enduring cruelties.

The second officer asked for other details, he could tell from her accent that she wasn't Italian. Lila nodded, yes, she'd come to Naples and worked for a while in a shop on via Duomo. Her family needed money. She often used this story, and Rafí laughed at it, because, let's face it, she'd never worked upright in her entire life, and, best of all, even if in some crazy alternate universe she did find herself a job men would always smell her out, because first and foremost she was a whore: where would she be without those American servicemen she was so fond of, and those good clean Scandinavian boys from NATO who were always so generous with their drugs? Lila also cringed at the idea, but it made a better story than the way she passed her days. For Lila time divided between doing something and doing nothing, and she dreaded time spent on her own. Alone at the Stromboli she felt like baggage, like substance without worth.

The officers began to ask questions she couldn't answer, and Lila began to tire. Perhaps she needed a moment to herself. Lila shrugged, she'd told them as much as she knew. Nothing further would occur to her.

When the door reopened Arianna leaned into the room. Her neck now purple, her face swollen and pulpy, her eyes panda-wide and bruised. Stopped at the door she leaned slightly in and whispered, 'Lila. Lila? We can't stay.' Arianna looked back into the corridor then stepped into the room. Behind her, and this made no sense, stood Rafí. 'We can't stay. We have to go.' Arianna held out her hand. 'You understand? We can't stay here.'

Lila called to Arianna, and a second, more formidable wave of nausea overcame her and she thought that she might faint.

'I had to call him,' Arianna whispered. 'This is only for tonight. We take our money and we leave like we planned. Tomorrow. We go tomorrow.'

Rafí hovered at the door, anxious and uneasy, eyes on the corridor.

Arianna was right, they should leave, but Lila couldn't rouse herself, all energy and self-determination gone. Arianna held out her hand, now impatient. 'Now. We have to go now.'

Rafí supported Lila on his arm, one T-shirt held to her chest, the other across her shoulders. As soon as she stood a chill passed through her and she thought that she might collapse. Rafí lumbered her through the hospital corridors without a word, taking an emergency exit so that they came out onto a parking lot edged with trees that seemed to her to be another country perhaps. Not Italy but America. A flat periwinkle sky. A low-lying mall too wide to be part of the city she knew. Barefoot, Arianna walked ahead and scanned the lot for the car. A technician in blue overalls sat smoking in the shade, the ground soft with pine needles. He looked at the three and blew smoke into the branches, indifferent to their hurry and disorder.

☆

Marek waited until the afternoon to call the brothers. He sent them photographs he'd taken of the Citroën, and asked if they still needed a driver. *I know the city,* he wrote, *if there's anything you need during your stay. Don't hesitate.* He tried to imagine what they might want, two men in Naples, and couldn't picture taking a holiday with his own brother, who in any case would never know his own mind without his wife. A hot summer, almost too hot to move, and hadn't Peña said the brothers didn't know the city, and they barely spoke the language. He knew from military service the kind of trouble men could make for themselves, it wasn't that they specifically sought it out, but given the opportunity, trouble would happen. If they wanted opportunity, as in *company,* he could help with that.

He waited in the cafe and stood at the window, an eye on his apartment and the magistrate's driver, who lounged against his car, half-hopeful of a call from Tony. A call came mid-morning from the brothers. Did Marek know of a doctor? One of the brothers had been punched in a fight and he needed a doctor. Could Marek bring someone to the hotel? It wasn't anything that needed any fuss. They would appreciate his discretion.

At first Lanzetti wasn't interested.

'I'm a pharmacist. Take them to the hospital. Take them to a clinic.'

'They don't want trouble,' Marek reasoned. 'They know how things work here, how simple things become complicated. They just want a doctor.'

'They don't want the police. This happens all the time.'

Marek shrugged. It was possible, a fight in a bar could lead to all kinds of problems, and no one would want to make a report, no one would want the police involved. He needed the work, but didn't want to spell it out. 'If I do this. If they trust me—'

Lanzetti turned his hands over, palms up as if to ask, *And this should involve me? This should be my problem?* 'You drive them to a hospital. You take them to a clinic. You bring them to a *farmacia.*' Out of politeness he asked where they were, and offered to find out the nearest clinic or pharmacy.

'Hotel Grand, in the hills.'

'Castellammare?'

'On the mountain.'

Marek stepped back from the counter. Before leaving he thanked the doctor for his advice. Before he reached the door Lanzetti had changed his mind.

Marek followed two white vans along the escarpment's terraced walls, vines and fig trees and creepers close on one side, a blue hole on the other. As he came up the hill, Lanzetti pointed out the view, and told him how the Americans at the end of the war had first seen Naples from the very same place. The view struck Marek as a piece of information: a set of facts. So this is where the Americans stood, Lanzetti explained. First they came over the top, then round the side through the valley, and others, even later, came by sea. In four days a mongrel group of partisans with a wise eye on the Americans' progress had rid the city of the Germans. It wasn't just a view about recent history, the capped top of the volcano, the thick plates of lava, and the dangerous proximity of the city spoke as a present reminder to an ancient event every boy knew by heart. Marek patted his pockets for cigarettes as the car crept upward and asked Lanzetti if he smoked.

Lanzetti said they could stop, if he wanted. They needn't hurry? He asked this as a question, and Marek drew over and said no, there was no particular hurry. He stopped at the crown of the hill where the road levelled out to a viewing station.

'I have decided to spend more time.' Lanzetti paused and lit a cigarette and Marek rolled down the window and blew smoke out over the view. 'More time *being present*. Does that make sense? To make sure I enjoy what is around me. My son. Good food. A beautiful view. I know how ridiculous it sounds.'

Marek looked past Lanzetti to the view, mindful of the edge, which fell at a discomfortingly sharp pitch. He saw the view as a phenomenon, a plate of land bounded by mountains and sea with an imperfect cone smack in the centre. If you drew up the centre of a tablecloth you would have yourself a model of the bay, the same flowing curves, the same dimensional scope.

'Last year I lost my father. Now I am the adult. He brought me here a number of times. It is always a good view. Don't you think? There are walks from here to Vico Equense, or over the top to Ravello.'

In front of them a man sat on his motorbike, head turned to the view.

'My wife has taken my son to her brother's.' Lanzetti looked out at the view as he spoke. 'There have been some disturbances at the palazzo. She's unhappy. She's always unhappy. She makes the boy unhappy.'

Marek remembered finding the purse on the coach. The accident wasn't his first death, and certainly not his first accident. The summer before, driving on the Tagenziale, a motorcyclist, a man in black and red leathers, had inexplicably sprung from his bike and spun over the parapet, head over heels, gone. The bike toppled as soon as the man was loose, parts shattering and spinning across the lanes, and Paola shouting in pure disbelief. Did you see that? A cross-wind, the smallest of bumps, a curving bridge, elements long in place that predetermined the young man's startling tumble and thump onto a roof, a balcony, a road. There were other deaths that summer, his father, Paola's grandmother, relatives dressed and laid out in grey rooms in sombre calm, a little dignity returned to them, but these two incidents where men appeared to be snatched, grabbed and thrown, were the measure to him of how life, and the taking of it, was a matter of simple whimsy.

Marek parked between the same two white vans, now being unloaded of decorations and tableware. They followed a man bearing flowers into the hotel lobby. The bouquet, a generous spread of cream-coloured lilies and green ferns, swayed a little obscenely as the man scampered up the steps. Marek, out of place in combat shorts, waited at the entrance and phoned the brothers. All about the lobby and the entrance staff prepped tables, windows, carpets, cleaned and arranged with practised focus. A wedding, without doubt.

A man came out of the hotel, brisk and direct, hand extended and asked Marek if he was the driver from Naples and was this the doctor. Marek shook the man's hand and the man indicated that he should come with him.

They drove in silence down the mountain. Once they joined the autostrada Lanzetti began to ask questions.

'Did he say how this happened?'

'His nose? A fight.'

'A fight?'

'In a bar. I think he said.'

'Did he say where?'

Marek said no. 'It was broken?'

'Yes, but not so bad. There is a bruise, a small swelling.' Lanzetti unfolded his arms. 'And how do you know these men?'

'I don't. They've asked me to drive them.'

'You work for them?'

'I will. They need a driver while they're here.'

'And you know what they do?'

'I only met them today.'

'So you know nothing about the fight? Because there were scratches. It would unusual for a man to scratch.'

'He said it was a man.'

'Perhaps he didn't want to admit.'

Perhaps, they agreed, perhaps. Marek dropped Lanzetti at the palazzo then returned the car to English Tony. He walked back along via Tribunali, a small and indirect detour, but he wanted to think. It wasn't his business what the brothers were doing, now they had guaranteed a steady two weeks of work.

☆

When Lila woke she found herself at the Stromboli lying on her side on the mattress, the T-shirt twisted about her midriff, a clear enough memory of the journey back but nothing after they arrived. An argument swelled about her. Arianna's voice rose hard above Rafi's, insistent on one question. 'My money. Where is the money? My money. I want my money. Where is my money?'

Rafí shouted back, face to face. 'You think you can work now? You think anyone wants you?'

Why had they gone to the hospital without coming first to him? It was the wrong day for this. The men he owed money to would not be happy to know that he wasn't in control of his women. 'Do you have any idea what this means? How this makes me look?' The difference between having something or nothing now depended on them.

Arianna settled on the bed, one argument streamed from her.

Wasn't he supposed to watch out for them? Wasn't that the one small thing he was supposed to do?

Hands dug deep into his pockets, Rafí slipped back to the doorway.

Lila couldn't work after the beating. Arianna insisted. 'She can't. It isn't possible.'

Slumped back on the mattress Lila let the argument fly and felt the small room collapse about her.

She woke a second time to see Arianna lunge from the mattress and spit at Rafí. Rafí cowered and blocked her blows with his forearms. Arianna flailed, untiring. The dressing flapped loose from her wrist.

Throughout, awake or gone, Lila could feel the unending arrhythmic cough of Rafí's dog. She'd let that dog free sometime. She and that dog would go separate ways. She'd rather see it dead than live out on the rooftop.

When she woke a third time the argument had shifted pace, and Arianna sat on the floor hugging her knees and Rafí leaned over her, swearing that he would find these men. He was emphatic. If Arianna knew where these men, these brothers, were now, where he could find them, he would kill them, he swore. He would find them and he would castrate them.

And later still Arianna sat with her head in her hands, sobbing, saying this is crazy, crazy. Alongside this, Rafí talking. It was the wrong day, entirely the wrong day, he had somewhere else to be, he was in default of a debt, the total, by default, now doubled. Lila and Arianna needed to understand this, because he couldn't run around after them, waiting on them, doing the things that needed to be done for them *all of the time*. In any case the Stromboli was closing down, in two months they would be out of a place to live.

In her sleep Lila pawed at her arms, wanting to wake but unable to rouse: she recalled details of the assault with a terrifying clarity – the sour breath of the younger brother as he beat her and how boyishly happy her fear made him, how bold he became, how certain. How he drew on the cigar before he stamped it onto her skin. When she held up her arm to protect her face he grabbed her wrist and bit deep.

*

She woke with Arianna crouched over her, whispering, sobbing, eyes an unreadable black: 'I can't stay here. I'll find somewhere. I will come back.' Arianna stroked Lila's hair, a roll of cash in her hand. 'I'm sorry,' she said. 'I'm so sorry.' A kiss and a promise to return.

☆

Peña returned the boy's trophies: the small soldiers, a racing car, the diver with the yellow aqualung. She set them in a single line close to the door then returned to her apartment to call Salvatore to find out who these men were and exactly what had happened. But Salvatore was not at work and refused to answer her call, although she left message after message. 'I'm not happy,' she said. 'I was very specific that there should be no trouble with the residents. Tell them that I want to speak with them.' But she knew, even as she spoke, that these words were nothing more than a gesture.

The toys remained in place for the entire day. Afterward, the only sounds to come from the apartment came from Arturo Lanzetti, and slowly Peña came to realize that Anna Soccorsi and her son Sami were gone.

FRIDAY: DAY F

Paola wasn't sure she could find the time. Today? Tonight? This weekend, she excused herself, she had plans, work to complete. He could see for himself. All of that, that right there. All of those clothes needed stitching, they weren't going to do themselves. And when she was done it would start again on Monday. Marek couldn't believe his ears. He laid out the brochure, pointed to the hotel. Was she crazy, or being deliberately stupid? This was a five-star hotel with a spa, a swimming pool, a gym, a chef of international renown, with three fully-staffed restaurants one of which sat on a promontory with a view of the entire gulf, and all of it was for free. The brothers were away for the weekend, and they could use their room. Why was she was turning her nose up at the opportunity, except to be spiteful?

He expected a denial, but no, Paola admitted, if that's how he chose to see it, that's probably how it was. But think about it, she said, whoever gives anything away for free? Things that looked too good to be true, as a rule, are pretty much always too good to be true. 'We aren't the kind of people who get given things for nothing.'

Out of his building Marek saw the magistrate's driver again waiting beside the car. The car was parked in almost the same place and the man adopted the same position – leaning against the car door with his arms folded. The difference this time was that the man faced Marek's building, and not the magistrate's. The driver's expression appeared stern and focused, expectant. Aware that he was being watched Marek stepped into the café and decided to take a coffee.

To his surprise the man unfolded his arms, stood upright, and came across the street.

Standing next to Marek the driver took off his sunglasses and asked for a coffee.

Both men stood at the counter and slowly stirred sugar into their coffee.

'It's hot.'

'Indeed.'

'The coffee is good.'

'Very good.'

Both men nodded and then drank their coffees.

The driver smiled. 'The thing about coffee,' he said, 'is that you can never make it the same yourself. It's impossible. It always tastes better away from home.'

Wishing Marek a good morning, the magistrate's driver put his sunglasses back on and walked back across the street to take his position leaning against the car. This time he faced the magistrate's building.

It always tastes better away from home.

Marek was certain that the man was mocking him.

He returned to the apartment and found Paola in the shower, and became intensely aggravated, as if she was preparing herself for a man and not for work. He couldn't believe she wasn't yet working. Marek waited in the bedroom. He stood back from the window and watched the driver to see if there was any signal, any interest even. He searched quickly through her belongings, the pockets in her jacket and trousers, then in her bureau, looking for receipts, notes, messages, anything that would indicate a separate life. But still, he could find nothing, except a life that was ordered, regular, and constrained by work.

Paola came out of the bathroom with her robe open, her breasts and her stomach equally round and white, and appeared surprised to see Marek. She ruffled the towel under her hair. 'Look, I'm not going to change my mind.'

'Who is that man?'

Paola covered herself and peeped quickly out the window to see the driver, her expression indicated that the man, clearly, had some appeal.

'I've no idea.'

Marek was not convinced.

'Everyone knows who he is. He's there all day, every day. He's the magistrate's driver.' The whole street could recognize the man and Paola could not? It simply couldn't be true that she hadn't seen him before.

'And why are we talking about him?'

'If he arranged a weekend in a five-star hotel would you go with him?'

Paola had no idea what he was talking about; she let the towel fall from her shoulder. 'This isn't about you, Marek. It's about work. You know? Work? I don't have time – I really don't have the time for this.'

'But you'd go with him?' Flustered, Marek gestured out of the window, and pointing at the driver he said that he would go down there now, and he would tell the man that he could have her.

Paola, still confused, called him ridiculous and returned to the bathroom. 'I'm going to dry my hair.'

Suddenly angry she returned to the room.

'I don't know what you want, Marek. Tell me? Tell me what you want, because it isn't clear to me. You want a child then you don't want a child. You don't want a holiday then you want to go away for the weekend. You complain about the city, all of the time, and yet you stay here, you talk about going to a hotel which has the best view of the city when you hate the city. I don't know what you want. And now this? I mean seriously, what do you think is going on? How can you not trust me? How dare you say these things when you are disloyal yourself? Tell me, which is worse, doing something, or constantly considering it? You are such a child, Marek. You're this little boy who believes all these things about women. I'm tired of having to work so hard.'

Stopping herself Paola returned to the bathroom, an apparent calm settled about her as she leaned toward the mirror, her mouth set firm as she drew the brush in long forceful strokes through her hair. Marek watched her hand search across the counter top and fail to find her lipstick. 'Fine. You want to go to this hotel. Let's go. It's free. Great. Let's go and see how free it is.'

Once again Marek had the feeling that he had won nothing.

At ten o'clock Marek reported back to Lanzetti that he had returned to the hotel the previous night. The brothers had called him with a proposition. Lanzetti excused himself from work and invited Marek for a coffee at the *alimentari*. They stood side by side at the counter. Marek checked the street and was happy not to see the magistrate's driver nor his car. Lanzetti asked after Salvatore and left the change in the dish. Marek leaned into the counter with a book and a map in his hand: *Napoli, Ischia, Capri. Touring Club Italiano*. On a sheet of notepaper Paul had written out street names and features.

'Paul?' Lanzetti pointed out the name.

He knew their names now, Marc and Paul. 'Paul is the younger brother.'

'And you know where they're from?'

'South? You know I'm not sure. Gap? Gad? Gappe?'

Lanzetti said he didn't know. He hadn't spent time in France, but he could ask his wife when she called this evening. 'Everything French,' he said, 'she loves it all. She loves the wines. She loves the food. She likes that man. That singer.' He couldn't remember names, admitted to it. 'Faces. I see faces and remember the medicines, the strengths. But names.' He shivered quickly to change the subject.

'How long have you lived here?'

Marek counted the years. Three, he thought. Perhaps a little longer.

Lanzetti picked up the book and fanned through the pages. Did Marek speak Spanish?

Marek shook his head. He hadn't meant to pick it up, but it was with the map, and maybe, thinking about it now, he could look up some of the names, at least he could pick out the names of places and see if he knew them.

'And you don't speak French?'

'English. It's easier, their Italian isn't good. It's basic but it isn't good.'

'They don't speak Polish, then?'

Now Marek smiled, he was just getting the measure of the man's sense of humour.

Lanzetti read out loud from the book. Did any of this sound familiar? He didn't know it. 'A mystery? *The Kill*. It must be?'

Marek thought as much. 'It's Paul's, he says it's about Naples.' The book wasn't old, and the story was set in the mid-forties, just after the war, but they were curious about seeing places mentioned in it.

Lanzetti asked if he could borrow the book, just for the night, just to take a look. 'I always have a book. I like to read to my wife,' he said, 'at night. When she's here. My son reads to me, and I read to my wife. If it's any good I will order it for her.'

'They were looking for places from the book.' Marek opened the map. 'I'll take them after the weekend. They wanted to find a farm, a vineyard. In the city.' Marek spread his hand to flatten the paper, from what he could see on the map there was no such thing.

Lanzetti asked him to repeat the question. There was one possibility, up above the neighbourhood marked as Cariati. He didn't know what the neighbourhood was called, or if it had a particular name, but just under the Castel San Elmo and the Certosa, there was an area, a hill, he explained, steep, and terraced into small and spare fields. As far as he knew it was run by an association, and there was an orchard, a place to grow asparagus also, some olive trees, from what he remembered: maybe there was also a small vineyard. He'd been there twice with Anna, once for a wedding, then a second time for a feast to celebrate the end of the harvest. There were some sheds, lean-tos, one with a wood-fire oven, and food was brought to be cooked there. Tables were set out in a double row under the shade of the olive trees. 'It's steep, and it's not anything you'd notice, but the area is entirely countryside. You can see over the city, the whole bay, from Capri to Nisida. It's very beautiful, but from the city it doesn't look like much except wasteland.'

Lanzetti folded the map in half.

You could reach the place by a church. 'Here,' Lanzetti pointed to the map. San Sepulcro, first an old path with proper steps to start, then a small rural path. 'The association keep goats up there, a donkey.' From what he could remember. 'Wild cactus, olive trees, and yes, I suppose a vineyard, grass, not at all what you'd expect in the middle of the city, and it's very steep. But why would they want to see this?'

Marek said he didn't know. They were just interested, he said. But it didn't seem so important.

So this is what they want? Not a driver at all, but someone who knows the city. Someone to confirm a few ideas taken from a book? 'How well do you know the city?'

Marek shrugged and said he had a pretty good idea.

'But you drive? For how long?'

'Two years.'

'In Naples?'

'In Naples. Yes. To the airport. To the city.' Marek wove his hand back and forward. Lanzetti laughed a little.

'What do they want with the room?'

Marek looked up, blank. He hadn't asked. At first, because they were businessmen, there was the idea that they needed the room for storage, but now, meeting them, they clearly weren't here on business.

'They are away for the weekend, and they've offered their room.'

'At the Grand?'

'At the Grand. Tonight and tomorrow night. They've already paid, but they have to be somewhere else, and they want the room when they get back.'

Lanzetti saluted him. 'You must have made an impression.' Marek smiled and said it seemed so. 'You are a lucky man.'

He drove to Salerno and parked beside the docks under the overpass. It was a good place to smoke dope. Marek set the tobacco pouch on his lap and began to make himself a small joint. At midday the prostitutes came out to meet the long-haul drivers waiting for the ferries and deliveries, the men who slept in their cabs before the drive back north. The police drove regularly along the road beside the docks and parked between the bulky red containers off-loaded from the ships, so that it wasn't always possible to see them. Marek watched the docks and the road, and made sure that all of the doors were locked. One prostitute wandered through the shade, made her way dolefully between the trucks and flat-bed lorries parked up alongside the pillars supporting the motorway. Leaning into the windows, or climbing up to the cabins and calling to the drivers, the woman solicited business. Marek smoked and watched, with his hands cupped over his crotch.

And this was the deal: if he wanted the hotel for the weekend, if he wanted a little luxury, he had to find two women. One (and this was easy), an Asian woman, Japanese, who worked for or attended, or lived above a language school close to the palazzo. This was pure curiosity, someone they'd seen a number of times at the station and going into the school, and they wanted clarity, they wanted to know her name. The second woman (a little trickier) worked as a prostitute. A she-male, Paul had said, a very particular she-male. Looks just like a woman. Exactly, every part, with only the one small exception he supposed (ha-de-ha). Paul spoke with fascination and mock-horror, and wouldn't let the subject go once it was raised. The task was simple. Marek didn't have to find her, as in *bring her back*. They just wanted to know her location, where she was, because, as far as they understood, she wasn't in Naples any more. They just wanted to know either way. Marek didn't like Paul's humour. He didn't like the word *she-male* either, and if he thought about it, he didn't like much of anything that came out of Paul's mouth. He knew Paul's type: the wiseacre loud-mouth who became quieter and more unstable the more he drank.

Marek asked for his money upfront, and wanted assurance that the arrangement with the hotel was legitimate.

Marek thought he knew who they were talking about, from watching the women outside the palazzo, he thought he knew. He concerned himself with this, the familiarity, not the issue of whether or not he should be helping them, because, in truth, he didn't understand what this was, and yes, the offer of a luxury hotel for one entire weekend was worth a few hours of idle enquiry. They wanted to know where she was, this she-male, this star. Simple and straight.

The woman walked with her hand out to steady herself. Her hair, an acid yellow, long and crimped, tugged back from her face. She wore a silver jacket and a frayed denim skirt, short and too small to allow her to step easily onto the kerb. From the way that she walked, busy but unsteady, she veered toward the cars in thick-heeled sandals that slipped from her feet, it was clear that she wasn't sober. When she approached Marek he wound up his window and looked blankly ahead, ignoring her. He needed to take a photograph and he didn't have his phone ready. The woman waited at the window, and then knocked. Marek continued to ignore her. He watched her walk on and lean into another car, once he had his phone out of his pocket he flashed his lights. The woman drew out of the car, turned and paused, and Marek flashed the lights a second time.

When the woman returned Marek ignored her and re-lit the joint. The phone sat on his lap. He didn't know why he was doing this, but he wanted to ignore her. The woman tried the doors, front and back, but found them locked. She knocked on the window again, but quickly tiring of him she slammed her hand against the glass and walked off. Marek waited until she was back at the car, and again flashed his lights. Leaning half-in half-out she shouted at him, and gestured that he should go fuck himself, but this time Marek held his wife's small red leather purse up to the windscreen. The women squinted back. Marek continued to flash the car lights and the woman returned, a little unstable on thick heels, shouting, what, what, what did he want? Marek opened the window just wide enough to squeeze the purse through, and he held it there, undecided whether he would let it go or not. When the woman came to the window she curled her fingers over the glass, and asked what it was, what was in the purse. Her voice and hands unfeminine, her make-up crudely defined her lips and eyebrows. Close to the glass he was certain now that he recognized her but doubted that this was the one the brothers wanted. Her face, thickly powdered, eyes and lips drawn with delicate care, but her eyes were dark, a little red, and very distant. She took the purse, looked quickly inside, and tried again to open the door. Finding the door locked, she pulled down her top and pressed her breasts to the window. He took the photo and managed to catch her face before her breasts spread against the glass. A small necklace, the letter 'A' on a chain, trapped against the glass. Laughing, she backed away, then hitched up her skirt and waggled her ass.

Marek squinted into the sun as he drove away. Between the shipping containers he spied a man on a moped. He doubted that the prostitute would keep the purse. The money would go to the man on the scooter.

As he drove back he regretted that the lipstick, which had passed over Paola's mouth, would now belong to a prostitute.

Marek came through the hotel to a terrace and a lawn prepared for another wedding banquet. The Grand Hotel sat on a wide plate high above the gulf; the walls and stuttered tiers of gardens could be seen from the city as a series of white slim-stepped blocks on the mountainside. As he followed after the waiter (a waiter, a clerk, who exactly were these people?) he made a note of the pool, the Jacuzzi, a sign for the spa, the viewing terrace called *Napoli a Piedi*. The man led Marek by tables laid out across a lawn to a lower terrace and a view of the city starting at Castellammare and ending only where the broad sweep of coast rubbed out at the horizon. Marek, as invited, sat at a table with his back to the cliff feeling the suck of all that space behind him, made worse by a swimming pool built right into the edge. He sat with his arms folded, thinking how odd it was to have so much water abutting so steep a drop when the whole point of water was to find the lowest point in any landscape.

'Would you like something to drink while you wait?'

Marek lit a cigarette and blew smoke out over the terrace. A day spent zipping back and forward, but not unproductive. The smoke hung over the drop. The idea of it, suspended, slowly dissipating, made him uneasy. Two nights, two days. Paola would be in her element. When the man returned he told Marek that the brothers had already checked out, but that the room was ready.

He wanted to check the room before he brought Paola, see if the brothers had left anything, luggage, belongings, so that he might get a better understanding of them.

The room faced the bay, and he was surprised to see a large bed and a single cot, but no luggage, and no keepsakes.

Late-afternoon Marek waited outside the language school. He recognized the sign for the bakery – he'd come to the small square many times and sat under the palms, drank at one of the two bars because it was literally just around the corner from the palazzo, a last stop on a night out before going home. The faint whiff of dope hung in the shadows under the long and weedy palms. The older parts of the city divided into micro-neighbourhoods (he'd heard Americans talk this way about their cities), so you could speak of Forcella, Sanita, Fontanella, as if they were distant towns, when in reality they might be side by side. Those really in the know could shave these districts even closer, so that you might refer to half-streets, blocks, as if they were distinctive, unique cultures with particular habits and codes. This idea only served the city's bad reputation, despite the mythology that the poorest neighbourhoods held the best eateries, the finest tailor, the original pizzeria, the freshest mozzarella / *sfogliatelle* / pasta / *limoncello*, the cheapest shoes, it spoke louder about the mysteries of clan-like associations, habits of use, of gangs, of safe and unsafe, when in reality after three years all Marek could see was a jam of dog-poor neighbourhoods scrabbling for breath. In Poland that kind of romance would be seen for what it was, a useless snobbery about poverty. As an outsider the best way to see Naples was from a boat or a hill, where it looked coherent as one single effect; come down to street level and everything started to fracture.

Marek couldn't quite work out what he was expected to do. If he asked in the school he would have to give reasons for looking for the woman, reasons he didn't understand himself. He had no name, which made this stranger, and he didn't understand the aim of this – except for his reward. In the end it wasn't hard at all. He stood at the doors, buzzed the doorbell and said he was looking for . . . and then he mumbled. When the reply came that they didn't know who he meant he gave the brothers' description of the woman.

'She's Japanese. Short. Black hair. About thirty-five but she looks younger.'

'Oh! Mizuki?' The voice sounded mechanical, metallic.

'That's right. Is she there? I'm supposed to meet her.'

'She isn't very well.'

Marek got the information he needed, the girl had been stung by a wasp two days ago and had to go home. She was all right, they insisted, but she was staying in Portici. She'd be back next week. They expected.

Marek said thank you. He'd done his work. Now it was time for his weekend.

SATURDAY: DAY G

Rafí had a new watch. A Seiko. He told Lila that he didn't want her to leave. He wanted to find the men, he wanted to find them and hurt them. This was a promise. Arianna had gone. It would be easier without her, and Lila would be safe as long as she remained at the Stromboli. She couldn't help but follow the reflections from the watch, the way sunlight splintered off the face, bright and sore.

'She took everything,' he said. 'We have nothing. She took your clothes, money. The rents. My savings. Everything. It's all gone.'

Lila pressed for details, had Arianna said anything about where she was going? Why had she left? Had he seen her? Had she called? Lila could see herself wearing upon him. Pushing.

He liked her more when she talked less, he said. What was so hard to understand?

'She took everything. Your friend. This is how she treats you.'

And this was true, Lila remembered Arianna crouched over her, promising that she would return, money in her hand rolled in the same way that Rafí rolled his money.

And later: Lila wasn't the only victim. Arianna had also spoiled his chances. This was typical, just his luck, to get stuck like this. The money he'd saved, yes some of it was Lila's money, but most of it was money set aside from the rents, the money he'd borrowed, money which could have set them up anywhere they wanted. Madrid, why not, or Barcelona again? Barcelona hadn't been so bad. He could probably go back there now. He could have opened a nightclub, a nice little place with a select membership. He could have, it would've been possible. A private club providing for every taste, every possible experience, but no, in robbing them Arianna had ruined these chances. He was done with Naples and with this way of living.

Rafí took off his shirt and straightened his back. He asked Lila how old she thought he was. His family were mixed blood, Spanish and Arab, and this was where the fine dark looks came from, the olive skin, the heavy balls. The women were freaks, he said, weak, feeble, little more than creatures, but the men were vital and strong. It was a pity for Lila that he didn't go for whores, because he knew how much she liked him.

Arianna would not come back. Couldn't Lila see this? Rafí held Lila's face close. Why would she come back, he asked. Think it through. What would she come back for? Every cent was gone.

Rafí left her in the afternoon. Lila lay awake, aware for the first time of other noises hiding behind the dog's incessant barks. Behind this animal hid a whole city, and deeper even, behind the traffic, the crude honk and buzz, the gasp of brakes, the market shouts, beyond these sounds were others, more ancient. Bells first, through which you could map the entire plain, the distinct differences between one church and another, the tinkering off-colour sounds, out of tune and out of time. And something else, something more than the city's daily shouts and murmurs, sounds she could not calibrate. When she couldn't sleep Lila saw herself poised above the muddle, neither rising nor falling, but holding place above the rucked red roofs, the churches, the palaces, the archives, the ancient halls and houses. No longer running, no longer falling, but suspended above the city.

Lila woke to smell burning. A small column of black smoke curled and collapsed on the balcony. She recognized, without interest, a pair of her shoes, the T-shirt from the hospital, and Rafí dropping these items one by one onto a grill. He was burning her clothes. From the flat roof two floors below came the crazy coughing barks from Rafí's dog.

Rafí, done, stood in the doorway, with blackened hands and a pair of tongs, telling her that she should stay where she was.

'I've thought it through,' he said. Lila didn't have to work at Fazzini or on the corso. She didn't need to go to hotels any more. Until they had to leave he would bring men to her. She didn't need clothes. She didn't need shoes. 'I'll provide what you need.'

And one more thing: with Lila momentarily out of action he'd devised another plan, involving Cecco. Everything now depended on Cecco helping out and pleasing a few of his friends. They had to take opportunities when and as they came. These friends, they wanted a boy.

Rafí dug his phone out of his pocket, and worked a bad smile as he scrolled through finding photographs. Cecco on a bed, soft, loose and compliant on Rafí's dope. Cecco arranged across a bed with his shirt hitched up, eyes closed to half-moons, arms propped behind his head. Cecco with his legs spread wide, so deeply relaxed that he appeared as something hunted, a trophy. He showed Lila the photographs and said they weren't half-bad, given that the camera on his phone was a piece of shit. Rafí's concentration did not last long, and while Lila could not guess the details of this new plan, she didn't doubt that he would replace her.

She came down in the late evening and waited outside Rafí's door. Hungry, she wanted food. Rafí stintingly provided what they needed, going out after midday to bring back ready-cooked meals from an *alimentari* opposite the Fazzini, usually something simple, pasta and beans, or pasta and tomato, which they shared sitting in front of the small balcony overlooking the roof. While he ate, Rafí would coo to his dog and taunt it with scraps. Lila had never needed to remind him before, but there was no coffee, no bread, no sugar, nothing sweet at hand, and she had woken hungry and dizzy.

She sat on the stairs and waited and listened, but could hear nothing inside. When she knocked there came no reply. The door was unlocked, and opening it she found Cecco asleep in Rafí's room. She'd never slept in Rafí's bed.

SUNDAY: DAY H

Amelia Peña returned on the Sunday morning, and found the basement door ajar and a white plastic shopping bag tucked inside. The bag was heavy and the sides scuffed with what she took to be brown paint. Inside she found a hammer, a pair of pliers, and a saw-tooth blade on top of a bundle of damp rags. The rags were wet and sticky, and looked like clothes. When she looked at her fingertips, she recognized that this was not paint or thinners, but blood. Beside the clothes curled to the plastic lay a piece of meat, pink and mottled and dry, and beside the meat a single tooth with long white double roots. The tooth, perfectly formed and specked with red pith, convinced her that this was real and not some kind of fakery. It took her a moment to realize that the meat, with its velvet upper surface and slick underside with a single ridge, was, as far as she could tell, a human tongue.

☆

Marek's problems started when he checked out of the room. While the brothers had paid, they'd also left a package at the desk for him: a box containing a pair of latex gloves (large), a disposable white suit (large), covers for shoes (size 42 to 50), what looked like a shower cap (medium), a pair of industrial goggles (one size, adjustable), and a two-litre bottle of bleach. Paola stood by the windows to the patio, her back to the desk, her bag between her legs. Marek asked when the package had been left and the clerk replied, on Friday, when the gentlemen checked out.

'And there was no note?'

'Just the box.'

'Why didn't you just give it to me when I arrived?'

The clerk pointed to a note which stated, quite clearly, that the package should be presented to Marek Krawiec when he checked out on Sunday.

Marek asked when they would be back, and the clerk looked blankly back at him.

'I'm sorry?'

'What time do they get back? Do you know what time they return?'

The clerk logged on to the computer, found the reservation and said no. The room was booked for another couple for the entire week. They had no reservation for Mr Wolf and Mr Rabbit. He smiled as he read the names. Funny that. Funny names.

Marek said no. Those aren't the names. 'Check for Marc and Paul.'

'Last names?' The receptionist looked from Marek to the screen.

'It will be the same last name. First names: Marc and Paul.'

'No,' the clerk adjusted the monitor. 'These are your names. Marek and Paola.' He made a creditable stab at pronouncing Marek's last name. 'Car-wee-ack.' No one could pronounce his name.

'No, no. I said Marc and Paul. Not Marek. Not Paola.' Marek spelled out the brothers' first names and the clerk still couldn't find them. First or last.

They'd paid in cash on Friday morning (everything in cash from Mr Wolf and Mr Rabbit), and there was no further booking, no apparent intention to return.

Marek didn't want to talk this through with Paola. Mr Wolf and Mr Rabbit? There were people with nouns for last names across the globe. Everything in English sounded funny: Mr Vest and Mr Trowzer (lawyers in Gdansk), Mr Grass (his French teacher years before in Lvov), Mr and Mrs Shyte (Pennsylvania, backpackers he'd met in a London hostel, unremarkable except for their last name); it didn't even have to be translated into English: Frau Frau (a nurse in Dusseldorf). In New Zealand a town pronounced Papa-fukah. Not quite right, but there it was. Wolf and Rabbit were probably spelled some other way (Wulffe? Wapett?). Although, weren't they brothers, Marc and Paul? They hadn't said they were brothers, because, being obvious, it hadn't needed saying. Marek had just assumed that this was fact. Wolfe and Rabbit was some joke between them, another example of their humour which he just didn't get. If Wolf and Rabbit was a joke then what about Marc and Paul, apostles both?

His telephone began to ring on the train back. Ring and cut off. When he checked his messages he found five calls, all from the supervisor Amelia Peña. Peña's messages were incoherent. The situation wasn't helped by a poor connection. Something terrible had happened and if she could not reach him she would have to call the police. When Marek called back the line was busy. As the train came into Torre Annunziata he made another attempt, and when Peña answered she spoke in a rapid staccato, repeating herself and the exact words from her last message. She was sorry, she said, sorry she couldn't reach him. She had called many times. She was sorry, the basement door, she said, a bag. Something about a bag? Salvatore wasn't around, she said, he wasn't even in Naples right now, and she didn't know who else to call.

Marek didn't understand her urgency or why it was necessary to call the police. Whatever her problem he had plans for the day. As far as he knew everything at the palazzo should be in good order. Paola spent the journey looking out of the window, head turned so that he couldn't see her face, not even in reflection. This gesture, if that's what it was, summed up the weekend, where she had participated but was barely present.

Mr Wolf and Mr Rabbit.

He would be back, he said, he would not be long.

At this Peña's voice became fearful and brittle.

She had found a plastic bag in the entrance. A shopping bag. There was blood smeared inside the bag, and worse, much worse, something so bad she didn't dare say. She hadn't dared go down to the basement. Couldn't.

They walked from the station to the palazzo and found the door locked. She's made this up, Marek told himself, Peña has concocted some plan or she's stupid, or maybe crazy.

He rang Peña's bell and her face appeared briefly at the bottom of the grille in a small square peephole cut into the door, her eyes wide and red, glassy and fearful. She had locked herself inside and in her anxiety she could not draw back the bolt. Paola drew an impatient breath, and said more to herself than Marek that Peña was a drunk dwarf. She wasn't even the proper supervisor; no one paid her. It's not official. 'And now she's locking us out of our home.'

When the door finally opened Peña stepped away in a doped slowness and slipped back to the whitewashed wall.

Paola pushed through, and used her overnight bag as a block between her and the supervisor. She gave Marek a look as if Peña was drunk, as if this really was all too much.

'I'm going up.'

She was sorry, Peña said, hardly acknowledging Paola as she walked away. She reached vaguely to Marek, feebly caught his arm, her voice fragile and diminishing, and whispered, sorry. So sorry.

Impatient with these apologies Marek asked what was she sorry about. What was this exactly? What did she want?

Peña pointed to courtyard, to the basement door, to a white plastic shopping bag. Even at this distance, Marek could see the blue lettering that served as a logo for *Salvatore Alimentari*. The bag looked fat, the sides folded over as if tucked, as if waiting to be collected, the sides scuffed with muck.

Marek walked directly to the bag and gruffly pulled it toward him and was surprised at the weight. Inside, he found a hammer and a sawtooth blade, a pair of pliers, some shorts, and a T-shirt sopped with something like oil, sticky and dirty. He opened the T-shirt with his fingertips, still not thinking, a little repelled at the feel of the material, but just not thinking, and out skittered two teeth, two human teeth, with long white double roots. At the base of the bag a piece of meat, impossible – a tongue. He dropped the clothes. '*What is this?*' Wiped his hands down his shirt, looked to Peña and said he didn't understand. What was this? Blood? Real blood. Teeth. A tongue?

Peña held out the keys and said that he should go to the basement, she would not go, and Marek said she was crazy, why had she waited, this was a matter for the police?

Except.

It wasn't a matter for the police.

Not at all.

When he returned to the courtyard Marek came quickly out through the service entrance onto via Tribunali. Certain that he was going to be sick, he leaned forward and regulated his breathing. The room's heavy stink followed him out, and the effort not to retch brought tears to his eyes. Marek curled up in the doorway and hugged himself hard.

It was impossible that this could happen. Impossible to accept what he had seen, a room fouled with thick gouts of blood, a pool of it misshapen with skids and slides, the colour bright-edged and black-centred, wet and crusting.

He had bought the plastic.

He had prepared the room, painted it, left it white, layered with plastic, not draped, but taped and nailed and dressed, and what he returned to was far beyond his understanding, a room so thick with blood that someone had dragged and swum through it, soaked themselves and left their imprint.

Plenty of people would have seen him coming and going over the past week.

He called the brothers, could hardly hold the phone with shaking, but let it ring and found no answer. He called again, and again, and thought he heard a sound from the bag – and there, in fact, was the phone, set to vibrate, beside the tongue.

Outside, distant, he could hear sirens and car horns. The traffic on via Duomo stopped and began to stall along via Capasso.

Sensing Peña behind him he spat on the pavement.

Had she called the police?

She could not remember.

'You must remember. Have you called the police? Have you spoken with anyone else?'

Peña shook her head, no she had not called anyone else.

'Nobody has seen this?' He pointed to the bag. 'And the room? Has anyone seen the room?' A T-shirt with a star.

Again Peña shook her head.

Marek shook his head. 'You haven't been down there?'

Peña gave another quick shake. No, no she hadn't looked. What was down there?

'Nothing.' Marek shook his head. 'Nothing.'

They shook their heads together, willing this to be true.

'There's nothing down there.' He held up the keys. 'Let me keep these for now.'

Peña nodded, eager to be rid of any responsibility.

'Has anyone come in or out? Anyone from the palazzo? Has anyone seen or looked into the bag?'

Once more she shook her head, and Marek again felt hopeful.

'Did you see anyone go down into the basement this weekend? What about the brothers? Has anyone seen Marc or Paul?'

She didn't understand him. She hadn't met the men.

'The men who rented the room? You haven't met them?'

'Salvatore,' she said, but according to his sons he had returned to

Bari, for his health. They knew nothing about a basement room, and nothing about two businessmen.

Lanzetti. Marek decided he should speak with Lanzetti.

What was he going to do about the bag? Peña pointed back to the courtyard. Marek followed after. He picked up the T-shirt, returned it to the bag and again took note of the pattern, badly stained: a white star in a white circle.

One of the brothers had killed the other, he was certain of it. He pinched the keys hard into his fist. A white star. A white circle. The same star and circle as the bakery. The bakery and the language school. A far worse idea occurred to him. They had murdered the Japanese girl. This was why they had asked him to find someone. This was why they had paid him so well. The clothes in the bag were not clothes likely to be worn by either of the brothers, but neither were they women's clothes.

Marek had painted the room. Bought the materials. Dressed the room in plastic. He'd helped them search for a woman. He began to understand his part in this, the realization yawned open, the bleach, the gloves, the package at the hotel. An expectation that he would clean up. And the tongue? An emphatic demand that he should shut his mouth.

He told Peña that it was a joke. The tongue, the blood, were fake. The clothes were real enough, of course, but everything else was some kind of elaborate joke. Peña appeared to accept the answer, although the idea produced no change in how she appeared.

Paola, seated at the sewing machine, leaned through and gave a hi, as if the weekend had not been awkward, as if nothing had happened, which was in many ways the problem. Nothing had happened: no arguments, but no agreements either. She'd tolerated the weekend, suffered through it as if this were something he'd especially wanted to do, and just this one time they'd do it, right, but it wouldn't become a habit, OK, it wouldn't be anything she'd care to repeat. Paola leaned from her chair, hands holding a T-shirt steady under the needle, to peep into the room with an apologetic hi, as if she realized now just how childish she could be sometimes. 'What's that on your shirt?'

Marek answered *paint*. He'd wiped his hands down his shirtfront. Two smears that looked nothing like paint.

Paola slipped back into work, and left him alone while he sat at the toilet, tried to control his breathing, tried to hold down his retching or keep it to the moments when she was sewing, when the machine peckered through the material and the sound stammered through the walls. His eyes were watering from the effort to regulate his breathing, he didn't know if he was crying.

She asked if he was OK, what was keeping him?

'I think, I don't know, maybe I've picked up something. The steam room.'

'The chicken,' she said, 'undercooked. Oh god, we both had it. I'm feeling a little that way too.'

He'd never thought of her as superficial, but now it struck him. If he was feeling sick, she had to be sick too, or sicker. The idea of Paola came to him, entirely apparent. As ridiculous as a small dog. It wasn't stitching clothes she hated, not in itself, it was the dread that this was the limit of her expertise, that she wasn't any better than any other peasant who stitched and sewed. Italian through and through, she felt she deserved better. She hated him, treated him with contempt. This was clear. Because he was Polish, because he earned his living when and where he could. They weren't a couple. They were two people making do.

He thought that he should like her more. That he should want to hold her, be close, feel someone living, just to feel loved. But he just felt sick. He thought he should be able to tell her exactly what he'd seen and she would know – without pause – to offer comfort. But she would blame him, she would tell him: *nothing is free.* Didn't you see what you were doing? Didn't you ask yourself: *what is this for*? Did you have no understanding, no perspective? She would tell him nothing that he did not know.

He stayed in the bathroom, lodged his foot against the door just in case she had the bright idea to check on him. He always knew what to do, in every situation, he always knew the answer. He'd speak to his brother. Lemi would know. And then he realized his brother couldn't begin to calculate the complications or the dimension of it. Every way he looked at this he was in trouble. He would be held responsible. Culpable. To the end of his life.

The room would have to be cleared. Either him, the police, or someone else would have to tear down the plastic, pack it in bags, take it elsewhere. It would not stay like this. It could not.

*

88

Marek kept the basement keys in his pocket, where he could feel them digging into his leg. He closed the shutters, lay on the bed, tried to sleep so that he didn't have to explain himself, but didn't want to close his eyes because the room stayed with him. He told himself it wasn't real. It couldn't be, he'd taken it wrong. They'd butchered an animal, that's all, some dog picked off the street. That's all this was. Not a joke but a prank, although how could this in any shape be seen as something funny. A tongue in a bag. Teeth. A room drenched in blood.

At five o'clock he heard a knock at the door, and felt his heart stop then quicken. This would be the police and they would take him now. They would want to know why he was asking at the school about the Japanese woman. Why had he bought those materials? Whoever were these people, Mr Wolf and Mr Rabbit?

He heard Lanzetti's voice and rose immediately. Paola at the door – uncommonly nice, even welcoming. She held the door open and invited the pharmacist in, explained that Marek wasn't feeling well, a stomach bug from a short trip, but here he is.

'Ah, the hotel.' Lanzetti smiled and looked to Marek then Paola. 'How was it?'

Paola nodded, too eager, surely she knew she didn't need to play it this way. 'He's picked up something. Stomach.'

'Have you been sick?'

Marek shrugged. It wasn't much of anything. A little rest and he'd be fine.

'Water,' Lanzetti smiled. 'Make sure he drinks lots of water. He's sweating. People dehydrate quickly. You have no idea how quickly, it's so hot. If he isn't well in the morning come by and I'll give you something for it. Some salts. Something also for the stomach if it doesn't go.' Lanzetti held the brothers' book in his hand. 'I came to return this.' He offered the book to Marek.

Paola stood at the door, looked hard at the book, and Marek felt that he needed to explain himself but couldn't think of anything.

'It's . . .' Lanzetti paused, turned the book in his hands, his expression showing some distaste. 'It isn't nice.'

'Nice?' Paola gave a short scoff.

'It's hard to say,' Lanzetti looked like he would rather explain this to Marek alone. He held the book out. 'It isn't what I would usually read.'

Marek didn't want to touch the book. He turned and Lanzetti

stepped into the apartment. Paola asked if he would like a drink, and Lanzetti appeared relieved. He asked for water, if that would be all right. It was hot this afternoon.

Once Paola was in the kitchen Lanzetti asked Marek if he knew what the book was about.

'The subject is – it's a little strange.' Lanzetti looked quickly to the kitchen. 'It's about a building, a palazzo such as this, a place where a lot of people live, and how the main character takes revenge on them because they didn't stop an event from happening, an event which involves his sister. He has a room, a basement room . . . and he turns this room into a slaughterhouse.'

And now Marek was paying attention.

'He prepares this room . . .'

Paola returned with the water, ice clinking in the glass. 'I have to work.'

Lanzetti accepted the glass with a smile. He gave a small and formal bow and apologized for stopping her. He stood and Marek stood as if in a confrontation, then they both walked to the kitchen.

'I'm not sure I understand. But there are elements from the book that are familiar.'

'Elements?'

'A word was scratched on the door, on the main door. This word was painted on the doors of collaborators at the end of the war. It's mentioned in the book. I think your friends, although this doesn't make sense, believe that this is the same palazzo as the place described in the book.'

'And the room?'

'The room. The room is where a killing takes place. Only it's staged. It isn't real. He wants the people in the building to be punished. So he pours blood onto the walls and floor and makes it look like a slaughterhouse. He makes it look like the people in the building have been killing American soldiers and selling them as meat.'

'It isn't real?'

'No. It's staged. It isn't real. The man uses blood he's stolen from a field hospital. He uses body parts. A tongue. A hand. A foot. All taken from the hospital. He leaves these where they will be found to incriminate a doctor, a lawyer, a magistrate, because he blames them for something that has happened to his sister.'

Marek accepted the book.

'It's not even a good book.'

Paola slept beside him, uncommonly affectionate, first spooning, then, because of the heat, lying separate but keeping a hand at the small of his back. Marek lay awake, now confused. So they had a book, a story, a script to follow, and what had they done? He knew blood, he knew the smell, but had no way to know if this was real. If this was animal blood, how could such a quantity be stored? A human has seven litres of blood. This they had taught him in the army. Seven litres, which, with an arterial cut will vent a fountain two or three metres, and take three to four minutes to bleed out. There were ropes hanging from the ceiling with tethers made from duct tape, and spatter on the ceiling and the wall. An elaborate hoax if it was a hoax. He wanted to ask Lanzetti about the mechanics of the hoax, the similarities with the book. He wanted to know the ending.

It was clear that Marek needed to return to the room and remove anything that would identify or connect him, and then he would leave the city. Take his money and go.

MONDAY – TUESDAY: DAYS I & J

Marek spent the day in bed, turned to the wall, the same thoughts racketing endlessly without result and couldn't sleep. In the late afternoon he rose, and decided he had no choice. Before he returned to the basement he contacted English Tony and asked for a car. It didn't have to be the Citroën, but he needed a car as soon as possible. Tony said that he could take the Citroën and Marek asked for something different. Anything would do, it was just to move Paola's bags, and he didn't want to spill anything in the Citroën. Already he was explaining too much.

'Take the Citroën,' English Tony insisted. If something happened he could clean it. Just take a little care and fill it up. It's only shirts, right? This is what she does, she stitches shirts?

Marek drove back through piazza Garibaldi, passed by every kind of police imaginable, municipal, state, carabinieri, finance, firemen and paramedics, you name it. Every one of them idling at the piazza.

Back in the basement he waited at the door, dressed slowly in the white suit, the slip-on booties, the hairnet, the goggles, the latex gloves, stared at the door, a heavy door like something from a ship, painted and repainted so the surface had a roundness, a way of appearing smooth when in reality it was deeply scratched and picked. He couldn't enter the room, couldn't make himself touch the door handle, and found himself stuck.

One week ago – was it? – the argument with Paola, a joke of hers about him being gullible. It wasn't that he was stupid, that wasn't what she was trying to say. Maybe it was the military training, or something, but he always did what she told him, always. She just had to speak in a certain way and he'd jump to it. He couldn't remember the comment but she'd said it was almost the same thing – doing what you're told and being stupid. Almost the same.

How could he not have thought of this?

A room covered in plastic.

THE KILL

How could it not occur to him?

He made the decision, physically leaned into the door until he had no choice but to step forward and touch it. Once inside he walked about the perimeter, his nose and mouth buried in the crook of his arm as he tugged the plastic sheets free from the walls. He shielded his face as the plastic slipped down, and trod carefully, because whatever this was, it wasn't only blood. Although he had carefully covered the walls and double taped the seams, the sheeting had separated on the floor and a large pool of blood had settled underneath, and there were bare footprints, already dry, tracked across the concrete. Marek attempted to fold the sheets without coming into contact with the blood. With only one side torn down, he looked about the room and understood that what he was doing was unwise.

Behind the door, set beside what remained of the roll of plastic, he uncovered a shoulder-bag. Under the bag, placed tidily next to the wall, he found a pair of brown trainers and socks, left side by side as if someone had undressed there. None of this seemed fake to him, the hairs caught in the tape strapping, the pattern and pooling of the blood, the hanging tether – but he told himself that none of this was real.

He packed the plastic into six black disposal bags, slopped bleach onto the floor and left it as it was.

Back on the street he found Cecco leaning nonchalantly against a parked car, happy with himself. Marek checked the street and when he saw that it was clear, he came out with two of the bags. Cecco watched, then offered to help him load them into the car. Marek signalled a gracious no.

'If you need a hand,' Cecco offered, 'I could drive.'

Marek opened the car door and began to load the bags onto the back seat, and wedged them behind the seats with his foot. Straightening as he backed out of the car, he smiled back at the boy and wished that he would leave. It was the car he was after. This is what held his interest.

Marek parked the car on via Consolo. He washed his arms and neck in a fountain in a piazzetta with boys playing football around him who knew better than to pay attention. He rinsed out his shirt then he checked himself in a shop window and was surprised by his expression, stern, sober, and pale. Inside the shop the owner sat in a chair fanning herself and avoiding eye contact.

Out on Corso Garibaldi the police attended to the traffic. A cat-call of sirens, close and threatening, ran down Corso Emanuele. Marek walked the long way round to via Capasso avoiding the groups of police, mindful not to appear suspicious; he had never seen so many police before, but realized that he must have, he'd just never had a reason to fear them.

He waited in his apartment, certain the police would come, told Paola that he was still feeling unwell. He waited curled on the bed, arms wrapped tight about his chest, and stared hard at the wall, convinced that the police were playing a game. His fingerprints would be all over the room, all over the car, and he didn't doubt that they would soon come after him. The police would trace the car, contact Tony, then they would come for him.

After midnight he began to feel hopeful. It was possible, just possible, that they hadn't discovered the car. Parked alongside other cars one road away from the palazzo it would not be so obvious. What was there to notice? Even if they did find the car, how would they know to come to him? Fingerprints would take a while to process, by which time he would be out of the city. No. A new problem struck him. The car and its contents combined were less of a worry than Peña. The woman was so stupid that if the police came to speak to her information would pour out of her, unstoppable, and she would tell them everything about the bag, about Marek preparing the room, and once they associated Marek with the room, they would quickly piece together what they needed. And Salvatore? What was the deal with Salvatore?

At two o'clock Marek decided to return to the car. He came carefully down the stairs and checked the courtyard to see if there were police in the building, and was surprised to see the entrance as it usually was at night, the hefty wood doors closed, windows and shutters open on the upper floors, only one or two lights showing in the front of the building.

The car was still on the bridge, undisturbed. He walked by it, not looking at the car, but looking up the street for any sign that something was not right. Satisfied, he turned about, and hurried back with the keys in his hand.

The late afternoon heat had drawn out a fatty stench from the clothes. Marek wound the window down. The car started on the third attempt with a rough choke. Marek drove with his head toward what draught there was, a buffet of hot air with the soft feel of cloth.

He took the smaller roads following the coast south toward Ercolano and sensed, for the first time, the possibility of success. The headlights broke across concrete walls and glasshouses, on one side were simple townhouses and workshops, on another a broken line of warehouses which appeared largely abandoned. Turning a narrow corner he was forced to an abrupt stop, in the middle of the road an abandoned dumpster, so solid, he thought of it at first as some kind of creature, something ancient. Marek laughed, tension broken, he turned left and headed inland and soon he was back among housing. He drove now with the lights off, aware that the car would draw attention to itself. He turned again and headed for an unlit area and found himself on a pumice track with stark concrete high-rises on either side. The road came to a halt at a dry sloping scrubby field.

Marek stopped the car, turned on the headlights: from what he could see he was far enough away from the housing estate and into a wasteland. He could burn the clothes and bags here. This, he thought, was too easy, as if he had some natural talent. The idea disturbed him.

Under the plastic bags he found a litre can of engine oil. He threw the clothes into the field and when he returned to the car he thought he heard a cough, a definite cough. Marek stopped and listened and squinted up the track. It was nothing, he was certain, but nevertheless he needed to hurry. As he reached for the shoulder-bag he thought he heard the sound again. Not a cough this time but someone walking, the crisp break of dry grass underfoot. Marek paused and again stared hard into the night, and again discovered nothing. He swung the shoulder-bag out into the field, then, following the light cast by the headlamps he walked after them opening the can of oil. It wasn't a cough this time but a huff – Marek stood over the clothes, he doused them with oil and was surprised that the clothes would not ignite. He attempted to light them with a handful of dried grasses, but again it wouldn't catch. He plucked more grass, wound the strands into a knot and tried again. This time the grass caught, but the flames died as quickly as they had started. Behind him the first handful he'd thrown aside quickly caught fire – and just as swiftly died. If he couldn't burn the clothes he would bury them. Unable to see where he had thrown the bag he searched the field and stepped carefully through the grass

– and there, again, a rustle. This time he was certain he heard someone approaching.

When he turned back to the car Marek was surprised to see a dog. Bleached white in the headlights, the animal appeared big and strong, with fluorescent eyes, a heavy black mouth; it stepped lightly through the grass. Head dipped it picked up the scent of blood and took a position between Marek and the clothes. As Marek moved forward the dog hunched in threat. He kicked sand, threw stones, a clod of earth, and the animal dodged and weaved back, swift and lithe, it came threateningly close. 'Just go,' Marek hissed, gestured. 'Go. Go.' But the creature set its shoulders back and gave a slow rolling growl. Behind the dog and the clothes the grass again began to burn with a soft crackle.

It was just becoming light, a pink hue opening at the horizon, the hills, barely described, becoming distinguishable in the last of the black night, a smog caught about the bay.

Marek returned to the car aware that it was becoming bright enough for him to be seen. People would shortly be rising, heading to work. The car would be easy to remember, the clothes would not, just clothes on a wasteland, dried and dirty. He saw the estate now, highrises built on a flattened section of land, turned to the bay, closer than he'd imagined. Further away, at the edge of the wasteland were the abandoned factories he'd driven by. He would dump the plastic in one of the buildings. The dog, now settled in front of the clothes, watched him back away.

He drove slowly back down the track. In the early morning light, the warehouses appeared less ominous. At the junction he remembered to slow down for the dumpster. He turned the car into a small alley and parked. Along the verge lay a pile of rotting flowers. He hauled the dumpster inside the factory. One wheel caught on the threshold and he hoisted it up, then shunted the dumpster across the room, the noise starting up a dog in the distance. The floor was gritted with broken glass, cushions taken from a couch set beside the remains of a small fire, among the ashes were several syringes. It was light enough to see now, and he quickly took the plastic out of the car, bag by bag, to the dumpster. Breath held, head turned, he worked quickly. By the last run it had become bright enough to see that the small alley ended in a steeper slope of smooth black basalt which tipped directly into the sea. He walked to the edge, and decided to dump the bags into the sea.

Hefting the bags back out of the dumpster was an unpleasant business, and one of the bags flattened at the bottom of the dumpster was difficult to reach. Once most of them were down to the shoreline he began to look for stones to weigh them down. He found pieces of concrete in the building, but not enough, so he tethered the bags together and weighed down the first.

He undressed by the shore, washed out his clothes then laid them on the stones which held a body heat from the previous day. He worked naked, made sure the bags were securely knotted one to the other, then carried the heavier bag with him and he picked his way slowly into the water. The sea was cold, welcomingly so, and gave him the odd sensation of being both awake and revived, while also being exhausted, so much so that he seemed to be observing his own movements, how he waded slowly through the water, how tedious it was to draw the bags one by one in a slack chain behind him.

He dropped the bag at his feet when the water was head-high, nudged them still further with his foot, and was pleased to see – at last, something was working – that all but one bag was submerged. Gouts of air belched from the bags as they sank, and holding the last bag he squeezed out the air, compressed it, turned his head away so that nothing would spill over him, then ducking under the water he felt for a stone, and lifted it over the last bag to secure it.

A shoal of small silver fish began to gather about him. The bags now submerged sent out a powdery rust. Marek also, his chest and arms specked and fouled, gave off a dusty cloud, and the fish, tiny, glass-like, sparks of light, flashed about him, feeding, and seemed miraculous.

Marek sat on the rocks and smoked. He had done well to separate himself from the basement room and the brothers, but while he might have broken the obvious links, there were, he guessed, many other connections. A body, if there was a body, which would have its own story, then Peña, and Paola, Lanzetti, and maybe even Salvatore, who could each connect him to the brothers. Without evidence, without the room, there would be nothing concrete. He didn't know how he would manage if the police questioned him. Brushing away mosquitoes he looked back along the coastline at the grey outline of the city and thought that he had never seen a place so beautiful or heard a sound so lovely as the slap of the waves against the shore.

Marek dressed and returned to the car, relieved for the moment.

The car, however, would not start. He had run out of fuel. Marek returned to the shore, swearing, cursing his bad luck. Hadn't Tony said as much, warned him she just runs out and dies. How could he possibly have let this happen? If he bought fuel in Ercolano he would be remembered, he would be connected with the place. If he left the car, he risked it being damaged or stolen. His only option would be to return to Naples, buy fuel in the city and come back for the car. This, he guessed, would take no longer than two hours.

Half an hour after he caught the train, the first of the bags, tugged loose by the current, floated free from the stone and came to the surface. The incoming tide drove it back to the shore and it pulled behind it the others so that they could be seen from the shore as black rounded humps bobbing at the surface.

The solution came easier than he expected. As soon as he arrived back at the palazzo he found the boy Cecco idling in front of the *tabaccaio*. Marek signalled to him and called him to the palazzo and asked if he could drive. Of course he could drive. Did he want money? Of course, he could always use money. If he wanted he could come with him to Ercolano. Marek laughed while he explained the situation: I need someone to buy some fuel, that's all. 'I can trust you?'

Cecco nodded. He could be trusted. He would be careful.

Marek took the train back to Ercolano with Cecco, had the boy buy a canister, then walk to a garage to buy fuel. At the last moment he decided that Cecco could also collect the car. He didn't want to be seen, and thought no one would pay attention to the boy. He gave clear and direct instructions. Find the car beside the warehouses and bring it back. Did he understand? If he brought the car back to the station he could pick up Marek. 'I've someone to meet,' he lied, 'come back to the station. I'll meet you here.' That's all he was asking. How difficult could that be?

Cecco nodded. He knew nothing, and that was good. The less he knew the less he could blab to the police.

Marek traced his change of luck back to the accident. He did not know how to describe it. It wasn't that he was unlucky; it was something infinitely more complex.

He paid Cecco generously, told him to be quiet about the errand, then left him at the station. He drove away from the city toward Salerno and with the mountains to his left and in front, determined to perform one last task. Pagani was joined to Torre del Greco and the larger sprawl of Naples, one town blending without break into another. Smaller barn-like houses butted beside villas and developments. Paola always pointed out Nenella's, a family house shared by three generations, isolated by busy roads that cut by on all sides.

When he arrived Marek parked and waited. He smoked and considered the absurdity of driving so far to meet a woman he had often ridiculed. He wasn't sure either what he wanted to ask.

The door opened directly onto the street, he watched a woman come out and manhandle a wheelchair onto the road. The chair was cumbersome, and strapped into it was a young boy, one arm on his lap the other held up to his chest, crooked, his head slightly twisted. The traffic could not see her, and came fast round the turn, coming dangerously close to the wheelchair. The woman lumbered the chair out onto the road, and once it was on even ground it seemed to move by itself. The woman, the child's mother or aunt, walked beside the boy to protect him from the traffic. She walked with a little difficulty, a slight twist in her hips, an awkward gait, a plastic shopping bag hitched into her elbow that flew over her hands as the traffic passed close by them.

Marek considered returning to Naples.

The house sounded busy. Children upstairs, shouts coming from the kitchen, full of people who could not be seen. As no one answered the door Marek came timidly into the hall and then into the kitchen. Two women worked together, busy, preparing food, and they didn't immediately notice him. When they did they sent him back down the hall and said he should go into the room on his left. Behind the building, through the open kitchen door, was a small courtyard, and he could see parts of cars and scooters parked up beside stacks of salvaged wood.

Nenella was younger than he expected, not much older, by appearance, than Marek himself. She wore jeans and a shirt with an embroidered design across the shoulder. Her hair was short and dyed a deep chestnut; she had none of the airs that he associated with faith healers and readers. There were newspapers spread out across the floor to either cover or collect, and at the back of the room, dark because of the drawn shutters, a fat old dog with rheumy eyes stretched out. Nenella appeared momentarily unsettled, surprised by Marek.

Disappointed that the woman appeared so ordinary, and a little ashamed to be explaining his doubts and troubles to a stranger, Marek began to stammer. Starting with the accident he described the difficulties and indifference that had settled upon him. Now anxious about what he was saying Marek began to sweat, and admitted that he did not know what he was doing.

After five minutes Nenella stopped him. There was nothing she could do. There was nothing to fix. She sent him away saying that she would not read for him. He would not conceive, she said, because he should have died that day. Every day after the accident came from a new life. He was a baby, she said, new-born, and there was no business between them.

He called Paola as he drove back and said that his mother was not well. He gave no details and used the tired language of those who don't have time to explain. *She'd taken a turn for the worse.* She was seeing a specialist, he didn't know when exactly, but it looked like they were running out of options. As far as he knew there were no further treatments possible. Lemi was coming from Frankfurt, they would stay at his cousin's then drive to his mother's house in Lvov. He didn't know how long this would take. He hoped to be back in a week.

He returned to the palazzo one last time, collected his passport, left what money he could on the table. Just as he was about to leave he heard a key in the lock, and Paola came into the apartment on her own. He waited in the bedroom and said nothing as she crossed through to the bathroom. He wouldn't normally be in the apartment at this time. So it was strange to him that she locked the bathroom door after herself, a piece of information he would not have guessed. He crept out of the bedroom and came slowly up the hall not wanting to make any noise, and not wanting to alarm or alert her. He thought of her without him, how his absence without an explanation would be cruel, and would hold her unnaturally to one place, where ordinarily, if they simply parted, she would be able to continue. She would understand the shape of such a departure. She would stay in the apartment, he could be certain of this. It wasn't easy finding a place as good as this to live, certainly not at the rate she paid. He would stay with her, while apart, for long enough to ensure that he could hear about the palazzo. If anything happened, if the police started to make enquiries he would need to know. For the interim he would stay at his brother's. He would wait, bide time until he could feel confident.

Then he would disappear. This much he had decided. Without Paola, without his mother, he would be untethered, and while this felt like a necessity, he realized that he had expected more with Paola, that while they weren't perfect, they fitted, and that – he'd never thought of it so clearly before – he had expected to grow old with her.

The last details: the edge of parquet meeting the marble floor at the main entrance. The marble yellow and cracked at the wall, but bleached where it had been cleaned over many years. The weight of the door, and how, slow to draw shut, it became easier mid-swing. How the key needed to be turned twice to get the latch to properly cross the gap. These details would stay with him longer than the physical memory of Paola, how she lay beside him on their final night, her hand curved to the small of his back, how she muttered in her sleep when she slept on her side, small whispers, the subject: he could never guess.

WEDNESDAY: DAY K

Early on Wednesday evening Niccolò Scafuti, a security guard for the Persano-Mecuri chemical dye plant in Ercolano, reported the discovery of bloodstained clothes and a small black cloth shoulder-bag a few metres from the road on scrubland behind his apartment.

Built in the early nineteen-seventies, the Rione Ini estate dominated the south-eastern boundary of Ercolano. Poorly constructed of pre-cast concrete sections, the buildings overshadowed the surrounding wasteland. Only four of the planned twelve high-rise apartments were completed, although the foundations, drains and sewers were laid for the entire complex. The land about the estate remained tracked and broken, levelled in the spring and summer by a sloped field of grasses busy with red, papery poppies.

Niccolò sat out on the balcony and waited for his sister to return. At five o'clock the incinerator on via Tre Marzo burnt paper waste and sent up a plume of white, feathery ash. In the late afternoon a cool breeze blew in from the sea, and the heat rose off the concrete and caused the falling ash to momentarily pause, hover, then rise.

At six o'clock Niccolò took a plastic sack and slingshot and headed directly for the wasteland. As he walked through the scrub he followed a path running parallel to the road, his eye open for small pea-sized stones. The day had been frustrating, much of it spent manually raising and lowering a barrier as the new security passes would not work. The drivers coming into the compound waited for his service but did not acknowledge him. When they did talk they'd look at him, take a moment, then deliberately slow down.

Beside the track, partly hidden by the tall grasses, lay a brown shoulder-bag. Further to his left, in a one-metre-wide clearing, he discovered a small rubbery hump of clothes, as brown as the bag, which appeared to be dug out of the ground from a small scratched hole. He cautiously inspected the clothes, busy with ants, set hard and coated in sandy dirt. It was only when he opened out the T-shirt, saw the cuts, a series of small slashes, and noticed how the heavy stains stiffened the cloth that he realized they were stained with blood.

Niccolò looked back along the path to see what else he had walked by. Close to the road the grass was scorched in a wide path, and he guessed that an attempt had been made to burn the clothes and the bag. Alarmed at what else he might find, he checked carefully to see if there were other areas burned or flattened in the field – then he returned to the bag when he was sure that he was alone.

He waited a long time before deciding to open the clasp.

There needed to be a certain kind of hush before it would happen. A kind of white noise filling the background and him focusing down, concentrating on the one thing – and then without any kind of prelude or announcement he would disappear inside himself. Just vanish.

There were triggers. Flickering or flashing lights, almost any tight pattern; reading – the simple action of casually passing his eye along a line of printed words was often enough to snag him. A length of sunlight slatted through a blind, or light cutting into a room catching dust and vibrating, and he would lose focus and become fixed in a kind of endlessness, a loop. In such moments the world flew away from him, a kind of flutter, and gone. Words within a moment of being spoken became lost. His sister would coo to him, singsong, 'Hey, hey, Niccolò? Where are you?' sometimes kindly, sometimes impatient, as if there was a destination, a place he retreated to, but these events were nothing but absence, the moment of leaving knitted to the moment of returning, and while they were brief, he had no notion of their length. These weren't jumps forward, sudden segues, but steps out, lapses. He'd worked in security for two years, or nine, depending on how good his memory was that morning.

Bent over the brown hump of clothes with a breeze running through the grass, Niccolò couldn't be sure how much time had slipped by, if those were the same dusty clouds burning off in a late-afternoon sun, the same flies rising, so dizzy and fired they batted into each other and into his face. His thighs ached and he settled onto his knees. He couldn't figure out how long he'd waited, just as he couldn't be sure, exactly, what he was doing. His hand settled on the clothes and information began to return: the sack, the slingshot, the heat, the ants, the flies, the clothes, the field, the reason for walking through the field, the time of day, the scents of scorched earth and something less pleasant. He couldn't stand cats, never could, he remembered now.

The material, crusted with dirt, unfolded to a T-shirt, a pair of shorts, and a fat wad of rags. The T-shirt slit with two parallel cuts at the navel – one long, one short – and slashed on either side at the lower stomach and just below the armpits. Ants ran up his hands and he shook them off. Done with the clothes, Niccolò carefully opened the shoulder-bag. He pinched the clips to release the buckles then cautiously opened the flap. A natural thing to do. You find something so you check inside just to see who it might belong to, naturally.

Niccolò returned to the estate with the contents of the bag tucked inside his sack and then he decided to contact the police.

Within an hour of Niccolò's discovery the police had cordoned off a small area of the field, and the clothes – a pair of corduroy shorts, boxer shorts, a T-shirt with a five-point star design – were photographed on site and carefully packaged. A preliminary search was made of the area but nothing of interest was immediately discovered.

Against all logic the evening wind brought heat. Reporters began to assemble at the perimeter of the wasteland. People hurried from the estate toward him to be stopped by the police. A slight haze wrapped about the figures. Still dressed in his uniform, Niccolò stood beside the police vehicles and folded his arms high over his chest so that the company insignia could not be seen; but the police had gathered the information they needed and asked him, not unkindly, to return home with the assurance that they knew what they were doing now, and thank you. You've done a good job. You've done all you can. We know where you are if we need you. Certain they would want to speak with him further, Niccolò took a new position outside the taped perimeter. With the sun low over the bay, light began to strafe between the buildings and their shadows reached almost to his feet – for one moment every detail held his attention. The gathering crowd, the police unpacking their equipment, the waiting huddle of reporters, the sun and the shadows and a light wind raising dust between the buildings, grey in the street and white in the sky.

Niccolò returned to his apartment and waited for the police to seek him out. Even without him the event drew interest. More people idled in the street than usual, and they stood in small groups, the men with their shirts open or rolled over their stomachs, an expectation that a body might be discovered. He practised his explanation about how he'd come across the clothes so that he would not sound confused. On the table he laid out two books on forensic science, course textbooks bought second-hand at Porta Alba. He waited, but the police did not come.

Frustrated, Niccolò returned to the balcony and waited for his sister, mindful of the street outside and the television inside playing an American detective show, dubbed well enough for the mouths to almost match the sounds. Away on the wasteland, under bright arc lights, the police walked in a line across the scrub. A second team combed the edge of the floodlit field, and he felt a slight anxiety and exhilaration as the line progressed through the field – but none of them, not one, looked like they would come to speak to him any time soon. Inside the apartment the sack with the contents from the shoulder-bag lay on the floor. If he wanted, he could simply walk out there and tell them what else he'd found, then they might speak to him, only he wasn't even sure what he'd taken and he knew that this might not be a sensible idea.

When he decided the police weren't coming, he put everything back in the sack, and tucked the sack where Livia wouldn't move it. He looked through drawers, and found in the kitchen where Livia had stacked photographs of his wife and daughter, removed them from their frames, although he could not see why. Tomorrow he'd take the sack to the paint factory, sort through what he'd found and dump what he didn't want to keep.

Niccolò stood on the balcony with his hands on his hips. He could feel the attention of his neighbours, and knew that he was being watched with small quantities of something that resembled respect. Police vehicles remained parked alongside the wasteland, and the press and crews assembled a temporary camp at the head of the field. The bright lights, the gathering crowd gave the evening the appearance of a festival. Two police teams worked their way toward the shoreline, one passing through the abandoned paintworks, the other passing through the rows of greenhouses, uncertainty in their staggered movement. Niccolò watched the white vehicles crawl along the road while the men walked ahead.

When Livia came home, he insisted that she watch the news with him. Niccolò described his discovery and his discussion with the police, and just as he began to work himself up a little (*they told me to come back. I waited, I was here. I did exactly what they asked*) a report from the Rione Ini estate came live on the television. It was a jolt at first to recognize the estate and they both pointed at the screen with surprise. The item was presented once in the main news and again on the summary fifteen minutes after, and later still on the local bulletin. Each time the segment appeared it came as a small shock, and he watched the wasteland on both the television and in reflection in the glass in the balcony door, satisfied that he, Niccolò Scafuti, security guard for Persano-Mecuri Ercolano, was the root cause of this. As soon as the clip was over, Niccolò scanned through the stations to see what coverage they were giving the event. He described the discovery to his sister again to fix the moment he came across the clothes.

Livia sat with him, occasionally dozing, legs stretched across the floor, her back to the wall, because these days this was the only way to remain comfortable. It was sad about the clothes, she said. It was the saddest thing.

THURSDAY: DAY L

Eight days after the assault three men came to the Hotel Stromboli for Rafí. Warned by a telephone call, Rafí scrabbled for his clothes and told Lila to get downstairs and tell them he wasn't about. The men, already inside the Stromboli, banged on doors and drew out residents to the landings. If she could delay them he could get out onto the roof where they wouldn't find him. They were peddlers, kids, he said, petty dope dealers he owed money to, and while they didn't pose much of a threat, he didn't doubt that they could do some damage if they decided on it.

As Lila searched for something to wear Rafí shoved her to the door and told her to hurry.

She met the men on the stairs, already halfway up, halfway running. Behind them the traders who sold belts and purses shuffled at their doors. Lila flattened herself against the wall and allowed the men to pass without comment or resistance, and they looked, as Rafí had said, young, like people playing a role, nothing much to worry about.

The two rooms on the top floor led one to another in a simple inverted 'L' and offered no place to hide. Lila followed after, immediately behind, and watched them turn over the mattress, search through the bedclothes, and when they found Rafí crouched behind the kitchen door – eyes squeezed shut, hands clamped to his face, groaning child-like, volume rising, as if this game was being played to the wrong rules – they demanded money. She watched them wrestle Rafí out, and backed away bumping into the door, the doorway, the wall trying to keep out of their way. Rafí at first pliant, disbelieving, snapped to life and began to struggle. He twisted, thrashed, kicked, lunged at the door, grabbed the lintel. The three men stumbled over the mattress, dropped him, scooped him back up, each of them shouting instructions. Rafí writhed in fury, octopus-like, took over the room with a pure and vicious energy sucked right out of nowhere.

As the brawl shoved past her out onto the landing, Rafí, face up, back arched, flipped over and grabbed a fist-full of Lila's hair. With Lila as an anchor the group collapsed to the floor. Too stunned to think, Lila punched out and hit Rafí in the crotch – at that moment the fight was lost and Rafí rolled into a ball, gawping, all of his fight gone.

Bowed forward, dizzy and wincing, Lila pressed her hands to her scalp, not quite sensible of the fact that she was the cause of this lull: three grown men, each twice her size and strength, had failed to subdue Rafí, and with one nudge (it really wasn't that much more), she had levelled him. One of the men helped her to her feet as the others took time to laugh and swear and rearrange their clothes, tuck in shirts and smooth their hair. For a moment they looked back at the room, taking account for the first time, and she felt in the way they looked from her to the hurly-burly of bed sheets and upturned chairs, that there was no difference to them between the battered room and the people who occupied it. As if she had no idea of the shabbiness of it all.

But she was all right? Right?

When the three men finally dragged Rafí down the stairs his expression, his final look before he was hoisted out of view was of surprise and betrayal, as if she should be running after him, shouting at least, putting up some kind of resistance. Instead, Lila listened to the men clomp and struggle down the stairs then returned to the room, stood tiptoe on the mattress to lean out the window and watch the sidewalk – but no one came out of the door. Hearing shouts downstairs, she hurried to the kitchenette to see Rafí sprinting full pace across the flat roof. Two men half out of Rafí's window withdrew as the dog went crazy, spinning at the end of its chain, lunging for them. When she looked for Rafí he was gone.

Lila sat on the mattress and waited for the men to return. She heard them come up the stairs and stop on each landing to demand payment from the traders, who each, at first, feigned disbelief, unable to understand Italian, some spoke in French, some in English, and she slowly understood that the men had come for the rents, rents that Rafí had collected. Collected and kept.

They searched the entire building. Room by room. Insistent that there was money somewhere, that the boy had stowed away the rents. How frugally he lived. By the time the men came to Lila they were irritated and tired.

'And you,' one asked, 'know nothing?'

Lila would not move, and the man drew up the blind to take a good look at her, to get light into the room for the search.

'Did he do that to you?'

Lila drew her hair forward and shook her head. While the men searched the room she sat on the floor, and when they left the man who had spoken to her said that they would be back. 'Why,' he asked, 'are you still here?'

Alone, Lila waited at the window, the day already a shape she did not recognize. She waited expecting Rafí to return or Cecco to appear, knowing it was unsafe to stay. Clearly, this would all be her fault. She counted the pins that fastened the hotel's name to the wall, she noted how they were corroded through, and how people coming out of the station squinted up at the building as they came into the sunlight, and how, tethered to the flat roof two floors below, Rafí's dog lunged at the length of its chain as if to choke itself.

It was impossible now to look at the room without seeing it for what it was, chaotic and dirty. She could smell Rafí on her hands, a stink of sour bedding and stale clothes and his sweet and peppery aftershave.

Rafí's keys lay on the landing with his shirt. Further down, almost to the wall, she found his lighter and cigarettes and a silver mobile phone. Her scalp stung, and she carefully straightened her hair and drew out loose strands. It was shit that he was caught, shit that he was so stupid or unlucky or both, shit that she knew no one better to be with and no better way to live, shit that there was no food and only three cigarettes, shit that there was no money, shit that she would have to wait for him, and it was shit that she could not find his drugs. The pills, which should have been in a hole behind the light switch, were not there. The dog's bark cut through to unsettle her; hard and loud, its whole body concentrated on the task.

She returned to the upper windows overlooking the piazza and watched the station. She stood with the sun in her face and made noises to the dog to gain its attention.

The dog sat down and looked up, suddenly placid.

Determined to do something about the dog, Lila made her way down to Rafí's room.

An old wood-framed bed dominated the small room. The sheets rucked back. The pillows bunched together. Rafí's clothes and shoes were scattered in loose heaps across the floor. His shirts hung on hangers on nails above the bed. Kicked from under the bed were cartons of cigarettes, contraband with Greek markings that he sold in clubs. The small sink was ringed with stains, above it a set of scents and colognes on a glass shelf. There were newspapers on the floor, kept as wrapping.

As Lila took stock, the dog tugged on his chain, followed as she moved through the room, paused when she paused, peered through the window as if intelligent. As she sat on the bed and summoned the courage to deal with the dog, it lunged forward, the chain snapped tight and slumped behind him, striking the roof with the sound of dropped coins.

Now the idea seemed foolish: it would be impossible to loosen the animal's collar without being mauled.

Under the window she found a patterned blanket, little more than a rag. She'd watched Rafí thrash the dog, whip it with the blanket until it cowered, thin-ribbed and panting, as far as its chain would allow. Lila braced herself, stood up, and opened the window.

The instant she opened the window the dog cowered back, shivering, haunches flinching. She held out the blanket and the dog slunk off, tail tucked tight away, ears back.

There was little out on the roof, a cardboard box of a kennel, an upturned water bowl, the dog's chain and the pole it was attached to. Padlocked to itself the chain wrapped about the pole and the pole lodged into the stub of a vent that butted out of the roof. Unless she could lift the entire pole out of its socket she would not be able to release the dog. The idea wasn't going to work. As the dog circled wide of her the pole jolted in its housing, and when the dog stopped tugging the chain slackened and the pole straightened up. Once the chain was slack Lila found that the pole could be twisted with ease. A small plastic wedge poked through the lip of the stub and kept the pole upright. With this removed the pole slid out of its housing, and as she hoisted it up the chain rode down and slipped free. Unaware, the dog lunged forward for the blanket and hurtled over the lintel into Rafí's bedroom, the chain snaking after.

Money poked out of the empty socket.

A single twenty-euro note.

Lila laid the pole down and picked up the note in disbelief. Pulling out one note, another came with it, and with that note came another, and another. She sat down to look at the money, checking either side to make sure that it was real. She was not lucky. Never this lucky.

She reached into the hole and unthreaded more notes until she held in her hands more money than she could count. Deeper still the hole was stopped with a scrunched plastic bag. Lila knelt down and tugged out the bag then reached further into the pipe, finding another bag containing yet more money, tight rolls of ten-, twenty-, and fifty-euro notes. The pole itself was also stoppered with plastic, and still deeper were tucked more rolls of money. Gathering the notes together Lila stuffed her sleeves full, then left the plastic and the pole out on the roof.

Back in Rafi's room the dog leapt onto the bed and turned first on the shirts, tugging them off their hangers and worrying them. Spoilt for options the dog began to nip and tear at the sheets, then the mattress, and wrenched out hanks of stuffing until it could squeeze its head into the holes. Done, the dog sat on the bed and looked back at the roof, the mattress now ragged, with hollowed-out pockets. Thick drifts of polyester, a fine white fibre, settled about the room.

Lila held the blanket up, ready to throw it over the dog's head. She crept cautiously back through the window. The door was closed and the dog watched her edge slowly about the side of the room, her back to the wall, and he growled with rising threat. When she opened the door, just wide enough to squeeze through, the dog sprang to its feet and began to bark.

Safely in the stairwell she leaned her head against the door, and thanked the dog. It was impossible to know how much she had taken, as it was impossible to guess where the money had come from – in such a quantity – or why it was stored on the roof. The only certainty was that the money was either Rafi's or belonged to one of his associates, and Rafi, the little shit, had done nothing, less than nothing, to earn it. What Lila had not earned she deserved.

Lila made her way directly to the Stazione Centrale. Dressed in Rafi's shirt and trousers and a pair of plastic sandals – the toy panda clenched in her arms – she walked out the door taking a simple A to B route, off the pavement, between the bollards. She headed across the road, under the station awning into the darker concourse to the ticket booth to the first free window. She walked in a daze with a crisp fifty-euro note pinched ready in her fist. She'd tucked money into clothes, arms and pants, before remembering the toy. The toy panda, misshapen, stuffed with money (loose, scrunched, wadded, rolled and folded) appeared more forlorn than before. Heat bloomed from the blacktop. And in making that walk Lila understood that she was breaking something which could not be fixed. She would never be able to return, she would not see Rafí again, if she did, she was certain he would kill her.

Once at the booth she stood blinking, sunspots in her eyes, thinking 'oh' to herself, 'oh' at her alarm to be standing exactly where she intended, 'oh', to have completed the simple walk without interruption. To her left the police lounged in a glass-walled office. To her right the carabinieri loitered in pairs, some on motorized carts scooping through the terminal in predatory arcs. Youths, boys she recognized, hung about the automatic ticket machines and lazily scanned the station, the groups, the people waiting, the small queue forming behind her. Lila kept the toy clutched to her chest.

She looked square at the man behind the glass, his hair slicked back in one smooth hood, dwarfed by his computer and the broad desk on which he leaned. Feeling queasy with the heat, Lila kept her composure.

The teller leaned toward the glass.

'Rome,' she said. 'No, Milan. No. Yes. Milan,' then, to be certain, 'Milan.'

He twisted his head to hear her. He tried Italian. English. French. Then returned to Italian.

'*Dove?*'

'*Milano.*'

'*Che giorno?*'

'*Si.*'

'*Oggi? Stamatina?*'

Lila pushed the money through the tray before he asked, before the details were decided. It was an effort to stand still, to not shout at the people behind her that they needed to back off. She picked the first of every option.

'*InterCity—*'

'*Si.*'

'*Diretto?*'

'*Si.*'

The man looked at the money. '*Eurostar?*'

'*Si.*'

'*Andata e ritorno?*'

'*Si.*'

'*Andata?*'

'*Si.*'

'*A che ora? Adesso?*'

'*Adesso?*' with some exasperation.

'*Prima o secunda? Prima?*'

'*Si. Prima.*'

She held her breath as she watched him type.

'Fifty-four euro.'

Lila leaned into the glass.

'You need four more euro.' The man held up the fifty-euro note and four fingers. Lila's stomach tightened, she couldn't see the problem until the man pointed at the price. Jittery at the realization that she would have to open the small pocket in the panda's stomach in the middle of the station, Lila wasn't sure what she should do.

The clerk twitched the fifty-euro note between his finger and thumb, and before her eyes the note divided into two.

The teller, equally surprised, saw that he now held two fifty-euro notes. 'Together!'

'Oh?'

'*Cento euro?*'

'*Si . . .*'

'*Cento.*' The clerk slipped the money away and drew out her change. After counting her notes and change he slid the ticket and the reservation stub into the tray then wiped his fingers on his cuffs.

Lila walked by the police and caught her reflection in the long smoky stretch of glass. She began to lose confidence, and doubted that she had properly thought through what she should do. A skinny ghost of the person who had arrived at the same station five months earlier, she doubted that she could manage without Rafí and Arianna.

With the ticket in her hand, Lila found the exit and stood facing the security cameras mounted over the automatic doors, defenceless in the station's broad angular forecourt.

The concourse and forecourt were now full and people moved slowly through the muggy air. Among them a young girl, slack and dead-eyed, hand feebly held out for money. Lila recognized her. The women who were out of favour, untrustworthy, or most likely sick were sent to the station to beg and steal. Lila watched the girl and felt again an extreme urgency that she should leave. Police waited by the barriers checking tickets. Above her, with infinite slowness, the clock ticked up to the hour.

Forty minutes after the train should have departed it was still at the station, delayed without announcement or explanation. The air-conditioning struggled against open windows and open doors. Lila sat beside the window with Rafí's silver phone tucked under her leg and the panda safely stowed on the rack within view. Three other women sat in the same compartment, one with her feet curled onto the seat, a large suitcase wedged between them so that Lila was obliged to sit upright. She wore sunglasses with a small diamante cut into the frame.

'I'm going to miss my flight,' she complained to the other two women in the compartment. She made the calculation, totting hours on her fingers. If it took two hours to get to Rome, one hour to get to the airport, plus, because you never know, another forty-five minutes waiting for the bus outside Termini station, then she was already running late, and you were supposed to be there two hours ahead of time. She would be in trouble if she missed the flight.

The other two women, students, sat with heavy textbooks open on their laps. One of the students' arms was bound in a sling and her friend tended to her, opened a drink, and asked if she was hungry. They stretched out side by side, shoes slipped off, bare feet on the seats, blocking the exit.

Lila sat on her hands to stop them shaking. It occurred to her to switch to another train, but none were leaving the station.

The longer they waited the more likely it would be that Rafí would return to the Stromboli, in which case he would find the dog loose, his room destroyed, and he would know to check for his money. Lila looked up at the toy, she couldn't remember if she had set the pole back in its slot.

Indifferent to the delay the two students tried to sleep, and the woman opposite Lila stared out of the window, arms folded, clearly angry. Passengers loitered on the platform, resigned. Some talked on their mobiles and others leaned out of the windows, smoking and watching the station, buying iced water from the vendors, everyone loose in the heat. Lila kept her eye on the panda and began to believe that she would never leave the city.

When the first announcement came the passengers on the platform applauded. The next train to leave was bound for Messina.

The trains were running again and surely the train for Milan would be next?

Rafí's phone gave a sharp trill and vibrated against her thigh. Lila jolted.

The woman opposite pushed back her sunglasses and pretended not to watch.

Lila listened for an announcement, a sign that they would soon be gone. If the train started now she swore she would never return, this was a final warning to underscore how urgently she needed to leave. Once they were out of the city she would talk with the women and ask what they knew about Milan.

The phone rang a second time.

There was no need to answer, no need to know who was calling. She was on a train and would soon be gone.

Looking at the small screen Lila saw the two calls from Cecco's mobile. She pressed her forehead against the cool window. The train on the opposite platform began to move, starting with a slow and smooth tug. Messina, she could have been heading to Sicily.

An announcement came with the small singsong of the station's call. The next train to depart was the Eurostar to Rome. Caserta would be next. No mention of Milan. The station stops were read out and she listened to the list and decided that she would take the very next train that was leaving.

She recognized him immediately. Rafí. Running headlong up the platform beside the grey Caserta train. Unmistakable in his loose white shirt, his scruffy black hair, that sloppy mouth, open, fish-like. Lila tried to draw the curtain but found it fixed in place. Throughout the night with the two brothers, through all of the brutality, it had never occurred to her that she would die, but she understood as a cold and clear fact that if Rafí found her and the money she would die. Rafí would have sent Cecco along one platform to check one set of trains while he checked another. The two of them would be here. Rafí hurried along the carriages pushing through people, passing parallel to Lila but searching, for the moment, the wrong train.

The woman flying from Rome sat upright, alert, and passed a glance to the students.

The announcement came, the next train to leave would be the Eurostar to Milan from platform eleven.

Lila sat down and looked up at the toy. The women also looked up. Passengers on the platform gathered at the doors.

If she held her nerve she would soon be gone. She was unlucky, she knew this, but how unlucky?

Rafí returned down the platform looking, as he ran, toward her train. He was much too far down the platform to see her. The announcement came a second time. They would soon depart. He would not make it.

And there he was, suddenly, as swift as a devil, hands up to the glass, looking hard, staring into the compartment, his face red and tight. Lila fled the compartment. She stumbled over cases, she made her way down the narrow corridor busy and blocked with people finding their seats. At the door she stopped and thought to ask for help, but Rafí already stood before her. For four hours Lila had been lucky.

Rafí walked Lila off the platform with his arm locked about her shoulder. She looked down as she walked and watched herself return, the toy tucked under her arm. The train began to slide out of the station.

'Where is Cecco?' Rafí's grip tightened, fingers digging. 'Was he with you? Where – is – he?'

Two carabinieri loitered at the entrance and Rafí steered Lila through clustered groups of travellers and past the news kiosk to the food hall. Walking through the food hall they came out of the terminus to the corner of piazza Garibaldi, to banks of white taxis, loitering passengers, men smoking, and he pushed her along the side of the station. Seeing two more policemen, a van marked 'carabinieri', he tugged her back and they returned to the food hall. Lila cringed as she walked, the toy tight under her arm. The station tannoy echoed through the concourse. More departures, a second train to Roma Termini.

He made her sit then slid beside her to keep her at the table. What was she doing? Why was she leaving? Did she think she wasn't being watched, that there weren't people who would tell him what his women were doing? Did she think after Arianna's little trick that she could slip away, just disappear, and do whatever she fancied? And where was Cecco? What did she know about Cecco? What had Cecco told her? Did she know where Cecco had gone?

Lila could not speak, and Rafí looked at her expecting information, his face red and his eyes small. What had Cecco told her? 'Was he on the train? Did you meet him here? Was Cecco with you? Was this his idea?'

She knew nothing and shook her head. Cecco was not with her, she said, and she didn't know anything. The men had frightened her this morning and she didn't want to stay on her own. That was all she knew. Lila forced the panda into her lap, fists on its belly.

Rafí shook his head and scoffed. 'You're lying. Who found the money? Did you see anyone on the roof? Did Cecco take the money?'

'What money?' Lila looked up and met his eyes, surprised that her voice could be so small and so convincing. 'You said Arianna took everything.'

Rafí rolled his fist across his forehead. A station guard hovered close to their table and they both became silent until he moved on.

Lila repeated blankly that Arianna had taken the money, hadn't she? She wiped her nose, then her hand on her trousers. As soon as the men had come this morning she'd left. She was frightened. They told her to go. She didn't understand what was happening. They told her to get out. Arianna had the money. Hadn't he said so?

'Where is it?'

Maybe the men who came this morning took the money. They let the dog free.

Rafí shook his head. 'No. No.' This didn't make sense. 'They're still looking for me,' he spelled out the situation. 'Why would they still be looking for me if they'd found the money? That's what they came for.' And as for the dog, no stranger had let that dog free, no stranger could come anywhere close, he'd deliberately under-fed it, kept it mean, for this explicit purpose. Whoever let the dog free had to know the dog. Which meant one thing: Cecco had let the dog free. 'Did Cecco come back to the Stromboli?'

Lila shook her head.

'Don't,' he said. 'Don't shake your head, don't cry, and don't draw attention to yourself.'

Lila nodded and wiped her eyes.

Rafí leaned closer, wrapped his arm about her shoulder, the table cut into his gut, he wiped her tears from the tabletop. 'I know what happened. I know that Cecco came back to the Stromboli. I know he found the money. He's the only one.'

Lila's hand closed over the scar on her wrist.

'Now tell me where he is.'

She took Rafí's phone from her pocket and slid it along the table. *Cecco – 3 Missed Calls*, registered dimly on the screen. She leaned forward and spoke clearly. 'He hates you. Every time he talks about you he says how stupid you are. He can't stand you.'

Rafí froze. So it was true. 'Where is he? Where is my money?'

Lila sat back, drew the toy to her chest and hugged hard. Her expression set as if she didn't know, as if she didn't care.

Unwilling to return to the Stromboli, Rafí arranged to meet Cecco at the Montesanto station. Lila watched from the station steps as Rafí became increasingly anxious. The waiting crowd grew thicker and mixed with the more active crowd scouring the market, so that commuters stood static beside the busier shoppers.

She thought it impossible that so much could go wrong at such speed. She looked down upon the market hating the stink and bustle, and uncomfortable to be out in the open she held the panda tight to her stomach and let her fingers press into the rolls of cash, outlining their shape even as she looked at Rafí, and she wondered why she had ever thought of him as smart.

Rafí came back and called Cecco a second time. How long could this take? Why wasn't he here already? As he listened to the reply he slowly straightened and looked up, patience draining out of him.

'What do you mean you're in Pozzuoli?'

Rafí listened, appeared to agree, then said he couldn't stop at the Stromboli, the men who were after him would be back, and he wasn't going back. He needed money and a place to stay. Lila noticed that he did not mention her. Rafí repeated: he had a handful of coins and that was it. He needed money.

'No,' Rafí disagreed. 'It isn't the same.' He hawked phlegm to his mouth then spat on the pavement and looked to see if anyone would disagree with him. When he said he only had a couple of euros, that's exactly what he meant. He needed money and he needed a place to stay. Lila watched Rafí cock his head, and for the first time look square at her. He held the phone up, his expression a mess of irritation and pure disbelief. Cecco had hung up. When he redialled the call would not go through. Rafí held the phone out and swore at it.

Cecco, Rafí said, the fat bastard, was dead to him, dead to the world.

He grabbed Lila's arm and pulled her up the steps toward the station. The platform, busy with people returning home, made it easy to bypass the gates and the guards. Slipping onto the train they stood close to the doors in the thick of the crowd and Rafí looked among them for bags that were open, and people who were distracted. When the train doors closed with a final decompression, Lila realized that she would not escape and began to hope for some other intervention. A wreck. A flood. A fire. A derailment. Some terrible affliction.

Within an hour of arriving at Pozzuoli they found Cecco at one of the bars facing the small port. Keeping their distance they watched from the shelter of the small tourist shops; if Cecco intended to go to Proceda it would be difficult to follow, but even he had enough animal cunning not to trap himself on an island. Rafí had managed to steal a pack of cigarettes on the train, slipped from a woman's open shoulder-bag, but for the moment was still without money. Lila smoked and found herself strangely unbothered, a little dizzy. How delicately Cecco held himself when he was alone. Two fingers pricked out as he held his beer.

'Get rid of the bear.'

'No.'

'Get rid of it.' Rafí raised his hand. 'You look stupid. People are noticing you.'

Lila tucked the toy to her stomach, leaned over it and drew on her cigarette. She couldn't help but shiver.

'You look stupid.'

'Stupid.' Lila repeated, her voice flat and factual, her arms clamped about the bear, shivering. 'Stupid me.'

Cecco stayed at the bar all evening and kept to himself, contented, perhaps even self-satisfied. Later, after talking on his mobile, he left the bar and began to walk away from the small marina. The road curled up the hillside and ran under the railway through a short steep tunnel carved into the tufa. Rafí stopped at the mouth of the tunnel and Lila followed after. They watched as Cecco entered an apartment block set on its own. Four storeys high, the building squatted into the hillside beside a small orchard raised from the road, paint peeling in soft folds on the undersides of the balconies. The street was open and Rafí decided to return when it was dark. Until then they would wait at the station and keep an eye on the road.

☆

Niccolò woke early. Livia could not sleep; uncomfortable and nauseous, she asked him to feel her brow. Brother and sister slept in T-shirts and shorts for decency, side by side, back to back, although this was becoming uncomfortable for her. Livia swore in her sleep, cursed and muttered so that she was always present in his thoughts. Sometimes the child stirred inside her and she would exclaim, often nothing more than a sharp intake of breath, but enough of a disturbance. The notion that something swam inside her turning, shifting, possibly even dreaming, made him uneasy.

'Am I hot? I feel hot.' She worried that something might be wrong but wouldn't say so directly, and it was left to Niccolò to divine this information out of her. Having slept poorly / very little / not at all (her status changed with each mention of her night), Livia demanded attention. Niccolò sat with her, clumsy with sleep, and when he reached for her stomach, because this is what he thought she wanted, she flinched and told him not to touch her.

'Why do men do that?' she asked. Angry now, Livia told him to get up and prepare for work.

By the time Niccolò had dressed Livia was sitting at the table drinking hot water, calmer and less concerned, colour back in her face. 'I'm OK.' She gave a tight smile that said she was still not quite herself. It had been a hot night and the heat had made her uncomfortable. 'I'm fine,' she said. 'Go. You'll only make me more anxious.'

He said goodbye from the door and as she waved she told him to head directly to work.

Niccolò returned to the wasteland to find the cordon taken down from the field. After only one night the police and reporters were already gone. The wasteland was still sectioned with stakes and tape, but the vans and cars and massive steel stanchions that held the arc lamps were gone. With nothing left except a few posts and lengths of tape snagged in the flattened grass it was hard to believe that the wasteland had attracted any attention at all.

He drove his scooter by the abandoned factories on his way to work. You could walk to them quicker, straight down the hill toward the bay. After the crossroads the road led directly down to the shoreline, the factories, the railway, the water. He drove slower by the market gardens and the rows of covered greenhouses, the plastic sheeting fogged and tracked with condensation. To his right the factories now: most of the buildings were without roofs, many had their entrances and windows bricked up and sealed. Heat rose from the stony fields of sparse and scorched grass which, some summers, held a lone mule.

The scooter made a feeble warble as he passed the first buildings, a thin wail thrown off the concrete wall to the road and fields. He slowed as he came to the last building, an old paint factory, and stopped at the small alley that led down to the railway bridge and the shore. Discarded on the steep slope lay bags of trash, ripped open with papers and plastic. Bound, rotten and dried bouquets of flowers spilled out. Flies broke loose from the weeds as Niccolò hitched the scooter onto its stand. He shouldn't be riding. He shouldn't be lifting. The agreement was that he would walk to work. When you've come this far, remember, it doesn't have to be everything at once. Niccolò checked to make sure he was not being watched or followed. A loose group of boys played football on the pumice road above the wasteland, and a white dust hung in the air.

The police had searched the paint factory the previous night and strings of black and yellow tape stretched across the doorway and lower windows.

As he approached the entrance Niccolò walked as if he intended to follow the alley down to the sea, but ducked quickly under the police tape and slipped inside, where he waited, head up, attentive, to ensure that the building was empty. Children often played in the building (possibly the same children who sometimes pelted him with stones when he rode to work). With its shattered walls daubed in graffiti the factory made an attractive haunt. Slogans and obscenities scrawled across the concrete named people he did not know.

Safe inside, Niccolò no longer felt the urgency he'd felt in the apartment. In the first room, cut into the floor, was a square metal tank with a round mouth, in which he dumped objects he no longer wanted. The animals he'd caught on the scrubland, cats mostly, stunned or dead, things he'd found, items he didn't need. Niccolò walked about the hole, scuffed a half-brick to the rim and tapped it over. The drop could only be a couple of metres, three at the most and the water would not be deep. Now disturbed, the water stank. He thought of the things he'd dropped into the water – the cats, the cans, the playing cards – as things which passed through a mirror to an inverted world: from his hands to someone else's.

He sat close to the hole, then carefully laid out the contents of the bag along the edge. After considering them for a moment, he divided the objects into two groups.

In the first line he laid out the blue notebook, a charger for a mobile phone, a black and white postcard of the port at Palermo, a wallet containing only receipts.

The second line, closer to the edge, included a receipt for the Hotel Meridian in Palermo, a mini-audio player with a crack in the plastic face, a small bottle of medication for insect bites, an open pack of chewing gum, a soap packet, a razor with a used blade, a novel with the cover torn off, a pocket-sized Italian–English dictionary.

In one last pass he looked through the items again and selected only the small blue notebook, which he returned to the sack. Its pages were greasy with oil, the ink smudged, and the paper translucent. Written in a small slanted hand that he couldn't read or in any case understand.

With one gesture he swept everything else into the tank.

The two other members of the B-4 security guard at the Persano-Mecuri chemical dye plant, Federico Taducci and 'Stiki' Bashana, met late on Saturday afternoons and occasionally in the evenings before work to play cards, sometimes at Bar Settebello in Ercolano, and sometimes at Federico's small apartment on the outskirts of town, less occasionally at a place closer to Stiki in Torre del Greco. Two years ago the shifts were managed with only one guard, but after the theft and assault, two men now monitored the facility during the night and one maintained security at the gate during the morning and through the afternoon.

Federico, a widower, always failed to invite Niccolò – not that Niccolò especially wanted to play Scopa or Sette e Mezzo – but he did want to be invited, and besides, Niccolò was the closer neighbour. Stiki lived in a single room in one of the larger blocks overlooking the train station at Torre del Greco. Younger than Niccolò by only two years, Stiki seemed much younger. He studied engineering, and worked nights to subsidize his studies. Always obliging, he smiled frequently but seldom laughed, and Niccolò mistook Stiki's poor and formal Italian as a sign that he was uninterested. At night Stiki slept while Fede played cards solo or taught himself English. Fede bought one American newspaper a week and made a show of completing a word puzzle. Niccolò often looked at the paper, but could make no sense out of it.

On this morning Federico stopped to speak with Niccolò. Fede greeted Niccolò warmly and asked for news about the investigation, they had both seen the news before the start of their shift and followed the reports on the radio. This is why he was late, no? The police had business with him? Stiki, ready to leave, loitered for a while, his backpack slung across his shoulder.

Niccolò bowed his head modestly and confessed that both the police and journalists were gone.

'Gone? Already?' It was mysterious, he said, very strange, they had listened to the news through the night. 'Are you sure?' Fede narrowed his eyes. 'You're not hiding anything, right? If there was something you'd tell me?'

Niccolò opened the windows and started a small fan. The booth carried a stale smell of sleep that Niccolò found unpleasant, but he could smell something else, as if the stink from the paint factory had clung to him, stuck to his hands or clothes.

'Don't you think it's strange?' Fede gave a reasoning shrug. 'They leave after one night? One night. Think about it. It's suspicious.'

Stiki agreed. It was suspicious.

Niccolò recognized that the two men were not entirely serious and said he didn't see how.

'It makes you think, though? No? Something is going on,' Fede considered. 'I'm telling you, there'll be more news tomorrow and they'll come back. This isn't over yet. You'll see.'

The men laughed as they walked away, an earlier conversation continuing between them. Niccolò completed the discussion: 'So you're helping with the investigation?' He looked at his reflection in the glass, ran his hand through his hair, ran his finger along a crease that started at the crown and circled round to his left temple in a perfect groove. If he tapped his head he could hear the difference, seriously, a completely different sound because it wasn't bone underneath the skin.

'Yes, I'm helping with the investigation.' He answered himself in a shy mumble. 'There are very many details to consider. It will take some time.'

Niccolò spoke to himself now, where before he used to sing. During the night he used to stand in the stairwell in the empty offices of B-19, call his wife and sing to her while his voice, hollow and lovely, drew strength from the darkened halls.

*

Once Fede and Stiki were gone Niccolò settled down to read the notebook. The wind carried sage and the slight scorched scent of fire. He lit a cigarette although they were not permitted to smoke in the booth and the memory of sweeping the evidence into the cistern came back to him. This gesture, a simple and decisive swipe, dismissive, was not in his language. A gesture borrowed from his sister. The thought, once solid, unsettled him. He took the notebook out of his bag, swept it off his desk, picked it up, and swept it off again. No, this was not his gesture. He sniffed at his fingers, and it became immediately obvious that the cover of the notebook, saturated with fat, was the source of the smell.

Livia returned home as the evening news concluded. She sat heavily on the side of the bed and twisted off her shoes, her mouth set in a tight line as she smoothed her hand over her shoulders.

'They stand at the entrance,' she said, 'those boys, right by the door so you have to push past them. How old are they? I don't like it. Always a group of them. My neck,' she complained, 'and my back, all day. There's something bad in the kitchen. I could smell it as I came in.' Livia made a face. 'What is that smell? Something smells bad. What is it?'

Niccolò leaned into the doorway with his arms folded and said that he was careful now to smoke outside and lean over the balcony so that the smoke did not enter the apartment. Afterward he washed his hands and brushed his teeth as she didn't like the stink of cigarettes on him. The bother of it meant that he was smoking more at work and less at home.

'I'm not talking about cigarettes.' She screwed up her face. 'Can't you smell it? It's like something has died.'

For an hour Niccolò indulged his sister, he moved the furniture around, checked behind and under the fridge while she sprayed with disinfectant, but the source of the smell could not be discovered.

'Men are so dirty,' she said. Which was not true as Niccolò kept his rooms clean and in order. Livia's clothes, her cups and plates, her shoes and papers littered the small apartment.

She asked him to sit down and said they needed to talk about the upcoming assessment. 'They will want to know how you've managed,' she said, 'they'll ask you questions, they'll try to trip you up, and you know not to tell them that I have been here. They won't want to know that I was here. You know not to say anything about that. You also shouldn't say that you've been using the scooter. Not right away. They'll want to know that everything is fine, that you are coping well. Tell them about work. Tell them that you cook and clean for yourself. Just tell them what they want to hear.'

Niccolò said he understood, this didn't need talking through – he didn't say, although he hoped that this was true, that once the first assessment had occurred that she would also leave. She hadn't come to look after him so much as to punish her husband.

FRIDAY: DAY M

As Niccolò steered his scooter around the barrier Fede came out of the booth, a little swagger to his walk, the *Cronache* folded in his hand. Stiki slumped in the booth, asleep, with his head to his chest. On a single-ring stove beside him was a pot of noodles.

'I imagine you haven't seen this?' Fede thrust the newspaper forward.

Niccolò set the scooter on its stand then brushed his hand over his hair. He took the paper out of Fede's hands.

'He was American. The man who was stabbed. A student or a tourist. Have they told you this?'

Niccolò shook his head as he read.

'And . . . there's a witness. Someone at the Circumvesuviana station on Friday morning – that's five days before you found the clothes.' Fede squeezed Niccolò's shoulder. 'What did I tell you? Didn't I say there would be news today? It says that a woman has come forward who recognized the star on the T-shirt. She saw someone at the station wearing the clothes you found. On Friday. In Naples. The T-shirt comes from America, it's unlikely there are more like it in the country. It's exactly as I told you.'

Niccolò looked hard at Fede and saw that he was serious. He didn't remember Fede telling him any of this but didn't want to openly disagree. Fede's face being creased and rubbery, was the hardest of faces to read.

'The police are certain it's the same person. They're looking at videotape from the security cameras to see which station he came from. It also says the person is almost certainly dead.' Fede pointed to the article. 'Here. Wounds to the lower stomach, chest, upper . . .' he ran a finger across his neck, '. . . within four minutes.'

The two men sat side by side on the concrete step beside the security booth.

Niccolò opened the newspaper across his lap and focused on

where the hillside dropped to a smooth blue plate of sky. Aquamarine. The tips of the city's towers visible at the edge in a tawny haze.

'I know,' Fede interrupted his thoughts. 'It's a bad world.' He slapped the paper with the back of his hand. 'But you know what. Everything moves forward.' The man stood up and looked down at Niccolò. 'Some family is going to thank you for finding the clothes. If it wasn't for you this might not have been discovered. When they sort this out some family is going to be grateful. I wouldn't be surprised if there wasn't some kind of recognition, some kind of a reward.'

Niccolò slowly re-read the article. Please, no more rewards, no more meals / speeches / flowers and plaques, no more interviews, no more presentations. He studied the two articles with care and re-read sections that were unclear to him until they began to make sense. The police wanted to hear from anyone who'd travelled on the six thirty Trento express or the six thirty-five Circumvesuviana into Naples on the previous Friday, or anyone who was in or around the station from seven fifteen in the morning until eight thirty. An image of the five-pointed star was reprinted, bold, white on black, accompanied with a map of the Circumvesuviana line marking all stops to Naples. An editorial called for witnesses to come forward, and an appeal was made to hoteliers asking them to report unfilled or cancelled bookings and ensure that all visitors were properly recorded as required. He began to count.

'I know,' Fede sucked in his breath, 'four minutes is a long time.'

Niccolò took the night report and logbook to the main office and waited a little while in the entrance, knowing that Fede would not be able to linger. When he returned he sat with the small blue notebook on his lap and kept it concealed under the counter. Happy to be alone he studied the tidy, sloping handwriting, his eye ran over words he couldn't understand. A fan blew warm air into the booth. On the first page, written in capitals he found an address and what he thought to be a name and serial number. N. CLARK, -0626.

The police had said that they would get back to him if they needed help, and given this new witness he was certain that they would need more information once they understood a little more about the situation. He wouldn't wait for the call, he would make his own investigation. It was almost two days now since his discovery, and during those two days Niccolò had been walking in a different world, breathing different air, separate and expectant. In the long hours sat monitoring cars and staff in and out of the dye plant, he nursed the idea that he was being tested and observed, as if the event itself, the murder of this student, was some kind of creature.

Closing the book Niccolò decided that he would conduct his own investigation, then he would contact the police and hand the notebook over to them along with his findings. He would say that someone left the little book outside his door, or that he had found it in a part of the field that they had not searched, or perhaps that he had found it a place that they had searched just to make a point of their uselessness.

Disappointed with the day Niccolò re-read the articles in Fede's newspaper and could not shake the idea that whatever had happened was predetermined, that all of these people and coincidences combined to make the event not only inevitable, but possible. As if the event itself had some kind of intelligence, an ability to decide what would happen and who would be involved.

The evening was slow and Livia contrary, whatever mood he was in was bothersome to her, and she had no interest in speaking about the investigation, nor in hearing his ideas.

'Stop,' she told him. 'Don't make this into something it isn't. Just stop. Take a walk.'

Avoiding confrontation Niccolò did exactly as Livia asked and took a walk and returned to the wasteland and the line of empty factories with his slingshot in his pocket to smoke and think a little about Livia and the baby, but more about how he would start his investigation. When he reached the factory the stink was now so foul that he couldn't enter. And then it occurred to him. If the clothes were dumped on the wasteland, and the person wearing the clothes had been seen on the Circumvesuviana train, then they must have walked from the station to the wasteland.

He couldn't decide which station the student would have taken. If he was a student or a tourist he would have alighted at the Scavi stop. This seemed the most logical. It was always possible, of course, that it was not the victim who took the train in the first place. In which case whoever had committed the crime would have taken the train from the city and brought the clothes with them, and they could have used either stop, Ercolano, or Ercolano Scavi.

As he walked the route, he began to think his logic was wrong. If the student was heading into the city, then why were the clothes found here, outside the city? And supposing the person who committed the crime did travel to Ercolano to dump the clothes, then there was no guarantee that they, like the victim, had taken the train. This walk was a waste of time. He needed to go to the station in Naples to see who came on the trains, and who left. To think about this properly, he needed to be at the station himself.

Later, when he settled into bed beside his sister and lay on his back, he doubted that he would sleep. It didn't help either that Livia slumbered soundly beside him, out almost before she laid down, mouth open, breath softly chortling; even in sleep she sounded dissatisfied. He longed for the baby to be born, and he longed for her to go.

As he lay in bed he retraced his walks from the wasteland to the station, the night leaning on him as a palpable pressure, thick with possibilities: an American on a train, a woman at the station, clothes on the wasteland, and the hint that this all connected to him. It was likely that the person who killed the American student was also on that train with him that morning.

☆

Mizuki rose early, dressed, sat on the balcony, then fell immediately into a deep, recuperative sleep. At seven thirty she was woken by a call from Lara. She watched the phone vibrate and allowed the call to go to message.

Mizuki took her morning shower then returned to the balcony. She held out her phone to read the screen and saw two missed calls.

'Mizuki. The police came to the bakery yesterday. They wanted to know if the bakery have ever printed their logo onto any clothing.' Lara paused, little more than a short intake of breath. 'I'm talking about the bakery under the school.' She paused again. 'The sign, the star sign. Mizuki. Are you there? They were asking about a T-shirt. Call me.'

Star signs? Mizuki didn't understand. She looked out at a wall of closed shutters and thought about the school and the palazzo, then remembered the small tin star that hung above the portico.

Lara called again, and again Mizuki allowed the call to go directly to message. 'Mizuki. Have you seen the news? Call me. Have you heard? It's on the news, right now, on the radio, on the TV.' Lara carefully explained: a T-shirt with the same design as the bakery logo had been discovered cut and bloodied on wasteland outside the city. But stranger still, someone, a commuter, had come forward convinced that they had seen a tourist, a young boy, wearing this T-shirt at the Circumvesuviana station last Friday morning. Mizuki felt her chest tighten, and was surprised that this was anger, not fear. She had come to Naples to experience something, and here was that something – and she'd missed it. *She wasn't there.*

Lara left a message asking to meet.

'I'm worried,' she said, 'you haven't called me back. I thought it was you. Did you contact the police? I'll be at the station before class. I'll meet you outside the station at eight.'

Mizuki came directly into the city. Once at the station she looked for the brothers, but they were not on the platform, not on the concourse, nor waiting, as before, under the long overhang from the station to the street, nor in the bright sunshine waiting by the taxis. Their absence came as a heavy disappointment, just to see them would offer some kind of solace – but what would she have said that wouldn't have ended in some kind of disappointment?

Lara waited outside the station. Not ready to talk, Mizuki took the exit through to the main station and walked from Stazione Centrale all the way around, through piazza Garibaldi, back to the Circumvesuviana so that Lara would not see her, but she could see Lara. Her phone sang in her hand.

Mizuki returned to the cafe she where she had spoken with Lara and listened to the message as she watched the station through the window. She had seen the clothes on the news and felt sad that a relative would have to identify them. Until they found the young man these clothes would be the only record of what had happened. The clothes were made in America, this is what they were saying now. But the coincidence about the star was very strange.

'I thought it was you,' Lara said, and as Mizuki listened to the message, she saw Lara come into view. 'The person who came forward. The woman who spoke with the police. I thought this is why I haven't seen you.'

Lara's final call came later that night while Mizuki was considering if she should or should not pack. Mizuki accepted the call but did not speak.

THE KILL

'I know how this is,' Lara spoke. 'I know how this feels. My father, when he died – I had to collect his jacket from the police.' At four thirty one summer afternoon her father had taken off his suit jacket, laid it carefully across the passenger seat, and before he could settle into the car had suffered a heart attack. 'I brought everything back. Things they had taken from the car, and my mother, the first thing she did was check through the jacket, to empty his pockets as if she didn't trust him.'

When Lara began to ask what was wrong, why had they not spoken, *She didn't understand what she'd done*, Mizuki hung up.

She would not pack. She did not need these clothes. She did not want them. Everything that was bought to fuel this character, this failed escape, would be left.

☆

Rafí had spent the night watching the flats while Lila attempted to sleep in the shelter of a small hut, her head resting on the toy bear, her arms locked securely about it. Several times she woke up, immediately alert, and thought she could just walk away, sneak down the hill: to where though, and to what? Woken by the sun and troubled by mosquito bites along her arms and neck, she watched Rafí, who in turn watched the apartment block, eyes fixed on third floor, which he believed to be where Cecco was staying. When he stood up, she stood up. When he walked she followed. Stray dogs, curious at this early activity, followed lamely after. Weak from lack of sleep, Lila ached and was thirsty, and despite the sun she was cold. How strange to have so much money in her arms. She could buy food, she could buy cigarettes, she could buy cola and Sicilian pastries. She could hire a taxi to take her anywhere she could imagine, but she couldn't find a certain opportunity to escape from Rafí. All this money.

They lingered at the port for an hour, dissatisfied with each other, unspeaking and uncertain. The bear clutched tight in defiance. Rafí sat with his back to her and turned on occasion to give a look of utter disgust. Both were surprised to see Cecco walk immediately by them, close, but so preoccupied he saw nothing but the pavement ahead. Cecco wandered along the promenade, paused to see what the fishermen had caught, then ambled by the ticket office.

Rafí tightened the distance between them. He was learning

nothing, he told Lila, this watching and waiting was a waste of time. If he wanted his money he would need to get closer, and when Cecco clambered delicately down to the rocks, Rafí came closer. He signalled Lila to stay back.

Cecco sought out a broad flat rock and settled down, he rolled his shirt high over his stomach and gave himself up to the morning sun. Rafí climbed down and Lila hurried after: if she ran now Rafí would catch her, she wouldn't even make it off the promenade. Cecco lay with his belly exposed, his hands flat to the rock, defenceless.

'So this is what you do with yourself.'

Rafí stood with the sun over his shoulder so that Cecco had to squint at him, hand shielding his eyes. Cecco managed a small hello and looked feebly about him. His gestures, his expression were the sure signs of a guilty man.

'You're sweating.'

It would be easy to pick up one of the smooth black rocks and belt Rafí while he was preoccupied, and who would stop her? Maybe not to kill him, but leave him useless for the rest of his life, with just enough brains to understand what had happened to him and why.

Rafí squatted beside Cecco, patted his friend on his shoulder and asked where he was staying.

'So? Pozzuoli?'

Cecco gave a nod and then shrugged. He noticed Lila and appeared momentarily relieved.

'Tell me about it.'

'With everything. I thought. You know. Why not? Just.'

'Just keep your head down.'

Cecco sat up on his elbows and nodded earnestly. 'I was going to call you today.'

'That's funny, because I've been trying to call you.'

They looked at each other, stalemate.

'Where are you staying?'

Cecco pointed up the coast to Lucrino, but looked back at the town. There was a woman, he said, a friend, but it was a small place.

Rafí settled on the rock beside him. 'I don't mind,' he said. Big or small it would suit him fine. He'd had a rough night.

Cecco's woman was not what Lila expected. Cecco passed her photo about. In the picture Stefania sat beside a man in workman's overalls, perhaps on the same rocks they'd come from. In another she held a ball, just caught or ready to throw, a posed picture. Ridiculous. Shapely, old, homely and content, with deep black eyes drawn in kohl and dark hair bleached to a brittle gold, the woman had married twice and more or less lost both husbands, Cecco explained. She worked at the *tabaccaio* on via Capasso, and every time he went in he'd spoken with her and got to know her a little.

'Enough that she looks after you?'

Cecco couldn't look at Rafí, as if ashamed. He took back the photograph and set it on the small side table. Rafí joked that widows were accommodating, especially the fat ones. He bent down to squint at the photograph and said she looked familiar. The apartment comprised three small rooms, a bedroom, kitchen and a sitting-room cramped with a plump couch and a large television beside a small veranda. There was no evidence of children, and few photographs or certificates.

Rafí sent Lila out to the small hallway. She backed out and watched him scope the room, possibly figuring where Cecco might have concealed the money. The room was busy, unkempt, with small girly keepsakes, china dolls, and soft toys with embroidered clothes that she sold at the shop. On the couch in small boxes were more soft toys with names and hearts sewn onto small jackets, and china ballerinas with real lace skirts. In the kitchen along a small folding table lay lengths of pastel-coloured ribbons cut to the same length with a package of porcelain figurines ready to be assembled and decorated, and she understood that this was how Stefania spent her evenings. Cutting and stitching.

Lila smoked at the veranda doors and took long considered draws. Cecco also smoked, fingers crushing the cigarette. When he caught Lila's eye he gave a private shrug, a *what is he doing*, and Lila, in response, shrugged back. How odd this was, how interesting, everything Cecco did just made him look like a thief.

'You have a paper? A newspaper?' Rafí asked Cecco.

Cecco looked down in deference. He wiped his hands on his shirt. 'I need a paper. Go,' he said, 'get me one. And get some food.'

Cecco nodded, yes, he'd go. There was one thing though, something important he'd forgotten to explain.

Rafí said that he could tell him when he came back.

Cecco shook his head. No, it was important. Her first husband was a security guard at the port.

'And?'

'And he's dead.'

Rafí, lost for words, looked like he might hit Cecco. Exactly why was this a problem?

'Because her second husband was in the carabinieri, and he isn't dead.' She spoke of him as if he was dead, but he wasn't. The man was violent and she'd finished with him years ago, but, and this was the problem, he was obsessed with her and sometimes watched the house and deliberately caused trouble.

'Just get a paper and get me some food.'

Cecco backed out of the room to the door. Lila could hear him running down the stairs.

With Cecco out of the apartment Rafí hurtled through the rooms. He swept the ornaments off the table, took a paring knife from the kitchen and searched swiftly through the boxes, first opening them then turning them upside down, emptying the contents onto the hard tiled floor until it was covered with small bites of packing foam and shards of shattered china, tiny painted heads and arms and legs, whiter than sugar. The money was not in the boxes. It was not in the drawers, the side cabinet, the dresser. It wasn't in the cupboard. Under the couch, under the cushions, under the bed. Neither was it stuffed into the pillows or mattress. Rafí reached over the bedroom cupboard and again found nothing. When he stepped back, hands on hips, he looked to Lila, then beyond her, and Lila followed his glance to see Stefania at the doorway, dark eyes, silent, aghast at the chaos and destruction. In five short minutes Rafí had emptied every container and destroyed everything he touched in his search for the money. Scattered among the broken porcelain were pieces of dried pasta, lentils, and pulses. Stefania cringed as he came quickly after her. With the paring knife pointed at her neck he told her to sit down and keep herself absolutely silent.

Stefania swept aside the brittle shards of figurines and slowly sat on the floor, her back to the veranda door.

'Tell me where he has hidden my money.'

Stefania shook her head and Lila shook her head to warn her.

'Where – is – my – money?'

Rafí held back her head to expose her throat and drew his arm full out, ready to swipe.

'Where?'

Stefania pointed to the television. Behind it was a package containing thirty euro, a measly find compared to the size of his loss.

Lila could see Cecco returning through the tunnel, a newspaper in his hand, an anxious hurry to his step, and in total contradiction, a broad smile – when she pointed, Rafí turned, and for no reason she could understand, his face tightened with fury and he bolted out of the room.

Rafí rushed upon Cecco in the stairwell and stabbed him in the gut. As Cecco tumbled back Rafí criss-crossed the knife over his face, then fell upon him.

'Where – is – my – money?'

Rafí stuck Cecco until the blade became slippy. Lila hurried partway down the stairs, the bear in her arms, and stopped when she saw the fray, the mortal horror on Cecco's face, how Rafí pinned him down so he could not protect himself, and how Rafí could not hold the knife without also cutting his own hand.

Cecco babbled, and Rafí let him talk. He knew nothing about the money, nothing. He'd come to the Pozzuoli because Rafí wanted him to do things with those two men. Rafí, his one true friend, had asked him to do things he did not want to do and he had come to Stefania confused and troubled and Stefania had taken him in without question. She was his friend like Rafí was his friend. He'd done nothing, nothing. He swore. What had he done? Rafí was like his brother. Whatever he had done he was sorry.

Rafí fastened his hands about Cecco's throat.

Lila flinched away as Stefania passed her, swift and ghost-like. She saw the woman, saw the hammer, but did not properly figure what was about to happen until the act was done. Stefania stood over Rafí and without pause or haste swiped him on the temple with one hefty clout.

Rafí fell sideways, turned, rose on his hands and knees so that he straddled Cecco, then stopped and hung his head. The four of them stuck in place: Rafí on his hands and knees, Cecco under him, Stefania poised with the hammer ready to strike again, and Lila, witness to it all, on the stairs.

Rafí squatted like a dog. Cecco, bloody chest, stomach, and nose split open, cheek gashed, slid from under him, mouth open. Lila could not calculate how long they waited, attention fixed on Rafí, who slowly leaked – blood dripping from his nose – but otherwise remained completely still. Finally, Stefania turned to Lila and offered the hammer and Lila came slowly forward, the toy clutched to her chest. She took the hammer, stood over Rafí, but could not strike. Instead she sunk to her haunches and looked closely at Rafí's face. Wall-eyed, he stared both at the floor and through it, and remained fixed in place.

Cecco raised his shirt in disbelief. The wounds, four small and bloody mouths, puckered his stomach. He looked to Stefania and asked why, and she said she didn't know. Cecco shook his head in a small shiver and asked again, 'Why?' Why had she hit Rafí? He didn't understand.

Stefania brought towels and a bucket of water. She locked the door, pushed the bolt to secure it, then threw the towels across the floor, gave Cecco her apron and helped him tenderly to his feet. With Cecco on the stairs she took a plastic bag out of her pocket and drew it over Rafí's head, when Cecco began to sob she stopped and explained that he was bleeding everywhere.

They laid Rafí across the back seat of Stefania's car then covered him with wet towels. On Stefania's instruction Cecco and Lila were to take Rafí and leave him, she didn't care where, but not the police, and not a hospital.

Cecco, wrapped in bandages, sat at the wheel, sweating, mouth drawn, his breath compressed, his face swollen, already black and plum-like, pulpy at the cuts. He drove carelessly, indecisive, as if driving some route from memory. Lila peeled the towels back from Rafí's face – also swollen now but bloodless, eyes black and blown, eyelids fat and slug-like, his hair matted flat. Not dead, certainly, but not fully alive. She held her hand, then the bear over his face and wondered what he could see, if anything registered. There was a warehouse, Cecco said, an old paint factory. They'd take him to Ercolano, call the police, tell them where they could find him, and then, as Stefania had instructed, he would return to Pozzuoli where she would again check his wounds. Lila wondered if she had any part in these plans.

They followed the bay, houses and developments on either side, until the bay-side, gorgeous with sunlight, swung close to the road, leaving room for abandoned factories, train tracks, a few open fields of scrub, then row after row of long plastic sheds running down the slope, greenhouses, the plastic sweated and tight. Cecco, bleeding from the cuts to his nose and face and the deeper wounds in his side and back, said he was beginning to feel sick and weak. He pointed out the road to the station and said, not unkindly, that they were here, and she should go. It was better if she looked after herself now. He was sorry that he didn't have any money. His voice came faint and exhausted, and he shook his head. She should hurry. She should go.

Raff's eyes were dry and fixed. His breathing now shallow and brief pulls, too brief to be of use. Cecco wept with his head down, his hands on the wheel. When Lila closed the door he drove away. In the end it was that simple. She opened the car door, slipped out, then watched it drive toward the bay.

Lila waited on a bare platform with the sun full on her shoulders. From the stairwell she could hear voices, a couple arguing in Spanish, and their words rose sweetly recognizable, a sound intermittently lost to passing traffic on the nearby autostrada. She read the sign, ERCOLANO SCAVI, and spoke the words out loud, repeated them until they fell into a rhythm. She looked left to right, then approached the rail and looked down the road at a campervan, rust running along the roof. She would speak with these people, or she could wait. Or she would sneak into their vehicle. Or she would walk to the service station she could see beside the motorway and clean herself up. Or she could find himself a car parked outside the services. Or she would wait in the shelter on the platform and tell someone how she had been mugged. Or, she would call the police and describe to them how Cecco could be found in an abandoned factory hugging the body of his friend who was not dead but almost dead. Or?

As she stood in the sunlight, dizzy and sticky, the toy in her arms, possibilities opened one by one by one.

SATURDAY: DAY N

Mizuki sat looking at herself. Her hair freshly cut and treated, heavy, black, so that it curled just under her ears. She'd never worn it short before. With the right glasses she would look boyish. No disguising her features, but an extreme enough change to mark a distinction between the woman who had come with such disorganization to Naples. It irritated her to have her nails manicured, and she did little to disguise her impatience with the woman – who asked, in any case, too many questions.

Her mouth, small but full, took on a slight shell-shaped plumpness, and the plum colour took attention away from what she considered now were heavy jowls and the distinct flatness of her eyes.

When the dress arrived she left it on the bed and waited for the woman to leave.

Mizuki took the box out of the bag, slipped off the lid and parted the tissue. Her hand ran over the material, a warm grey flecked with gold, wool threaded with silk so that the dress found its own weight and smoothed itself to her hands – and she could see, just in the whiteness of her hands against the colour and heft of the cloth, how well this would suit her.

Once dressed, she opened up the jeweller's box, set square on the table. She leaned forward to buckle the chain about her neck. Her eyes small and black. She was again a woman not out of place, a handsome woman, lucky enough to afford her tastes.

Lara's Saturday class would be over in ten minutes. Mizuki watched the clock. She could invite her to the hotel and they could speak one last time before she left for the airport. There would be time.

As the car pulled out, the grand facade of the opera, the Castel Nuovo, the fountains and piazzas reflected across the window. But she sat looking forward, scanning for men on the street, her mind elsewhere, her hand resting delicately at her throat. Keiko, she said to herself. Keiko. Possibilities. Always. Possibilities and happenstance.

MONDAY: DAY O

He woke certain that what he wanted would be found in Naples.

Niccolò rose quickly, closed the door between the bedroom and the kitchen and called Fede to explain that the police wanted to speak with him. He needed to go into the city. It would take all day.

Niccolò was careful to sound perfunctory.

Fede agreed to cover the first two hours of his shift, after that he would tie the barrier back and they could manage without a guard. If it couldn't be helped, it couldn't be helped, but couldn't the police give them more advanced warning? Uninterested in debate Niccolò said that he had to go.

Niccolò dropped his keys. As he stooped to pick them up he caught his reflection in the frosted glass of the bedroom door. Behind the glass, in the dark, Livia slept. Fearful of spiders, wasps, mosquitoes and blood-borne diseases she preferred the shutters closed. 'I'm a magnet for disaster,' she claimed, 'any kind of trouble,' although this was simply not true. The air from the room was still and warm and baby-sweet. He reached for the keys and caught his face half-lit, and believed for a moment that the reflection was someone else's. He waited expecting the reflection to move independent of him, to pick up the keys before he picked up the keys.

He prepared breakfast knowing that Livia needed to be away early. He took his time showering and dressing. He dressed as usual in his uniform, but once Livia had left he changed into casual clothes and laid his uniform out across the bed ready for the end of the day.

Checking his watch he made sure he had plenty of time. Niccolò stood in front of the mirror and took measure of himself. Uncomfortable, he undressed, folded away the clothes, took a second shower, selected new clothes and re-dressed.

He rubbed oil into his hands and tousled his hair, then combed it, then gave himself a parting, a clean straight cut, so that his hair no longer fell forward to disguise the edge of the plate. He studied himself in the mirror and began to feel satisfied. While he found it difficult to associate with this face, he understood that it was his and how it felt, increasingly, less like a mask. The student's notebook wrapped in plastic safe in his pocket. As he came across articles about the case he clipped them from Fede's newspaper and folded them between the empty pages in chronological order.

At the station Niccolò bought a ticket from the tobacconists'. After franking the ticket he walked up to the platform and stood where he could watch the other passengers.

The train was not crowded. He stood with his back to the door so that he could see about the carriage without having to move. People read newspapers or sat looking out of the window, there were few discussions. At Torre del Greco passengers began to move toward Niccolò's end of the train. At the far set of doors he could see two men in carabinieri uniforms. While most people avoided looking at him, the officers caught his eye, and Niccolò nodded back, and couldn't help but smile at the idea that they were probably on the train for the same reason.

Niccolò studied the passengers and considered that none of them looked strong enough to abduct and stab a young man. He knew that it was a mistake to assume that the person who committed the assault would stand out in some way or even look interesting. He knew that once some discovery was made, the assailant would, in many ways, be a disappointment. But still, the possibility remained that the man responsible for the stabbing would be on the train.

The station in Naples was busy with police and carabinieri. Up on the concourse, the police watched people coming out of the station and up onto the street. Uniformed men stood in threes and fours, armed and prepared, and immediately outside the station, under the shade of the concrete awning, carabinieri waited beside black vans marked with official insignia, and Niccolò guessed that there was to be a parade or demonstration.

Niccolò came slowly through the market stalls at piazza Nolana, his hands in his pockets, hoping to see why there were so many police, for some kind of reason to materialize. But no demonstration emerged. Disappointed to have discovered nothing Niccolò walked through piazza Garibaldi and further, along via Carbonara, hoping that something would occur to him now that he was in the city. As he hadn't read the paper that morning, he bought *Il Mezzogiorno*, and decided to take a coffee and see if there had been any developments overnight.

The front page carried an image of the star: a simple black square with the white outline of a star set in a circle. Inside, on page seven, he found an article about the graphic and how it was used in the city by a publisher, a printer, a chain of bakeries, and as a logo for a biscuit produced by the bakery. He read slowly, took breaks so that he would not become addled, so that he would not lose himself. This is what he needed to focus on. The star. This was the reason for his journey. Niccolò remembered the biscuits. Surely everyone knew of them. The tins were stacked in every shop and market for weeks before and after Ferragosto. It wasn't a tradition, as such, but this is when he always remembered seeing them. He also had an idea where the bakery was located – although the newspaper had indicated that a number of bakeries produced the star-brand biscuits.

Uncertain of the neighbourhoods Niccolò walked first through I Miracoli and found the roads forced him up the hill; the streets became steeper and narrower and took him away from where he sensed he should be heading. At first, catching his reflection in shop windows, he did not recognize himself. But this was no confusion, instead he saw himself as someone who lived in the city, someone who belonged on the streets, a man with authority. The almond sellers, the gypsies asking for money, the shoe salesmen, the women at the markets, they all knew him, or knew his type: an independent man going about his independent business.

The further he walked the quieter the streets became, until he was surrounded by buildings five or six storeys high, their fronts rose directly from the black-cobbled road and their backs stumped into the hillsides. One row of houses topped another, butting higher at each level, so that the road appeared to rise through a canyon of dank grey rock. Turning back, he returned through the market on via Vergini, then seeing a street sign, via Arena di Sanità, he followed the street through to a long curved piazza and regretted that he had no address and no map. Even so, he couldn't find the bakery.

Stopped on the piazza with only a general notion of his location, he decided to return to the station. Once on via Carbonara his thoughts now ran on other subjects. When he stopped at via Capasso to wait for a break in the traffic, he looked down the small street directly at a red tin sign of a star in a circle mounted under a porch.

The dimensions, colour and design of the star were identical to the star on the missing student's T-shirt, the sign duplicated in Fede's newspaper and this morning's *Mezzogiorno*. The discovery astounded him. He walked to the entrance and found the small portal-door open. Niccolò peered into the courtyard to smell fresh bread and see what looked like apartments rising above the central courtyard. On the brass plaque beside the doorbells he read the names of the businesses: a language school, a furniture 'fabricator', a lawyer, a seminary. It took a while for the information to sink in and seemed oddly coincidental, so odd that it might not be a coincidence at all, but some deliberate design.

Niccolò stopped at the entrance perturbed, unsure of his discovery. The longer he looked at the tin sign, the more significant it seemed.

He waited two hours, standing first immediately outside the door, so that every time it was opened he could see into the courtyard and understand a little better what was inside. He thought it best to wait, to stay open to the coincidence and see what might develop. Contented with the discovery he was happy to allow whatever might happen to unfold without prompting. At eleven o'clock he heard voices echoing as they came to the door, and a whole group of people came out of the courtyard. They came out in threes and fours, Americans, French, German, busy with chatter. The students from the language school held the door open for each other, they ducked as they came out, and Niccolò waited with his back to the wall, close enough to see each individual, and some, noticing him, nodded politely. The students, mostly women and girls, spoke English, although he heard German, and a little tentative Italian. Two boys, Japanese, ducked out through the doorway, and Niccolò waited, not sure if this also meant something. When the door closed behind them the students walked on and the street became silent.

After twenty minutes with few people coming in and out Niccolò began to consider moving on, and just as he debated the idea the door opened, and out stepped a young girl dressed in a short skirt with black skin-tight leggings.

The woman crossed directly in front of him. Short, with black hair cropped in a boyish cut, she hurried, half-running, through the shade of the street out into the sunlight, and headed to the broader piazza where she joined a small group of students and followed after them into an *alimentari*. Niccolò, with nothing else to do, came cautiously to the shop. Looking through the long windows he couldn't distinguish her from the other students. Finally she emerged from the shop alone with a blue bag tucked under her arm. As she walked the strap slipped from her shoulder and she occasionally corrected it.

The student crossed directly in front of him. Niccolò automatically shied away, when he looked up again she was heading through the market and the tight streets of the Centro Storico, stepping aside for the cars and motorbikes and making her way to the open parade of via Cavour. Turning once the street opened out she hurried toward the metro, and came directly down the subway steps, walking so purposefully that he was sure she was taking him somewhere he needed to see.

Niccolò followed the student down to the platform, and stood close enough that he could have touched her shoulder without having to stretch. Niccolò seldom came into the city, he disliked the forced proximity of strangers, the crush and chaos; through the rush of the morning he had found no time to consider where he was, but now, deep under the city, he felt at ease. He fidgeted with the student's notebook in his pocket. His fingers slipped over the plastic sheath.

Nothing particular singled out the student, she was a plain girl, thin, possibly haughty, a little masculine. There were other women on the platform and girls dressed in shorts or short skirts shouting as they came to the platform, heading to the northern beaches. One talked to a friend and lazily looked him up and down.

He stood beside the student on the train, turned three-quarters away from her, and refused a man asking for cigarettes. The girl appeared not to notice as the man spoke to her. Coming through to Campi Flegrei the train broke to the surface. Looking directly out of the window he watched the hotels and apartments on the broad cliff surrounding the back lots. He waited for her reflection when the train hit shade to show in the window.

Alighting at Campi Flegrei, he let her walk ahead, and followed via a bridge over the platform down to the street, it was clear that she was familiar with this route. The avenue was broader than the tight city streets. Ahead, running behind apartment blocks was the steep sweeping rim of a crater, the crest edged with finer houses and palm trees.

He followed her through a car park to the doors of an apartment and stopped at the steps as she paused at the doors and checked through her shoulder-bag for her keys. As she leant over the counter she looked back, and for the moment, before she turned and walked into the building he was certain that she had seen him. She seemed, he thought, to be looking for someone.

A group of four men playing cards inside the entrance looked back at him, and he thought that he should leave.

He returned directly to the train station.

Finding Niccolò just out of the shower Livia asked why his work clothes were laid out on the bed.

'You need to help put things away. They're going to be here at any minute. Why are you taking a shower now? You do this deliberately.'

In an attempt to broker reconciliation, Livia's husband's parents had invited themselves for the evening. They were passing through, they said, nothing more. Livia begged Niccolò to stay. 'Do this one thing,' she begged. 'For me. I ask very little of you. They are checking on me. They don't like that I came here, and they are suspicious.'

Niccolò knew how critical her father-in-law was and was well acquainted with her mother-in-law's particular fussiness. The evening would be soured by the couple's disappointment in Livia.

'I've bought cold meats, cheese, and bread. Do you think that's enough? They said they wouldn't eat.' Livia stood in the bathroom and watched Niccolò dry himself. 'Don't,' she asked, 'please, please, don't mention the clothes. Say nothing of the clothes. I'm begging you. They are going to be here soon. You need to hurry up.'

Niccolò stood naked in front of the mirror. He parted his hair in the same way he had parted his hair that morning. He refused to be hurried.

'So? Why are your clothes on the bed?' She didn't understand. 'And why is your hair different? You didn't go to work?'

Niccolò shrugged and said the police had called and asked him to come into the city.

Livia immediately appeared alarmed.

'You went to Naples?'

'I took the train.'

'I don't understand why they would want to speak with you? What else do they need to hear?'

Niccolò said he didn't know.

'What did they say?'

'I didn't see them.'

'You didn't see them? They called you in and then they didn't speak with you?' She shook her head, immediately angry. 'Do you have a name? Who was this?'

'It wasn't anyone. It doesn't matter.'

Livia paused, then made herself smile. She stepped closer to Niccolò and apologized. Her tone became lighter, easier. 'You're right? This is your business. If they call you in and then they don't speak with you it has nothing to do with me. I promise I won't interfere.'

Niccolò nodded. There were things that she didn't want to hear. Details about the clothes. Details about the murder. New ideas.

Livia waggled her hands. 'I don't need to know. I don't want to hear how many times that boy was stabbed, or what else they've discovered. I don't want such details in my head.'

Niccolò watched from the balcony as Livia kissed her in-laws goodbye. She waited as they got into their car and kept her hand raised in a minimal wave, crisp, precise, until they had driven out of sight – then immediately dusted her hands. She glanced up before returning to the building. Hearing the door close behind her, Niccolò flicked his cigarette into the street and returned to wash his hands and brush his teeth. On the table the remains of their small supper: olives, cold meats, bread, cut tomatoes and artichokes.

As Livia cleared the table she said he should not let them talk to him like that. 'You could defend yourself a little more, you know.' She stopped and grimaced, hand at her stomach. 'I shouldn't have eaten so late. Why do we always eat so late?' She gathered the plates together. 'Did you notice how they agreed with me? You watch, he'll call tomorrow. I'm telling you.' She paused and asked: 'Don't you mind how they speak to you? You barely said a word. It wouldn't hurt if you stood up to them. Just once. That's all you have to do. Stand up to them, and they will respect you.'

She spoke to the police later in the evening, broke her promise and called them to complain. She held her hand over her stomach, sometimes looking at Niccolò, and sometimes at the wall as she cleared up the confusion.

'Someone called. I don't think he would make that up. Someone invited him into the city,' and then, with genuine anger. 'That isn't how it works.'

He knows what she will say. This is his story, although, to be honest, he's sick of hearing it. Two years, she'll say, he nearly died. They held him down, she'll say, a foot on his neck, she'll say, they beat him with a metal pole. She'll try not to tap her head as she talks. She might give the detail about how he came across them, a band of men in one of the warehouses stripping out the units. She will explain how, even after the police had caught them, they couldn't really explain why they'd done it. *We'd already got what we came for.* When it was done they took the pole with them and drove away, and nobody knows this except Niccolò, how he managed to get himself to the security barrier. From the warehouse to the barrier. It wouldn't take two minutes to walk, but it took him all night and he made it on his belly, with his fingers in the dust and his toes pointing and pushing to drive himself forward across a concrete lot, across a rough stretch of scrub, across the open parking lot, all the way to the security barrier. The report says that the men dragged him, propped him up against the barrier and left him, but no, Niccolò had focused on the barrier and made it the whole way by himself. He knew what lonely was, he knew what effort was and what it cost him, that crawling on his belly to that barrier was something almost beyond him, an ocean to swim, or like turning bone to metal through pure force of will. He knew that when you have to focus on your breathing you are in trouble. He understood that everything comes at you one moment at a time, and when it came down to it he either made it to the barrier or he didn't. He either survived or he did not.

Livia had one or two stories about her brother depending on her mood. Story one was always the attack, how she had heard this on the national news, about how she had stood up and screamed and screamed with grief. Story two, more often than not, was the story about how his wife had left him, taken their daughter and moved back north to Rivara, because he did not know who they were. He knew who they were in common ways, he could remember their histories, the birthdays, the courtship with his wife, but these events no longer had content, and while he knew enough to sometimes feel guilt, even that was not sustained. He knew that he had loved his wife. He just didn't currently understand what that meant. She told this story when she was angry, or when she wanted to become angry. She didn't speak about the day he married, his daughter's birth. She didn't explain that she had taught him to swim, and how beautiful he was, my god, how incredibly handsome, floating free of her arms, just loose, present, so very alive, and that every day she had to steel her heart because she was looking at someone who both was and wasn't her brother, and how her only wish was to have him back. She didn't speak about how easy he was, about how, before all of this Niccolò Scafuti didn't have one miserable bone in his body. She hid the photos in his apartment for herself because she no longer believed in that perfect world.

Niccolò arrived early for work and sat in the booth frustrated. On the horizon hung one long grey cloud, smog rising from the city.

Fede sent Stiki up to the main building with the report and the logbook, he wanted to speak with Niccolò. Out on the counter were his study books, an English-language primer and an English-language newspaper. Niccolò was in no mood to talk, but seeing the newspaper, he asked Federico if he could read English.

'Yes. Of course. My reading is better than my speaking. With reading,' he explained, 'I can take my time. As long as the subject isn't too technical. That's why a newspaper is good.' Fede set his books away, and slipped the small and worn dictionary into a drawer beneath the desk. 'I can manage. So did they say anything? Yesterday. The police?'

Niccolò took the student's notebook from his pocket and set it on the desk. The notebook was almost full now, fat with newspaper clippings.

'What's this?'

Niccolò pushed the notebook across the desk.

Fede picked up the small book and looked through the pages, slowly turning and reading. 'Do you understand any of this?'

Niccolò shook his head and asked if Fede could make any sense out of it.

'No, it's difficult.' Fede frowned at the pages. 'Tricky.' The writing was small and slanted, difficult to read. He glanced quickly through the other pages; his head made a small bird-like peck when he came to the clippings. 'What are these? What is this book? Where is it from?' Fede closed the book and looked at the cover. He didn't understand. 'Surely this is evidence? Why haven't you handed it to the police?'

Niccolò said that the police didn't know about it, yet.

'But I saw them myself, they had a whole team of men, they wouldn't have missed it?' Federico placed the book down on the desk. 'You found this in the field? Why didn't you give it to them yesterday?'

Federico opened the cover. 'If this is the American's notebook it might be important. It belongs to his family.' Federico opened the cover. 'You can't keep it. You understand? They might be able to tell who he is. His family will want to know. You should call them immediately. I mean now. You should tell them now. Any news about this person is important.'

When Stiki returned he stood outside the booth and asked what was wrong. Fede shook his head and said it was nothing. Nothing he needed to explain.

Sparrows squabbled in the dirt.

Once they were gone Niccolò attempted to settle into work. Taking out Fede's books he spread them across the desk, then adjusted the seat, raising it so he could sit comfortably and face the view.

Little happened for the first hour. The plant was located on the outskirts of the town and the road led directly to the factory. Lovers searching for discreet roads and parks would make their slow way up the hill, but few stopped long. From the cubicle he could see the edge of Naples, a vast yellow spill slipping into a solid blue sky. Aircraft coming in and out of the airport slid slowly beside the hill, gaining height over the bay.

Disturbed by his discussion with Fede, Niccolò could not settle. He spread out the newspaper and kept the notebook underneath. Throughout the morning he considered what he should do, and the problem bore into him. He should take the notebook to the police, he decided. He could say that he'd found it on the wasteland after the search, that there was an area close to the houses where everyone parked their cars. It would be better to be rid of it.

Fede returned in the early afternoon and asked directly, coldly, if Niccolò had gone to the police. Irked by the question, Niccolò shrugged him off. He'd come all the way back to ask him that? Fede stepped into the office and asked immediately, 'What's that smell?' He saw ash on the ring burner, saw how the wall was scorched, and turned in disbelief to Niccolò. Niccolò, as usual, was due to take the report forms and ledger to the central security office, and he used this as an excuse to leave Fede. When he returned from the main building he was pleased that Fede had gone. He sorted through the newspapers stacked under the desk, and looked quickly through them to see if there were any reports he might have overlooked before he threw them away. The day was bright; a soft wind came off the bay directly onto the mountain, and with it came a sweet smell, and again the faint brittle stink of fire.

Livia had wanted to talk that morning. Her in-laws wanted to visit again on Sunday afternoon, there was progress she said, real progress this time, and if her father-in-law was as rude to Niccolò as he had been on the previous night, she wanted him to say something. Niccolò could not remember what the man had said. The man wore glasses with thick black rims and thicker lenses so that his eyes appeared glassy and wet, he was short, and his teeth were yellow from smoking. Niccolò could not see why Livia was so intimidated by him.

At four o'clock Niccolò was called to his supervisor's office.

The supervisor's office was in the central administration building, a set of concrete oblongs abutted one to another; the windows zipped in a long black line across the entire complex. The dye-production plants were glass boxes with slanted glass roofs, surrounded by concrete offices. It was only his second time in the office, the first when he picked up his employment papers and the Chief of Security who had seen him came out to shake his hand, and from that one gesture Niccolò had always thought well of the man.

Niccolò had seen the chief a number of times, talking at meetings and holding discussions. The man habitually spoke in an unbroken monotone so that he could not be interrupted.

Now, on his second visit, Niccolò walked quickly wondering what this could be; the reviews were completed for the year, and in his report he had done neither well nor badly, which his manager assured him was a good sign given the length of his employment.

As soon as he entered the office Niccolò could see that his guesses were entirely wrong. Three senior officials stood about a desk: his manager, the section manager, and a police officer. The police officer asked directly for the notebook, and Niccolò, in honesty, said that there was no book. After speaking with Federico he had set the book on top of the stove and burned it.

The three men appeared surprised. The officer invited Niccolò to sit down.

'You've destroyed evidence? Do you understand what you are saying, what you are admitting to?'

Niccolò shook his head. He locked eyes with the police officer. Pinpoints of light vibrated on the tabletop, the floor, the tawny walls and doorway shifted in relation to each other. The pure complexity of the moment he found himself in. Unlike other absences this one shuddered down on him, and Niccolò fell heavily, his cheek on the floor, his shoulder hammering his chin as he quickly seeped away. Light first, voices after; the officer calling for attention.

FRIDAY: DAY Q

In the late morning Niccolò returned to the abandoned paint factory with the police, and it was a shock to leave the confines of the cell and return to Ercolano.

That morning two magistrates had come to question him. They wanted to hear again about the factory in Ercolano.

Was there anything Niccolò wanted to add to the list of evidence he had thrown into the tank?

Niccolò shook his head. It was hard to be exact, he had thought through the night, trying to remember, but nothing else had occurred to him. Cats, he said. Mostly cats.

Was there anything particular about the factory, anything he could describe?

Niccolò apologized. No. Nothing occurred to him.

The chief magistrate said that it was of no issue if he could not remember, and Niccolò said that he was thinking, but it was difficult to describe an empty room. He had only ever gone into the first room. He didn't much like the building, and didn't feel safe going in there, as there was only one entrance and no windows.

The men waited in silence.

Could he describe the factory?

Niccolò nodded, and looked to the chief magistrate as he answered. There was only one that you could get inside, because the commune had recently sealed the others. And this factory was on the opposite side of the road to the wasteland and the market gardens. A path ran down from the wasteland across the estate and eventually brought you to the road and the factory. The other factories, as he had said, were fenced off.

Could he remember what was inside the room?

Again, he shook his head. There was nothing in the room. Nothing at all, and he hadn't looked into any of the other rooms. As he'd said it was entirely empty except for a tank, in the first room. A tank set into the floor. Is that what they wanted to know?

There was nothing else to remember about the place? The tank. What shape was it? Was it square or round?

The hole into it was round, but the tank itself might be square. The water was about three metres down from the hole. It probably wasn't that deep. It was filthy, the water was black and it stank.

The magistrate asked if Niccolò could draw a map, and could he show where the building was in relation to where he lived. Niccolò said that he could, it would not be as hard as trying to describe the place. Even though he'd seen it a good number of times, he couldn't remember anything distinctive. There was graffiti. Writing on the walls.

As the magistrates left, Niccolò rose in his seat, and raising his voice a little, began to repeat what he had said. It was easy to know which building it was because all of the other buildings had been sealed by the commune. Some of them had been bricked up, but for one reason or another they hadn't sealed this one. He didn't know why. The others were all secured, and there was no way into them.

Leaving the room the chief magistrate quietly thanked him, and Niccolò thought that there was sadness in his voice.

The officers' heads jolted in unison as the squad car came steadily down the grey pumice track, silhouettes in their flat caps. Dust rose behind them in a long and low plume, obscuring the steep rise to the mountain and the two cars behind them.

The three police cars drew up beside the building. Two policemen waited on the opposite side of the road, between them stood an old man whose trousers were tucked into his socks. Further up against the wall leaned a bicycle. Niccolò recognized the old man as Italo, one of the market gardeners. He didn't know his last name, but knew that the old man was difficult and disliked. It was the only reason that he knew the man. Italo grew dahlias in an allotment opposite the factory, and earlier that morning he had cycled by the building and heard boys inside throwing stones. There was something about their haste, the way they ran away from the factory and their pause on the hill that made him curious about what they were doing. Inside the warehouse he found cushions from a couch, and a split bag of lime, the room was empty. The boys had taken the dumpster from his land two weeks ago, he complained, a theft he had reported to the police. They had slashed

THE KILL

the plastic in his hothouses and cut the irrigation pipes, but it was neither the theft nor the vandalism that justified his call to the police, it was the stench from the factory.

In one day the smell had become much worse, the boys had disturbed something, and as the police stepped out of their car they paused, recognizing the smell, and unwilling to go closer to the building they decided to wait. The investigating magistrate joined the police and the old man, and discussed what they were to do.

Niccolò sat alone in the car. He could see into the factory through the doorway, and he watched the two policemen approach the tank, hands covering their mouths. Standing at the entrance another officer threw a small stone. The stone hit the metal plate with a round boom, and a black storm of flies rose in a malignant buzz.

The three policemen backed out of the room and agreed that, clearly, something wasn't right, and this was perhaps a matter they weren't adequately prepared to handle. The magistrate shouted across the road to the men that nothing was to be disturbed. They were to wait.

Italo complained to the investigator that he knew exactly who the boys were, their parents worked for the cooperative, and he'd spoken with the police a number of times about their thievery and the damage they caused. He knew their names, and he knew where they lived. He'd given them the names before.

The first officer called across to the magistrate and said that they should take a look in the tank and see what it was. Supposing the experts and specialists arrived and all they found inside was a dead dog, or rotten fruit, or any of a number of things that had nothing to do with their investigation? How stupid would they look?

The second officer disagreed, it was unlikely that anything vegetable could smell that bad. Had he smelled anything that bad before?

They all knew what it was.

Both men hesitated and agreed they had never seen so many flies in one place. It was a bad sign.

Italo asked if they were going to do anything now that everyone agreed on how bad the smell was. The magistrate stood with his hands on his hips. Turning slightly he agreed that they should pry back the plate and disturb as little as they could. He looked at Niccolò as he spoke, but Niccolò sat still, his hands cuffed together on his lap.

Is there anything we need to know? he asked.

Niccolò shook his head. The heat was making him sleepy.

The first officer returned to the room with a stick. He pushed the cushions away, then tapped the metal plate covering the tank. On the floor were marks indicating that the plate had been recently dragged into place. He grimaced at the stench and shoved the plate back with his foot. Flies swarmed up as the lid slowly shifted back. The officer leaned over the pit, hand to his mouth as he squinted into the hole. He turned his face away but kept his place. He needed a torch, he said, it was too dark to see or guess what might be inside.

The second policeman shrugged and gingerly approached and he seemed to stare for a long time, squatting over the hole, squinting. Cupping his hand over his mouth he walked briskly out of the building. Out in the sun, a good distance away, he breathed fresher air. Then standing upright he said that there was something in the tank. The white back of splayed legs. It looked like a body.

Turning to the squad car, the magistrate asked Niccolò if he had any idea who it was.

Niccolò held up both his hands to scratch his neck, in the heat it was impossible not to yawn. What, he asked, what was he asking?

The police set up a barrier along the road to redirect traffic through the town. The only vehicles that arrived were the ones attached to the investigation, squad cars, a forensics van, and almost as an afterthought, an ambulance.

The magistrate sat beside Niccolò and said that he should just tell him now what he knew. Hey? Why not? Identification would be attempted on site to see if the body in the tank matched the basic description of the missing student. So why didn't he simply tell them what he knew?

Livia was allowed to speak to Niccolò on the evening of his second day in custody.

'They came to the school and brought me home.' She sat at the table with her head down. She tapped her head, indicating the bandages about Niccolò's head. 'They told me you didn't want me to know.' She spoke calmly, her voice fading into the room.

Niccolò sat upright, he remembered to set his shoulders back and raise his head. There was work in Rome.

Livia caught her breath. She listened to him silently and appeared startled by the news. Niccolò continued to talk. There would be opportunities in Rome. When they released him he would go immediately and look for work. Why should he stay and struggle here? His mind was made up.

'You can't go to Rome because you don't have the money.' Livia shook her head. 'Niccolò. They have dismissed you from work.' Livia steadied one hand on her belly, the other at her mouth as if to delicately tease out the words or finish them so that he would clearly understand her – and looking at her he tried to measure if this was anger or pity. 'Do you understand what is happening? Do you understand what they are saying about you?'

Niccolò again reminded himself to sit upright. He said nothing. It was obvious that he was helping the police. She should understand this. Tomorrow they were to take him back to the warehouses in Ercolano again, and this would all be cleared away.

'Niccolò?' Livia shook her head, her hand now clapped to her mouth. 'How have you become so lost when I have always been by your side? How did you manage these things?'

Niccolò folded his arms and closed his eyes.

Eyes swollen from crying, Livia slowly regained her composure.

YEAR 2: MR RABBIT & MR WOLF

MONDAY

The magistrate agreed to meet with Finn on the understanding that his name would not be mentioned and there would be no direct reproduction of any of the material he would present. Finn agreed without hesitation and arranged an earlier flight so he could make his way directly from the airport to via Crispi in Chiaia in good time to meet the magistrate at *Prima!* – a café he'd picked for such a purpose on his previous trip, the kind of venue that deserves a tracking shot, a slow reveal of the space and the few mindfully solitary characters in it; white tiles, a god-damned chandelier, smocked waiters, a canvas-covered patio (in a word: Europe). *Prima!* sat beside an intriguingly unnamed jewellery boutique just up from Ferragamo, Emilio Zegna, Armani, and further over – piazza del Martiri. Pleased about how his day would focus down from Paris to Naples, to Chiaia. He liked the economy of it – the first day of his second visit to Naples. He'd be working as soon as he set foot in the city. The very moment.

He wanted to use his time efficiently because he only had the summer. He needed to be *effective*. In less than eighty days he would be a student again, one of a number, pushing a student loan, a coffee habit and unsociable hours; but during the summer he was a writer with a project. A writer with a project and a publishing contract. A sophomore (soon to be final-year) student with an agent and a contract, about to hold a discussion about a notorious and unsolved murder with a respected anti-Mafia magistrate. Hard to believe how the year was working out. In travelling Finn had focused his luggage down to two items: a small backpack; a soft hold-all. Both could be slung over his shoulder, and he fostered this image of himself, as someone mobile, focused, unburdened but connected. The contents of his luggage reflected this ambition: in both bags he'd carefully wrapped a wealth of goods, a laptop (new), a portable hard-drive, two USB memory sticks, a DV camera (borrowed at the last minute from his sister), a phone, and less convenient, the assorted cables and plugs because they've yet to figure out the proper portability of these items. Along with this were his notebooks. These books were precious, seven already filled with his tiny writing, a compact concentration of notes from interviews, his own impressions, research from the sites, scraps of papers, tickets, receipts, things discovered while out and about, and he'd been smart enough to choose small books and marked each one with his mobile and home number, email addresses, and a note on the first page suggesting a reward might be paid if they were found and returned.

Finn wanted to test-drive a way of life – this is how he'd phrased it to his sister – see for himself if he was cut out for writing. While he loved college – what wasn't there to like? – he was working it hard and didn't see the point in waiting around, holding on for blind luck and good fortune while amounting debt. The whole point about ambition is making sure it happens (name one other sophomore to secure a publishing contract). Carolyn agreed, besides, he was older than the other students, and that five years made a difference. They talked this over, endlessly refining, because beyond choosing a smart college and a sensible course with professors whose references would really matter, nobody really considers the bigger picture, not really, and just because his family were loaded didn't mean he could ignore these things. No one really figures this through. Most people just let things happen to them, like they're lucky. Not that Finn wasn't lucky. Moderately good-looking, modestly intelligent, white, and with parents who didn't mind bankrolling the project while he waited for the advance, just so they could brag that their not-yet-graduated son had a publishing deal and was writing in Naples, Italy for the entire summer (and your kid has an internship, er, where exactly?). From Finn's perspective everybody gains something this summer: the parents, the college, the publisher, and certainly (not least of all), Finn himself.

Finn ordered coffee, spoke Italian well enough to feel part of the general rush, although Spanish was the language he swam in. The value of the magistrate would come in the form of names, not anecdotes (which Finn already knew), and through inflection – the weight he placed on certain events, and the sequence in which he ordered them. Aside from this, a senior magistrate who wasn't willing to go on public record but still had something to say (unofficially) would make an excellent introduction to his book, not to mention the boost it gave the project: people were still interested. Finn couldn't imagine a better situation. He didn't expect to uncover anything new, not after a year, but he did expect to find new people and new perspectives – much the better if they wanted to remain anonymous.

As a figure, the magistrate didn't disappoint – reassuringly familiar (as if cast into the role) – tall and thin, slightly wild grey hair, a hint of stubble, a man both preoccupied and focused. Distinctive, Finn thought, an air of instinct about the man, an intelligence and concentration he'd like to describe. As expected the information was less than revelatory: the magistrate ran through what he knew to be happening.

1. Since his release from custody, Niccolò Scafuti had returned to his apartment at the Rione Ini estate on the outskirts of Ercolano, where he now lived a solitary life. If the magistrate had any personal regrets, it was the involvement of Scafuti in the investigation and he wished that the man had not taken the walk that night and discovered the American's clothes and brown bag. But he didn't think, a) given the circumstances, b) Scafuti's unwise decisions, and c) what they knew at the time, that anything could have played out any differently. Scafuti had destroyed evidence, it was unfortunate, a criminal offence which had caused great damage. Who knows what might have happened if they'd read the notebook?

2. Marek Krawiec. Now here was an entirely different situation, and the magistrate remained clear and absolute about the fact that Krawiec could not be interviewed, and neither would he be coaxed into any kind of acknowledgement of where Krawiec was being held (most likely Rome). The case was under judicial review. On this the magistrate remained firm. Marek Krawiec could not be interviewed. He could say, though, that investigators were hopeful about finding the missing bodies. Krawiec was still emphatic about his innocence.

3. The palazzo, of course, was indeed the palazzo at via Capasso 29 close to the Duomo and the tourist district – everybody knew this and it had featured in many news reports over the year. This didn't stop a rumour that this palazzo was not the actual site of the murders – that there was some kind of cover-up because somebody important lived in the building where the killing had actually occurred. This was plainly untrue.

4. Evidence. There were many other rumours which were not true: the evidence taken from the basement room on via Capasso and discovered on the shoreline at Ercolano was not destroyed or lost, and was not mishandled or contaminated as many reports had speculated.

Much of the blood evidence was destroyed by the sea, but even so, there was plenty of other evidence to confirm Krawiec's presence in the room (which, interestingly enough, he never denied).

5. The missing student, otherwise known as 'The American', 'The Student', or less frequently as 'The First Victim', seen once and only once at the Circumvesuviana station dressed in the hunter-green T-shirt with the five-point star design, had not yet been identified, and no other remains had been discovered. The DNA from the shirt, shorts, undershorts, matched the blood evidence on the plastic taken from the room and recovered from the shoreline, and these were assumed, until new evidence or Krawiec told them otherwise, to belong to the American. The American was picked up probably before he had a chance to check into a hotel. The only blood evidence belonged to the American.

6. The man known as 'The Second Man' (the body discovered in the abandoned paint factory in Ercolano) had never been mistaken for the missing student – 'The American', or 'The Student'. This death, the autopsy demonstrated, could be attributed to a combination of factors: a blow to the head, the resulting haemorrhage, and drowning after he was dumped in the storage tank. Because of evidence found in the tank with the Second Man – the novel, a wallet, a digital player – assumed to be items taken from the student – this 'victim' had always been looked upon as a co-conspirator, although they were unable to establish his identity.

7. The body of Mizuki Katsura, AKA the missing 'Second Victim', had also not been traced nor recovered. And here the magistrate wanted to talk about what he called the situational context. 'Imagine,' he calmly laid out the facts, 'in a region of four and a half million people, how many more transient people come and go who are not accounted for?' Some legitimate, but a good number without account. There is immense opportunity here for exploitation. Both victims were linked by one known circumstance; they were both known to have passed through the Circumvesuviana station in the early morning. A friend at the language school confirmed that Katsura saw two men, had noticed them at the station, and commented on it in her class. The magistrate believed she had seen both Krawiec and the Second Man hunting, as it were. Katsura's belongings were found in the room she had rented in Portici. The name and address she'd given the language school were not genuine – who knows why?

THE KILL

8. The star. Now here's a coincidence – which might one day be explained by Krawiec when he finally talks. Fact 1: Mizuki Katsura went to school in a building on which there was a sign showing the outline of a five-point star held within a circle. Fact 2: The American, and this is still all they really know about him, wore a T-shirt with the same design. Again, there were theories about this, many wild and ambitious, semi-occult ideas. To the magistrate this spoke of something both deliberate and accidental. A coincidence, which, examined in the right light, would open up a methodology, systems of thinking, habits which could be key in definitively identifying Krawiec and the Second Man as the killers.

9. The existence of the Brothers. From the start the killings were considered as crimes which had to be committed by more than one person. The logistics of erasing not one, but two people would require resources not open to a single individual. Krawiec's story about brothers from France was exactly that, a story, a fancy, implausible at best – a ploy to get the system tied in knots while they chased down phantoms. The people who could supposedly confirm the existence of these brothers, other residents at the palazzo, had never in fact met or seen them. The building supervisor, Amelia Peña, was a fantasist.

Which brings us to, 10. the most contentious issue of all: the relationship between the murders and the book *The Kill*, published anonymously as a fanciful memoir by Editiones Mandatore, Madrid, in 1973, then by Universidad di Seville in 1997, where it was presented without the introduction as a work of fiction: one in a series of novels published as 'crimes in the city'.

The magistrate regretted the coincidence very much, and wished that the link had never been drawn – another attempt by Krawiec to muddy the water, this one, wildly successful. True, a copy of the book (the '97 edition) was discovered in Krawiec's apartment. The magistrate had to be honest. 'The book, this *Kill*, is not about Naples. It doesn't mention the city, the region, the country. Not once. The city in the book bears no comparison to the city in reality. It is a work of imagination and a truly regrettable coincidence.'

'So you've read it?'

'It has been a while now, and I no longer recall the details.'

'But the details are very similar.'

'They appear similar.'

'A room prepared with plastic. The body cut up and left in the palazzo. The blood.'

The magistrate shook his head.

'In the novel, there are other items. What happens with the feet, if I remember correctly. The bones. The organs. An ear. Teeth. Some hair. A tongue. Evidence is deliberately scattered in places to incriminate people who live in the palazzo. There are elements that seem similar, but a number of important pieces aren't there.'

When asked if he believed whether Marek Krawiec and the Second Man had collaborated precisely to realize the murder described in *The Kill*, the magistrate shrugged.

'To what purpose would they do this? They abducted tourists. These were crimes of profit or opportunity. Pure and simple. To recreate a fictional event is something much more imaginative, even intellectual. Something well beyond their scope. And they would have to have read the book. Marek Krawiec does not read or speak Spanish. He has the book, but he can't read it. Perhaps he knew something of the story, and perhaps this is part of his fiction, along with the brothers, another invention.' The magistrate asked Finn to consider. 'The practicalities are more convincing. You abduct someone from a train station. What are you going to do? You rob them, take from them whatever you want, or do with them whatever you want to do, and because you have already exposed yourself to certain unnecessary risks it becomes necessary for you to kill them. This is a city of four and a half million people who live on top of each other and who know each other's business. So what are you to do? Such murders involve dismemberment because you cannot walk out of a palazzo with a whole body, not without being seen, but if you divide something into small enough parts, and if you are a little clever in how you dispose of these parts, it is possible that you will never be discovered.'

'But there are connections between them?'

'Unfortunately, there are general connections, yes. But it has been a year since I read it. Without the book this is not such an interesting case. Without the novel nothing distinguishes itself above other such events. It's possible that this aspect of the case, which has been greatly speculated over, has meant a certain kind of concentration, an inclination toward the more sensational elements, which has, in turn, distracted us from asking the proper questions.'

The magistrate folded his hands together and smiled, closing the discussion about the book.

'Why did the evidence point only to one killing?'

He looked directly at Finn. 'Because we found only one crime scene. They wouldn't have risked committing a second crime in the same place. The evidence from via Capasso indicated only that the American had been killed there. Although this was considerably degraded. It might be possible that two people were killed there, although only one dismemberment took place.'

'And you believe Marek Krawiec to be the main instigator?'

'I do. Krawiec's skill, if this is the right word, is in his "everyday-ness". The issue – let me give you my experience – is that wickedness is not as interesting as you might hope. Krawiec appears normal, a neighbour, someone who can be trusted, because, for most of the time, this is exactly who he is. In most circumstances he is entirely ordinary. There is nothing exotic about him, and nothing immediately apparent in his personality that would show him capable of such violence. If you want to understand him you should speak with the people in the palazzo who were familiar with him. They also were convinced by him, and managed to draw them into his version of the world. This is typical of someone who is dissociative. They will insist on a reinterpretation of events, and they will draw people into their schemes and ideas. I don't think Krawiec was the sole perpetrator, but I consider him to be the sole author.'

The magistrate had one last thing to say: 'People come here believing all kinds of things about the city – I'm sure you have your own ideas – that it is violent, corrupt. It is hard to refute the facts. The city has its problems. There are many issues. But it does seem, and this is perhaps truer when speaking about Naples than any other city, that stories are written and ideas are decided long before anyone has actually arrived. Do you understand? It is a problem to be spoken about only in one way, to have one kind of discussion, or one common language. To believe in occult signs and coincidences is to lose sight of the facts, and to indulge fanciful ideas. We have enough problems without this becoming more mysterious than it already is, especially because it involves two missing visitors. We still don't have many answers at this point about what happened. At the moment there is very little truth, what we take to be truth is based on rumours and lies.'

As Finn walked the magistrate to his car, the man's driver straightened up and opened the door. Finn's last questions involved Mizuki Katsura.

'Nothing was found in Tokyo. I even hired someone and they found nothing.' Mizuki Katsura did not exist. Had the magistrate ever considered this?

The magistrate paused before ducking into the car. 'We don't have her name. But that doesn't mean she didn't exist. Clearly someone under this name attended classes at the language school, and some-one under this name has disappeared. In Europe we should be especially careful of such an idea. Many people who fall victim to crime are undocumented, or have chosen or have no choice but to exist in ways which remain officially off the record.'

'So you believe that there were two victims.'

'There are three, remember. The man at the paint factory is a victim as well as a culprit.'

Finn nodded in agreement.

The magistrate lowered himself slowly into the car, then fixed Finn with a gaze, cold eyes, grey, white-rimmed and a little clouded. 'I will give you the ending of your book,' he said, with just an edge of a wry small smile. 'Consider how smoothly this was achieved. I do not believe that this is the work of a novice. It is possible that Marek Kraw-iec and the man found at the paint factory had a criminal career which involved the disappearance of considerably more than two people. Krawiec also might have had experience prior to his arrival here. What better place to disguise himself? What you must write about, if there is any need for clarity, is the history of Niccolò Scafuti, and the damage done to the city.'

Finn watched the car draw away then looked with satisfaction at the boutiques along via Crispi. A profitable meeting, which provided both a beginning and the end. As soon as he was on the metro Finn checked his mini-recorder. Nothing you could broadcast, not in terms of quality, but still useable.

Hotel Grimaldi – between Corso Umberto and via Nuova Marina – was close to the palazzo on via Capasso, and cheap (Finn wasn't being irre-sponsible with his money, and didn't want to make the mistake of being too remote from his subject, just comfortable enough for a good, critical distance). The room held a wardrobe, a dresser, a bed, a sink; the shutters for the window could not be folded back as they hit the side of the bed. Finn left a voicemail for his sister, and then typed. *They have beds here like school beds*. And thought as the message slowly fed its way through, a dial turning on the screen, that this was the beginning of her day, the end of his. She wouldn't yet be in New York, the message would arrive before her. Out in the bay a ferry rounded the jetty, the sea soaked blue.

While he unpacked he began to consider the month ahead. He would find his meals close by, eat during the day with Rino. He would write for four hours in the morning, arrange his interviews and site visits in the afternoon, write late into the night. There would be no evenings out, no time wasted. With twenty thousand words already written – the first three chapters had secured the contract – he had a foundation for the project; although he already guessed this would need to be refigured. Unlike his fellow students, Finn had discipline. He could organize himself, and he could focus. By the end of the month he would transform the notes and the research into a complete and serviceable draft: something in the region of seventy to eighty thousand words. Which meant three thousand words a day. Not a problem. He could achieve this. Having secured a book, Finn had his mind on a larger target, film, and while his mother could advise on publishing and help with contacts, with filmmaking he was completely on his own.

Finn, still busy unpacking when Rino arrived, asked the clerk to let him up. He'd advertised for a researcher at two universities, and picked Rino Carrafiglio, a Ph.D. student at the Orientale. He'd formed an idea of the man from their correspondence, and thought of him as someone in his early twenties with whom he would have easy and intense conversations. He'd pictured himself in bars, cafés, trattorias, which only Rino with his detailed understanding of the city would know, either planning or unpacking their interviews, tapping into the core of the crime and the city itself, stripping back, in long and late discussions, the artifice and the deceptions to discover what was really happening. In reality Rino looked like a taxi driver, end-of-shift bags under his eyes, unshaven, and miserable, with thinning hair, short stature, and a wrinkled shirt; he looked like a dirty old basset-hound. A few hairs stuck over the back of his collar. He could be twenty-something, thirty, late forties even, Finn couldn't tell. Finn did little to hide his disappointment, and regretted sending money in advance to secure assistance (money he could have used on a ticket to Amsterdam, London, or his return to Boston). He had a certain expectation of Italians – which the magistrate had not disappointed. The magistrate looked the part: a long grey face, thin and graceful, a man who appeared cultured, whose knowledge seemed to be reflected in his owlish and groomed manner. Where the magistrate held authority, Rino, on the other hand, just looked worn and sad. It didn't seem right after all of the work he'd committed to the project – two weeks in Naples, two weeks in Rome, two (crushingly disappointing) weeks in Struga, Poland, chasing up a mother who was dead, and a brother who could repeat one phrase in English ('He didn't do it'), visits obsessively described in little black notebooks. He'd already over-sold Rino's abilities to his agent and editor, and determined now that he would take no photographs which included the man.

Finn took a while to hide his valuables while Rino waited. The cash on top of the wardrobe. The traveller's cheques in their envelope under blankets inside the dresser. His passport under the mattress. The laptop inside its soft case slid under the wardrobe. The portable hard-drive in the bottom drawer of the dresser, among dirty laundry. The spare USB sticks which contained copies of all of the drafts of the book and correspondence were easily concealed, one in his wash-bag alongside the shaving cream and toothpaste, the other in the interior side pocket of his soft hold-all. He'd also bought a bottle of rye and he placed that beside the bed.

Rino stood by the door with his hands in his pockets and licked his lips.

On that first evening, for a small additional fee, Rino brought Finn to the Bar Fazzini. As they passed the palazzo on via Capasso, Rino pointed out the carriage doors but didn't say until they were inside the bar that this was the place, you know, that's where it all happened.

Immediately into the bar Rino picked two men and told Finn to keep an eye on them. 'Here,' he'd said, 'are the people you need to speak with.' Finn couldn't guess why he'd singled them out. The men, evidently brothers, had dressed for the meeting; both wore suit trousers and long-sleeve shirts, both combed their hair straight back, and both were clean-shaven with light skin and small wet black eyes. The younger brother, slight, reed-thin, pinched his forefinger and thumb at his crotch as he spoke. The older brother, larger and more solid, was the man to do business with and Rino paid him all of his attention. With broad shoulders and massive hands, the man looked like a chef and was a chef. He looked out of proportion, as if he had built himself, choosing a thick body out of mismatched parts.

'Salvatore and Massimiliano.' Rino grandly swept out his hand. These, he said, were the brothers Marek Krawiec had based his alibi on. From these two men he had invented the French brothers. Massimiliano worked at the *alimentari*, the small kitchen and food shop under the palazzo on via Capasso. His brother Salvatore worked as an accountant but was often at the store.

Finn asked when the brothers had first met Krawiec and the men shook their heads. It hadn't worked like that. Salvatore had only recently moved up from Bari. He'd never met Marek Krawiec.

Rino, thoughtfully, began to explain. 'But there were photos in the *alimentari* of them together when they were younger. Lots of photographs.'

'So he knew you?' Finn spoke directly to the older brother, Massimiliano.

The man shook his head. At that time he also was not living in Naples. 'But in the store there are photographs of us that the man would have seen. It is unbelievable that he would do this.'

Rino nodded. It was true, there were pictures. Their father, who ran the store until last summer, had pictures of his family everywhere.

'It's like that film.' Massimiliano leaned forward, confident about his information. 'Where the man makes up stories from what is around him. He sees something and he includes it in his lies.' He nodded, sincere, eyes closed. 'This way, everything sounds true because everything comes from somewhere. Everything sounds reasonable.'

'So your father ran the store?'

Alimentari. The brothers nodded. They served and sold food and wine. Salvatore wanted to get back into property again, just as soon as he had his licence.

'And would it be possible to speak with him about Marek Krawiec?'

Their father, much to their regret, was no longer with them. The family hadn't managed the shop for very long, four years. 'Do you know what it takes to run a business like this?' The whole fuss with the palazzo last year hadn't helped.

'So what's your father's name?'

Salvatore answered, '*Salvatore.*'

Massimiliano answered, '*Graffa*,' at the same time. 'After the sweet – you know, the pastry with the sugar. Because he's fat.'

'Because he sells them.'

'So he's alive?'

'He's back in Bari.'

'Can I speak with him?'

The men shook their heads. He wouldn't talk. He had nothing to say. They wouldn't want to burden him.

The interview was going nowhere. The brothers knew nothing about the affair. Not one thing you couldn't find in the newspaper or discover on the internet. Even so, this could still be useful. News isn't news, after all, without colour and detail. Information requires the inflection of experience. Finn understood exactly what he had going. What he didn't understand is why no other journalist had jumped onto this. So he asked details about the city, about the Italian south, about what they knew of the crimes. Throughout the discussion Rino kept nodding, and gave his own little affirmations, *yeah, right, OK, like I told you. Exactly*.

The small bar remained busy through the evening. At some point the ceiling fans were turned to the highest setting and the doors that made up the full front were lodged open, all without effect. The sticky night air, honey-sweet, became acrid with sweat. Finn stood at the counter beside the brothers, and while they spoke he took notes in a small black notebook, keeping it as discreet as he could manage, the book held low, at his hip. He wrote about the meeting, small clues and reminders, alongside what he was recording, so that when he had time he could fill out the episode with more detail.

'Is this all you wanted to know?' The older brother, Massimiliano, tipped his finger on the notebook. He spoke in English and set his arm about Finn's shoulder.

'I don't know. What else do you know?' Not his best question, but still.

'What's this?' The man's finger ran down the spine.

'It's nothing.' Finn closed the book and tucked it into his back pocket.

'You write nothing?'

Finn felt himself begin to flush.

The man nodded. 'Where are you from?'

'Boston.'

The man curved his mouth, impressed. His voice sounded softer than his brother's, the accent a little more marked. The man leaned into him, angular and uncomfortable. 'You should be careful who you speak to. Not everyone is happy to remember this story. It might be a big city, but this is personal, and you might want to show some care.'

Finn gave a gesture, a half-shrug indicating, naturally, he would show discretion.

'Do you smoke?' The older brother tapped Finn's arm. 'Do you want to come outside to smoke something?'

The four men walked to the alley behind the Fazzini. Muffled beats came from the bar, the blue lights of televisions hesitantly illuminated rooms in the wall above them.

The older brother took a cigarette out from a packet. He licked along the length and tore off a strip. 'You'll like this.' He smiled as he concentrated on the task. 'This is a nice. A little different. You smoke this sometimes? It's OK?' Gripped in his hand was a smaller packet, a lighter and papers. He looked to Finn for his response.

Finn said yes.

When the joint was made Massimiliano rolled it between his forefinger and thumb and eyed it, pleased. 'This is good,' he said again. A scooter's buzz sounded in the night. The four of them waited but the scooter did not appear. The younger brother lit a cigarette and leaned back against a car.

'Twenty euro,' the man said, his expression held, expectant.

'Sorry?'

'For the joint. Twenty euro. It's good. You'll like it. Twenty euro and we'll all have a nice smoke.'

Finn took out his wallet and tried not to show how much money he had. The older brother took the note, pocketed it, then lit up the reefer. Then handed it to his brother.

The younger brother blew smoke up in a long measured calculation. 'Have you seen the palazzo,' he said, blinking. Then shook his head and sniggered as if he had no clue what the answer might be, and Finn thought in these casual gestures was seated a small element of threat. In the humid air the smoke rose and flattened out above him.

'Do you want to see inside the room? The basement room.' Salvatore used the word *basso*, although technically this was not one of the *bassi*, but a simple underground storage room. 'We can show you the room.'

Salvatore leaned into Finn. 'It's true,' he said. 'We have a key. If you want to see inside the room we can show you. We can take you tonight if you like. Only if you want, of course.'

Salvatore snorted, a little incredulous. 'Of course he wants to.'

Massimiliano spoke deliberately, answering to his brother through Finn. 'He's in a mood. He wanted to go to a party tonight, but instead.' He took the cigarette out of Salvatore's hand. 'So, we can show you the room but it's expensive.'

A light blinked above them, on and off. The four looked up. Rino, who had yet to receive the reefer looked a little disconsolate.

Massimiliano offered the joint to Finn. 'So how much to see the room?'

When Finn raised his hand Massimiliano drew the joint away, then slowly set it to Finn's lips. 'Take a little, breathe lightly and hold it, then let it go down slowly.'

Finn nodded, and did exactly as he was told.

At the first proper toke Finn immediately felt dizzy. He held the smoke in his mouth and felt it soak softly into him. This, he thought, wasn't grass. Not even close.

Massimiliano set his chin on Finn's shoulder and looked up at his face. He smiled when Finn smiled. 'I said it was good.' He took the joint out of Finn's mouth. 'Don't blow out yet. Just let it . . .' He smoothed his hand through the air, and Finn felt the smoke run free through him.

'So how much are you looking for?' he asked.

The men looked eye to eye.

'Three hundred euro and we can take you there tonight. You can have a look now.'

Massimiliano took a drag himself, a deep, slow intake. He leaned his head back, wrapped his arm about Finn's shoulders. Looking up at the sky he held his breath, then slowly, in what seemed to be an infinitely beautiful moment, exhaled with a satisfied hum, a soft guttural roll. He offered the cigarette back to Finn.

'I like the name. Finn. It's a good name.'

The two men held on to each other. Massimiliano, inexpressibly big and soft, seemed permeable, his arm still about Finn's shoulder. 'You have three hundred euro. It's nothing. You can afford this.'

'How do you have the keys?'

'For the shop. Everyone has keys.'

*

Massimiliano opened the small portal door to the courtyard, and as he held it open he warned that there wasn't a great deal to see (now the money had changed hands), but a trained eye could pick out the right details to get a close picture of what had happened. The two brothers led Finn across the courtyard to an unlocked metal door. Rino followed behind, his hands in his pockets. Finn ducked through the doorway and found to his surprise a steep set of steps carved into the rock to form something like a tunnel, the top of which was rounded, the steps themselves small, steep, and worn with use. A blue electric cable threaded down the steps, and Finn, feeling increasingly more of an interloper, consciously ducked to make himself smaller – still feeling a soft buzzing blur from the reefer (surely something more than just a regular reefer).

The four men came carefully down to the basement. The air, cooler underground, set up the hairs on their arms, a stale reek of mildew made them hold their breaths. At the bottom, Massimiliano pushed forward and indicated a door set into the right side.

The door, small, metal, chipped and battered, had the lock punched out and the handle removed so that it could not lock. Salvatore pointed this out. 'They took the door handle as evidence,' he said, smiling. 'Look, they cut it out.'

The blue cable ran along the corridor into the room, and he could see through the doorway a set of photographers' lights to the left and the right. Finn had the feeling that the brothers had brought a good number of people into the basement, and the likelihood of it costing three hundred euro to every person was slim. He took in breaths, held them, slowly released, and thought that he would not be able to stay for long because of the overbearing reek of mould.

The room itself was entirely stripped, smaller and cleaner than he had imagined. A strip-light in the corridor shed an oblong of sour yellow into the room. Of all the reports Finn had read, none had given much of a sense of the space and just how tiny it was.

Massimiliano leaned into one of the corners. 'There are more caves under this,' he kicked his heel to scuff the stone. Then stamped. 'Can you hear that?' A small boom, perhaps nothing. He stamped again. Moments later another faint boom, deep below, possibly imagined. 'You wouldn't think that people used to live here. When they built these old palazzos the city introduced a stone tax. You couldn't bring stone to the city, so most of the palazzos were built from stone dug out from under them. You have buildings five or six floors high which lean against each other and that's all that holds them up.'

Salvatore held out his hands and shook them, made a rumbling noise and Finn realized he was talking about an earthquake.

Rino, uncomfortable, sweating, bowed his head. He was sorry he said, but he would have to leave. The basement had a bad smell, the room was too confining. Finn felt uneasy as the man scuttled out. The remaining men did not speak as the scuff of Rino's footsteps tracked back to the courtyard hollow and fast.

Finn realized that he was alone with two men, brothers, in a basement where two men (brothers according to Marek Krawiec) had cut their first victim, another American, to pieces. Salvatore said that he would turn on the electricity for the lights and disappeared after Rino, leaving Finn and Massimiliano to face each other in the basement. Neither speaking. As if a plan were now in action. The light from the corridor fell on the man's shoulders but not his face, which seemed to Finn to hold a desperate expression. Finn began to compose an excuse in his head. Massimiliano watched him without a word.

With a loud click the basement lights completely failed, both Finn and Massimiliano were swallowed by thick, clothy darkness. This is it. Finn felt himself weaken, become dizzy. He had walked directly into this, and any questions he'd had about how the brothers had enticed the boy to the palazzo were gone. It was that easy. A little curiosity. A little smoke. If he ran there would be Rino and Salvatore to contend with, there would be no escape. His sister, he thought, would be hearing bad news.

A timid apology echoed down from the courtyard, and with a third click both the photographic lights and the corridor lights suddenly brightened. The glare, so instant and so bright, brought Finn and Massimiliano's arms up to cover their eyes. Finn began to laugh with relief. He was sweating and he could smell himself even above the mould, sour and bitter, and he could taste bile. For the boy, he thought, there had been no such relief.

They lowered their arms slowly, blinked and grinned and grew accustomed to the light. Massimiliano cleared his throat, and, as if obligated, explained that the holes, these holes, were where the plastic sheeting found at Ercolano had been pinned to the stone. Starting at this line here, and ending there, close to the doors. The police had brought two sheets back and rehung them, and found that whoever had prepped the room had taken considerable care to make sure that the sheets were held taut and flat. It would have been a difficult job and it would have taken two people. The tape used to hold the plastic together was cut, sliced, and set at regular intervals to prevent the plastic from sagging. 'A professional job.' Massimiliano nodded almost in admiration. The sheets on the roof were stuck with a double row of tape. It would have taken some time to complete. The mattress was taken out of the room before the final attack. It was possible that when they removed the mattress they also disturbed the plastic on the floor, which is how there came to be such a large quantity of blood underneath it. There was, Massimiliano cleared his throat, another possibility. From what they could tell, the American was suspended at the centre of the room with his arms above him, however, it is possible that he was standing. Out in the field they discovered the lengths of tape used to bind him. He was hog-tied, ankles bound to his wrists, and hoisted, belly down. Before this happened he was kept hanging by his arms, possibly for two days. Depending how high and how firmly he was raised he could have disturbed the plastic on the floor, kicking or thrashing. The event itself had probably occurred over three days, two at the very least, as there were three different drying patterns in the blood. They knew one thing for certain: the boy had been bled before the final event, and then slit open.

How the plastic was removed was another story, and it was certainly done in haste. There was evidence that someone had begun to wipe, perhaps mop, but this was only in one small area close to the door and this was started very soon after the killing, thirty-six to forty-two hours. The woman denied cleaning the room, and in truth it was unlikely that she was able or strong enough to tug down the plastic. 'She's a dwarf,' he said, cutting his hands at hip height. 'It's just not a possibility.'

Finn tried not to think of where he was, and that a young man had been strung up and gutted right where he was standing. According to Massimiliano the boy would have died within four minutes, and four minutes, after waiting three days, was a long time. It's also possible that he would have remained conscious for much of that time. Whatever the scenario, there would have been time for him to realize exactly what was happening.

It must have occurred to Massimiliano, just as it had occurred to Finn, that he could do to him whatever he liked.

A line of sweat ran down Finn's side; he held his breath, and despite Massimiliano standing close beside him he felt utterly alone. It was more than this. He felt useless, and sad. And while he could see the logic to how he had come to this place it just didn't make sense once he was there. What he had taken as a public phenomenon, public property, was nothing of the kind. The boy was taken from a train station, brought to a room, any room in any basement, and gutted.

Finn had never properly felt alone. He'd moved from infatuation to infatuation, falling from one kind of love into another, and he'd distracted himself with the idea of it, so that he could not remember a time when he wasn't preoccupied with thoughts of someone else, so that a presence sat with him at all times – except now. At this moment, for the first time he could remember, Finn was not in love, and neither was he surrounded by family, and he felt alone and wretched.

Remembering his mobile phone, Finn took it out and began to take photographs, and used the activity to avoid making conversation, and as a way of concluding the visit.

TUESDAY

Finn woke in the early morning with the sun full on his face, his mouth open and dry, unsure for a moment where he was.

He waited for Rino on Corso Umberto. His chest ached. He felt seasick, out of balance, his throat unnaturally sore. He hung his head and breathed slowly, his conscience was beginning to prick. The visit to the basement had brought home exactly what he was involved in. Confronted with the room itself, he'd felt his interest to be sordid, a little shameful. He was earning money writing about the killing of a fellow American, and it seemed random to him who would be receiving the money to write the book and who would the subject of the book – as if their positions were interchangeable. However he justified his interest and motivation, he came back to this fact, *he was earning money from a death*, and it didn't feel good. Last night had cost him close to five hundred euro.

Rino was late. A bad sign. While Finn couldn't complain about the previous night, he couldn't say either that the basement visit had happened as a result of Rino's research. This had come out of the discussion – which was otherwise useless. Finn waited where they had agreed: Corso Umberto, beside the *farmacia* and opposite the Banco di Napoli. Or was it inside the *farmacia*?

Finn checked inside and found Rino waiting at the counter with a pack of disposable diapers in his hand and a queue of assorted women in front and behind. Rino poked his finger into the plastic wrap as he waited and left divots in the packet. The store, with its glass shelves and white boxes, seemed unnervingly antiseptic, at odds with the muddle outside. Behind the counter stood a woman, a girl, and an older man, each dressed in white clinician coats. When Rino reached the front of the queue he allowed the woman behind him to be served. When the girl became free, he again allowed another customer ahead of him, but when the man became free he stepped immediately up.

While the man said nothing about this, Finn thought the pharmacist had noticed that Rino wanted to be served by him.

Finn picked through the toothbrushes while he waited, and didn't become especially aware of any problem until he looked back at the counter and saw the pharmacist pointing at the door and heard him give Rino instructions to leave. Finn came closer to the counter, not quite sure if this was private business or something he needed to be involved in. Rino appeared to be holding his ground.

'You have a son,' he said, 'what if something like this were to happen to him? What would you do if someone was not telling the truth? What would you say to this man?'

The pharmacist, clearly addled, his face white with outrage, as if unused to being challenged. The man shook his head and asked Rino to leave. 'Go.'

'No.'

'Go.'

'No.' Rino stood firm, a little petulant but unmovable. 'I'm not going.' He pointed at the pack of diapers. 'I would like to buy these.'

The pharmacist picked up the diapers, looked over his glasses at the price, sharply rang it into the till and asked Rino for the money.

Rino laid the coins one at a time into a small dish. 'Imagine. You hold on to something for so long. Keep it inside. Is this healthy? Is this advisable? Imagine when something else comes to light, the trouble that this would cause.' Rino buzzed his fingers at his temples to indicate confusion. 'Imagine also the kind of father who would set such an example to his son? I have a son, and I wouldn't want to set such an example.'

The pharmacist pushed the coins back across the counter, took the diapers and placed them behind him. There would be no sale.

'You think you know what is good for my son, or for my family?' The pharmacist leaned forward his voice now low and threatening. 'If you return I will call the police.'

Rino stepped back, gave a small gesture, and lifted his arms lightly from his side as if this were of no account. The police, he seemed to indicate, would possibly also have these questions. Rino caught Finn's eye as he turned about, then remembered, suddenly, to pick up the money.

The two of them walked out onto the street. Rino, in no apparent hurry despite the pharmacist's threat, patted his pockets for a cigarette. The pharmacist looked after them as Finn closed the door and made a dismissive gesture to the women as if this were nothing. But the gesture, Finn thought, being too emphatic, and grumpy, seemed disingenuous – and the women, who might be expected to be curious, simply continued with their work as if this had happened before.

'This man,' he said, 'his name is Dr Arturo Lanzetti. The very same Dr Lanzetti that Marek Krawiec claims came with him to the hotel in Castellammare and gave treatment to one of the brothers. Dr Lanzetti says that this did not happen. Marek Krawiec also says that Dr Lanzetti told him about the content of the book, *The Kill*. Dr Lanzetti says that this did not happen, although he has read the book, he says that he read it after Marek Krawiec was taken into custody. He says he knew nothing about the room, and knew Krawiec only in passing as they lived in the same building.'

Finn looked up at the sign, a small outline of a neon cross. The store windows almost empty except for posters for eyewash in which a young woman looked to a blue sky, white letters furred with beams of light as if offering a religious experience.

'You think he's lying? Do you believe the story about the brothers?'

'I've no idea. We need to find another *farmacia*. Life will not be worth living if I forget this.'

Rino drove to Ercolano. He pointed out the volcano as they came out of the city and spoke about the earthquake, 'Nineteen eighty-seven. The city was hit. Many of the buildings were weakened and later con-demned, but they weren't taken down. At the same time all of these factories were closed down, and there was a plan to build here – hotels, places to live, shops. But this never happened. Instead they made them so they could not be used. After they found the body the com-mune had the doors and windows closed so no one could get in.'

'This is it?'

'This is where they found the Second Man.'

He drove over a small crossroads and parked beside the building. When Finn locked the door, he said, 'Don't worry, there isn't anything to see here.'

Finn walked down the small alley, a slip-road to the shoreline. A wall of striated concrete on one side, the factory close on the other, so that path – barely broad enough for a car, became deep. A black rail-way bridge, and the grey shoreline beyond.

A haze out to sea hid the horizon, hid the sun, so the sky and sea faded one to the other in a glassy bright plain. If they make a film, Finn thought, they should use these locations. The places where it happened. Finn had ambitions he'd yet to formulate properly. He walked along the shoreline, back and forth, stood on the stern grey blocks, smooth, massive and locked together: arms folded he looked back at the factory to imagine the event playing out – not as it might have happened, but as it might be filmed. A crew gathered in the road huddled ready because this would be taken in one long shot, the camera beside the door, a set of tracks for the camera down the alley to the shoreline: and there, the actors playing Krawiec and his accomplice arriving in the Citroën, parking. Krawiec giving instructions: an urgency to his gestures and movement. The Second Man unloads the large bags – unwieldy, tied at the top – and brings them to the shore, while Krawiec smokes with the car door open. Krawiec is the one to manage the body, cut up by this time and sectioned into manageable pieces which are also packed in plastic, blood slipping into the creases. The Second Man manages the sacks, which are full and lighter, and they rustle. Krawiec's packages are heavier, much smaller, and tape binds round them. The camera will follow Krawiec, because this detail is important. They will want to give themselves options, and the entire scene will need to be shot right from the start (the car arriving) twice, because there are two questions the film will need to answer: 1. Why did they kill, and 2. What happened to the body – and this scene will resolve that issue. They wouldn't need to specify the victim, well, not the first, because that would undermine the basic mystery. Everybody knows by now that nobody knows who this was, and there's no point in spoiling this with invention. Instead it would be more interesting to look further into Mr Rabbit and Mr Wolf, now these deserved inventing, fleshing out. These men should be made physical. OK, there was the whole absurdity of it, obviously, it's a crazy idea, but an appealing idea also, who doesn't like the idea of two men, tourists, who kill, and take their instructions from a pulp novel. The very randomness of it. They come and go, and no one is ever caught – it's morbidly satisfying, knowing you'll never know.

In the film, in this first version – Version Number One – Krawiec unloads all of the packages: these heavy little sawn-up pieces of Victim Number One. He lines them alongside the water, and here the filmmakers will need a calm day so there are no waves, just this dopey lapping, the water coming up and folding over, not even touching the bags, although the stones are wet and there are clouds of tiny black flies. And Krawiec, seen from behind, will crouch and open up the packets, slit them one by one, and dump out the contents – piece by piece until he is done, roll them into the water so that the water clouds with blood, until he closes the knife against his thigh. Trouble is, with this version, if they found the bags, you've got to believe they would have found the body.

In Version Number Two, Krawiec will arrive with a small dinghy of some kind. An inflatable. It could even be in its box, bought for the purpose. And this will need to be done carefully so it doesn't become stupid. Krawiec brings this craft down to the shoreline first, and maybe this isn't all one shot, because you're going to want to see him inflate this, and see those details, the nozzle holding the valve; Krawiec working up a sweat because this shouldn't be too easy. If this is shown to be an effort it's going to look more plausible. Once the boat is inflated, he's going to press on it with his foot. He's going to test it and make sure he's satisfied, maybe give it a few extra pumps. Only then is he going to unload the backseat of the small packages, and the Second Man is going to be standing at some distance tying his sacks together and making a job of it. Krawiec will load up the dinghy. Piece by piece. A hypnotic back and forth. Done, he'll tug the boat into the water, then, with his pocket knife he's going to give the dinghy a little nick, just a small – the smallest – puncture, then push it the final distance. He'll come back to the shore holding a rope that's tethered to the dinghy and it's going to take several attempts, and there's going to be some tension here, because if that boat deflates too much it's just not going to make it, because those gentle waves are pushing the boat back alongside the shore, not taking it out. Finally, Krawiec will have to wade, then shove hard, and out it goes, a little slow, a little dreamy. The small craft, obviously weighted down, is picked up by a current and taken out the whole length of the rope.

And maybe here you'll see the boat up close, the shoreline distant with Krawiec standing, rope in hand, the line leading from the boat all the way to the shore, and further to Krawiec's right the Second Man is on his knees still working on those larger bags, still busy with his knotting, and water begins to fill the craft, slowly pooling about the black bound packages, trickling in at first, then faster, so that half the dinghy folds under the waterline, half of it submerged, and the packages tip out, and then the whole thing, flaccid, just sinks, then sits softly under the water making bubbles with this blue line of rope going all the way to the shore. That sea reflecting like it's thick, like sugar syrup.

Back with Krawiec he tugs the dinghy to the shore, hand-over-hand, it doesn't look like much, a more or less empty black bladder that he hauls to the shore, water runs off the rope. Krawiec winds the rope about his arm, the way that fishermen coil lengths of rope. He folds up the dinghy. When he stands up they're almost done. There's no need to show what happens with the bags. Everyone knows this part of the story. He will kill the Second Man with one blow, a rock or a hammer. One strike. And it will mean nothing to him, this little piece of business. Or, alternatively he'll just shove him into the tank like it's an afterthought, and the man will hit his head as he tumbles. Either way, Krawiec will put little thought into it, but great energy. As the magistrate said, Krawiec is ordinary, he's not so special, but when he kills the violence comes with extraordinary force.

Finn took photographs from the shore, 360°, a whole revolution. He wanted to see inside the factory, to see the tank, but couldn't find an entrance. The windows and doors bricked up with some care, small ventilation blocks set up in a row, the holes too small to see through to anything. At first he couldn't find Rino, and didn't understand that the pebbles landing at his feet were dropped from the roof. When he looked up he saw Rino on the flat roof.

'Ready?'

He didn't want to be hurried, and even while he was paying Rino for his time, he didn't like to cause delay and had to think through if he wanted to get to the rooftop or not before they called in at the Rione Ini estate (although he had the feeling that Rino wasn't keen), and wondered if he would he regret not climbing up.

In preparation for Finn's visit, Rino had kept his eye on Niccolò Scafuti for a week but hadn't learned much: Niccolò Scafuti no longer worked, remained in the same apartment as before, but was seldom seen outdoors. Much of what he needed was brought to him, and the days when he was feted and celebrated by the Christian Democrats, the charities, the good people of Ercolano, had long since passed. Finn had a collection of photographs of dinners and presentations held in honour of the hero Niccolò Scafuti. All of this before the discovery of the clothes on the wasteland, before he was taken in and charged with murder – which had to be, as the magistrate acknowledged, the worst mistake made by the investigation. Finn wanted to speak with him, to straighten up the story.

They walked from the paint factory, followed the road beside a line of glasshouses up to the estate. Finn asked why Rino wasn't interested in this, he seemed reserved. Was he reading this right? And Rino said he doubted that Niccolò would want to speak, a good number of reporters had tried, they'd pestered him, and whether or not this was the reason he didn't appear to ever leave his apartment he didn't know. You'd have to figure what kind of trauma that would bring for someone normal, you know? Let alone some guy who has had a fistful of brain removed and half of his skull constructed out of steel.

'I wouldn't stay.' Rino plucked a piece of grass, trimmed it down to the stalk. 'I'd take myself somewhere new and start over. Once you've lost your family and your neighbours you have nothing.' What had happened to Scafuti was criminal, but it was done and there was no way to undo that fact. Rino pointed at the school where Rino's sister had volunteered one summer to help kids who hadn't passed their exams, who otherwise wouldn't move up a grade. 'Most of those kids have family who've spent some time in jail, or were otherwise in trouble, one way or another.' What made this ironic was that Niccolò Scafuti, once a hero, was now seen as some pervert who'd cut up a body, planted the evidence and 'discovered' it, to keep himself in the picture. And nothing backed up these ideas, even the stupid things he came up with, all by himself, about the notebook, about a star. His co-workers had made good money telling his story to the papers. 'Once it's in people's heads, there's nothing you can do. I feel sorry for him myself.'

Rino had a way of making Finn feel responsible. Finn couldn't figure out how he managed it and whether it was deliberate, something in his delivery, the way he spoke without expecting a response, or if it was something Finn felt anyhow but didn't yet understand. It didn't matter because, after less than one full day together, he was tired of the man's company.

Finn rang the number. Took a photo of the lobby door while he waited. Rang again. Buzzed another number to be let in. Photographed the side of the building, had Rino point out exactly which apartment Scafuti lived in (from the right: four along, one down), rang the buzzer, took another photo and then stood back in the street with his arms folded. The buildings, mirror copies of each other, had clothes and plants out on other balconies. Not shambolic and not quite messy, but disorganized, like the people who lived here didn't have much time to consider what was around them, or bother about their clothes being in their neighbours' view. A few people hung about, women at balconies, a small group of boys at the head of the wasteland who stopped to look for a moment and then continued with their game.

'We should go.' Rino encouraged Finn to leave. The two of them walked to the wasteland, as Finn wanted to see exactly where the clothes were discovered, because this at least needed to be fixed in his mind when he was writing. They lingered for a while. The scrubland was dry and tawny with long grasses bent over, paths worn through, some scattered empty water bottles, but not much of interest. He took some pictures, and took pictures of the apartments from the wasteland, but didn't think he'd use them. It didn't look like much, even with the side of the volcano in view behind the shoulder of the school buildings, broody and slightly improbable – a purple slope where there should be sky. He couldn't think of anywhere less prepossessing, only the presence of the mountain gave it any kind of dark mood.

Finn wanted to understand Scafuti. In many ways the man was key. Here you have someone who is celebrated in his community, who has this whole other life going on. Rino didn't follow. What other life? Niccolò Scafuti barely had his life together, two years ago he was just out of rehab for a head injury. Two years before that he was just an ordinary man running security up on the mountain. This man didn't have another life.

'So what about the cats?'

'What about them?'

'The cats he killed. He killed all those cats. Dumped them in the tank.'

'So he didn't like cats.'

'With a slingshot.'

'They were strays. Nobody missed them.'

'But you don't kill cats. That's not normal.'

Rino shrugged. 'Cats are cats.'

Finn didn't want to leave the question alone. 'But it isn't normal.'

'Who knows? They piss everywhere. They shit and breed. They need to be controlled.'

THE KILL

A figure stood out on Scafuti's balcony, leaning on the railing, but when they approached the figure slipped back inside, and no amount of ringing would draw him out.

On the return drive Finn asked questions about Rino's family, but Rino remained reserved and delivered answers as plain facts (My son is nine months old. Portici. All my life. She works for the commune and teaches adult literacy), as if he disapproved of what they were doing. Two weeks before while emailing these facts had come out easier, more conversational (My son keeps us awake, when he sleeps he sleeps for two hours, three sometimes, he has his mother's lungs. How he can cry!), but one week spent waiting outside Scafuti's apartment had soured him, and the visit revived this dislike.

Finn would rewrite the start of his book. It needed a statement, something to set it up, about how, years after, the crime still held purchase in the community: the magistrate who won't be named, a suspect who won't answer his door. He'd start the story properly with the cats. A man killing cats. He wouldn't start at the basement. This image would set Scafuti up as a creep, the villain, but he'd slowly recover the man's dignity, work against type, until, by the end, you would feel the injustice deeply. They'd have to make a film of it.

Finn called his sister, ran through some of the issues. The two-killer theory had its problems. First, how did Krawiec and the Second Man know each other? He just didn't see it. If it was all Krawiec's idea, how he would find another person and then get them involved. Krawiec's theory that there were two other people, the famous brother hypothesis, had its attractions and smoothed out all of the problems, but it just wasn't plausible and there wasn't any evidence to it. If there were two brothers, and if they were following the narrative from *The Kill*, then key elements were missing. This is a story about a man, a fascist, who won't accept his country's defeat and humiliation, who punishes the people living in his building, his palazzo, for collaborating with the Americans by making it look like they are murderers and cannibals, like their acceptance of the occupation is only skin deep; after starving for years, the army is seen as meat. The book is about revenge. It's about creating havoc.

Finn read out the opening of the book, translated it to English for his sister and couldn't be certain if she was or wasn't listening. 'I am not a cruel man. I'm not stupid or vicious. I'm not wicked. I am not an animal. You must not believe what you have read. There are many facts about me you do not know and would not easily guess: I am a sentimental man; I like to help when I can help. I prefer not to interfere in other people's business, and keep where possible to myself and trouble no one. I am a private man.'

Couldn't she see it? This was all about someone being provoked. Had Krawiec been provoked in some way? Was Krawiec following the narrative? 'I am a sentimental man.'

Other structural elements did not stand up, the room, the blood evidence, the organs, the teeth and tongue. The book was about the building. It's all about the palazzo.

And then the magistrate had said something interesting, something he probably should have picked up a long time ago. There were two versions of *The Kill*. There was the version which read as a crime novel, and then there was the earlier version, which had an introduction, which was marketed as a confession, a testimony. The publisher of the second edition had cut the introduction because they felt it didn't work with the main story.

Did she see the difference, he asked? Could she see how different this was?

He could tell she wasn't listening. Finn spoke to his sister about a killing, figured out details, gave her information because he couldn't otherwise talk to her. When she needed money, he asked for it from their father, because she didn't want them to know it was for her.

Finn curled up in bed, couldn't quite fit the frame, the bed slightly too short, so he either slept on his side with his feet curled (uncomfortable after a while), or he stuck his feet between the bars which meant that he couldn't turn over and had to wake in order to pull his feet out and then slide them back once he'd found a new position. It didn't work, this sleeping in shifts.

He finally lay diagonally across the bed, flat on his stomach, arms folded under his forehead, and legs out in the air, and woke twenty minutes later splayed out, superman. At one o'clock the air-conditioner began to squeak so he found his earplugs, which seemed, all things considered, a sensible solution. At midnight he was woken by a small tremble, a vibration – his phone, which he'd tucked under the pillow, as always.

Finn struggled to read the number and found the ID withheld. He answered with a more timid hello than he would have liked, and was surprised to find himself speaking with a woman.

'Where's Rino?' the woman demanded – as if midnight was an acceptable time to call a stranger and ask for someone's whereabouts.

Finn had to think before he understood what he was being asked for: Rino? 'Who is this?'

'This is his wife. Where is he? He's supposed to be home.' She sounded more irritated than worried, her voice an outright demand, as if he had some special knowledge, or was the cause, of Rino's delay.

He told the woman that he'd sent Rino home early, like, really early. He lowered the phone to cancel the call and then couldn't help from asking one last question.

'How did you get this number?'

After a hesitation the woman answered crisply. 'Rino gave it to me.'

Finn thought he could hear laughter in the background – something close to a donkey bray.

'He gave you this number?'

More braying laughter.

'But he has his own phone?'

'He isn't answering, *culo*. That's why I called you.'

Finn bridled at being called an asshole and at the hee-haw laughter behind this. 'Just don't call this number, all right. Never call this number again.'

As he hung up he could hear more hefty chuckles above the donkey-laugh which seemed to choke on itself, a laugh that was also a haughty gulp.

He should have turned the phone off. Right off. Instead he checked his messages and email, and felt that the glow from the small screen, blue and just bright enough to pick out the white sheet, the edge of the pillow, as if sensing and measuring the rising humidity, which now, thanks to the air-conditioner, closed in, a kind of seepage, the air quickly thickening. Finn lay on his stomach, felt sweat bristle in the small of his back and he thought again about the student and wondered if Krawiec had stayed in the room the whole time, watched him strung up, ankles to wrists, and taunted him, or left him alone at times. This information mattered, he wanted to know if the student was toyed with, tortured. He felt the dimensions of the room, could sense exactly where and how he was located, the distance of the walls and floor, the pitch and angle of his body. He could sense it all. The boy had suffered, and it mattered that no one properly knew how much, and that no one knew his name.

The second call came forty minutes after the first. The number, again, withheld.

'If that whoreson isn't home in five minutes you can tell him not to come home at all. You tell him—' and this time the woman's voice tumbled into laughter and she couldn't quite complete her sentence. Once again a donkey-like laugh buckled through from the background like this whole thing was a dare. He hadn't heard Rino laugh. She hung up, then called back immediately.

'I think he's been kidnapped.' Again, that laugh, a little more distant but a little more explosive.

'I'm tracing the call,' Finn lied. 'It just takes a second but I can do it. There. I've got it. I'm passing this on to the police.'

'*Culo*, you'll do no such thing.' The voice sounded angry now, she hung up herself.

The phone rang again. Stopped. Then rang again. Nearly two o'clock.

He resisted answering, allowed the call to go to message, managed not to check the message, until – with the phone under the pillow, his arms supporting his head he realized he wouldn't be able to sleep.

The message started with a string of expletives: *culo, pezzo di merda, frocio, succhiatore, pompinaio, leccacazzi, affanculo.* 'You come here and you think you know who we are.'

The phone rang regularly after this at intervals which cut shorter over the hour. Every fifteen minutes, every ten, every five. Finn switched off the ring, turned off the vibrate, but the small screen still lit up each time a call came through and each time a message was stored, and he fought against the urge to check the messages. Finally, when he decided to switch it off he was surprised to see that the calls had come from Rino's phone.

He checked the messages and heard Rino, at first apologetic: 'I'm in a situation,' he said. His voice a little bashful, hushed, and a noise about him, which Finn identified after replaying the message, as a number of men quietly pushing over some discussion. 'I need money. Badly. I can pay you back.'

The second and third calls reiterated the demand with a little more emphasis. 'Pick up. Answer. Come on. I know you're there.' Finn couldn't tell if this was frustration at receiving no answer or desperation because he really was in trouble.

The phone rang in his hand. Finn didn't intend to answer but his thumb hit the keyboard.

'Hey, hey. Are you there?' Rino sounded indignant. 'I need a little help. It isn't much, I can pay you back.'

Finn didn't respond, and waited for some explanation.

'I need seven hundred euro. I swear I can pay you back as soon as the banks open.'

The phone crackled and another voice cut in gruffly and demanding, 'Just get the money. Do exactly as he tells you.'

Then Rino – 'I need the money tonight. I know you can do this.'

The call cut off and Finn switched on the bedside light and sat upright and blinked, really unsure what was going on.

Minutes later the phone beeped. An SMS, again from an unmarked number, with the simple instruction that Finn should walk to the piazza Nicola Amore, right where Corso Umberto crosses via Duomo, and wait. *Portico, Café Flavia, 20 minutes. €800.*

He arranged his clothes ready to dress, picked the socks out of his trainers, half-hurrying, then paused because he was working up a sweat and something about this whole thing just didn't convince him. He sat on the bed, looked about the room for his clothes, and wondered what he was doing. A demand for money for no reason, coming in the middle of the night: why would he answer this? Rino didn't sound drunk and didn't sound particularly under pressure, and Finn had paid him, transferred a good deal more than this already, in advance. He had no obligation to go out.

€1,000. A new demand.

And how safe would this be? Walking the streets with a thousand euro.

Ten minutes later another message. *You'd better be on your way.* A definite threat.

Minutes after: *Room 32, Hotel Grimaldi. Your light is on.* His hotel, his room.

Then finally: *Bring €2,000. Mr Rabbit & Mr Wolf.*

Finn re-dressed, tucked his shirt into his pants. Two thousand euro? Rino wasn't worth two thousand euro. One, maybe, at a stretch.

But two thousand? Not a chance. A meeting with Mr Rabbit and Mr Wolf would be worth much more than two thousand.

He had the money, as it happened. This was all of his money for the month. It troubled him more that these people knew his hotel room, and, more likely than not, this would make him a target. If he didn't go to the café they would come to the hotel. If he did go to cafe this could all be resolved.

He wrapped the notes in a sock and brought it with him to the piazza. Mr Rabbit and Mr Wolf? The mention of these men, he had to admit, was alarming and deeply unexpected, and sent the whole night off kilter. Finn waited in the portico outside the Café Flavia, the metal blinds down, no lights in any windows along the curved arcade. The road ran in a circle about the piazza and a centre island barricaded by temporary plywood barriers and a sign saying 'Metro'. Above the hoardings some indication of roadworks, or digging: the sketched tops of cranes and heavy equipment. No traffic and no people. Finn stood under one of the arches, in view, in case anyone was watching, the money in the sock in his fist, in his pocket.

He heard the scooter come down the corso – a feeble wavering zip. When it came about the piazza the scooter continued, made an entire circuit, and when it returned to view a second time the man slowed down and crawled hesitantly toward him. A skinny man in shorts, very tight red shorts, with a striped T-shirt, a white helmet, sunglasses, a ratty beard, set his feet either side of the scooter to hold it up. Red shorts and white shoes. No socks. Sunglasses at two thirty-five in the morning. The man whistled through his teeth at Finn and signalled him forward.

'You. Money.'

'No.'

'Money.'

'No.'

'Money. Now.'

'No.'

The man appeared to speak little English, and Finn, although he spoke Italian very well, had no inclination to help him. The man set his hands on his thighs, as if Finn was being entirely unreasonable.

'Money!' he insisted.

'Rino,' Finn replied. 'Mr Rabbit. Mr Wolf.'

The man lifted one foot to the scooter's running board then started up the motor. Finn watched him slowly ride away and disappear around the corner. Something laughable about a tall man on such a small vehicle making such a stupid noise.

He couldn't hear the motor run up the corso, so he followed the arcade round and saw for himself, the man on the scooter stopped at the side of the street speaking into a mobile. Finn crept close enough to hear pieces of the discussion.

'I asked him. I said. I told him to give me the money. That's what I said. I think he wants . . . I didn't ask. OK, say that again,' a pause, 'again. OK. No. OK. One more time.' The man cancelled the call, and stood up to wedge the phone into his pocket.

Finn approached him and asked in Italian what he thought he was doing.

'Your friend. They will slit his throat. You have the money?'

'I want to see him.'

'You can't see him.'

'You can't have the money.'

'Give me the money and tomorrow you will see your friend.'

'He isn't my friend.'

Finn started to walk away. The man started up his bike. He followed Finn with some difficulty, the front wheel weaving awkwardly, the pace being too slow to keep the scooter steady.

'Why don't you give me the money? They will slit his throat. It will be your fault. You will be to blame.' Now the man was sulking.

Finn gestured that he could care less. Before him, he saw a sign for the Questura. 'Call your friends and tell them I want to see Rino, or they won't get the money.' He pointed at the sign. 'Do it before I get to the police station.'

The man stopped his bike, and called OK, OK, to get Finn to stop. He stood up to take his phone out of his pocket, spat on the pavement, sat down heavily and cursed under his breath as he made the call. '*Ciao, ciao*. Yeah. No. He wants to see him. I have . . . I did . . . I said that . . .' He gestured at Finn. 'He wants to see him now. OK.' He handed the phone to Finn. 'They want to talk.'

Finn dug his hands into his pockets.

'Take the phone.'

'No.'

'Take it. They want to speak with you.'

'I want to see Rino first.'

'Take it, *culo*. Take the fucking phone.'

'If I take the phone I'll smash it.'

The man recoiled, and began speaking very quickly into his phone. In a hurry he started up the scooter, and with phone pinched in his hand he swung back into the street and sped off. Finn watched him disappear, then continued walking. The thin whine died away, but didn't disappear completely. He was almost at the doors to the Questura when he realized that the sound was getting louder.

The man rode on the sidewalk and came right at him, head down, and fast. Finn, now past the police station, had reached a long wall and could find nowhere to step into. He began to run, too slow and too late.

Struck by a punch in his side he hit the wall and rolled to the pavement. Unsure exactly what the mechanics of the accident were he fumbled to his feet. The man had driven up and shoved him, hard enough to knock him down, and Finn winced, automatic, just folded over, expecting something else. Instead the man turned his bike around and returned. He used the scooter to block Finn against the wall, all of this within paces of the Questura.

'Give me the money.'

'I don't have it.'

The rider pointed to Finn's pocket.

'The money is in your pocket.'

Finn reluctantly took the sock out of his pocket and handed it to the man.

'You come to the Fazzini. The Bar Fazzini. Your friend will be there. One hour.'

Finn sat down in the street. The scooter zipped up the sidewalk, raced toward piazza del Municipio with a throttled croak sawing up the sides of the boulevard. Denying that he had the money and then handing it over was, well, as stupid as it gets. The corso opened up at the piazza, broadened into a neon-tinted night. Lights on the heights at Castel St Elmo. They'd found a boat in the piazza, hadn't he heard this somewhere, or maybe lots of boats, some entire Greek fleet imprinted in the mud under the piazza, right smack in the centre of town. You couldn't lift a paving slab without history leering back at you insisting your insignificance. Winded, Finn tried to catch his breath.

*

Finn decided to return to the hotel, but wanted first to check himself. He could have been stabbed. You heard about this happening all the time: people in shock who don't know that they've lost an arm, a kidney, half of their spine ripped out, who walked up the street like la-di-dah, to collapse from blood-loss, shock, inattention. Finn found a side alley behind the Questura and stripped down to his boxers and checked himself, and saw in the dull yellow light only a slight graze on his elbow, a round imprint on his right hip that would surely blossom to a bruise. The man had shoved him, knocked him down – the whole thing was immature, barely man-to-man. There wasn't any blood, and once he'd reassured himself that he hadn't been stabbed, he checked his body for broken bones. Pressure? Wasn't that it? You check for pressure points? See what aches or hurts, or is just outright unbearable.

Everything checked out, nothing really wrong here (but how close was that?), no blood loss, punctured organs, broken bones. But seriously – how stupid was that? Why had he even answered the phone? His watch had hit the wall and it grieved him to see the face cracked, but nothing else was damaged.

He walked quickly, limping at first, one side seeming a little larger, the bump to his hip limiting his stride, and elbow aching as a hint of how serious this could have been. He became angry as he walked and couldn't console himself with the idea that this was all experience, all useful, all material for the book. The kind of story he could tell in an interview. *Oh the kidnapping. Yeah. Well, Naples – beautiful by the way – nice place, but troubled, very complicated . . . let me tell you . . .*

Finn took via Umberto back to via Duomo, to via Capasso. He walked fast to walk out the ache.

The Fazzini, as before, bright and busy, with a younger noisier crowd. The bar ran along the back wall, a broad wood counter stacked with glasses, and blocked with people, quite a crowd. But no Rino. No thugs. No kidnappers. No hit-and-run scooter-rider.

He half-ran, half-hopped back to the hotel.

Lights on in the lobby, the door unlocked (at three in the morning) and no night security: bad signs. Unwilling to wait for the elevator he hobbled up the stairs, four floors, to find the door to his room open, *as he expected*, the lights on, the room in disarray looking something like a film set with the bed pulled away from the wall, the cupboard open, his clothes thrown out of the drawers and scattered, paper torn from the blank notebooks littered the bed and the floor. Everything gone.

Someone must have given them a list. Just written out exactly where he'd hidden his laptop. His portable hard-drive. His sister's camera. His phone. The two USB sticks. His remaining traveller's cheques. And not one, but every single notebook from the trip. Even his copy of *The Kill*.

This was no simple theft, but a complete strategic wipeout – erasing every piece of research he'd collected on the murders. In taking the computers and the notebooks they'd stolen every draft and every scrap of information he'd collected, along with the correspondence. Some of this stuff he couldn't begin to consider replacing. Finn buckled over at the doorway. An instant stab of grief at all the detail and experience now lost to him: all of his careful and particular notes that could not now be recreated. He'd sat with Lemi Krawiec for six long hours while the man repeated endlessly that his brother was innocent, and how he didn't know the facts because he didn't need the facts. *He was innocent.* All the while Finn had taken notes, he'd written about the kind of airlessness trapped in that room, the space between these protestations, the protestations themselves and how by their insistence they held a kind of dogma, that the more times they were repeated the more it could be believed, and the more likely it was that this would be true: until nothing else could be considered except that single fact: *Marek Krawiec is innocent.* And this was gone. The precise description of the decor along a mantelpiece, Krawiec's mother's house, the petiteness of it, sullen and ordinary, of Lvov at night, how capsule-like the city seemed, of the people seated facing the windows at the respite home in Lvov, the women on buses, the silent trains and trams. Everything lost: the airport and how coming into it the aircraft pitched through a layer of fog – fog so you knew you were in the heart of Eastern Europe, right on the edge of another period entirely – how this worked as an image of what he would and would not find – *coming through fog*. OK, not great, but apt. The petrochemical works, the roadways, the fields and fields shaved of produce, and the intensity of it all, that one man could come from this flat monochrome to a city so bumpy and opposite and butcher two people. Just how, exactly, is such a notion seeded in someone, so that it becomes essential to act on? He'd formed some sense of Krawiec – not so much from his brother, but from experiencing the same spaces – of how casually cruel the man would become, of how the landscape predicted this, made it so. He was close to understanding how such a crime comes out of a limited number of options, so that it seems both possible and inevitable, something to do; he understood a connection between flat landscapes and wet fields and industrial parks and chemical plants and how an impulse drives an idea to become an inevitable action. He'd come that close to understanding.

On the door handle, a last touch from the thief or thieves: the housekeeping sign saying '*Thank You For Your Stay: Gratuities.*'

He checked the dumpsters outside the hotel, went through the trash, dawn now and his side beginning to ache, and found nothing. The hope, at least, that the notebooks would be scattered somewhere because they were of no earthly use to anyone else. As he bent over the dumpster, moved cardboard around, he remembered a description in one of the newspapers about the discovery of the clothes in Ercolano – and didn't like the idea that there could be more in the dumpster than trash or stolen goods.

WEDNESDAY

He packed his rucksack in the morning. Without his papers and note-books and equipment he didn't have enough to fill the soft hold-all. He hadn't slept, and through the night plans were made and disassem-bled, ideas on how he would return home because he had less than nothing, and how he'd have to undo the publishing deal because he didn't have the material any more, or even the heart to start over. He hadn't slept, and he had to go back to the Questura, chase up his report, because the police who'd come had told him there wasn't any-thing to do until the morning because this crime didn't register to them as being something worthy of any kind of attention. He couldn't even call Rino because all of his numbers were on his phone, his email was on his laptop, and nowhere would yet be open.

After the police, Finn checked in his bag at the Stazione Central. His head rang with humiliation; they'd laughed at him, asked him to describe with particular precision exactly where he'd hidden his valu-ables. *So you hid the money on top of the what? Exactly where?* He couldn't expect any sympathy back home, because this whole thing, he had to admit, was kind of shameful. He'd set himself up: bragged about his summer, his contract, rubbed it hard into other people's faces, and in one night he'd managed to wreck it all. The police had contacted Rino, who said he had no idea about any kidnapping, assault, or rob-bery. Last night was the same as any other, he ate at about eight o'clock, watched TV, argued with his wife, and was incredulous, as was his wife, about this entire idea, and Finn understood that words were said between the police and Rino that undermined him, although he did not know exactly what.

Finn stood in the concourse and looked up at the grey boards flick-ering city names and routes above him. Passengers waited on the platforms, some smoking, most sitting, pressed down by the heat, mopping their foreheads and necks as if expressing regret. It was stupid, foolish to trust Rino, to have paid money to the man. A mistake he swore he wouldn't make again. It was hard to estimate the amount he'd lost, all in all. Now he had twenty euro, just enough to find a place to email his parents and explain the whole stupid episode in some kind of shorthand they would understand. How much would he need to return home, end the summer in Massachusetts? How much would that humiliation cost? He wouldn't ask his parents, he'd ask his sister. Carolyn would lend him money, and he'd pay her back, as long as she swore to keep this to herself.

What to do? Tired and too sickened to eat, he walked through the platform, and found a bookstore. Feltrinelli. And there, facing the door, a small display of *The Kill*, a new Italian translation with the introduction restored, as per the '73 Editiones Mandatore original. The cover: a blood-spattered picture of an Italian palazzo. Finn stood in front of the display completely forlorn. Here it was, a last piece of mockery to rub home his failure. Two days in Naples and he was through. He picked up a copy and walked out of the store without making any effort to disguise the book.

He sat for an hour on the concourse, faced the bookstore entrance, and read the introduction in one sitting.

Finn called his sister collect, could hear her laughing as she accepted the charges – *This is going to be good, bro.* He told her quickly about the theft, about the night with Rino and some skinny thug on a scooter, and how, everything done, Rino denied the whole thing.

Carolyn laughed. Couldn't help herself. Thought this was funny, better than expected. But he was obviously OK, OK? because they were talking. So he's been stung right? This is what it was. A sting. This Rino had orchestrated the whole thing. Obviously.

Finn couldn't see the logic.

'Where did you find him?'

'Online. The university.'

'And you know that he goes to the university? You've seen him there, met his friends, spoken with his professors?'

'I've spent one day with him. His email address is through the university.' And then he remembered, it wasn't. Rino had given an excuse, *The university email is sometimes inaccessible. The server is slow and often fails. Use this address.*

'So he could be a student, but he could also not be a student. Doesn't really matter.'

'They kidnapped him. Someone kidnapped him and threatened to slit his throat.'

'Someone *said* that they'd kidnapped him. Big difference. Do you know anything about him?'

Finn struggled for ideas, of course he knew things about Rino, they had spoken for two months, the man had completed research for him, sent photographs, sat outside the estate at Rione Ini for an entire week and watched Scafuti's apartment. He knew all of the sites and all of the places relevant to the murders.

'Sounds like he just got sick of you.'

'Thanks.'

'Seriously. You can be tiresome. Anyway, it's not like anything bad has happened. You just got played.'

Finn didn't like the term and wouldn't answer.

'So why have you called? Are you really broke? Have you called me to sulk? It's just money. It's just stuff, right? Money and some computers, which were probably holding you back. You've bruised your ass, that's it. I wish my lessons came so easy. There isn't anything permanent. There isn't anything to really worry about. You're OK, and you have yourself a story.'

'I'm OK? I've lost all of my work. All of my equipment.'

'You're fine. It's just some constraint someone's given you. They've taken all of your toys. You just have to work with that. I love you, Finn, but you're a pain in the ass, and someone has played you. Which, you know, you kind of earned. Now you have to work with that. I'll get you money, but you can't come back. You just can't.'

Finn spent the day walking. He tucked *The Kill* into his back pocket and took the *funiculare* to Vomero, roamed through the grounds of the Villa Floridiana, then followed the roads along the steep scalloped flanks zigzagging down via Falcone, Francesco, Tasso, to Corso Emanuele – the bay, sharp silvers and sparkling blues, to his left then his right – all the time feeling the pressure of the book squeezed into his pocket. As the late morning sank into a placid afternoon he slowed his pace and realized that he'd stamped about the city without looking at what was around him. Coming down to the *lungomare* he found a place to sit on the seawall and watched joggers and couples pass by. The idea of coming to Naples wasn't just to write the book, but to gain experience of the city, to prise under its surface and become, chameleon-like, part of the situation, someone tapped into the heat and the bustle, open, as only an outsider can be. How stupid was he? He'd come to Naples one time to test the water, and was startled on a walk to Capodimonte by his first view of the city where he couldn't believe the sight of one unbroken mass of housing, so busy and detailed, so hectic and impenetrably thick, carpeting the hills and the swoop of the plain all the way to the volcano and further to the distant mountains, and he became certain that here among this fractured chaos something would speak to him. Now he had to admit that he'd penetrated nothing.

He pulled the book from his pocket. It wasn't only the city he'd misread, he'd also been misled by the book. Without the introduction *The Kill* was little more than a story about a man who manufactures a crime scene with body parts stolen from a hospital so his neighbours are accused of murder and cannibalism, a strange story, bloody and blunt. But with the introduction it became a story of someone lost in a defeated city, whose actions were prompted by the occupation, a hatred of the occupiers, and a deeper hatred of people he saw as collaborators: his actions, in this context, were justifiably provoked. An entirely different story.

Finn returned to the station feeling less and less happy as he came up the corso. He had to walk by the Questura just to see in daylight the place where he was knocked down, and he began to wonder now how much it would cost him to stay in Europe for the rest of the summer. Six thousand euro? Would that see him clear for the month? He came up via Capasso, and as soon as he caught sight of the palazzo he decided to stay. Maybe losing everything wasn't actually so bad? Carolyn had a point. He could strip everything down to pen and paper. He took a coffee in the café opposite the palazzo. Looked to the shops, the wedding boutique, the *alimentari* with Salvatore and his brother Massimiliano, the doorway with that weird imp of a woman, and thought the story here wasn't the killing, he had this wrong, right from the start he'd had it wrong, the story wasn't even the city, much like *The Kill* the story here was about the palazzo, about what was happening immediately around the crime.

*

By the evening he'd received the money wired by his sister and rented a room opposite the palazzo on via Capasso – procedures, both, which he expected to be much more laboured. Finn paid for one week and assured the landlord that payment for the month would come in two days, and found him not only amenable but sympathetic. By the time Finn returned to his room sweating and laden with supplies (six-packs of sparkling water, beer, long-life milk, biscuits, and chocolate), his head was busy with new plans.

His room faced the palazzo, and if he stood at his window he could see a broad wine-red wall with regular, deep-set, shuttered windows, on the lower floors the small Juliet balconies, the rooms inside black and unknowable. He divided the view into quadrants to guess occupant by occupant who might have lived there for more than a year (most, he assumed). At street level he could see the entrance, the vast black doors, the tops of heads, the fanned black cobbles of the street. Tucked beside the door a wrapped spray of flowers, dirty and bruised, and behind them other flowers, what might be a candle stub, and beside them a small upturned crate with a cushion.

The landlord came to ask if he was settled, and Finn looked about the room and realized that he was settled, and that, with little more than a writing desk, a handful of pens, some paper, he had everything he needed. He wouldn't dwell on last night, because most things are replaceable, right? Everything depended on him, on what he wanted to achieve.

The landlord lingered and Finn realized he wasn't in any hurry to start his work. Tonight, tomorrow. He could write any time, but the opportunity for a discussion would not always be available. So he offered the man a beer and invited him to sit at the window overlooking via Capasso, and gave himself the one constraint – he wouldn't talk, he'd leave it to the landlord.

Window by window the landlord described the occupants of the building, their occupations first, then their foibles: pharmacist, speech therapist, accountant, the two brothers who ran the *alimentari*, a lawyer, at the door the supervisor, in the street the magistrate's driver who seemed to be there at all hours. Outside the Fazzini there would be prostitutes, and while you can't see the bar, you can see the women, loitering among the scooters, talking, loud, calling one to the other.

'The two Frenchmen, the brothers – not Salvatore, not Massimiliano.' The man pointed at the palazzo with his beer, he'd seen them himself. Only one time, but he'd seen them, they weren't fiction. Few people believed that Krawiec was guilty, except the police. 'There isn't much,' the man admitted, 'that happens here that doesn't get noticed.'

Finn asked him to be clear. 'You saw them?'

'I saw the brothers. Plenty of people saw them. They came at night, they never stayed long. Many people saw them, except the driver.' The man nodded down to the street. 'He's there most days, but he says he never saw them. It might be a question of keeping his job.'

Finn took a long look and realized it would be hard for anything to happen here, night or day, without someone seeing or hearing. A figure in the palazzo, faced into the room unaware that he could be seen, practised voice exercises: 'peh-peh-peh-peh'.

As soon as he was alone he set the table in front of the window. He tore pages from the notepad and labelled the days: A, B, C, D . . . wrote a list of the occupants as he could remember them: the doctor, the supervisor, then added the participants: Marek Krawiec and his wife/g-friend, the Second Man, the American Student, Mizuki Katsura, Niccolò Scafuti. Then a list of places: Ercolano, field and paint-factory. Via Capasso. The Language School. The Circumvesuviana station.

MONDAY

Finn called Carolyn and told her he was staying, not just for the summer, but for as long as it took, which might mean deferring his final year. *It's different this time*, he explained. He was considering Krawiec's story, and taking it seriously; no one had bothered to do this. For Finn this meant going right back to the root, which wasn't, as you'd expect, the Spanish novel. He asked his sister if she knew how he'd first heard about the killing. Not the novel, but the *actual killing*? It happened through a chance meeting, in a hostel in Portland, Oregon, on a mid-term break, and in one long evening, after they'd exhausted the usual conversations about the weirdness of campgrounds, fears of bears and deer-ticks, the hassle of travelling by Greyhound, he was told a story by someone who'd spent the previous summer in Italy. Naples, Italy. This man – there's no point even trying to remember his name – said he'd sat opposite two women on a train, and one of them had started talking about how she was the only witness in a murder case. There wasn't much to it. She'd stepped off the train to see a boy at the station with two bags – a shoulder-bag and a duffel bag. Key to this was the fact that he was wearing a green T-shirt with the design of a star set in a circle on his back. There wasn't anything else to it. She saw this boy at the station. Nothing more.

Then one day, on the train again, with everyone reading the newspaper with a picture of the dark T-shirt with the star design, she'd caught a headline saying that the person who was wearing the clothes had, more likely than not, been killed.

It took her a while to figure out what to do, but eventually, she decided to have a word with the police.

Next time she was in town she went to the Questura, and she spoke with the people at the front desk and was immediately taken to the top man. She told him what she knew, and he asked her to describe the clothes, and then he took her to a room where he showed her the actual clothes. At first she thought they couldn't possibly be the same.

They didn't even look like clothes. The T-shirt was cut, stained, so wasn't even the same colour. The shorts were rust-coloured, this weird brown, and she realized that this was blood. Except for the blood, the stains, the cuts, the clothes were exactly the same. She was positive. The only thing was, she couldn't exactly remember what the boy looked like because it wasn't like she'd really noticed him, she'd just walked past him. And this is where the police did something really smart. This investigator had the man who did the photo-fit pictures walk her through one of the offices and ask her to look at the men in the office. As they walked he asked her if the youth she'd seen looked anything like this man, or that man. And the woman, who's really uncertain, started to give answers like: he wasn't so tall, his hair was shorter, his nose was this way or that way, and this gave the photo-fit guy a really good idea of what they were looking for. Clever, no?

At the end, once she was done, they made up a picture of this guy composed from different faces, and with a little work they managed to figure out exactly what he looked like – not just his face, but they managed to get a good idea about his height and weight, just from walking through the offices and her answering questions. I mean, that's really something. That's clever.

Finn told his sister what he was writing, in great detail: three thousand words on Saturday, seven thousand words on Sunday, and today, a day of revision – and then a description of the content. He read passages to her, but nothing too involved. His desk overlooked the palazzo entrance, the doors were right in his eye-line, he could look sideways from his paper and see it, and had quickly learned about the habits of those who lived inside and those who visited. It wasn't unusual for people to come to the entrance and just stand there. People came all the time to loiter in front of the doors, and it was hard to tell exactly what they were doing. Some took photos. But a good number just gawped in a way that could be boredom or grief and left flowers, candles, notes and tokens, and while the supervisor cleaned everything away almost immediately, she was too superstitious to remove the candles and tokens, and they become dustier and greyer by the day. It's the kind of thing that causes more pain over time, he said. Sometimes the Italian sense of melodrama took over: on Saturday three black sedans pulled up just short of the entrance, highly polished and dressed with fine strings of white flowers, and in the middle car sat the bride, who would be married, he guessed, within the hour. The doors either side of the bride were open and a woman attended to her, arranged and fussed over her dress. Beside the car, smoking, the bride's father in a new suit, visibly more anxious than his daughter. The girl's mouth was drawn into a pout and what details Finn couldn't see he imagined: the pearlescent lipstick, the nails impossibly long and polished the same colour as her lips, her black hair carried back in long ringlets and covered with a mass of toile, delicately edged with petals that needed to be plucked away from her face. The girl's face was undeniably round, he could see this, hamster-like sulking jowls, and when she talked she tended to set her mouth in a broody scowl, her neck and arms also were plump, child-like – but when she smiled she became exceptionally pretty, in a girlish way that made Finn suddenly sentimental. It was lucky, he thought, to see a bride among all this bustle, poised before her wedding, it improved his mood to see her in her last independent moment, cosseted and fussed. But it wasn't an accidental pause. The bride's father threw away his cigarette, took the bouquet from behind the bride and laid it at the foot of the entrance. No prayers, no pause, which surprised Finn. The bouquet was placed with care, leant in the corner so that it would not get kicked and would not be in the way, another man handed him a football shirt, Napoli blue, with Maradona's number, No. 10, which the man folded, number showing, and laid beside the flowers. Once the man had set the flowers and shirt in place he returned to the car and settled without a word beside his daughter, and within a moment the three cars continued slowly down the hill toward the bay.

The brother of the bride, Finn thought. It had to be someone close who'd disappeared – and for this boy, as for many others, there was one day when he needed to be accounted for, included in some way in the family's continuing life.

Carolyn repeated, *That's sad. So sad.* He called her every time he saw someone paused in front of the doors. One man, old, knelt for an hour on the cobbles. *Sis, sis. Listen to this.*

Finn took his lunch at the *alimentari*, he sat with Salvatore and caught up on the news. In the evening he began to translate the start of *The Kill*, as it set a context for his book. What I'm writing isn't about the crime so much, he explained, but the people in the palazzo. What he didn't know he invented, and began to find a kind of veracity to this invention.

*

Finn didn't tell his sister about the emails he'd received. The first came the day after an interview in the *Corriere* in which Finn requested new information on the killings. Information he promised to treat with discretion. I'm not the police, he'd said. I write. The email came from a commercial account: *If you want to know what happened,* it read, *we'll be happy to show you.*

More messages from other fake accounts. In each email the same message.

If you want to know.

This also, although he could not put his finger on it, appeared to be another echo. Another book, another film, a way of saying – if this was serious – that an idea once seeded has to yield fruit.

We will be happy to show you.

Future tense. Perfect.

The Kill

(page 1) 'First. I am not a cruel man. I am not stupid or vicious. You must not believe what you have read. There are many facts which you do not know and would not easily guess: I am a sentimental man, I help when I can help. I keep to myself and trouble no one. I am a private man, and perhaps this is a failing. In sum, I am no different than any other, excepting the reports in newspapers and those written by hired experts in which I am described as a maniac who does not have the temperament to stop or to quell an idea which could otherwise be expressed in violence: whatever boundary prevents you from undertaking an experience is no boundary to me. The accusation stands: that I have murdered my brother.

I do not intend to argue or rehearse my defence. Understand, I have no desire to lie – it is in my interest to lay everything out clearly and honestly, and this is my intention. Even so, the task is not easy as I have been confined for a considerable time and questioned on so many occasions that the most basic facts now seem either to be confused or to indicate some grossly wicked intention – so that I no longer know the truth myself, although I wish, sincerely, to tell the truth. Doctors assigned by the court regularly put questions to me, and these questions – which I am required to answer yes or no – imply readings and meanings beyond the range of a simple answer.'

(page 4) '. . . When asked if I have committed violence, I must answer 'yes', as there are many forms of violence which are casually enacted, day to day. Is it violence to deny food to a person? *Yes.* Is it violence to withhold employment? *Yes.* Violence to portion charity to one person and not another? *Yes.* Is it violence to display your wealth, or at the very least does the display of wealth justify violence? *Yes.* Is it violence to hold a conflicting opinion or position on any given subject? *Yes.* Is it

wrong to set yourself above others to take advantage of them? *Yes.* Is it not also wrong to set yourself lower, in such a position that others must take advantage of you? *Yes. Yes.* Ask yourself: if you are weak, why have you not yet been taken?'

(page 5) 'In examining my past experts have found and reported in depth and detail the root causes of my disturbance. If you believe what you have read there will be no convincing you otherwise, and you might ask instead what else has this man achieved? *What other crimes are we unaware of?*

Let me explain myself.'

(page 5 cont.) 'Much of this is nothing, half-remembered (rooms roughly laid out, tables and fireplaces; an afternoon sky edged by pine trees and rooftops. Certain smells which draw images of the city: a skinny dog running the length of a street; a doorstep opening to a courtyard with water dripping on flagstones from wet clothes). There is nothing specific or entire until I am six years old, and even this, I suspect, is borrowed from a newsreel, a history I have mistaken for my own. Although I have a full sense of the occasion I can't claim it is authentic.'

'(. . .) what could be a carnival? Certainly, a celebration. A parade? A boulevard busy with people nudged shoulder-to-shoulder, immobile for a moment, expectant but sombre. A city canyon, the windows and doorways along a route marked with shoddy home-made bunting full on every floor: women, only women, leaning out, waiting, heads turned to the city gate. There are people along the rooftops also – still, poised, silent. These people are silent because they are defeated, and they have come out of cellars and holes and shelters which were intended only to be temporary but have become their homes. And from these hovels they have watched their neighbours and their families die, and many strangers also. Above anything else they are exhausted. Neither do they look like women: they have shaved their hair to rid themselves of lice, they have haggard faces and colourless skin, they wear unbecoming clothes and have long ago shed any kind of vanity in how they present themselves. They are nocturnal, bloodless and famished. This manly crowd is silent, there is no gossip or chit-chat, none of them are bearing a child (although this will shortly change), all softness has been scraped from them, scoured by days spent underground, and nights spent foraging. But still, they know to present themselves when the occasion requires. And then a sudden eruption, a cascade of paper, white and yellow, papers ripped from ration books, passes, identification papers, contracts with the living and the dead, and memberships of now, or soon to be, illegal organizations, all torn to tiny pieces and flung so that the air flickers. Among this paper snow fall petals and flowers – stemmed flowers in what might be my first memory of real flowers – and while I couldn't have seen them before, I knew exactly what they were, and didn't wonder where these would have come from, because this is the end of a war, and where would these flowers have grown? How could we have flowers but not food? With this, just as sudden, another burst, a mighty shout, unified, a roar of loving cheers, arms raised, hands waving and hands clasped, frantic and happy. Children, girls, are heaved to shoulders, held high. I remember being held aloft and seeing only heads, arms, upturned and expectant faces, many in tears, and there, at long last, making slow progress, the first in an interminable line of green-grey military vehicles, the jeeps the tanks the trucks, being struck with flowers and paper. I remember the men on these vehicles, and how they arrived unsmiling, jolting, unimpressed, sober men, statuesque and unmoved, bruised by war, who kicked the flowers from their vehicles, swept the paper away, looked on us, half-starved, with disgust. I remember the physique of these men, how they seemed bigger, broader – a different species – biggest among them, their fat and round commanders. The faces of these generals set with distaste. We welcomed you, we offered you open arms – the soldiers who'd fought in the marshes, the beaches, and lately to our disaster the mountain crests – the men who starved us (our memory is not so short), the army who stopped our water and poisoned the air, the men who nightly bombed our homes and churches, sucked oxygen from the houses with fire, shot us in our streets and squares, killed women and children like bored farm-boys hunting rats: for you we crawled from basements, crypts, and shelters, and stood on the ruins of our city to present to you the last of our politicians, the collaborators, their wives and their children. Under the brightest blue sky we gave you our city, and we gave it to you out of love.*

---

* This was not the experience related by the Americans – see Part 2, pp. 64–67, where there is a discussion about resistance fighters in the main square, and the discovery of a building loaded with explosives which did not blow.

The very next week we lined the streets and performed the exact same welcome for the British.

This was not the end of war. Although we believed that it was.'

(page 9) 'I am allowed to read, and have been given histories and accounts both of the war and of the city prior to the war. And while these versions of what happened are not incorrect, they largely miss the point. Remember: your arrival was our defeat. For twenty-two years we happily supported the government and way of life knowing that hard choices needed to be made – unpopular decisions for the benefit of all. The government didn't arrive by accident, and while they disappeared overnight, taken to courts and tribunals, some summarily shot, remember – this was our choice because it worked. Full employment. Acceptable housing. Food. And future hopes – not only for ourselves. And our inclination to that government, our allegiance to those ideas, did not disappear as quickly as their bodies.

(. . .)

The city thrived, ten years before my birth. Everything new: stations, trains, trainlines, trams, roads, the first motorways, an opera house, public gardens, cinemas, a grand post office, municipal buildings and swimming pools. We asked for homes and they built us homes. We lived on the edge of the city, in new houses. At that time ground hadn't yet been broken and the city hadn't overtaken the neighbouring villages, spread out to take over the farmland.

You can't imagine the countryside and how it was. The wine and olives from this region were famous, as was the oil with its curative properties – all of which sounds like Spain, and while there is a strong Spanish community here, it is not Spain. It is, or was, handsome; we enjoy a fair climate and moderate weather. The countryside is, or was, pretty in every season: the vines held the winter mists, spring was brief, the sunflowers followed a full summer sun, and autumn, the longest, truest season, when the twilight is unnaturally long, was the time best spent here – the basic structures remain: there are rivers (now channelled), a close curve of mountains, a bed-like cultivated plain leaning into a broad-curved gulf where the city tumbles to the sea, and while it is not Spain, you might believe that you were in Spain. Now that the city has become so vast these seasonal subtleties pass unremarked: it either rains or suffers an oppressive heat. The winters are wet. The summers are hot. The periods of transition are almost unnoticeable. Outside the city, away from the concrete the climate is more temperate. All this is before the Americans. Before their tanks and progress, their factories, their processing plants, all, now, abandoned.'

(page 12) 'Shortly after the relief of the city, I witnessed, close-hand, a death in the vineyards, a young workman, cut in the thigh with a pruning knife, bled into the dirt, arterial, beyond help. He knew this, self-wounded, and I felt the weakening pulse at his thigh; held my hand close above his mouth until his breath expired. I looked into his eyes for a long time and fancied that I witnessed something, although I am certain now that this was only a naive desire; in any case I found it hard to leave – more out of science than sentiment – and having witnessed the process of his expiration, having watched a great quantity of blood leave him and saturate the ground, I became curious about the other processes now riding his body and in learning what other kinds of collapse were happening inside him: I wanted to know what was occurring deep under his skin. I inspected the cut but left the body otherwise undisturbed, (. . .) there is little point withholding the fact that this man was my brother.

(. . .)

The three-room apartment in which we lived does not deserve attention, situated on the first floor in a building seven storeys high, it housed at any given time no fewer than four, and no more than six of us. We shared mismatched chairs, a table, and little else. Four children, we shared one room and two beds. The boys bundled chaotically into one bed, a habit so ingrained that I still dislike sleeping alone. One apartment among many, our home was no different and no more decrepit than our immediate neighbours on either side. One mystery occurs to me now, which has not occurred to me before. At the start of the war, upon its declaration, the city lost about one third of its inhabitants, who took with them what they could manage and headed for the mountains or the sea and abandoned their homes. We did not take over these empty properties, then or later. Even at the start of the bombardment, when war came to our doorstep, we remained, as did the others, in the places allotted to us. Even in their absence we afforded respect to people who had abandoned us.

It is possible that the building dictated this. There would have been little use us occupying the other apartments. The professors, lawyers, doctors, clerks, the city officials and shop owners had their own entrances, their own stairwells. The tradesmen and labourers, along with those who could not find work, entered through the stairwells opening onto the inner courtyards. So that the building, as with many of the buildings in the city – and I think, in other cities, although I have not travelled much – folded about a core courtyard and kept separate the wealthy and the poor. In other countries these palazzi are known by their more proper names as *tenements* or *slums*, although, I believe, in other countries, they do not house the same variety of people. Opposite these apartments, as I have said, on the other side of the road, and therefore in the country, lay a vineyard, and more immediately a line of stone sheds, a place first for animals or produce, for olives and walnuts, for the safe storage of harvest, some of which were later adapted into workshops in which the goods brought from the fields were prepared. During the worst of the bombardment we temporarily fled the palazzi – taller, and easier targets for the mortars and bombs – and hid in the farm sheds. Although I spent much of my childhood in these buildings, either hiding or playing, I remember very little about the place, except how the musk of animals permanently coloured the air. The city, at this time, took on its own smell, of cooked and rotten meat, of the flesh of the dead.

What of the farm, which is now long gone? The owner, whose father had built the property, was killed early in the war, at the docks during an air-raid. On his death his family managed to buy their way out, and left all of the business (the managing of the land and farms, the harvesting and selling of its produce) to unscrupulous managers. But so productive were these holdings, and so rich the land, that even in the thick of war there was produce available – until, naturally, the final year, when the outmost fields abutting the river and mountains became the front line and the harvest was left to rot.

I have less useful information about my parents than I have about the place in which we lived. Both were sentimental, suffered at every slight grief or injustice, and easily took on others' troubles as their own. Before the war my father worked as a handyman whenever and wherever he could and was periodically busy and absent, or without work and constantly at home. When he was busy he lacked the wherewithal to collect what was owed to him – as this seemed to pain him, and people quickly learned of this weakness and took advantage, delaying and sometimes denying payment whenever possible.

Unskilled, he dug graves, trenches, irrigation ditches, and never received his proper wage. He laboured at the harvest, repaired walls, drains and roofs, and was always, in every instance, short-changed. I remember him in dirty, worn clothes, hands stained by labour, the skin on his face, hands and arms commonly rough and dark from the sun, the rest of him remained whiter than a plucked chicken.

My mother worked for charities and good causes, and before the war she avoided the city proper and worked in the local towns. Coming from the south we were used to working on the land, and while we lived in the city, we looked outward and worked the trades and activities that we understood in the neighbouring fields. Similarly, my mother worked at foundling nurseries and in the hospitals, she cleaned, learned to administer basic care. A skinny woman, she walked bent, peasant-like, head down. Prideful enough to henna her hair, she wore it high and drawn back tight. The pair of them, my parents, made little sense, one constantly robbed, the other constantly burdened as if grieving – and in the evenings they would bring each other to tears, and so, as I have said, they were largely useless.

Was I loved? I suppose so. They bragged over our achievements, small as they were, celebrated their children to others, held us up, but in such a limp way they always seemed on the edge of an apology. My younger brother sang in church, at fetes and fairs, travelled for a while with my mother and then with a band of penitents, and my parents talked about him as you might talk about a man who slurs or stutters, or a man who drinks, with a little shame, as if this were also a small failing, as if he could not help himself, knew no better than to sing in the way he did – and underlying this, always, a warning to my brother that this would not last, or that his ability to sing more beautifully than other boys was also a cause of pride which was to be monitored and kept in check.

The truth is that my sister and brothers gave my parents so few opportunities to celebrate that they were unused to it, and as a consequence did not know what to make out of the small pickings we offered them. A joke in the palazzo that my parents were related, brother and sister, which is patently untrue, helped to explain their simple pleasures, their inability to soundly reason, their love for the church, how they were able to dutifully abide the pressures of the times when others wilted under it. If I'm giving the impression they were attentive: they were not. Our education was a scattered affair. We were taught, sporadically, at the local school by a fraternity of monks, who delighted in my older brother and my younger brother (too stupid on one hand, too naive on the other), but whose interest I managed to escape. We shared the same tutors, the same amount of schooling, each of us managed the rudiments of reading and writing, and the most basic arithmetic, but we were needed in the fields in the spring to plant, train and prune, in the late summer for harvesting, in the autumn for storing – whatever influence the holy fathers had over our young bodies and minds, remained, at best, minimal. Our education came in the fields through practical labour: first we understood the length of the day, our own energies, we quickly trained in agriculture, assisted in making cheese, wine, and then we understood the currency of our bodies, that our labour, four children, was not enough to sustain the family, the fact our combined labours were worth less than the work of one man meant that we were obliged to pilfer food.'

(page 15) 'My younger brother's birth came alongside the first sugges-tion of war. I should impress on you that once the country was overtaken by war, life became a wholly different matter. First there was the skin, the day-to-day fact of it, and second there was the under-layer, the continuation of regular life: births, deaths (unassociated with the war); people continued to marry, breed, labour, sicken – and in this regard we existed almost as we had before.

My mother, a thin woman, took on a translucent quality when she was pregnant. Her skin became unnaturally pale, as if something fed on her and threatened her life. As her belly grew she became increas-ingly fragile – and looked, very much, like a fish, a sprat, with some bubo attached, so that she appeared infected. Our neighbours, all farmhands and labourers, bred hard – so little else to do – and as these women grew they took on an unsuppressed vitality and health, of which my mother appeared to be the exact opposite.

My brother's birth came in February. I watched her in the court-yard, cranking the mangle and managing sheets through the rollers, then all of a sudden doubled-up, hand to her belly, and brought to her knees. Secured in her room she bled heavily, and we waited for news, we sat in the kitchen as the midwife boiled towels, brought out spoiled sheets and bedclothes. Her yelps lasted through the night and were accompanied by deep guttural blows that sounded like wind on a roof, a rising storm that came in answer to my mother's cries, a kind of call and response of two animals. As she howled, the sky bellowed – and so my brother was brought into the world. These booms, this noise was neither thunder nor wind, but the artillery of the 112th sounding from the mountains. Already in view of the town, too far to effect damage, they made their guns sing to us little songs of threat, a boom, a drum-beat, an unrealized threat.

One detail. We needed a doctor. Three lived in the palazzo, so my brother and I were sent first to one, and then to the other, and finally, begging (as it looked as if both the child and mother would perish) to the last. While these good men were home, one assured us that he was called out elsewhere, another that he was sick himself, and the third that he would attend (he did not), and that we should return to my mother.

(. . .) On this first assault the Americans were repelled. Perhaps if they had not announced themselves they would have surprised the city, and if the city had fallen then, the region, and maybe the country would have slid quicker into their hands – but no, they told us where they were and were repelled. (. . .) Four years later they would not repeat their mistake. The 112th returned with fresh battalions and with the British in tow (somewhere, dallying behind, paddling up the beaches, moving in like hyenas after the kill). The Americans dropped their troops in the mountains from great aircraft and a great height, scattered them like dandelion drifts along the farther crests, speckled the ledges with paratroopers, and so they silently took the heights ringing the city, and from this vantage they prepared to kill, maim, starve, and punish. The lights of the city can be seen across the plain at night as a condensed and distant sparkle. Intensely signifying the kind of life, the plenteousness of the city, which they must have looked upon with hate: planning, night after night, how they would reduce it.

But this, this is four years ahead still, four years away from the night of my brother's birth.'

(page 19) 'I cannot talk about the American army without mentioning my sister – who I should have more properly introduced. E—, named after my mother's German grandmother, had her own mischief and needed watching. She could be still, as sound and static as a tree, and then gone. If you did not keep your eye on her you would miss her. But I cannot think of her right now. Not at this moment.'

(page 20) 'Against expectation, A— (they gave him a Spanish name) was not a fat baby. The first time I saw him he appeared greasy and paler even than my mother, run through with fine capillaries, as if made of goose-fat and red thread, infinitely vulnerable. So frail and vague he was not expected to live. Announced by the Americans boom, boom, boom, A— brought into the house a new and focused anxiety as we expected him to expire at any moment. As a consequence we lived those moments and felt them dearly, and sustained him second to second, minute to minute. For this period I remember being happy, and my devotion toward A— grew.

This birth brought little joy to my father, who would not approach my brother, feared any further attachment, and resented that the birth had cost so much physical trouble for my mother. As my mother recovered, A— remained delicate, and we all worked toward his welfare, either in the home or at what work we could find.

It is possible that A—'s frailty caused my father to ignore him. He robbed milk from my mother, leeched her limited vitality, he cried through the night, a thin noise, pathetic and unbroken, lamb-like. The midwife kept returning and brought with her chestnut oil, nutmeg oil, light scents to coax the baby to sleep. Even so, I do not remember my brother sleeping, he seemed to fight it, on the understanding, the midwife fancied, that he would be taken the moment he surrendered. While awake, he still lived.

I am not the man they claim. This is the evidence. I lived for my brother. I kept vigil over his cot – so small he was coddled in half a suitcase. We watched over him, and paid him every attention. I learned to feed him a weak broth on which he was weaned, anything to encourage and draw life into him. We raised my brother in the same way in which we had raised cast-off lambs.

(page 24) Here now is a version of an incident that has been used to demonstrate how black a people we are. (. . .)

The first assault by the Americans brought unintended consequences. In landing on the ridges, overtaking the small villages in the mountains on that first salvo, the Americans inadvertently woke a long-standing resentment. This resentment has no logic, or that logic is now lost and there is no pure reason why the cities in the plains mistrust the villages on the mountains (accept that they are thieves; known cheats, unreliable in business. They are cunning as gypsies, oily, calculating, and equally unclean. The women are loose and unprincipled). Accept that this grudge exists: to welcome a man from one of these villages into your home would corrupt your name, spoil your reputation. There is between the city and these villages no trust and no common ground.

Imagine the reaction, shortly after the birth of my brother, when it was discovered that these villages lay within kilometres of the American army. Think also of the outrage when it became known that not one man sought to warn the city (they claim not to have known, and were as surprised, as alarmed as the people in the city when the Americans began to sound their guns). Imagine what nonsense they expressed as justification. The simple fact that an entire battalion of Americans could spread through a landscape they did not know seemed too incredible to accept. These villages, these villagers must surely have helped.

In order to protect ourselves it became necessary to clear these villages. To move the inhabitants elsewhere so they could no longer provide opportunity and support to our enemies. As documented in film, in photographs, the houses of two of the villages were systematically destroyed. While there are a number of other villages, V— and C— were chosen, being positioned at either end of the crescent ridge. A seven-day warning was given to the inhabitants of V— and C—, and so they were driven out of their farms and houses: once vacated the villages were razed to the ground.

The occupants of V— and C— had nowhere to go, and no means of travel. Their animals were slaughtered, and given the poverty of the villages, it is unlikely that more than a few of them could have afforded to leave, or have bribed the officials to provide them with passes and identification. Instead, they came down from the mountains and set up encampments on the outskirts of the city.

By this time many had fled the city, as I have earlier described. And this train of refugees – as this is surely what they were – was moved from place to place and not allowed to settle. The hope being that they would move somewhere distant.

One group, of perhaps forty, certainly no more, men, women and children, settled on the roadside beside the farm in full view of our palazzo.

These people were wretched. They wandered ghostlike without complaint, sat by the roads and track without energy. Idle and indolent, they did nothing to support or help themselves. Discussions in the courtyard of our palazzo grew hot. *These people might seem passive, but they need food, they need water, and they will soon come to us for provisions and who knows what else.*

In less than a week these fears began to be realized. Small shacks were built, from our waste – spare boards and wood and cardboard were fabricated into shelters. The encampment pushed a little into the field, a semi-circle overtook one of the vineyards (it has to be said that no damage was afforded to the vines), and they stretched their squalor alongside the road as an affront.

My mother, familiar with such degradation from her work in the hospitals and hospices, was no better than our neighbours. In practice her charity did not extend far, while her sympathy might have reached other cities and other situations, it did not travel so much as one step in their direction. Her fears, numerous, of disease, theft, murder, were slowly realized with more misery than she would have imagined. First an outbreak of measles, then an unnamed fever the source of which appeared to be the fetid pond that grew in the bald centre, which took with it the babies and the elderly. And then, one night, a fire broke out, which razed five of the eleven shacks. Imagine us gathered at our window to watch the fire. Imagine our attention on the rising brightness, how people fled, approach and ducked, shied from the heat, of how they sought help but found none. This emergency certainly drew out the good people from our tenement who grouped at the road, and seemed for a moment to be ready to set aside their resentments at these gypsies. But no, they did not assist. Instead, as the emergency vehicles made their attempt to approach, our neighbours valiantly held them back, delayed them, detained them from reaching the encampment. What of the police? What of the fire brigade? What of our army? It is true that they arrived in great numbers, a battalion of trucks and water wagons, but while the fire spread they appeared to discuss the situation with our neighbours so that it seemed to be the army, the fire brigade, the police who were manning the very barricade which blocked them from the fire.

(page 28) Both of my parents attended the fire, they knelt with the neighbours on occasion to pray – for guidance, or a clean wind to lift the fire.

(page 29) The Americans, and later the British landed their armies in the south. Swallowed the islands, overran the east and spread like cholera with dangerous and undeniable speed. I do not remember the war, and while its history is physically marked upon the buildings – if you look above the boutique and shop windows you will see bullet holes in the stone and blast damage to the cornices and carved decoration. In some districts, close to the docks, there are still vacant spaces, sockets left by the bombing raids – the vacant lots soon grew a scant kind of grass, so that the city took on, in my early memory at least, a damp aspect, damaged and melancholic.

(page 32) The Americans took the Royal Palace and made the surrounding government offices their headquarters, leaving nothing for the British when they arrived a week later. The British settled at the outskirts, right under the city walls, and chose as their hub the vineyard, to use the old farmhouse and outbuildings as their command base. They managed to settle the land without destroying the vines, seemed to occupy us with an apologetic air. Later, on negotiation with the Americans, after the end of hostilities was formalized, they moved into the city proper and shared the government offices. In their absence, gypsies, who had been encouraged to settle, occupied the vineyard, growing in number from a few makeshift huts and huddled caravans into a larger encampment. They refused to settle in the houses and chose instead the outlying fields. They cared little for the vineyard, and the fields, which had survived the war, were soon spoiled. Our rooms looked down on an undisciplined, unkempt, unsanitary arc of tents and trailers. The vines were cut for fuel. The carefully tended embankments levelled. The irrigation ditches in-filled, so that the terraced field became nothing more than a mud flat.

I remember distinct moments from this period. The fire. The women. The women, brought from the south, were either camp followers, or women traded on the route through the country, from the beaches. Wherever they landed the men, who found almost no resistance, distracted themselves with women, and rather than discard them, collected them, adding to each regiment a sizeable retinue of girls. They were housed in the basement rooms at the palazzo, and I spent my time watching from the courtyard window as the women gathered and washed, or simply spent their days, a kind of endless waiting as if idleness stuck to them, glued them into deeper inaction. The soldiers had gathered women without any particular eye, taking, by criteria, women who were young first, comely second. The trek along the beaches, then inland across the malarial swamps, through the lowlands and foothills, and later, the mountains, had meant that few were lost through combat, but along the way the skinnier girls had become lost, or abandoned, or did not have the fortitude to last.

I have no real idea about how the women came to be in our palazzo. I know only that they were, and how they appeared thinner than seemed reasonable, and how they followed the soldiers without complaint. They washed; they worked on their backs. The British soldiers appeared not to enjoy this. The American, the Polish, the French all took to these opportunities, and there was no small amount of abuse, shouting, little displayed physically. But the women were spoken to as imbeciles. They were paid in food. Badly. Stale bread. Dried meats. Processed foods that were shipped in, offloaded and left to cook in their cans on pallets on beaches further south. One can of corned beef would service as pay, so that these women were worth less than canned meat. These women were worth less than rotten scraps. As supplies improved, so did their pay. One night a week the Americans would arrive and back a truck into the courtyard, and on this truck they would hold a barbecue, cook meats; they were uncommonly generous.

(page 34) Because of the dead the city was overrun with rats. Many had been trapped in basements when the bombing started, others were caught in catacombs, in the churches, in what passed as shelters, so the city took on a sweet smell which sank into a rank stench, recognizable as decay. The Americans brought us cats. This was one of their first gifts. Cats to kill the rats. The rats who had grown fat and large on the dead were easy to catch, and we were soon overrun with cats, who without live rats to hunt, turned to the same food source. They became aggressive and seemed to hold designs upon the living.

(page 35) The Americans reported the truck missing. They came another time in separate vehicles, but the truck was taken, assumed sold, as most other provisions and equipment were stolen away and resold, sometimes back to them. In this instance the truck was found, and inside, littering the truck-bed, were the bodies of cats, necks

snapped, slaughtered in the hundreds. As for the rats we would find our own solution.

(page 36) The loss of D— had a profound effect. While we did not play together, knew each other in passing, I thought of her as someone close, similar. Her proximity and encouragement (while she was free), and a discouragement (when she was incarcerated). Once she was gone – or unavailable – I turned to my brother A— for company. At that time I needed a compatriot. I needed to know I was not alone.

(page 40) Here I must speak about my sister. Here everything comes together and I should speak of the third woman who has held influence over me. So far E— has been absent, and there are many reasons for this, not least of all the considerable pain I feel at remembering her.

The episode of the cats caused a change in how the Americans treated their women. They viewed them afterward more coldly, as a resource, the men arrived now with briskness, as if keeping to an appointment, and no longer delayed to joke and play games, to tease. They also began to play small but cruel games. Through the Americans the black market thrived. In opening the city they brought back trade in two tiers, honest and expensive, dishonest and more various, and double the price. One young recruit, a handsome willowy man, a private from Kentucky, from whom I would not have expected such cruelty, brought with him packets of stockings which he gave to the women, there was one girl he was fond of, young, very small, from the mountains in the south, who had fine and dark features, and was known among the women as Mouse. The youth held back one packet, which he handed over with a kind of pride. Unlike the other sets of stockings, these were coloured, a faint but handsome pink. The women, at first delighted by the gifts, perhaps believing that some normalcy was now returning, that they had been forgiven for the episode of the cats, soon appeared puzzled, and as I watched a wave of doubt flickered through them. While the stockings were in packets, they were not new, some were rolled, and others carelessly folded, a sagginess to them that showed that they had been worn. These stockings, it later became known, were taken from the bodies of the dead or stolen from the homes of the absent. A whole new economy grew about the houses and apartments which had been abandoned, and also the houses of the dead. These places were looted – and I will not lay the blame solely at the feet of the Americans, I will not say that this was entirely about finding treasure, about taking trophies, but they caused this need, and the houses which had remained secure until now were plundered.

The women received gifts from the houses of the dead. Lamps. Carpets. Clothes. L— dressed now in a fine patterned silk nightdress, and wore over this a sheer white nightgown with cascading frills, a silly pretty thing which suited her. I watched as she received this gift, from a commander, who gave it to her in a box, wrapped in tissue paper, so that it appeared as a gift a lover might present his mistress, a fine token brought from Paris, to signify a small, perhaps intimate, occasion. It was of course no such thing. Shortly after other such boxes appeared and we learned that one of the boutiques on via F—, which had remained shuttered and unbothered through the barricade, was now forced open and looted. But this made a better gift, something she was happy to accept as it came from no one's home, from no other body.

She stretched the fine material over her arm, allowed it to smooth over her, the weight fitting itself to her body. In wrapping her arms about the commander she looked up and caught me watching. With one finger she gave a small tick-tick wave, indicating that I should not watch. I should keep out of this business. I should not be involved, because, clearly, all this would invite would be trouble. But even with this small admonishment, I had to admit to a fascination.

L— kept a good eye on the women. She did not interfere in squabbles, but quelled them quickly if they appeared to stay unresolved, or if the irritation escalated into a fight. More like the sultan than the chief of the harem, she signalled her displeasure and her pleasure with gestures: sent girls away, picked men when they arrived. An authority on her that even the soldiers obeyed.

She also gave advice: 'Would it be better to be dead?' 'If he enjoys you now, he won't hurt you later.'

On occasion a darkness fell over the group. The girls would become unhappy, or some incident, an argument with one of the men would infect the air. L— was not immune, and I learned when and when not to observe them.

One night L— came to our door. My father answered and shut it immediately.

My mother and sister wanted to see the visitor, and came after him to the door. I watched also, and saw, with a confused pleasure that it was L—. I could hear her laugh before the door was opened, and sure enough she stood in the landing with arms carrying something wrapped in a shawl. She offered this to my mother – and what might have been a baby proved instead to be supplies provided by the Americans.

Up close L— was pretty, the face of a china doll, round, with sweet small lips, blue eyes. Her cheeks a little chubby made her face while it was settled appear even jolly, although I had seen on a number of occasions that this was not always the case, and that she could set herself from silk to steel in a simple moment.

My mother wanted to refuse. I could sense this, so L— had to drop her hands to let the weight settle in my mother's arms. My brother came forward and took the bundle from my mother, and nodded his gratitude. His face as flushed as mine.

She offered us milk. Packaged eggs. There were cigarettes, she admitted, but they used these to trade for produce. There was no telling what the soldiers would bring, and rather than allow this to waste she thought we might make good use of the food. There were perfumes (she smelled so sweet herself), stockings, scarves, clothes, but it did not seem a good idea to offer those, unless they could be traded. But trade here, she seemed to indicate the building, is not safe.

On seeing my sister L— looked quickly at my mother and whispered, I am sure I heard it. 'You should not keep her here. You understand me? Take her to relatives. She is not safe.'

After this warning my parents did not allow my sister to pass through the courtyard unaccompanied. They attempted to keep her to the apartment, but found this impossible, and needed in any case the money she would bring in. She had to work. They hatched between them another plan, a fatal idea, that they could buy a pass for her so that she could leave the city, work elsewhere, somewhere safer. These passes were almost impossible to acquire and were gained through the permission of an adjutant, one of the military administrative overclass. I accompanied my mother to the offices, and we made our way through the vast lobby of what was once the central office for pensions and war relief, less than insects in the shadows of these lofty windows, which made me certain that this endeavour would not succeed. In front of us, a man who had once been a neighbour, who spoke without bitterness about how he had needed to choose between his daughters, whore one to save the other. He was there, on this occasion, to barter for his wife, and had brought with him what remained of her jewellery: her wedding ring, her engagement ring, a pair of diamond stud earrings, which he feared would not be enough.

The queue ran through the corridors, my mother told me to keep in place, then checked for herself and despaired when she saw that this line of people ran a ring about the entire floor then through the stair-well to rise, and who knows, run another circuit about that floor, maybe others also. The people appeared comatose, and this frightened her; resigned to whatever they might need to surrender, they brought with them small packages, clothes, food, boxes of jewellery, all to ensure that their daughters and wives would escape the city. It was not clear how many days we would have to wait, and if that wait would in the end be successful. Another plan needed to be devised.

This failure sent my mother into a depression. E— could not remain in the building, it was not safe, neither could she leave. To con-firm her vulnerability E— had been stopped that morning by the soldier from Kentucky. Clear that his tastes ran to the more delicate, the more defenceless of the girls, he singled out my sister as she brought water through the courtyard. The man watched as she passed, turned his whole body as she moved alongside him and toward the stair. He looked up as she made her way up the stairs, then gave a long and low whistle. The kind of whistle a hunter might give his dog, a signal that there was quarry to be had here. He had found something to hunt.

A short time after this, perhaps one or two days, the Americans performed a search of the entire building. Whether this was for secu-rity, as they claimed, a kind of census taking to ensure who and how many people populated these palazzi. They came to the door in their uniforms. Four men. Clipboards and rifles.

'This is how they find their women,' my mother fretted. Clearly they wanted more than women. They catalogued the rooms and con-tents, checked our food resources. It was certainly how they found their goods. And we listened afterward as they broke in to the empty apartments. Once those doors were breached, the contents would be pilfered. During the night we could hear the vacant apartments being looted, the soft bumping of furnishing, the splintering of wood: we dared not see who this was.

This situation sustained itself for a while. Once the apartments were looted it seemed that there could be little else that could be taken. And perhaps this might have been the case, perhaps this might have been the story if the women in the courtyard had not caused another upset.

(page 43) The young private, the youth from Kentucky, was found stabbed. The wounded man wandered, trance-like, out of the lower rooms, into the courtyard. He walked through the stairwells, vacant, seeming to have some quiet purpose, stepping as a cat through wet grass, lifting up his feet, but not sensate enough to express exactly what it was that he was doing, what it was that he wanted. His hands, slashed, showed defensive wounds, where, perhaps, he had tried to grab the knife. His handprints along the wall, small slides and smudges tracking his progress from floor to floor. We saw the blood, ignored it, then later, more worried about what fresh trouble this would bring, my brother and my father followed the trail up to the top floor.

They found him sweating and panting. In the darkness his tunic appeared black, the blood having seeped through his jacket.

Unwilling to touch him, they raised the alarm. One dead solder would be no end of trouble and they did not want to be involved, but considered quickly – which would be worse? To allow him to die and suffer whatever consequences the Americans would bring down on us, or perhaps, through intervening, be seen as people who had helped, at the same time appear as collaborators to our own.

My father could not make the choice. My brother, independently, sounded the alarm. Went down to the basement and roused the women, got the soldiers away from their women's arms and beds and brought them up the stairs to their companion, who now lay in a swoon.

They brought him down in a blanket, a makeshift stretcher, and laid him in the courtyard, still alive, but feeble from blood loss. The women came out, one by one, and held back to the courtyard walls, hands to mouths, frightened, recognizing that this would be no good thing. Ten of us could die, twenty, a hundred, and it would mean nothing. But one wounded American signalled a whole world of trouble.

The soldiers themselves appeared stunned. They stripped off the boy's tunic, demanded water and rags and found him stabbed once in the side, and once in the chest. The boy lay pale, his wounds agape. His chest raising and falling with laboured breaths.

The military police arrived alongside an ambulance, and the boy was dressed and taken away with some hurry, and greater fears that he would die. The courtyard trapped silence, no one dared speak, and it seemed that all, even the men who had spent the night here, were under suspicion.

(page 45) Let me describe now what was happening inside our apartment. How this event brought down a deeper distress. My mother at the table, too gone to wail, head in hands, believing that this would be the last that we would see of my brother. My father, useless, did not know what to do with himself and hung, waif-like at the door. My sister kept back, and I urged her to pack. We would hide her in one of the other apartments. They would not find her. We would say that she had already gone, that she was working elsewhere, that she was now in a city in the north, and that we had not heard from her. We could say that she had died. We would take her belongings, all evidence of her and deny that she existed, say that their records were incorrect, that there never was a girl here, that we had no sister, there was no daughter. The Americans would be bound to come and question us now. Our involvement would be examined. This attention would need to be managed if we did not want it to cause us trouble. Looking about the room, about the apartment, as bare as it was, it would not take much to convince them that there was no girl.

We hid her in another apartment, the room a chaos of broken furniture – it was not hard. She dug herself under the broken frame of a bed and slipped from view.

The Americans came in the night. They brought dogs. And now my mother's grief grew into song. She shrieked as they came into the courtyard as they broke the doors and rounded up the women, hauled them into trucks. I strained to watch but did not see L— but watched as the women were roughly gathered, bound, thrown onto the back of the vehicle like meat. They took them away and left a team of men to clear the room, who threw out the beds, tossed the clothes into the courtyard, and then set fire to it; sparks rose and sucked the air, a column of smoke billowed upward. They threw linens, bedding, mattresses, clothes and shoes onto the fire, not caring that this might spread, that the dry night air would carry sparks into other homes.

I saw the face of my neighbours at the windows, brightened by firelight, who each caught my eye, and each turned away, slipped back into the darkness, wanting not to be seen. The dogs howled at the fire, strained at their leashes, and here – finally – we come to the worst.

One of these hounds released by its minder hurtled up the stairs, and found its way floor by floor to the vacant apartment in which we had secured my sister, it sought out the chaotic heap under which she lay and began to bark and howl and scrambled at the furniture.

They found her, the soldiers. Brought her out. Took her away.

(page 47) My mother returned to the new ministry and came back exhausted, used up. They would not speak with her. Threatened her with arrest when she started to make a fuss. She begged, fell to her knees, offered herself in her daughter's place. Attempted to explain that they had taken her by mistake, that she was not one of the women they had herded in the palazzo. She was a girl. Her daughter. Surely they had daughters themselves? Surely they had mothers also, who they would not bear to see degrade themselves? Could they not see that this was a simple mistake. She would make no complaint. She would be grateful. She would spy for them, inform on the neighbours, collect information. She would do anything if they would release her child. She is fourteen. Return her to me.

The man she spoke to appeared not to understand. Refused to listen, and when he had to, sat without expression, a wall. Stones would have wept, she said, but this man saw nothing in front of him, nothing recognizable, nothing from which he could draw the simplest strand of sympathy.

Outside the building she was met by a woman, an American who hurried after her. This girl, she said, had heard her, understood her, and realizing that the adjutant would do nothing, explained with care that there was a magistrate. One of our own people, and that my mother should assemble witnesses, set out a record of what had happened and have this signed by neighbours. The magistrate would not ignore us, with evidence he could over-step the adjutant and speak directly with the military commanders. There was hope in this, a little hope.

On her return my mother explained what we needed to do. Using D.P.'s paper I addressed the facts of the night before. Wrote first our address and date as I had seen on official documents, set out the names of the people in the house, wrote my sister's name in capitals. After this we knocked on our neighbours' doors. If they had refused my mother, they could not refuse the testimony of others. There were men who had witnessed this. Neighbours drawn to their windows and balconies – she had seen them, I had seen them – keeping safe behind shutters, but watching; she had felt them, seen them, knew they were there.

Some, at first, admitted as much. Gave their condolences. Shook their heads in horror. That it would come to this. After everything. Daughters taken, stolen from their houses. Floor by floor we knocked on each of the doors, implored each neighbour the same. Come with us. Come to the magistrate, help present our case, prove that our daughter existed, and that she was taken from us. Sign here. A piece of paper, give some testimony, if not your name then a mark, a simple mark. None of them. Not one. Would sign.

Misfortune is a river, and once it has found its course it will widen its banks, flood wasteland, vineyards and farmland without discrimination, swamp and lay the plains to waste. The same day my sister was taken, the British stood by as the museums were looted. Done with our homes, our palaces and museums were now the target.

We determined to see the magistrate without the petition. If he were one of our countrymen he would surely help us. The streets, which by mid-afternoon would normally be quiet, were hectic with activity. Troops, American and British, lined the boulevards, the shops along the main thoroughfares were shuttered, the ministry itself closed. Police blockaded the main arcade, at the port the ships' guns faced inland. It became clear, as we ran from corner to corner, inching our way to the magistrate's court, that there were fears of an insurrection. By the time we passed the National Museum the looting was done. The doors lay open, and a white thread of smoke blew from the back of the building. There were shards, glass from the windows, stones used to pelt the doors, and papers scattered across the pavement and into the road. Tanks faced the building and the men now guarding (surely too late) wore visors and masks so their faces could not be seen.

The magistrate was not at the court, as we should have expected. Instead, at the height of the looting, the Americans had driven him to the museum, and there was no clear idea what had then happened to him, except that he had failed to quell the trouble.

We waited at his office. His secretary sat behind a desk and told us that it would do no good. 'There will be no other business now. They (meaning the Americans, perhaps the British) were working hand in hand with the looters. These weren't bandits. This was organized, carefully planned. Much of what they wanted, the prize of our culture was gone already by the time they arrived. The people they caught were passers-by. They will be shot. Under martial law. They will be shot.'

He knew nothing of our sister. Nothing about the women at the palazzo. Nothing about the entertainments, and did not seem surprised by the news. 'A car we could find,' he said, 'we know the names of every thief. A person.' He shrugged. 'They disappear. If someone is gone. I am sorry to report. They are gone.'

His office, decorated white and blue, held busts. Heads of state, former kings, and in the corridor also I noticed the bronze likenesses of our philosophers, a great deal of statuary in fact along the corridors and stairwells, none of it particularly fitting the surroundings. Watching me the magistrate's clerk said that we should go. There was nothing he could do, and nothing either that the magistrate could manage. Without verification of our claim we had no grounds to make a petition.

(page 50) My sister returned two days later at sunset as we returned, again, from the magistrate's office. (. . .)

I called on Dr P—, begged him to come see her, to help. Knocked hard at his door. Saw that his blinds were slightly opened. Called to him. Insisted that I knew he was in. That I would break the door. His voice, feeble but clear, refused to assist, and told me, directly, and with some shame to go away.

I ran to other doors, to other neighbours and asked for water, for towels, for a trough so we could bathe her. Door after door remained unanswered. About the palazzo hung a thick silence. The silence of people hiding, of people holding their breaths, of people closing their eyes and hardening themselves, making themselves as dull as walls and floors and stone. Not one person came to our aid.

(page 51) The morning after the return of my sister, my brother took himself to the vineyard and used a curved pruning knife to slit the artery in his leg. He lay with his back to the vine and bled himself of life. He left no note or explanation, which did not need to be voiced perhaps. I found him, and held him at the end. I sat with him long after, and thought hard over the facts and realized that everything I

had done to this point was driven by coincidence. The opportunities opened to me had come through chance alone. The misfortunes were otherwise, and were driven by situations which I believed I could not control. But now, it seemed to me that I could be less undirected. Less blown. More determined. If I did not I would end up used like my brother and sister. Here, as if to give example to the trouble which I debated, I was found with the knife, covered in blood, and arrested.

And so I was imprisoned for the murder of my brother.

YEAR 3

WEDNESDAY

Yee Jan waited in the cubicle until he could be certain that the students were gone. Some stuck around for extra sessions, one-on-ones that lasted an hour at most. Others dawdled to chat and wrap up the day, and took too long to say goodbye. Tonight they were filming at the marina and Yee Jan didn't have time to dawdle. *They* meaning a film crew, technicians, handlers, movers, a mix of lean and professional Americans and Italians (men) from Los Angeles and Rome: people (men) so serious and focused and so used to crowds they saw nothing but the job ahead of them. Yee Jan wanted to watch them for their industry alone. The crew wore military green T-shirts and vests with *The Kill* printed in white script on the front and the outline of a white star in a white circle on the back. He wanted one of the vests, although he was happy to settle for a photograph. Yee Jan leaned into the mirror and considered how this could be achieved. He pinched his eyelashes to tease out stray hairs. He'd come in early that morning specifically to watch the maintenance crew off-load lights from flat-bed trucks and prepare the cabins (technically trailers) and set them end on end on the broad sidewalk that ran alongside the port, and just as soon as he was ready he'd go back and find them.

Inside his satchel he'd packed another set of clothes and a small zippered make-up bag. He laid the clothes across the sink then picked carefully through the make-up and chose the lighter lipstick, flesh-pink, and a foundation which would erase the small open pores on either side of his nose and the oilier skin around his chin. He leaned toward the mirror, smoothed his hand across his jaw and satisfied himself that there was no sign of stubble. Certain now that no stray students roamed the corridors. he puckered his mouth, tested a line of lipstick, and thought it too much. The staff would stay until the evening and students would return for a film screening, a cooking class, a visit to the crypt or the roof of the Duomo, he couldn't remember the programme, but it usually started two hours after the final class.

It was a mistake to open the week with the story about the wolf: Lara had made a point of showing her disappointment. No stories about Naples, right from the start. Meaning: no bad stories. No bullshitting the Italians. In fact if you're going to say something that involves Italy or the Italians you better make it flattering: and best remember that as an American you know less than nothing about food, language, clothes, culture, politics, religion, especially religion, especially with Lara. No shit. Yee Jan practised his shtick in his head: remember, this is a country that voted a prostitute into government and a fat clown as Prime Minister, persistently, for like, eighteen years. Italians know every kind of shit about every kind of shit there is to know. They've heard it all. Italians are the Meistershitters. No kidding.

Personally, Yee Jan didn't understand what was quite so bad about the wolf story. It certainly went down easier than the introductions two weeks earlier when he'd announced himself as Princessa Chiaia. He'd given the word a kick, a little hot sauce, a little yip: Key-yai-ya. Bad idea. But like most ideas it came to him in a moment – and you just never know if it's going to work until it's out of your mouth. The group after all were all women, worse, wives, worse, military wives, and they had no sense of style, not one drop, and probably shopped at Target and T.J. Maxx, no Filene's Basement, not because they were poor but because they didn't know any better and had No Idea about the pleasures of Chiaia and the boutiques at piazza del Martiri (was it any wonder that their husbands were so fruity?) – besides, they didn't know him yet, hence, not one laugh. Instead they regarded him with the same kind of horror they might regard a falling phial of smallpox. But this time the tutor, Frau Lara, had taken umbrage, and she seriously couldn't see that a story about a wolf loose in the city was simply a story about a wolf loose in the city, nothing more. He meant it as a fable, if anything. Nothing more to it than that. Wolves are cute, come on. Who doesn't like wolves? Yee Jan pouted at the mirror, narrowed his eyes. Didn't a story about a wild creature slinking through the alleys and piazzas make the city that much more interesting, that little bit sexier, and best of all, didn't it seem ever so slightly possible? Besides, he'd yet to meet an Italian who didn't love to bang on about Napoli's special sense of mystery, a particular ancient unnameable beauty, a special something, a blah-blah-blah-blah-blah-di-blah, all in one breath and then slag it off as *terzo mondo* in the next? Bad logic, freakopaths. You can't have it both ways: you're either something of interest or you're not.

Yee Jan inspected himself in profile. The light in the toilet wasn't great but it gave him enough to work with. He squeezed the foundation into his palm first, presented his chin to the mirror and sneered at the sweet stink of the place, a sickly vanilla, somehow worse in the bathroom, which made little sense – the bakery in the front of the building, the toilet at the side, nowhere near the courtyard. What's that film where the woman rubs her arms with lemons to rid herself of the stink of her job? And what's her name? The man was Burt Lancaster. No forgetting Burt, who might have had an English name but surely, had to be, somewhere deep down, a pure genetic Italian.

In Yee Jan's story the wolf made a habit of coming into the city: she hid in the underground caverns that ran under the old town, or sometimes those catacombs dug into the rock at Fontanella. She didn't live here, no, instead she wandered in now and again, found her way from the mountains by tracking the scent of the city through waterways and irrigation ditches, all the way through those drab flat fields. She came in winter, in February with the denser snow, when the waterways were frozen, and when the meaty stink of the city clung to the earth and spread out for miles, scratch that, kilometres. She came here to give birth. This wolf, magnificent, canny, even wise, and had enough smarts to know when and how to hide herself and her pups in a city of nearly three million people – four point six if you include the entire metropolitan area – and she knew how to disappear, how to find food, taking cats, small dogs, maybe once or twice some impolite fat child (and so many of them good and porky). The people who spotted her (an old woman outside the Duomo, a trader on via Tribunali, the street walkers at piazza Garibaldi, a team of street cleaners on via Toledo / Roma, whatever you will) were luckier than they knew, because the wolf took a particular interest in the people who spied her – call it providence. If the wolf passed by you, if she saw you, if, for some small reason she paid you a little attention, allowed you to see her, you couldn't come to harm, for a day, for a week, it just depended.

Yee Jan's Italian wasn't great, that's for sure, but he could manage well enough to tell a plain story simply. A city. A wolf. The lucky few who stumbled across her. And he could tell these ideas as unadorned facts which provided a handsome certainty. Everybody knows it's not the embellishment that makes the story: it's the cold hard presence of possibility. This is why people play the lottery – because winning is always possible. Improbable. Really-fucking-remotely unlikely. But *possible*.

Yee Jan pouted at the mirror. A finger at the corner of his mouth. He held up the mascara brush but decided against it. The thing about make-up is making sure there's just enough, too much is a problem, but finding that distinctive point where you both are and aren't familiar is all about precision. More often than not it's the mascara and lipstick combination that tips the balance. These military wives could do with some lessons. Seriously. Why would you leave the house looking like a monkey had a party on your face?

By the time he found the film crew they had progressed from the portside to where the road curled about the bay, right beside Castel dell'Ovo. A line of silver-white screens bounced light from the sea to form a bright path across the road. As far as Yee Jan could make out, the shot involved a woman scurrying along the promenade and a man following after. Time after time the woman walked in a quick romp, skirt tight between her legs, hand up to her shoulder to keep her bag in place. The man came after in a long stride, close enough, smoking, sunglasses and a pinched face. People only walked like this in movies. When they stopped both the man and the woman wiped their faces with towels in a gesture that reminded Yee Jan more of tennis than filmmaking. Tedious wasn't the word. The woman walked, the man followed. Walked. Followed. Their movements matched by a camera running alongside, then everything stopped, tracked back to the start, and after long and digressive preparations (make-up, discussions, cables hauled back, the camera itself in one instance appeared to be dismantled, while screens were adjusted to accommodate for the changing pitch of sunlight, and plenty of pointing, everybody pointing) they began again. Tired of watching Yee Jan sat and finished a slice of pizza which he picked into pieces, this at least couldn't be faulted, mozzarella so fresh it sat in a light sap, only just set. He took a photo of himself with the slice held up to his mouth and didn't mind that people were watching. After eating he wanted to smoke, Bacall-style. It's the head that moves, never the hand.

THURSDAY

Before the class could properly settle the secretary knocked on the door and asked the tutor if Yee Jan and Keiko could please come outside. As soon as they came out the secretary asked if they could sit in the hallway for a moment.

'What do you think this is about?' Keiko whispered to Yee Jan in English.

'Fashion police.' Yee Jan whispered back. 'You're wearing two kinds of stripes.'

Keiko gave a complicit shrug and said she didn't think she'd done anything wrong. Not anything she could remember.

'You think we're in trouble? It feels like high school. Maybe it has something to do with money?'

Yee Jan thought it strange that they would be called out of class and then asked to wait. He was, after all, paying for the lesson he was missing. He listened to the tutor's voice through the door and the measured laughter of their fellow students, all a bit predictable. People didn't like Lara as much as they liked the other tutors, but he had to admit she got the job done. Yee Jan splayed his hands and inspected his nails. Today he wore mascara but no foundation.

When the office door opened, a student from Elementario Uno came out, book in hand, and returned to her class.

'It looks like they're speaking to the Asian students.'

Yee Jan strained forward. Printed on the back of the student's T-shirt a picture of a smiling cat, the face not entirely unlike her own, broad, almost round. He had to admit she was pretty. Inside the office sat two police officers. 'Why are the police here? Are we supposed to have our passports?'

Keiko took out her passport from a small wallet hung about her neck.

'You're such a victim,' Yee Jan said. His statement of the week, which he applied with sincerity, insincerity, irony, love, or anger to any situation. *Such a victim.* 'I told you about those stripes, didn't I?'

As they both leaned forward the office door was carefully drawn shut.

After a few moments the secretary came out of the office and in a low voice she asked if Keiko would come with her – then seeing Yee Jan's bag, she stopped cold. The secretary curled her hair behind her ear then pointed at Yee Jan's bag. '*Questa è la vostra borsa?*'

'Sorry? Am I going?'

'Your bag,' Keiko interrupted. 'She's asking about your bag.'

'This is *my* bag.' Yee Jan held up the bag so the secretary could see, then pronounced emphatically. 'Mine.' It was one thing learning Italian, quite another using that knowledge out of class.

The secretary looked seriously at the bag. Maybe the job didn't pay that much. Maybe secretaries across the city had to snatch and grab whenever they could.

'It's from Macy's.' Yee Jan pointed in the direction he thought was west. 'I know. Ironic. It looks like Ferragamo. You'll have to go to New York yourself.'

Used to Yee Jan's oblique ways the secretary straightened up then returned to the office.

Keiko looked at Yee Jan's bag. 'I don't think this has anything to do with visas or money. I think it's something to do with the bag?'

'*My* bag, victim. *My* bag. *I* paid for it.'

The news that a man had followed him was nothing extraordinary. This is Italy, Yee Jan told himself. As far as he could tell everyone seemed to be watching everyone else, and apart from an obvious, often hostile, curiosity, Italian men liked to make their likes and attractions clear. It wasn't much of a surprise that someone would take it further. Only this wasn't a simple harassing call, a bothersome stare, a whistle or a gesture. This wasn't a joking profession of love, a cock-grabbing insult, or a scout for a sexual service. This was a grown man waiting outside the school for him on three, certainly, possibly even five consecutive evenings.

When they showed him the footage the secretary Sandra burst into tears and had to leave the room. The police, uncomfortable with the procedure, continued, their faces red, flustered. Yee Jan wondered to whom they felt the most sympathetic, him, or the man who'd mistaken him for a woman – as this was the scenario from their perspective.

THE KILL

Everyone knew the story about the language school and the disappearance of the Japanese student (which explained Sandra's tears), but none of the students were aware that this had any effect day to day on the school or had anything much to do with the slightly heightened security around the palazzo, because, let's face it, this is Naples, so a camera above the intercom wasn't odd. A camera above the courtyard doors wasn't odd. A camera mounted in the window of the antiques store wasn't odd. The police knew next to nothing and seemed genuinely bored. They couldn't even be sure how many times the man had followed him. Three times captured on tape, but maybe four. Four or five, then.

In gritty black and white, from three separate vantage points, the image showed a man standing, and sometimes leaning, by the wall opposite the entrance. In the first tape the man stood with his arms at his side, he wore an unmarked baseball hat and a lightweight jacket despite the heat and humidity. Yee Jan thought he looked a little (and while he didn't like the word, he couldn't avoid it) *retarded*. No one stands that still for that long without having some kind of an issue going on. It didn't help that the crudeness of the image flattened everything into tonal plains. The longer Yee Jan looked, the harder he concentrated, the more the grey plains appeared to vibrate. In two of the segments other students came out and the man showed no interest, but as soon as Yee Jan emerged with his bag tucked under his arm (that handsome ersatz-Ferragamo with a white and brown body and long double-stitched brown straps, a serious piece of equipment), the man turned his head, then, once Yee Jan walked away, he followed after, looking ever-so-slightly undead. It was the walk. Definitely the walk. Evidently, Yee Jan or his bag had some kind of zombie-magnetism going on.

In the set of images from the second day the man waited in almost the exact same spot. This time he leaned back, shoulders against the wall, and bowed forward as soon as Yee Jan came out of the doors and followed after, not quite so zombie-like (in fact pretty ordinary, though somewhat languid) one hand running along the brim of his cap, a ring on his finger. The ring passed too quickly for him to see which finger (he suspected it was a signet ring, it would be too much to hope that a married man with some secret vice was following him, smitten). On the third day the man waited, hands in pockets, a little more anxious perhaps and wary of the street. When Yee Jan came out, among a burst of other students, he waited, held back, his right hand wiped his face and he walked out of view, more zombie than not, again following Yee Jan.

The director of the language school cleared her throat throughout the viewing. She spoke softly with the two policemen, then directly addressed Yee Jan in English.

'This isn't the first time. I think the film, it's possible, is making things worse.'

Yee Jan sucked the skin on his knuckles – which film? Did she mean the movie they were shooting on the seafront? The policemen didn't appear to care and he wondered at how Italians seemed to love their uniforms, however stupid they appeared wearing them because they always looked a size too small and were over-dressed in ornament. Just dumb.

'Do you know who he is?'

'No. Most of the people who come, come only once. And some-times, once they're here, they wait for a while. It's not clear why, exactly.' But this time there was a complaint from one of the students about a man waiting outside, and when the secretary checked the tapes, she noticed it was the same man coming time after time. 'We don't know for how long.'

Yee Jan sat forward, and repeated his question. 'Why is he here?'

The director shifted back in her seat. 'There isn't much we can do. It's a public street. There is the sign outside. Every time something comes out in the newspapers or a book – and now this film – we have people who come to the school, they go to the palazzo on via Capasso, then they come here to look at the sign outside. I have asked them to take down the sign. But I don't think it would make a difference.'

It sounded to Yee Jan like this would be the preferred option. Take down the sign, rename the school. Easy.

'Why is he following me?'

'Was. He was following you. This footage is from last week. He hasn't come back this week.'

'So why was he following me?'

At this the director looked deeply pained. 'Because,' she answered carefully, 'one of the people who disappeared was one of our students. A Japanese student.'

Yee Jan nodded, he knew the story. 'I'm American. The features are Korean.'

'I don't understand it either. But it's always the same. People are curious. It's an unfortunate mistake. I think this is what happens when an idea spreads. I think someone has seen you and just become fascinated with the idea.'

While the error was just about plausible – in a general sense – it was a simple fact that Yee Jan looked nothing like a Japanese housewife, not even close. In any case, Yee Jan had shown utmost sensitivity for the first couple of weeks at the school over the issue of his mannerisms and his clothes, and toned everything down. He'd kept to a simple wardrobe of dark T-shirts and black jeans. Although he sometimes changed after lessons, not one person from the school had seen him. Only slowly, over several weeks (and the difference becoming more noticeable this week), had he allowed himself to relax, to return to being human, feminine; his body becoming less constricted, his gestures broader, larger, and he'd started wearing a few more bangles, a little more make-up. He'd began to laugh again, that double laugh, the supple ripple that underscored and lit up conversations, and that coarse horny bellow that singled him out of any crowd. Yee Jan's laughter was a gift given generously. He began to address himself in the third person when he was forgetful, or if he made a mistake. He began calling the boys *girlfriend*, *girl*, *ragazza*, or sometimes *she*, in a manner which suggested affection, and enjoyed making a mess of the genders in class to amuse himself, his tutors, the other students.

It was possible with his black hair, the occasional clasp, the eyeshadow, the hint of eye-liner (nothing even close to the amount of make-up he wore at home), the plucked eyebrows, his mannerisms (that lazy, sexy walk, those smooth gestures where his hands followed one beat behind every motion), his height, his skinniness, that he could be mistaken for a girl – a girl – but not, no way, a middle-aged Japanese housewife.

There were too many questions. Did this man follow him because he looked the type – Asian and petite? Did the man have some kind of problem with his sight, or was he crazy? Was he certain about his choice, or did he consider, vacillate, become certain then uncertain? How long did he follow? Did he come all the way to Vomero, door to door, or did he give up at the *funiculare*? Did he intend to harm him? Or was it something else? Yee Jan had seen in movies how a slight gesture made without deliberate intention could fashion a whole world of consequences, happenstances, and while he didn't believe that this would occur in life, he wanted to know if the man believed that he had given him a signal, a please follow me? In any case: how curious was he, this man who wore jackets in the middle of the summer?

The police had a slightly different idea. Some of the people who came to the palazzo were from families with missing people. Since the disappearance of the first victim, and possibly because he wasn't identified, the case had brought the attention of almost everyone who had lost someone. There were forty-five similar cases in the region, of people who had just gone missing without any indication or any obvious plan or prior warning. The case was a touchstone, and sometimes people came to the palazzo or the school in the faint hope that there would be some kind of discovery or realization. Yee Jan found this unbearable.

The director said she didn't know what to do, because there wasn't really much that could be done. They had debated whether they should let Yee Jan know, and thought it sensible to see if he recognized the man. 'But really . . . other than that . . .' She raised her hands in submission.

The police asked him to watch the images again, just to make sure, and this time, Yee Jan noticed some differences. The clothes were the same, the baseball cap, the jacket, the hand to his cap, the same hand to his face. Yee Jan asked for the images to be replayed. Now he was used to the idea, something didn't quite fit. There was a something else, a piece they hadn't shown him on the first viewing where the man had made some kind of gesture to the camera above the door. It looked like sign language, he couldn't tell, being brief and perfunctory it passed almost without remark.

'It's a wasp.' The director dismissed the gesture before Yee Jan could say anything.

'That isn't the same man.' He cocked his head to think. 'Look.' He pointed at the monitor. 'They aren't the same. Their shoulders, this one is smaller, he's a little shorter and he isn't so broad.'

The policemen couldn't see it.

'His hand. He has a ring on the second day and not on the third.'

They all leaned toward the monitor. Yee Jan was right. On the second day the man was clearly wearing a wedding ring, on the third day he was not.

'It isn't the same man. I'm telling you.'

The police struggled to see the difference, but once the idea was suggested they couldn't claim to be certain that it was the same figure on all three occasions.

'It's all right.' Yee Jan gathered up his bag. 'It's happened before. I'm used to it, kind of. Seriously, I know what to do if there's any trouble.' Yee Jan pushed back the chair. The police shuffled to their feet but looked only at the director.

'I – we – want you to know that you are safe.'

Yee Jan didn't understand.

'Nothing is going to happen to you.'

'I don't know what you mean? You said this was nothing.'

The director corrected herself. 'The police have been keeping an eye on the school, and they –' she indicated the police, 'want you to know that you are safe.'

'Do you mean I'm being followed?'

The director shifted her weight. 'You were,' she said, 'but they don't think there's any need any more. It has been a week.'

Yee Jan's friends waited at the *alimentari*. When he came out of the school he looked first to the wall knowing that this was where the men had waited, then crossed the alley to the broader piazza in a skittish hurry – and it was easy to allow the sunlight, the promise of waiting friends, their expectation of news, and such strange news also, to diffuse the threat he felt. He knew that if he could talk this through a good few times he would be able to wrap the event in a protective shell, reform it as a harmless anecdote. Stranger still was the idea that he had been monitored by the police but had no idea about it. Yee Jan looked about the palazzo, but could not see anyone in uniform, or anyone who looked like the police.

The news came out in a flood. A single explanation delivered standing at the head of the table. He held his hands up against the flurry of questions, ordered a beer, then sat down.

'You don't understand,' he said. 'I'm losing my touch. He wasn't interested in me. He didn't want me. He wanted an ancient Japanese hausfrau.' Yee Jan shuddered and whispered to Keiko. 'It's so insulting. Epic eyesight fail.'

No, he didn't know what this man / these men, wanted, except to look, that it was probably some pathetic kind of curiosity that brought the lame and the inadequate to the language-school doors. They wanted to know about the Japanese student, the housewife, that's why they were there. It wasn't really much of a mystery, just people who had nothing better to do, and no other accident to gawp at. And it was all so last week.

'Aren't you frightened?'

'No. I mean, maybe if I'd known about it, then yes, but I had no idea. And there's nothing to be frightened of.'

The woman who asked the question was French, and she sat low in her seat with her arms folded, making herself as small as she possibly could. 'I don't like it,' she said. 'This place isn't safe.'

Yee Jan saved the best piece of information till last. 'I had an escort. All last week. And I didn't even know it. I had police, secret police, following me just in case. Who knows, maybe they're still here?'

On the *funiculare* back to Vomero, Yee Jan scanned the commuters, and wondered how many of these people, just out of curiosity, had walked by the language school at some point, just to place it, to know exactly where the school was located; to confirm for themselves that this was the very same sign they had seen a hundred thousand other times. He looked for a man with a baseball hat, a lightweight summer coat, but found no likely candidate. He looked among the passengers for someone who might be a policeman, and again found none, everyone looking so tired, so fed up and everyday he couldn't imagine any one of them rushing to his aid if things got sticky. What worried him most wasn't the current threat that some stalker might be after him – but that he hadn't noticed. The whole event had come and gone and he'd known nothing about it.

FRIDAY

Yee Jan decided to overhaul his look. He rose early and made sure he was first into the bathroom, where he washed his hair, then spent an hour sitting at the end of his bed waiting for it to dry with his make-up laid out. It was time, he decided, to do the whole business. He wedged a small hand mirror between the slats of the window shutter, and as he prepared himself he occasionally paused and looked out at the city, at the backs of apartments and closed metal shutters, over rooftops busy with aerials and satellite dishes. He took out the clothes he'd thought too risky to wear, and thought that unworn, as loose items without specific shape, the blousy almost translucent shirt, the chequered neckerchief, the mini-skirt (tartan, naturally), the chain-link belt from which hung raccoon-like tails, the black herringbone stockings, the patent-leather black Mary Janes, were nothing, literally nothing, elements of something perhaps, but of little substance in themselves. He stood naked in front of the window, hands on hips, then posed in front of the mirror and thought he was tiny, without clothes he barely seemed physical: I dare. I don't dare. I dare.

He wanted to see the video again, slowed down if possible, the man or men outside the language school, leaning against a wall, sullen plains of grey like this was early TV, Ernie Kovacs maybe, some kind of gag. He wanted to click through frame by frame, give the men the same attention they'd given him: only this time they wouldn't know it. He wanted to see that gesture, to see if this movement was conscious (a deliberate sign, a series of calculated motions) or something automatic (a wasp in his face, a complicated nervous tic). The director's answer had come too readily: it wasn't enough any more to know if one or two men had followed him, no, he wanted to know if one of the men had left a message.

There was no reaction on the *funiculare*, but crossing piazza del Municipio two boys shouted at Yee Jan and ran ahead, finding them-

247

selves funny, and these shouts were reassurance that he'd established himself: if someone followed him now, police or maniac, there would be a reason for it, an explanation. With his white face, finely drawn eyes and eyebrows, with his hair pulled back over his scalp, a broad soft collar (he'd chosen a butch office number over the blouse – hints of Chanel), he walked with the manner of a courtier, with delicate but confident steps, not quite primping, but mannered, definitely mannered: each footfall an assured but subtle, *me, me, me, me*. The wide reach of the piazza, this volume of space about him open and hollow, the air close enough so that he could feel himself swim forward, and he felt honest and good and happy.

The students of Elementario Due returned with clippings from the week's newspapers and chatter about the film, the visiting actors, and news of where they were staying. Everyone expressed amazement at Yee Jan's transformation, how perfect, how delicate he appeared, and how he seemed to flutter in front of them as someone they knew and someone they did not know. He soon bored of the attention, and became exhausted by the constant struggle to pick the simplest phrases, he ached to get outside and find the film crew (although, even this could offer only a momentary interest). As a boy in Washington State he'd felt the same kind of boredom, days on end. A dry dissatisfaction. Something akin to taking a journey, the sedation of watching the world slide by a window and holding no influence over the persistent slide of it all, of being both inside and outside, a passenger who is never really present.

The newspapers revived the story of the clothes, the assault, the missing Japanese student, Mizuki Katsura, the missing American student, and it all began to assemble itself. At first, Lara refused to answer questions. Everyone had an idea about what had happened, and while the tutor would say nothing the students became busy with speculation.

With some effort she attempted to steer the conversation to easier subjects: toward whatever they might have attempted in Italian on the previous night – but the news of a killing made for a better discussion than food or culture or travel and these students, now roused, became inexplicably fluent and direct in their new language. This was no ordinary Friday. Lara wouldn't just tell them directly to stop, to shut up, to do exactly what they were asked.

'She was singled out at the train station. They were waiting for her.'

Then Lara, provoked: 'There are people who have family – missing family. They come here to make a film, to tell the story about this, but they bring everything with them and have no interest in the city, and no interest in the people who have lost members of their family and who have no idea where they are.'

Tonight there was to be a demonstration. A silent protest, an hour-long vigil organized over mobile phones, devices seeking people from the region, calling them to a specific point at a specific time. They would find the location of the film crew and they would silently materialize and surround them in their hundreds. This, anyway, was the plan.

The second session did not improve. Having answered questions all week about why they'd come to Campania and what they liked best about Naples, students fixed on the subject. What they liked best about Naples today involved killing.

Yee Jan was surprised how uneasy the discussion made him: when he left the building for the coffee break he waited deliberately for a group and struck up a conversation so that someone would escort him across the courtyard and outside.

'Did you see him?'

'You know I can't say I saw him. I mean, the police said he was right at the main door.'

The question was repeated, time and again through the break. Have you seen him? What do you think he wants? What are his intentions? What do you think he is going to do? It was only when they returned to class and came round the corner to see the thin dark alley, the glass of the antique shop window, wet-looking, eye-like, that Yee Jan understood – these people are no better than the people who came to the school and stood outside. Everybody wanted that thrill of proximity. There wasn't one speck of difference.

Keiko met Yee Jan on the stairs and Yee Jan spelled it out. 'I have a theory,' he said, 'about why people are so curious. There's only one question, really. What's it like to watch somebody die?'

He refreshed his face at the end of the day, and when he came out of the toilet he found Lara at the entrance, waiting, somewhat deliberate, he thought. He planned to find the film crew at the Duomo and did not want to be delayed.

Lara sat in a folding chair beside the door, an invigilator, hands clamped between her knees.

'I thought you'd be here. If you have a moment.'

Lara had not spoken to him in English before and Yee Jan found this slightly alarming. 'You want to speak?'

'It's about what happened last week.'

Yee Jan waited but Lara couldn't formulate the question. Finally, she gave up and stood up and said it didn't matter.

'I know about the police,' he said. 'They told me I had my own secret security guard, or something like that. I had no idea. Did you know?'

Lara gave a small nod. 'They told us last week.'

'So everyone knew except me?'

'The other instructors were told.'

'Did you see them? The police?'

Lara shook her head.

'I should have been told.' Yee Jan smiled. 'Someone should have told me.' He let the statement stand. 'Have you seen it?'

'I'm sorry?'

'Did you see the footage?'

Lara nodded. 'They showed it to all of the instructors last week.'

'It was two men, wasn't it?'

'I don't know. It isn't clear.' Lara dismissed the question as she did in class when the answer wasn't what she wanted.

'Did you know her? The Japanese student. The woman who disappeared? Were you teaching then?'

Lara made a small gesture which Yee Jan took as a no.

'Has to be weird. The whole thing. Is there anyone here who knew her?'

'I was here. I was finishing my teaching placement.'

'So she was in an advanced class. But you'd know about it.'

'Everybody here knows about it.'

Yee Jan nodded and thought to leave. 'It's just, when something like that happens people treat you differently. If they know you were involved.' He could sense Lara measuring him.

Yee Jan made one single nod. 'And people don't know how to talk to you. Like you're sticky. A little toxic.'

'Look.' Lara dipped her head, eyes closing. 'This has happens a lot. People come all the time. Even though nothing actually happened here.'

'They said.'

Lara zipped up her bag. 'You said this happened to you before?'

So this is what she wanted to know? 'Not quite like this.'

'Sorry?'

'It wasn't the same.'

Lara looked up and waited.

'OK, the first time there was a guy in a car. He just drove up and told me to get in.'

'And you got in?'

'I recognized him. I knew who he was. I wasn't sure there was much of a choice. Anyway, *I always do what I'm told*. After I got in the car I changed my mind and he wouldn't let me out. I managed to get out, but for a moment I didn't know what was going to happen.' Yee Jan explained the situation directly and without fuss, his voice gently flattening as if what had happened was a little tedious or had happened to someone else, to a person perhaps that he didn't like.

'Did he threaten you?'

'He didn't need to.'

'But he didn't?'

'I don't know. I thought when I got out of the car – that was it. He'd – I don't know.' Yee Jan shrugged. 'I was just scared.'

'And nothing happened?'

But that wasn't really nothing. Yee Jan gave a polite smile. 'No. I saw him again. He tried the same thing. Told me to get into the car. This time he made threats, said he would tell my family things, make trouble for me at college, at work, and then he started making threats, just general threats. Stuff he'd do to the people I knew.'

'He knew you?'

'No. I found out later he didn't. I'd seen him around. I'd noticed him. But I thought he knew me, or knew of me, and he might know where I lived – and I thought he might do something.' Yee Jan looked up. 'It was two men, wasn't it? Last week. Outside. Not one.'

Again Yee Jan had the sense that he was asking the wrong question.

'You sound certain?'

'Do you think they thought I was her, this Mizuki?'

'I don't see how. She's been gone for two years.'

'Then why were they waiting for me?'

'I don't know.'

'It's because of the way I look.' A statement of fact.

'I don't think it's that specific. Or clear. The police think you fit a general profile. Being Asian. Something more general.'

Yee Jan didn't answer. 'So this has happened to other Asian students?'

Lara shook her head. 'We've had some trouble with younger women, girls – but I think that's not so unusual. That's an entirely different thing.'

'So, I don't understand. Why are the police interested if this happens all of the time? They have someone don't they. Isn't he in prison?'

'Everybody thinks he's the wrong man.'

Yee Jan nodded. 'Even the police?'

'I don't know.'

'Did they say anything else?' Yee Jan was surprised when Lara paused. 'They did? They said something else?'

'Not about you. There's a type of person who gets obsessed with this kind of thing, and there have been lots of people coming by because of what had happened. It's a problem the school have to do something about. They understand it's a problem, but they haven't done anything about it.'

'I know. They said. But did they say something else?'

'Not about you.'

A siren careened from the corso behind the school. Yee Jan cleared his throat. 'I'd like to see the tapes again. One of the men made a gesture.'

'It's an ambulance, that's all.' Lara stood up.

'So what else did they say if it wasn't about me?'

'It wasn't about you.'

'So it was about the men, then?'

'It was nothing.'

'They think it was two men, don't they?'

'Nobody knows. It's not so clear. And maybe not so important.'

'But they have been speaking with people here, so you know what they think. I mean people must have some idea?' Yee Jan stopped and became more direct. 'I think you know something.'

'I don't. There are so many rumours. Where are you staying?'

'In Vomero. It's OK. An apartment. You know. Why?'

'Are there other people with you?'

'Why are you asking where I'm staying? Is there something else going on?'

Lara folded the straps of her bag around her arms. 'There is a rumour,' she looked directly at Yee Jan, 'about the tapes. It isn't anything the police have said directly. But after they spoke with you they were interested in the tapes again and they spent some time looking at them.'

'So they do think it's two people.'

Lara shook her head. 'There's something else, and I probably shouldn't be telling you this, because it is a rumour, and it's only a rumour. But the gesture the man made, they think that he's saying something.'

Yee Jan waited. Lara slowly ran her tongue over her lips.

'I did know her. Mizuki. I thought I knew her. She came here to get away from her husband. She told me this. Before. Mizuki wasn't her real name. She paid for everything in cash, she gave many explanations, to me and to her class, about who she was, and she didn't seem to be someone who would not be telling the truth. Anyway. She stopped coming.' Lara's voice became quiet, the words less than vapour. 'She was here at the school and then she wasn't. We don't know what happened to her.' Lara cleared her throat and spoke louder, her voice caught in the room. 'I've watched the tapes. I watched them with the police. They think he's saying something to the camera. The man who followed you is saying something to the camera in the video. There are some gestures, but they think that he is saying something to the camera about a woman. They think this is a reference to Mizuki. They think he is saying that they did not touch her. They didn't touch the woman. They think the person who was waiting outside was involved, and they think he is saying that there was only one person who was killed and that they did not touch the woman, but it isn't clear.'

Yee Jan stepped back to the counter. 'Why were they following me?'

Lara reached forward to calm him. 'It's over. The police were watching you. Just in case.'

The film crew took up most of via Duomo in a one-block radius of via Capasso with their vans, stalls, and equipment. Lights raised on stanchions and scaffolding burned sharp into the street, silver caught in the shop windows and along the cornices and ledges. Yee Jan tried to push ahead to see what was happening and found his way blocked by a line of security guards and behind them a row of boards. He caught glimpses of the crew, but had arrived too late to find a good position –

and what he could see didn't interest him. They were filming the murder in the place where the murder occurred: a little bankrupt, he thought, a little unprincipled.

Yee Jan came out of the small street, walked by the palazzo onto via Duomo and found papers taped and pinned to the door – photographs and photocopies – on each sheet a face or a figure in a scratched monotone, and beneath each a date. A familiar kind of memorial. At the bare piazza in front of the Duomo he found a disconsolate group of six or seven protesters each holding a placard with one of the same images from the doors of the palazzo. The protesters, a shabby group, had dressed in black and wore black armbands, and looked, being such a small number, foolish. One of the group approached Yee Jan and offered him a handful of flyers believing him to be one of them. The man's expression was stern, possibly disappointed, so Yee Jan accepted without saying anything.

DOVE SONO I 41? / Chi sarà il prossimo?

Yee Jan took a piece of paper, on one side a list of names: Pascal Entuarde. Johannes Blume. Emilio Santos. Mizuki Katsura. In two years there were forty-one unaccounted people, forty-one missing.

The film crew divided into two groups. A group busy with the production, and a looser group at the margin, who waited, arms folded, some smoking, a little edgy at what was beginning to develop: as if a group of ten people was something to worry about. Yee Jan also felt that energy, as people began to gather in twos and threes at the Duomo steps. Eight people to start. Thirty people within ten minutes, and in twenty that number had tripled: the day, the fading light, began to hold an expectation.

Yee Jan picked up the flyers scattered across the piazza and added them to his own. And as the Duomo's bells began to ring a charge ran through the air. From the side streets, via Tribunali, along via Duomo more people arrived, many dressed in black, many with posters and all with unlit candles, the groups gathered without sound, all facing via Capasso and the film crew, so the noise of the gathering became a hustle of bodies and feet. Yee Jan stood in the centre and handed out the sheets. For Pascal. For Johannes. For Emilio. For Michele. For Mizuki. The vigil formed about as the small open square in front of the Duomo stopped with people – when the bells struck midnight the candles were lit and all conversation stopped without any instruction to do so. And there, brightening the darkness, a sea of light.

TUESDAY

The men wear baseball hats, one grey the other blue with a black visor. Both men wear lightweight summer jackets, windbreakers, similar to the film crew. Both men wear sunglasses in what seems at first to be an affectation, because approaching midnight on the piazza the only light comes from candles and the floodlights brightening the front of the church and the blank ends of the buildings either side – so in analysis there's little to distinguish them apart, regardless of how many cameras, how many phones catch them as they push through a crowd too dense to make room. The image loses focus with the candles, the fuzz and blow of light, as an undulating plain speckled soft and obscure, a sudden brightness dazing the image as the two men lug the boy through. The blackness – night sky, gaps between figures, hair – appears liquid.

Monica watches the image on her own, sits at the side of her bed, the remote in her hand to change to another channel. The image switches, a kind of flicker, as if something has been edited, and loses colour completely, shows the men as they push through, bodies angling sideways, shoulder first. In every example it's almost the same, or a version of the same sets of information: two men, on either side of what you'd take to be a petite girl, Asian, who appears to be drunk or stunned or stoned. The two men look like boxers in the way they duck forward, although the association makes no sense to Monica, perhaps because of how lean they seem, and their clothes, the caps, the coats, an attitude to them of stern and focused business. And the girl – who she knows to be a boy because this has already been reported and discussed, and because the screen carries his name – Yee Jan Lee – although this could be the name of a girl as far as she can tell, because this is the face of a girl, deadpan white, and eyes so small, would it be wrong to call him pretty? And something wrong with him, seriously wrong because he isn't walking properly, he's being held up by these two men who bully him through, propped on either side, and move as one brusque unit, no gentility about the shove and shunt and push, and there, in the register of the boy's mouth a turn, a down-turn, that might be pain. He's being swept through. Monica thinks of him as a girl because this is how the boy is presented, a painted face, luminous white, delicate eyes drawn in, a painted face with a slender feminine mouth, so much about this boy is soft. The boy's face sweeps by the camera, nothing more than a blur, his eyes are certainly looking into the camera, and there, a hand gripped on his upper arm. If he or she passed by you so close you could free him, hold him, keep him from harm. The videos insist that this is a present action, something happening continuously: the ongoing abduction of a boy in a crowded piazza. A counter beside the name marks the days he has been missing. 4.

She watches again.

A different view taken from the Duomo steps so that the field of people is specked with a pulsing light, the candles too many to account for, star points, a map of light, and she can see the disturbance, how the light appears to grow dense, block together as the three bodies push through, a small hole behind them which soon, water-like, refills itself. The buildings opposite glow with ominous long, hollow windows.

Again. Another view. Closer.

The crowd barely move, the threesome press directly toward the camera, shoulders first. No one steps aside to allow them through so they have to shove and lumber past the person taking the shot. The camera jolts, is held up to show a brighter set of lights, the film set beside the Duomo and the scaffold holding floodlights which turn night into day. Something about the crowd reminds her of an execution, a public trial. She's old enough to remember Tiananmen Square.

Monica watches because she has promised to do this, and tries to concentrate on the men, the boxers, the brothers, as they bump deliberately, shoulders set to knock people out the way, some small cries of protest. But every time she can't help but focus on the boy, it is impossible not to watch him, and she can't imagine how this could happen – an abduction during a silent protest, one body selected and removed.

She has to understand how this could happen. How someone could be picked out when surely all attention would be on him, everyone would notice him. She cannot help but watch the boy. The boy appears drunk, ill, out of it. The men have purpose, threat in their speed, which dares to be challenged – and this, the greatest shock of all, almost unaccountable, is their pure nerve to show themselves, join the very crowd protesting their actions two years earlier. Everybody is here because of these two brothers.

The news today is worse, if this is even possible. There is footage from the police, not from the demonstration but images taken a week before of a man waiting in a small street. This image is almost black and white, and at one point, showed slowly, the man appears to leave a message, make a series of gestures, his hand up, a signal she cannot read. The same baseball cap, the same jacket. A one point a group of people come out from under the camera, and there, among them, the boy from the piazza. Yee Jan Lee.

Monica sits and watches, unsure of the limits of her body. She can't feel her fingers, or sense anything other than her breath and chest, aware that it hurts to watch, but now, exhausted, she feels like she is starting to disappear. There is nothing about the brothers that she recognizes. Although they must have been there, two years ago, on the platform, in the station. They had to have been close, she must have walked right by them, there is no possible way she could not have passed them. She has taken the very same walk many times in the intervening years and looked at every detail and wondered, in a space so small, how could she not have seen them?

On his first visit the man made it from the door to the rack of magazines. On the second he managed a further two metres to the desk before changing his mind. On his third visit, which comes minutes after the second (they have all occurred in the space of one morning), Elisa, who always keeps an eye out for the weird ones, announces as the man steps in from the street that this is a travel agency for the purpose of booking flights and holidays. OK?

'You come here when you want to go somewhere.' She slides a brochure across her desk. 'If you want anything that isn't travel-related then you're in the wrong place.'

Monica, being less confrontational, asks the man if she can help, and the man asks if there are any brochures for America or England. Monica points to the rack at the brochures facing out with pictures of São Paulo, Rio de Janeiro, Buenos Aires, searching herself, and then and along a lower shelf, aha, Las Vegas, San Francisco, New York, and there it is, London. 'Where are you thinking in England,' she asks, and realizes she can't think of anywhere other than London. London, England, even though she has relatives who live in Manchester. She can't remember booking anyone a trip to anywhere other than America, North and South, in a long time. She tries to chat but it isn't easy this morning: to be honest everyone figures out their own arrangements these days (she's talking nonsense because she just can't focus). Everyone has a computer. She makes a grimace and the man smiles. After the smile he steps forward as if they are a little more intimate.

'London? OK? That's what you wanted?'

He gives a dismissive blink, a slight head shake, and asks if she speaks English. Monica answers in English.

'I do. A little.'

'You are Monica Cristobari?'

And here she realizes her mistake. There is no holiday. There are no plans. The man, like many others, has sought her out and now he will tell her why, they always do.

'Did you recognize them? The brothers? Did you remember them?'

Monica raises her hand to her head, unconscious of the movement. Elisa flies at the man as he speaks.

'My name is Doctor Arturo Lanzetti. I live at via Capasso 29. I have seen them before. I recognize them.' The man, walking backwards now, is repelled from the shop by Elisa with a loud *Out, out, out.* Monica, stunned, moves as if she is swimming. Before Elisa has the man expelled, the door closed, the lock secured, the bolt drawn, Monica has her jacket over her arm and speaks as if this is rational – she thinks she should be getting home if that's all right. And Elisa guides her to the back of the shop, insists that she sits down, swears at the man, tells Monica she should wait a moment, let him leave and she will call her a taxi.

'You shouldn't have come in today.'

Elisa returns to the window to check the street, but can't see the man because the market is busy. Monica shakes her head. 'It isn't going to stop, is it? It's never going to stop.'

The man stands on the opposite kerb until Elisa makes a show of calling the police, her phone held up dramatically, to demonstrate her intention. Once the police do arrive, purely coincidentally, the man disappears.

Elisa turns the blinds to direct the light from the street and close the view. A distraction? Is that what they need right now? Some noise? A distraction? The radio?

'He won't be back.'

Early afternoon, on a bright day, most days, the gold lettering on the opposite shop window shines across the floor, and slips slowly across the linoleum to the foot of Monica's desk. Monica would slip off one shoe and slide her foot into the path. Today she stands at the edge, mind blanking on ideas on how she can excuse herself and leave.

Elisa bins the newspaper, unread. 'I'm not in the mood for news.' No interest today in reading about the film or the actors – which out of respect has stopped production, or at least filming in town.

'It's – honestly. I'm OK.' Monica watches Elisa rearrange the draw-strings for the blinds: her blouse untucks from her skirt. 'It's just,' she shakes her head, still can't think of anything to say. 'Rude. The point shouldn't need making.'

This is how things are these days, the women agree, without any real thought, any conscience. Someone has an idea about something and they just go ahead and do exactly whatever they please.

Elisa always agrees with Monica, even when she disagrees, you're right, she'll say, then pick a word and stick with it. Most days Monica finds this funny, endearing even. Some days, though, it would be nice if this didn't have to happen.

'You're right. There's no respect for privacy. That's really the problem. That's honestly what this is about. If we're being honest about this, they didn't have to do it here at all. The film. And they've chosen the actual places. Honestly. The palazzo. Ercolano,' she hesitates, manages not to say the station, the abduction and it is still only an abduction, because no body has been found, the boy, carted away from the piazza, has disappeared. 'Can you imagine?'

Monica hums her disagreement. 'Can we not do this today?' Her computer fades into sleep mode. On screen a man swimming, a shot taken underwater looking up, spars of sunlight radiating about him.

That afternoon, while changing into her swimming costume, Monica feels a cold pulse pass across her lower back. She has stuck with her regular routine. Insisted upon it. She checks herself in the mirror and remembers a rash she discovered that morning. Not a rash, so much – nothing more in fact than a small area of dry skin, but it has now divided into two patches on either side of her spine. Monica prefers to keep out of the sun, and exercises in an enclosed pool. Her skin is snowy white. She seldom sits under direct sunlight.

Troubled by the rash she decides not to swim. There are chemicals in the water, she tells herself, which will aggravate the condition. Monica believes that this discomfort is caused by stress. *It would be strange if it didn't happen.* It's impossible to avoid the news about the film, or news about the boy, who was taken, they suggest, as a stand-in for the girl they didn't take two years ago. A fascination now with Yee Jan Lee, a boy, who by rights should not have looked so pretty. It's impossible to avoid the storm growing around the conviction of Marek Krawiec, who was right all along. It appears. An appeal is lodged. So who are these men, these brothers? And why would they come to the city to kill one boy then grab another? She isn't sure she understands. Uneasy with her part in this, she finds herself featured in reports in the *Cronache* and the *Corriere* as 'the witness', or 'the sole witness' to the first killing, and while her name has not become generally known, it's no secret that 'the sole witness' works for a travel agency located close by the Centro Direzionale. Her clients, her friends, her family all know the story and are all alarmed by the weekend's developments. *People being picked off the streets.* Truth is she's thoroughly sick of it.

By example: when Monica returns home her cousin Davide asks if it would make sense for her to take some kind of a holiday until everything blows over.

Monica, preparing the evening meal, her hands wet, pauses long enough to ask why she should have to stop her work and head off to some place – if it was even possible – where they hadn't heard of this case?

'Maybe China,' she says, 'or India? Or some place where people don't read?'

Davide insists that he's serious.

'And I go, and then the film comes out and there's a big fuss in the newspapers and all over the television. I leave again and then I come back. Then it's released on DVD – there's more fuss, I leave and I come back. And then it goes on cable, then RaiUno. And on and on.' She draws her hands out of the bowl, wet ring-less fingers. 'And then . . . perhaps someone will write a book about making a film about a story that is taken from this book which is taken from a real-life story that was copied from a story in a book. You know? Or maybe there will be a video game? Something they can play in the arcades? And then later they can remake the film, or make the film of the video game? Or maybe there will be some other imagined crime that these men can act on and make real?'

Davide visibly weakens under this reasoning – in his defence he's trying to suggest something practical.

'There isn't any escape, Davide. There isn't an ending. It doesn't just stop because we are tired of it.'

Despite herself Monica is becoming increasingly preoccupied by the three minutes or less in which she witnessed the young man at the train station. And this is two years ago now, two whole years. The man had sorted through his bags with little hurry, unaware of the people about him, as if he had somewhere to go, somewhere to be. Two years ago she become frozen by the event, caught in endless possibilities, so that the event itself became completely unreal, a fiction. What if he had not paused? What if he had taken a moment longer? What if she had spoken to him? Would the sequence of events that brought him to the small basement room in a dirty palazzo on via Capasso have played out differently? To add to this she wrestles with the uncertainty of what has recently occurred. Like everyone else she entertains alternative possibilities: perhaps the boy isn't dead, perhaps this is just like the book, an elaborate scam?

These ideas set fire to her skin. The rash won't quieten.

She calls a specialist recommended by her sister-in-law and makes an appointment.

THURSDAY

Monica takes the morning off work and turns up early at the specialist's office in Portici. The rash hasn't improved. Dr Novi carefully checks her back and asks after her diet and sleeping pattern. He washes his hands after the inspection and says that this is minor, although he is certain that it must irritate her, it's unlikely to be caused by the chlorinated water. More likely than not the condition is caused by stress (and this is something she didn't know?), although it was always possible that they were using different chemicals, or more chemicals than they should. He cannot be certain. He will provide a prescription for a salve, and suggests that if she wishes to continue her exercise that she swims instead in salt water where she will benefit from both the ions and the iodine, but failing that, there's a mineral pool in Lucrino, a small distance from the city. It is, he said, a far second best, because it might be better if she does not swim at all.

Monica sits on the doctor's raised bed, dissatisfied with the examination. She'd mentioned swimming only because this was easier than explaining about the cause of her stress. She can't be certain about his recommendation either. Can she or can't she swim? It isn't clear. Swimming offers her the one pure moment when she does not have to answer to her family, or to work. While she swims, in that brief thirty-five minutes each day, she is completely alone, and the isolation that the activity brings is a welcome and rare pleasure.

Immediately out of the office Monica takes the metro to Cavalleggeri d'Aosta, and in the heat and bustle her clothes irritate the skin, and send a small charge, a pulse around her back. She tries to scratch her wrist instead of her back but finds this useless.

The pool is new, less than a year old, and managed by a university. Monica changes in a private booth, conscious that her costume is old, and that chlorine is beginning to rot the stitching. The pool itself is steel, of even depth, and encased in glass, one side looks out to a bright view of a honey-coloured cliff, the lip of a crater, the other to a parking lot, and in the distance, the other side of the crater.

Monica is joined at the poolside by a young man. Like Monica the man has with him a towel, which he sets on the slate side away from the pool, and goggles, the straps wrapped about his hand. She watches as the man walks to the head of the pool and chooses the centre lane, and she considers quickly who she would be able to keep pace with, and picks the lane beside the young man.

On her first few laps she finds herself swimming faster than her usual pace. Her stroke, although clean, is usually underpowered, but once she is comfortable she begins to move with economy and feels the motion to be smooth and direct, and for twenty minutes she swims without a break, aware of the young man in the lane beside her. As Monica swims freestyle, the young man swims breaststroke, and they fall into an easy rhythm, swimming at points side by side. When she stops, the man continues, and she watches him set the pace for the lane with a powerful, simple stroke – as his hands dive forward his head ducks down and his shoulders follow in a sequence that is direct and uncomplicated. Unlike the other swimmers he causes little disturbance in the water, no splashing, and no hurry, just a smooth and considered series of movements. When she starts again, she finds herself falling into the same rhythm and is mindful to contain her stroke and make the movement as direct and uncomplicated as she can. Hand slightly cupped, she breaks the water, thrusts her arm full length, then folds it under her in a long swift swipe, and finds with this simple adaptation that she moves quicker, further, faster.

At the end of his swim the young man stands at the end of the lane. Tall and gangly, he has none of the poise and grace out that he commands when he is in the water.

Monica returns to the changing rooms exhilarated, not only by the swim but by the coincidence of swimming beside the young man. It is only when she sits to take off her costume that her mood changes and she remembers the boy at the station, and an unreasonable notion strikes her that if one man she had noticed disappeared, it could possibly happen again. As soon as the thought occurs she dismisses it. There was no killing, she tells herself. No such thing.

FRIDAY

Monica returns to the pool at the same time. As she walks into the building she's surprised to see the young man ahead of her, smartly dressed with a small backpack. He leans forward a little as he walks. She guesses that he has come directly from work, and wonders if the people he works with understand how exceptionally graceful he is in the water. Out of the water there's nothing exceptional about him, but when he swims everything about him seems in tune and in place. She stands beside him to pay for her ticket, neither smiles nor acknowledges the other, and the previous day's anxiety is remembered but not felt. The man has returned, of course he has returned. Nevertheless, if she hadn't seen him, his absence would have troubled her.

And so she swims beside the man again, each keeping pace, that one or the other sometimes breaks, and she finds this silent company comforting and imagines that a familiarity is growing between them. While she fights to keep pace she begins to recognize when her own stroke becomes similarly economical and pure. In just two sessions her stroke is beginning to change, she is becoming long, more decisive with her reach, so that the motion is unconsciously fluid. Afterward, she wonders if the man deliberately keeps pace with her, he made no attempt to force any other kind of contact between them. Out of the water they are strangers, in the water they are companions, and their bodies move at the same pace. She can feel his company as soon as she slips into the water. She is familiar now with the set of his mouth as he comes up for air, his quick efficient gasp, the hunch of his shoulders as he lunges forward, and the speed with which he pulls deep into the water.

This is, she understands, a distraction. The more preoccupied she becomes with the swimmer, the less she needs to think about the student at the station, about the boy at the piazza.

SATURDAY

On the Saturday, the swimmer does not appear, it shouldn't surprise her, but she finds it impossible to swim, and sits at the poolside waiting. That night her anxieties return in a full and wide-eyed sleepless distraction. She sits upright in bed, her back irritating, the nerve ends prickle, sharp and sensitive. The heat of the room and the oily stink of traffic catch in the night air, familiar to her as the station that morning two years ago. She sees it time and time again, the train door, the boy crouched beside his bags with his back to her, the shirt as it was on his back, and the shirt as it was, bloodied and cut. Why hadn't she delayed him? Why hadn't she spoken to him?

On the news the boy's parents, Mr and Dr Lee, who move like people who do not trust themselves, whose bodies might at any point fail them, who look torn by grief and unknowing. They beg for the release of their son. Dr Lee speaks in Italian, explains how much her son loves the city. Speaks in the present tense to keep him alive.

Monica watches the news. The footage of the vigil. The candles as a map or a sea, all comfort taken from the image. They show the brothers, a still of their faces which gives nothing away. A politician explains that Krawiec is to be released but banned from the country. She does not know how they can do this. These brothers, the politician struggles for adequate words, come to our city to feed on us, not once, but twice, like wolves. There are calls again for information regarding Mizuki Katsura, the thinking now is that the killers have taken her absence, her disappearance, the belief that she was killed to be instruction and script on the abduction of the boy. She must come forward. How then did they find the first American? Was this an accident? Did they choose him the moment she passed by, or had the decision already been made, the boy as good as dead?

She sits at the edge of her bed, her back needling. The room is close, the air sticky, and she tries to calm herself by thinking of the swimmer instead of the student at the station. But the substitution of one man for another will not work. The man in the pool and the youth at the station, while not similar, were also too similar, and the sound of the traffic, the scooters, the taxis, the night bustle of the city, while not like the sounds of the station, were not unlike the sounds of the station. The familiarity, the associations were uncanny and close.

She thinks of opposites, of things that are not there and memories that will not trouble her. Instead of heat, she thinks of snow. Instead of the city, she imagines herself above it, safely distant, alone on the mountain. Her immediate memory is of her first close view of snow. She was five when her father drove her to the volcano and presented it to her as if it were of his own making. It was winter, the first day of the year, and she remembers the long and steep road along the flanks of the mountain, and her excitement at how strange it was to be looking back at the city rather than out at the mountain. The inner cone sheltered by the separate shattered ridge of Monte Somma, and between the two peaks ran a long and lower field of rucked and fluid lines of stone capped and softened with snow. The trees, so thin and precarious on the steep lip, appeared sparse and burned, black against a thin white drift, and it is with this thought, the notion of a field of blankness, of coldness, of everything alien to the physical heat currently pressing down upon her, that she is able to slowly shut the chatter out her mind. And to this place she brings the swimmer, and the two of them sit, silent, side by side, overlooking a plain snowbound void.

There was no killing. There were no brothers. The city does not exist.

THE
KILLS

Although *The Kill* can be read and enjoyed alone, it is part of a larger project. It is the third book in a quartet of novels called *The Kills*. Together the four books (*Sutler*, *The Massive*, *The Kill* and *The Hit*) make up an epic story of crime and conspiracy.

The Kills is also a groundbreaking collaboration between a writer and publisher. Its creator, Richard House, has written and produced audio and video content that takes you beyond the boundaries of the book and into the characters' lives outside its pages.

To discover more about Richard House, to see the multimedia content that relates to *The Kill*, or to learn more about *The Kills*, go to www.thekills.co.uk

Sutler, *The Massive*, *The Kill* and *The Hit* are available separately as ebooks now. *The Kills* will be published in hardback and ebook on 18 July 2013.

   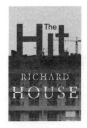